THIS ROAD WE TRAVELED

Center Point
Large Print

Also by Jane Kirkpatrick and available from Center Point Large Print:

The Memory Weaver

**This Large Print Book carries the
Seal of Approval of N.A.V.H.**

THIS *ROAD* WE *T*RAVELED

Jane Kirkpatrick

CENTER POINT LARGE PRINT
THORNDIKE, MAINE

This Center Point Large Print edition is published
in the year 2016 by arrangement with Revell,
a division of Baker Publishing Group.

Scripture used in this book, whether quoted or
paraphrased by the characters, is taken from the
King James Version of the Bible.

This book is a work of historical fiction based closely on
real people and events. Details that cannot be historically
verified are purely products of the author's imagination.

The text of this Large Print edition is unabridged.
In other aspects, this book may vary
from the original edition.
Printed in the United States of America
on permanent paper.
Set in 16-point Times New Roman type.

ISBN: 978-1-68324-133-1

Library of Congress Cataloging-in-Publication Data

Names: Kirkpatrick, Jane, 1946– author.
Title: This road we traveled / Jane Kirkpatrick.
Description: Center Point Large Print edition. | Thorndike, Maine :
Center Point Large Print, 2016.
Identifiers: LCCN 2016033913 | ISBN 9781683241331
    (hardcover : alk. paper)
Subjects: LCSH: Mothers and daughters—Fiction. | Frontier and
pioneer life—Fiction. | Oregon Territory—History—Fiction. | Large
type books. | GSAFD: Christian fiction.
Classification: LCC PS3561.I712 T48 2016b | DDC 813/.54—dc23
LC record available at https://lccn.loc.gov/2016033913

Dedicated to Jerry,
who walks many roads with me

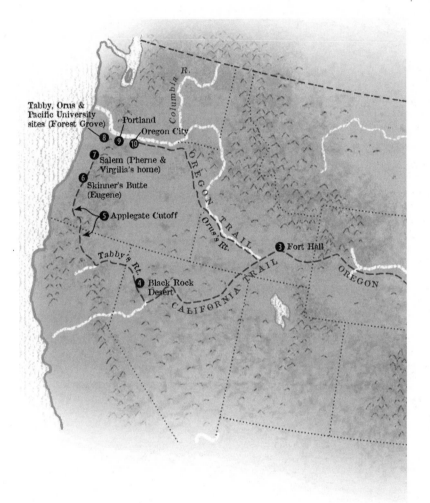

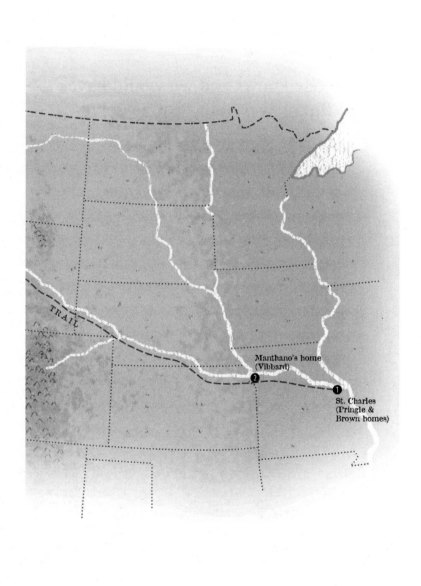

No one knows and we would have to figure everything out ourselves.

Rinker Buck in
The Oregon Trail:
A New American Journey

Cast of Characters

Tabitha (Tabby) Moffat Brown	matriarch of Brown family
Clark Brown (deceased)	Tabby's husband
John Brown	Tabby's brother-in-law and former sailor
Orus Brown & Lavina	oldest Brown son and his second wife; 13 children
Manthano Brown & Catherine	Tabby's youngest son and second wife; Young Pherne and other children
Pherne & Virgil Pringle	Tabby's only daughter and her husband
Virgilia	oldest Pringle daughter
Clark	oldest Pringle son

Octavius, Albro, Oliver (deceased)	Pringle sons
Sarelia Lucia, Emma Pherne, Mary Ella	youngest Pringle daughters
*Judson Morrow	ox driver
Jesse Applegate	originator of Southern cutoff trail
Captain Levi Scott	pilot, guide for Applegate cutoff trail
**Nellie Louise Blodgett	traveler on the Oregon Trail
Fabritus Smith	Oregon farmer and legislator
Harvey & Emeline Clark	independent missionaries in Forest Grove

*imagined character representative of people of the time
**based on a real person from another century

Prologue

It was a land of timber, challenge, and trepidation, forcing struggles beyond any she had known, and she'd known many in her sixty-six years. But Tabitha Moffat Brown decided at that moment with wind and snow as companions in this dread that she would not let the last entry in her memoir read *"Cold. Starving. Separated."* Instead she inhaled, patted her horse's neck. The snow was as cold as a Vermont lake and threatening to cover them nearly as deep while she decided. She'd come this far, lived this long, surely this wasn't the end God intended.

Get John back up on his horse. If she couldn't, they'd both perish.

"John!"

The elderly man in his threadbare coat and faded vest sank to his knees. At least he hadn't wandered off when he'd slid from his horse. His white hair lay wet and coiled at his neck beneath a rain-drenched hat. His shoulder bones stuck out like a scarecrow's, sticks from lack of food and lost hope.

11

"You can't stop, John. Not now. Not yet." Wind whistled through the pines and her teeth chattered. "Captain!" She needed to sound harsh, but she nearly cried, his name stuck in the back of her throat. This good man, who these many months on the trail had become more than a brother-in-law, he had to live. He couldn't die, not here, not now. "Captain! Get up. Save your ship."

He looked up at her, eyes filled with recognition and resignation. "Go, Tabby. Save yourself."

"Where would I go without you, John Brown? Fiddlesticks. You're the captain. You can't go down with your ship. I won't allow it."

"Ship?" His eyes took on a glaze. "But the barn is so warm. Can't you smell the hay?"

Barn? Hay? Trees as high as heaven marked her view, shrubs thick and slowing as a nightmare clogged their path, and all she smelled was wet forest duff, starving horseflesh, and for the first time in her life that she could remember, fear.

Getting upset with him wouldn't help. She wished she had her walking stick to poke at him. Her hands ached from cold despite her leather gloves. She could still feel the reins. That was good. What a pair they were: he, old and bent and hallucinating; she, old and lame and bordering on defeat. Her steadfast question, *what do I control here,* came upon her like an unspoken prayer. *Love and do good.* She must get him warm or he'd die.

12

With her skinny knees, she pushed her horse closer to where John slouched, all hope gone from him. Snow collected on his shoulders like moth-eaten epaulets. "John. Listen to me. Grab your cane. Pull yourself up. We'll make camp. Over there, by that tree fall." She pointed. "Come on now. Do it for the children. Do it for me."

"Where are the children?" He stared up at her. "They're here?"

She would have to slide off her horse and lead him to shelter herself. And if she failed, if her feet gave out, if she couldn't bring him back from this tragic place with warmth and water and, yes, love, they'd both die and earn their wings in Oregon country. It was not what Tabitha Moffat Brown had in mind. And what she planned for, she could make happen. She always had . . . until now.

Part One

— 1 —
Tabby's Plan

1845
ST. CHARLES, MISSOURI

Tabitha Moffat Brown read the words aloud to Sarelia Lucia to see if she'd captured the rhythm and flow. "Feet or wings: well, feet, of course. As a practical matter we're born with limbs, so they have a decided advantage over the wistfulness of wings. Oh, we'll get our wings one day, but not on this earth, though I've met a few people who I often wondered about their spirit's ability to rise higher than the rest of us in their goodness, your grandfather being one of those, dear Sarelia. Feet hold us up, help us see the world from a vantage point that keeps us from becoming self-centered—one of my many challenges, that self-centered portion. I guess the holding up too. I've had to use a cane or walking stick since I was a girl."

"How did that happen, Gramo?" The nine-year-old child with the distinctive square jaw put the question to her.

"I'll tell you about the occasion that brought that cane into my life and of the biggest challenges of my days . . . but not in this section. I know that walking stick is a part of my feet, it seems, evidence that I was not born with wings." She winked at her granddaughter.

"When will you get to the good parts, where you tell of the greatest challenge of your life, Gramo? That's what I want to hear."

"I think this is a good start, don't you?"

"Well . . ."

"Just you wait."

Tabitha dipped her goose quill pen into the ink, then pierced the air with her weapon while she considered what to write next.

"Write the trouble stories down, Gramo. So I have them to read when I'm growed up."

"When you're *grown* up."

"Yes, then. And I'll write my stories for you." A smile that lifted to her dark eyes followed. "I want to know when trouble found you and how you got out of it. That'll help me when I get into trouble."

"Will it? You won't get into scrapes, will you?" Tabby grinned. "We'll both sit and write for a bit." The child agreed and followed her grandmother's directions for paper and quill.

The writing down of things, the goings-on of affairs in this year of 1845, kept Tabby's mind occupied while she waited for the second half of her life to begin. Tabby's boys deplored studious exploits, which had always bothered her, so she wanted to nurture this grandchild—and all children's interest in writing, reading, and arithmetic. So far, the remembering of days gone by had served another function: a way of organizing what her life was really about. She was of an age for such reflection, or so she'd been told.

Whenever her son Orus Brown returned from Oregon to their conclave in Missouri, she expected real ruminations about them all going west—or not. Perhaps in her pondering she'd discover whether she should go or stay, and more, why she was here on this earth at all, traveling roads from Connecticut southwest to Missouri and maybe all the way to the Pacific. Wasn't wondering what purpose one had walking those roads of living a worthy pursuit? And there it was again: *walking those roads.* For her it always was a question of feet or wings.

Sarelia had gone home long ago, but Tabby had kept writing. Daylight soon washed out the lamplight in her St. Charles, Missouri, home, and she paused to stare across the landscape of scrub oak and butternut. Once they'd lived in the country, but now the former capital of Missouri spread out along the river, and Tabby's home edged both city and country. A fox trip-tripped across the yard. Still, Tabby scratched away, stopping only when she needed to add water to the powder to make more ink. She'd have to replace the pen soon, too, but she had a good supply of those. Orus, her firstborn, saw to that, making her several dozen before he left for Oregon almost two years ago now. He was a good son. She prayed for his welfare and wondered anew at Lavina's stamina managing all their children while they waited. Well, so was Manthano a good son, though he'd let himself be whisked away by that woman he fell in love with and rarely came to visit. Still, he was a week's ride away. Children. She shook her head in wistfulness. Pherne, on the other hand, lived just down a path. And it was Pherne, her one and only daughter, who also urged her to write her autobiography. "Your personal story, Mama. How you and Papa met, where you lived, even the wisdom you garnered."

Wisdom. She relied on memory to tell her story and memory proved a fickle thing. She supposed her daughter wanted her to write so she wouldn't get into her daughter's business. That happened with older folks sometimes when they lacked passions of their own. She wanted her daughter to know how much being with her and the children filled her days. Maybe not to let her know that despite her daughter's stalwart efforts, she was lonely at times, muttering around in her cabin by herself, talking to Beatrice, her pet chicken, who followed her like a shadow. She was committed to not being a burden on her children. Oh, she helped a bit by teaching her grandchildren, but one couldn't teach children all day long. Of course lessons commenced daily long, but the actual sitting on chairs, pens and ink in hand, minds and books open, that was education at its finest but couldn't fill the day. The structure, the weaving of teacher and student so both discovered new things, *that* was the passion of her life, wasn't it?

Still, she was intrigued by the idea of recalling and writing down ordinary events that had helped define her. Could memory bring back the scent of Dear Clark's hair tonic or the feel of the tweed vest he wore, or the sight of his blue eyes that sparkled when he teased and preached? She'd last seen those eyes in life twenty-eight years ago. She had thought she couldn't go on a day without him, but she'd done it nearly thirty years. What had first attracted her to the man? And how did she end up from a life in Stonington, Connecticut, begun in 1780, to a widow in Maryland, looking after her children and her own mother, and then on to Missouri in 1824 and still there in winter 1845? Was this where she'd die?

" 'A life that is worth writing at all, is worth writing minutely and truthfully.' Longfellow." She penned it in her memoir. This was a truth, but perhaps a little embellishment now and then wouldn't hurt either. A story should be interesting after all.

His beard reached lower than his throat. Orus, Tabby's oldest son, came to her cabin first. At least she assumed he had, as none of his children nor Pherne's had rushed through the trees to tell her that he'd already been to Lavina's or Virgil and Pherne's place. It was midmorning, and her bleeding hearts drooped in the August heat.

"I'm alive, Mother." He removed his hat, and for a moment Tabby saw her deceased husband's face pressed onto this younger version, the same height, nearly six feet tall, and the same dark hair, tender eyes.

"So you are, praise God." She searched his brown eyes for the sparkle she remembered, reached to touch his cheek, saw above his scruffy beard a red-raised scar. "And the worse for wear, I'd say."

"I'll tell of all that later. I'm glad to see you among the living as well."

"Come in. Don't stand there shy."

He laughed and entered, bending through her door. "Shyness is not something usually attached to my name."

"And how did you find Oregon? Let me fix you tea. Have you had breakfast?"

"No time. And remarkable. Lush and verdant. The kind of place to lure a man's soul and keep him bound forever. No to breakfast. I've much to do."

"So we'll be heading west then?"

For an instant his bright eyes flickered and he looked beyond her before he said, "Yes. I expect so." He kissed her on her hair doily then, patted her back, and said he'd help her harness the buggy so she could join him at Lavina's. "I'm anxious to spend time with my wife and children. Gather with us today."

"I can do the harnessing myself. No tea?"

"Had some already. Just wanted the invite to come from me."

"An invite?"

He nodded, put his floppy hat back on. "At our place. I've stories to tell."

"I imagine you do. Off with you, then. I'll tend Beatrice and harness my Joey."

"That chicken hasn't found the stew pot yet?"

"Hush! She'll hear you." She pushed at him. "Take Lavina in your arms and thank her for the amazing job she's done while you gallivanted around new country. I'll say a prayer of thanksgiving that you're back safely."

"See you in a few hours then."

"Oh, I'll arrive before that. What do you take me for, an old woman?" Beatrice clucked. "Keep your opinions to yourself."

Orus laughed, picked his mother up in a bear hug, and set her down. "It's good to see you, Marm. I thought of you often." He held her eyes, started to speak. Instead he sped out the door, mounting his horse in one fluid movement, reminding her of his small-boy behavior of rarely sitting still, always in motion. *Wonder where his*

23

pack string is? She scooped up Beatrice, buried her nose in her neck feathers, inhaling the scent that always brought comfort.

But what was that wariness she'd witnessed in her son's eyes when she suggested that they'd all head west? She guessed she'd find out soon enough.

— 2 —
Pherne's Watch

Pherne Pringle watched her mother make her way through the bladdernut trees with old Joey. She wondered why she'd harnessed the big old mule instead of walking. Maybe her foot bothered her this morning. Still, she insisted on doing such things herself. Perhaps she had news of Orus? Pherne's brother Orus still ran the Brown and Pringle clan, though he'd been gone for two years. She'd enjoyed seeing the changes in her husband, Virgil, these past two years without Orus's domination. Virgil had discovered how to linger, giving her a kiss before heading to the barn to tend the stock. His friendly teasing of Sarelia, Emma, and Virgilia and his congratulations to their sons, openly praising them, was something Orus dismissed as coddling whenever he heard an expression of appreciation.

Still, she missed her brother. It had been months since a stranger brought the last letter affirming that Orus was still alive last fall. If he came back and had inspiring words about the Oregon country, the question would then be, would they go west? Orus would, if he set his mind to it. Or he'd convince them all that what they had here was better. His wife, Lavina, would have no say. But she and Virgil, they had a choice, didn't they?

And what if Orus didn't come back? Could Virgil take over the running of two farms forever? It had been a hard two years, but they told each other it was only temporary. But what if it wasn't?

She stopped herself from thinking of that awful possibility and concentrated on scrambling the eggs for the second breakfast, Virgil having eaten bacon, biscuits, and gravy before heading to their fields.

Her brother had a way of stifling those who disagreed with him or who didn't see the world as he did. Orus's older boys tended their father's fields and helped their stepmother with the eleven children Orus left behind when he headed west. At least Lavina had a rest from being pregnant and nursing another infant. Childbearing took its toll on women, something men failed to under-stand. Orus's boys had turned to Virgil for advice on planting and harvest, and Pherne had watched with pride how her husband spoke to the boys as young men, capable, and not just barking orders as Orus did.

"Aren't you going?" Her mother hobbled into the house, having tied Joey to the post, and pulled herself up the steps with her walking stick.

"Going where? I'm fixing Virgil's second breakfast. Sarelia, push your grandmother's rocker here so she can rest."

"I'm not resting. Orus is back." Her mother's voice was the strongest she'd heard in weeks. "Didn't he stop by? He's planning a gathering at Lavina's. Well, I guess it's his place too. I got in the habit of thinking of it as hers."

"Maybe he stopped at the fields and told Virgil. I guess we better mix up some fixings. Blackberry biscuits would be good, don't you think?"

Her mother nodded. "But I'm heading on over. I don't want to miss a thing. He says we're heading west."

"Are we? Well, exciting things await then." Pherne frowned. "Virgilia, run and tell your father to hurry along. We've a gathering to step up for, like it or not."

Her oldest daughter helped her grandmother back into the buggy and saw her off before pushing through the rows of hemp as tall as trees where her father and brothers worked. They were one of the few farming families in St. Charles without slave help, and Pherne was proud that it was so, even though it meant more work for her family.

Pherne turned back to her dough boy to begin blending flour and water for her biscuits, while Virgilia, now returned, finished up the breakfast. Her mother was so excited about undertaking another journey. Pherne wished she could share that enthusiasm. Already Orus's presence disrupted her well-laid-out plans for the day, and here she was once again hopping to the fast

27

music her brother played instead of waiting for the peaceful slow waltz of her husband's.

And what about her children's wishes? Would they want to go? Sarelia was her vocal child who had actually inspired her mother's autobiography by asking so many questions. Emma rocked in the chair by the fireplace. She was Pherne's baby now, Oliver having lived only nine months. Pherne shivered, busied herself, rushing over the memory ghost. Emma had been quiet as a snowfall most days since Oliver's death. Could a child so young still grieve the death of her baby brother? Pherne swallowed, fingered the gold locket at her throat, tucked beneath her blouse. She let the grief still so fresh take her away. Then she took a deep breath and returned to her dough.

Yes, Sarelia was the verbal one; Emma her quietest child at seven. Albro, middle son, was her husbandry child, tending the sheep and cattle. He followed after his father as a dreamer. Octavius would want to go. Would Clark? Already fifteen, he was her studious boy, thoughtful, often engaging in philosophical discussions about the meaning of life and God's relationship to man as he worked in the family boot-making shop. And then Virgilia, her firstborn, seventeen, who was her helpmate. In ways, Virgilia was more like a younger sister than a daughter. She'd hate to lose the girl's baking, cleaning, and child-tending skills when the right young man took her fancy. But wasn't that what life was about, raising children to give them confidence to make their own lives, separate from their parents, letting them fly off into the future, giving them courage to face the inevitable losses? What if some wanted to go to Oregon and some stay? Break up her family? She stopped mid-kneading. The crust would be tough if she didn't calm down.

Virgil had come in from the fields, followed by his son. Was that a twinkle in his eye?

"Orus is back," Virgil said.

"You already knew?"

"He stopped in the field after seeing Mrs. Brown. He looks fit. Slimmer but strong." Her six living children moved around the log home as though in a dance, each knowing the steps that kept them from bumping into each other. That dance was all Pherne had ever hoped for as a young girl, to find the kind of love her parents had had, live a comfortable life surrounded by the things that brought her pleasure. Fine furniture. Jewelry. Books. And family, of course. She'd raise her children to be faithful and be kind to each other and their neighbors. Virgil had been the perfect choice. But now, disruption promised to raise its little head in the form of Orus Brown.

Virgil led the prayer after they'd swarmed around the breakfast table, and together they all said, "Amen." Pherne stood up to bring coffee to her husband. She turned and surveyed the scene. All she loved sat around that mahogany table, high-back chairs with carved harp-back design and arms (to help her mother push up out of the chair when she ate with them). Virgil had spared no expense to bring those luxury items on board ship to their Missouri home. What more could she ask for? She hoped they'd stay here forever.

Her eye caught her husband's as he passed the platter of biscuits. He winked at Pherne. She felt her face grow warm. She was pleased that Virgil had resisted Orus's pressure to go west with him to explore two years previous. She needed to tell Virgil that and not let him ever wonder who she saw to be the head of her family: It was her husband and not her brother. Nor her mother, either. She meant to keep it that way.

— 3 —
Virgilia's Hope

Virgilia bent over the washbowl in her second-story bedroom. She wanted to clean up before heading to her cousins' for this unexpected midweek outing. She could tell that her mother wasn't happy. But her uncle Orus was a charmer and storyteller and he was back after two years. His stories would become legend. His idea of living offered adventurous possibilities. Her mother harbored the past and hanging on to things while Virgilia found excitement in the future . . . but wariness too. The unknown could frighten. Fiddlesticks. Let the future rule! She wanted to have a husband and family one day, find the perfect mate as her mother had, but she also thought there might be more to life than tending babies and cooking and cleaning and gardening. She supposed she read too many novels and poems. But what had her mother expected? Her grandparents had started the St. Charles library and literary club. She was born to love books and stories and to think of the possibilities. Some of those stories spoke of faraway places, and the endings were always happy, weren't they? Well, not always. The unknown roads ahead promised boulders and holes that could sink a soul.

Virgilia undid the braids from the chignon that had rested on her neck so she could wash the sweat away with lavender-scented water. She ran her fingers through the amber waves that liked to tangle. She'd gotten the little girls dressed, and they stood outside awaiting the rest of the family. She brushed her hair, long strokes, the pull against her scalp a pleasant tingle. Much as she loved her younger brothers and sisters, she knew she didn't want so many little hands and feet surrounding her days, asking questions, sparring and sulking. She had few moments to sit and read. She hadn't had the luxury of working disagreements out with a big sister, being the oldest, and the boys—who were like triplets in their own world—didn't include her. She'd been commissioned into adulthood before she was four, helping out every two years or so when another baby appeared. She was eleven when Oliver—number eight—was born. Dear Oliver. No new babies followed. Her mother's childbirth sickness after Oliver meant even more care from Virgilia, given to her mother as well as her brothers and sisters. Thank goodness her grandmother had lived close by, and despite her limitations, her good nature and open heart gave Virgilia the strength to go on some days when she considered, well, just lying down and going to sleep, hoping she might never awaken.

In the next room she could hear her brothers Albro, Octavius, and Clark's low voices, and a wistfulness to have someone to share anticipation with ached in her chest. She'd like to find a friend with an ordinary first name like Nellie or Jane. Maybe because Brown was such a common name her grandmother had distinguished her three children with singularity: Orus, Manthano, Pherne. And her parents had continued the tradition despite Pringle being a distinctive surname in itself. Virgilia? For her father, she knew, but still. Why not Virginia?

She pulled hair from the brush and stuffed it into the hole of the porcelain container. Winter would bring time to weave the amber with small beads, making pins and hair decorations for her sisters and herself. She tied a blue ribbon around thick-as-pudding hair, pushing curls from her forehead, then rubbed a dab of glycerin onto her cheeks to keep them moist. Her mother said she had a perfect widow's peak, perfect blue eyes, and perfect skin, and that glycerin would keep it that way. Well, she tried. But the heat from the stove, the wind when she went out to milk the cow, and even the hot sun in summer when she shelled peas on the steps all worked to bring nubbins onto her face. It had gotten worse as she began her monthlies. They were miseries. Did every girl have such abominable abdominal pains? She laughed. She'd have to write that phrase down.

A good friend, that's what she wished for. She had a cousin. Young Pherne was a year younger than Virgilia, but she lived days away. They wrote letters sometimes, but it wasn't the same as sharing chatter, anticipating her uncle Orus's return. Would they go west? Would they separate after all these years of close living with cousins, or would they go as one large unit as the family had done heading to Missouri all those years before? She couldn't imagine them all not going. Then she would have Young Pherne to share secrets with. Or maybe Judson Morrow who had smiled at her across the sanctuary of the First Methodist. But he was shy and hadn't so much as said hello to her. And he was probably younger than she was, and no one knew where he'd come from or if he had family.

"Virgilia?" Her mother's voice followed a soft knock on the door.

"Yes?"

"I've gotten a knot in my necklace and your father's out at the wagon, waiting on us." Her mother entered the room, her voice soft as a rabbit fur, soothing.

Virgilia patted the seat next to her as she moved over on the bench. "Let's see if we can get it untangled." The gold felt cool against her fingers as she held the tiny chain. "Funny how it can get a knot in it while you're wearing it when it goes on without it."

"Oh, it's had that tangle for a while now. But today it annoyed me and then I couldn't get it unclasped. I suppose I should have left it until this evening. Your father will start shouting at 'his women' to hurry up. I'm not sure what I'd do without you, Virgilia."

"You'd do fine. And one day, you won't have me around. I hope. So enjoy it."

"That's a long way off, *I* hope."

"You were young when you married Papa."

"Twenty-two. That's old in some parts. But we found each other. In the library his parents started." Her mother's blue eyes glistened. "It's surprising how paths cross and then one day you see something you never saw before. It's like a bolt of lightning hits you and you wonder how you could have seen this man a dozen times and never noticed. There you are, in love."

"I can hardly wait, Mama. Here it is. All untangled."

"If only life offered such easy solutions."

"Pringle women, are you ready?" her father shouted, his deep voice lifting up the stairs through the summer heat.

Virgilia leaned over the balcony. "Coming, Papa." With an ivory stickpin, she held her thick blonde hair in a twist at the top of her head. She ran a bit of beet juice around her lips.

"You're only going to see your cousins," her mother cautioned.

"Orus is back telling stories. There'll be a crowd. Maybe I'll have one of those lightning moments, Mama. I want to look my best in case I get struck."

— 4 —
Orus's Report

"So I says to him, 'Shut up, White! Don't beg like a baby.' The Arapaho had tied our hands tight behind our backs, the rawhide cutting into our flesh." Orus held his hands up, wrists together as though bound still. Tabby saw the scars and winced. " 'Where is your old village?' I says to him. 'Come on, let's get this over with.' That's what I told those Indians. Stand up to 'em. That or die a coward."

"I wonder if you should tell such gory details, Husband," Lavina said. "We have impressionable children here."

"They may as well know what we went through and how we endured. Life knocks you down, Wife. Browns learn how to spring back up."

Orus was in his glory, Tabby decided. All eyes upon him. He'd gathered all the family save Manthano, of course, and a couple dozen St. Charles citizens too. He reminded her, not of his father who was a great preacher and orator, but of his uncle John who would launch himself into seaside bars filled with drinking sailors and pontificate on the virtues of giving up the brew. He never wavered, though she doubted he ever won a convert to his teetotaling ways. She could see Orus's audience had a few more who might be willing to head west, but the gory story he told now wouldn't do much to entice the masses.

"So White says to me, 'You'll anger them, Brown. Plead, that's what I say.' You all don't know, but White was once appointed Indian agent in the West. He's a doctor and maybe even a missionary, though I found a bit of his theology as warped as mine. Sorry, Marm." He nodded to Tabby. "Anyway, the usually certain-of-all-things Dr. White traveled back with me to the States and at that moment he proved more of a burden than the equipment we'd packed onto our mules. When some of his bravado might be useful, the man was a sniveling fool."

"Orus." This from Pherne. "That's no way to talk about a man of the cloth."

"Phooey." Orus waved his hand in dismissal of his sister's words. He took over a room and now held all rapt, sitting at the plank tables under shading trees.

" 'Indians respect confidence, boldness,' " I told White. " 'Keep your mouth shut and let me handle this,' I tell him. 'Well,' he says, 'I still think—' 'Stop thinking!' I said. I admit he sort of withered then, but sometimes a man's intellect isn't enough to get him through. It takes imagination and his body acting and understanding how another might see the world."

"Diplomacy was never your long suit, Brother Orus." Virgil grinned after he spoke and the laughter died down. Orus seemed not to have heard, grabbing a drink of sassafras.

Orus went on to tell how the men stumbled ahead of the Indians, who led his and White's horses behind their own. It was late April and they'd made good time in that year of 1845. Orus had hoped to be home by early summer. But then they'd been ambushed by these five Indians, and Orus allowed himself a moment of regret that he hadn't stood guard. He should have. This was his fault, but it was White's too. "I share the blame," he announced. "But White claimed to know all about Indians, so he should have seen the signs. What White contributed now was more trouble than help. What was done was done. A man comes to that place of knowing in a time of trouble." They'd been on the trail east for weeks, seeing no Indians and spending a few nights with a cluster of wagons heading west. "One of those trains had a black woman carrying a baby with them. Seeking freedom. There's that to be had in Oregon Territory, though not so much for colored folks."

"Will it be a free state?" someone asked. "Your Oregon."

"If it becomes a state and not a part of Britain first." He turned back to his adoring audience. "So Doc White and I take letters from that and other wagons heading west. Then days passed before anyone else crossed our paths, and the prairie gave a wide vista to see miles ahead. Sunsets worthy of Michelangelo's paints. We set our sails and figured free-sailing on to home. Forgive the sea talk, Marm." Orus grinned.

"You didn't expect trouble then?" Virgil spoke as he poked a potato fingerling into a savory sauce. Lavina and Pherne had covered the planks with hams and fresh-fried catfish and potatoes in various forms.

Orus shook his head. He reached for a peach, starting to eat from the bottom, a habit of his. "Back at Fort Hall, the soldiers spoke of small skirmishes, but things were described as calm. The soldiers told us that if we were headed east, the Indians weren't likely to bother us. After all, we were escaping their country, not coming into it. Well, that didn't work out as even a smidgeon of truth."

They had been leaving the Territory, but Orus told them all that he suspected the Indians knew they'd be back, bringing more white faces, wagons, cattle, sheep, who knew what all, unless the Indians could scare the hope and dream out of the Americans. That might be possible with some, but not with Orus Brown. "I decided then that if I survived, I'd be back to work the claim I made in Oregon Territory in the greenest country I've ever seen, with soil as black as that wagon-train woman."

And here he was. They would all be heading

west. Tabby saw the dreaminess on all the faces. Maybe not Pherne's, but all the rest of her family.

"As we entered that village"—Orus lowered his voice, leaned in—"dogs scattered like ducks on a pond, and women and children hustled aside to watch us pass." The children clustered forward. Tabby did herself, not wanting to miss a word. "I tried to make eye contact with everyone I could. Told White to do the same. We'd enter as brave men, nothing slovenly or cowardly in our demeanor." He stood straight then to show how he took on that village. "If we were to survive, it would take courage. Creativity. Maybe even a little compassion."

He spoke of hearing White mumbling prayers behind him. "I'm not a praying man—I know, Marm, you were praying for me—and I didn't mind someone putting up the request. But Papa always said that prayers demand action."

"And you're such a man." Virgil spoke those words. Pherne touched her hand to her husband's arm, wary of his tone.

"That I am, Brother. That I am. So I shouted, 'I want to see the chief.' I knew some Chinook, a trade language of the Indians. It's a mix of French and English and Columbia River gab. I didn't know the word for 'chief.' It hadn't seemed critical when I was learning words to trade for food and shelter. Most of that trading was done with the women, and I knew none of them would be chiefs.

"Those braves looked at each other. I couldn't gesture with my hands behind my back so I made a stern face, stood straight as an arrow, and ignored the pain of the tight leather at my wrists. I nodded with my head toward a tall Arapaho with regal bearing leaving a hide teepee and striding toward us." Orus kept his hands behind him, his chin held high, acting history out.

" 'I'm Orus Brown and I'm leaving this country if you'll set us free. If not, be on with what you're going to do to us.'

" 'You speak with brave words for one so bound.'

" 'English? You speak English? Well, praise the Lord.' That's exactly what I said, Marm."

Tabby clapped her hands. "Something sunk into your brain after all. Gratitude is a good place to start."

" 'Only small words,' this brave says. Then he talks to the Arapaho who brought us in. He spoke unintelligible things. White still mumbled, head bowed, a kind of murmuring moan, the backdrop to what sounded like an argument. I figured we'd been given a gift to meet up with an English speaker. All I had to do was turn that to our advantage. Maybe White and I would both get out alive."

"Were you afraid?" Virgilia asked her uncle.

"Afraid? No, Niece. But I was mighty attuned to the moment. So long as I had a next step to take, I couldn't let fear hold me from moving. We stumbled on into the circle of Arapaho, and that chief, the English speaker, set up a challenge. If we could run the gauntlet of slashes and lashes, they would let us go with open wounds and minus horses, tack, pack animals, and clothes." Orus's voice grew softer. "I was pretty sure I could do it, but White was emaciated already. And he's old. I wasn't certain he could. So I offered up myself, to run for both of us. I'd do it twice."

Tabby winced at the thought of her son facing whips and knives and who knew what all and doing it more than once. But she was pleased, too, that he would make the offer for another.

"Your father would be proud, to lay down one's life for a friend."

"Naked I made that run and naked I did it again. True to their word, they let us go, chased us out into the prairie, but they gave me my rifle and one round of ammunition 'because I was a brave man.' We wore old animal skins that stank, had no blankets. White carried water in his hand for me to drink and wash the wounds. We ate berries and then, as luck would have it, I shot a skunk. We didn't dare start a fire so we ate it raw. White says, 'We should ask the Lord's blessing on this food.' I tell him, 'I'll be d—sorry, Marm. I'll be dunked in tar before I thank the Lord for a skunk.' White says, 'I will say thank you then.' He asks the blessing and we ate."

Tabby frowned at her son's cursing. Virgil led the laughter.

Orus continued. "We'd been gifted earlier by meeting up with a botanist for the British Museum before we lost all to the Arapaho. We had supplies then that we shared with this learned man. He in turn gave us valuable information about what berries and nuts and other natural shrubs were safe to eat. Imagine that, way out there in the middle of nowhere. 'We are lucky men,' I told White. He says back, 'There is no luck. Only God's intention.' He would say something like that. Later we came upon a laundry line snapping in the wind. We grabbed pantaloons, shirts, and when the woman of the house came to stop us and saw our exposed bodies, old hides, smelly and all, she let us keep the clothes, fed us, gave us each a pair of old moccasins, listened to our story—that's a gift in itself—and after two days, set us on our way. I will always think more highly of a humble wife's willingness to give to others. Just as you always did, Marm." Orus saluted Tabby and then his wife. "The whole return was not as we had planned. White claimed it was his prayers that rescued us, and fine, I'll give him what credit he wants to take or give to others, as the case may be. I'm here and that's what matters." He ended with a flourish, and his adoring family and neighbors applauded. "And you all survived without me."

Was that a shining in his eyes, tears perhaps?

Not like her son to display such open emotion.

"And despite that ordeal, you want to return?" Virgil spoke again.

"I've built a cabin there on a little creek in the midst of a forest grove. It's in fertile ground not far from a mighty north-flowing river called the Willamette. Will-am-et is how they say it. We can all thrive there." He lowered his eyes, then turned to Tabby. "Well, maybe not all."

There it was again, that uneasy feeling that clutched at Tabby's heart.

Orus cleared his throat, and for the first time that afternoon Tabby heard no birdsong, no sounds of young children giggling. The world of sound had ceased. "Marm." She heard the change in his voice, wanted him to join the silence. He came over to the chair she sat on and knelt beside her, his hand on her walking stick. "It will be an ordeal, as Virgil says. You're lame. And getting on in years. I . . . I've thought this through. I don't think you can survive."

"What?"

"Excuse me, Gramo." Sarelia tugged on her grandmother's sleeve. "That's what you're supposed to say when you don't understand what someone has said—instead of 'what?' you say 'excuse me.' Isn't that so?"

Tabby patted her hand. "Indeed. But I do know what your uncle means." She swallowed back tears. "That I'm to be left behind."

— 5 —
What He Didn't Say

"I'm thinking of what's best for you." Orus rose, no longer squatted next to her hickory rocker. "The journey is long and arduous. There will be Indian skirmishes or worse, as I've just described. And you, you're sixty-five years old. And there's your lameness."

Virgilia brought her a glass of sarsaparilla. She chewed on dried cherries Lavina had placed in bowls around the table. "What would you have me do?" Tabby's heart pounded like a butter churn, thumping down both fear and betrayal.

"I would have you stay here, in a safe and growing town. Or with Manthano. He left the sea because of you, Marm. We both did. And now we've moved on to new lives. He'll look after you—if he doesn't decide to go too."

Tabby didn't like all this exploring of her fate with eyes staring. Or looking away. *They all knew about Orus's plan.* Why did Orus have to talk about it now? Why had he announced in front of the family and the neighbors his intention to go but leave her behind? He surely didn't need the support of many when he put out his proposal of them all leaving for Oregon—all but her. And she'd been feeling so proud of him.

"You still have purpose, Marm. But expressing it in the West, well, I'd be remiss if I took you into that at your age and in your condition."

"I'm too old to travel with you, yet you think I can stay on alone." Orus could be as impulsive as his father.

"You've got your old students here. Your home is secure. We'll make sure you have resources. It's what's best for you. It is. Do it for us if not for your own safety. You wouldn't want to hold us back, would you?"

Virgilia intervened. "Gramo, wouldn't you like a piece of my cake I baked for today, and the pies."

She had time to bake a cake? Orus must have been here for hours before coming to see her. Were they all aware of his plan and no one told her?

"I'm not of a mood for cake, even one of yours. But bring it for the others. I wouldn't want to stand in the way of everyone else's pleasure."

The girl's eyes lit up like a flash fire, either with the heat or having a reason to leave the large gathering if only for a few moments. Tabby watched the girl take a quick look down the lane before swirling her skirts and swishing into the house, that bright facial light suddenly dimmed to low ember. *She's waiting for someone.* Tabby's granddaughter was of courting age, and now that

Tabby thought of it, she was surprised no potential beau had been invited to this celebration.

"Mama? You don't want cake?"

"Phernie, I think maybe this old woman should head on home and get some needed rest for her aging, weary, lame, fatigued, exhausted, drowsy, apparently worn-out bones." She couldn't keep the hurt from her voice. "Surely don't need cake. Don't need anything as far as I can tell except gaining strength to watch my family disappear. Old as I am, I guess I'd better get started with that or I won't be ready by the time you all leave Missouri and follow Orus west. Come on, Sarelia Lucia. Help your old somnolent granny."

"What's som-no-lent, Gramo?"

"Something until a few minutes ago I didn't know I was."

She'd been knocked off her feet. Orus returned after nearly two years and lifted her up and swung her around as though she was a little stocking doll. So good to see him! And then, just when she imagined she'd be planning the move to Oregon —something she knew now she was ready for—he tells her, and everyone else, that it will be too dangerous. For her. She'd never felt her age before as she did at that moment. She was an old boot, too worn out for any foot. Useless, judged by her own son. She looked at her old feet and wondered if Orus might be right, but only for a moment. "Surely if I'm still here, the Lord has a plan for me and it wouldn't be to be separated from my family, would it?" Tabby asked her chicken. She stroked the bird, head to tail feathers. Jeremiah was an old man too and he trusted that God had a plan for him, a good plan, not to harm but to bring a future purpose and a hope. Beatrice's soft clucking acted as back music to Tabby's thoughts.

Stay with Manthano, Orus said. That her second son would want his mother close by after all these years apart was unlikely. That her daughter and her husband would remain that she might continue to be of help now and then to them and their children? Not likely either. "Have I no say in my own future?"

"Is this the biggest challenge of your life, Gramo?" She'd forgotten the child lingered.

"It could be. It just could be." She put Beatrice down and watched her "beak" her way toward her cage and the corn there. "You'd best head back, Child. I'm fine." Unharnessing Joey took the edge off her anger. Now it was sadness she had to put away.

Sarelia hugged her, then left, and Tabby watched her disappear through the trees. A nine-year-old child they let walk miles on her own back to the gathering but this old woman couldn't join them? Her heart ached at this first sign of the change, the great loss of her family so close to her. Had she been domineering and that was why her son didn't want her? Was it really so dangerous, the road to Oregon? Women and children had left in droves this past spring. Was it for her own good that he said she couldn't go?

She remembered being separated from Clark when the children were young, as he preached and worked around the region. How she'd turned down his marriage proposal twice before accepting because she thought him too old for her, too "stuffy" when she was an outspoken soul, not good for a preacher's wife. But he had seen through that façade to who she really was, and he told her that marrying him would be a good thing for her life. And so it had been. Was Orus merely following in his father's footsteps? Was his telling her she could not go an act of protective love? Maybe she had to listen.

Pherne rubbed Emma's feet, tucked Sarelia in, and blew out the candle light. It had been a long day begun early with Orus's arrival before dawn and ending with her mother harboring herself in her cabin, sulking. She did that sometimes, but this separation was considerable. And who could blame her? For her part, Pherne would be happy to remain in Missouri with her, and she'd tell her so in the morning. No reason for her to brood. They could go on as they had the past two years with Orus out west. She was glad Virgil hadn't said much during Orus's storytelling, and while they hadn't discussed it, Virgil wasn't an impulsive man and she imagined his wanting to stay right here too. She was a little disturbed that she hadn't defended her mother earlier, but she didn't want to take Orus on in front of everyone either.

"Mrs. Brown didn't take Orus's proclamation all that well." Virgil always called his mother-in-law by that formal name. He'd climbed into their four-poster bed while Pherne said prayers with the children, and he waited for her now as she sat on the bench before the mirror.

"I can understand." Pherne fiddled with her locket. "She's been raving about Orus her whole life, forgiving him for any number of escapades, and now this. It must be a terrible disappointment. But it gives us a perfectly good reason to stay. I'm grateful for that."

Virgil cleared his throat. "Not to go? Why wouldn't we?"

She turned to her husband. "You want to leave all we have here?"

"I helped fund Orus's trip and kept things going, hoping he'd have good news of Oregon. And he did. Does."

"You did?" She raised her eyes to his in the mirror, saw him with his arms behind his head, leaned against the headboard. It had been Virgil's parents' bed. Mahogany, heavy, polished to a fine sheen. His parents had brought it all the way from Connecticut. His hair, the color of tar, glistened in the candlelight. "But we have a life here."

"It'll be changing before long. I can feel that. Business slows. This slavery thing. It's wrong, you know that. If we remain, we'll be forced into it for commercial reasons, just as Manthano is. But in Oregon we can gain enough land—640 acres, Orus said—and it's destined to be a free state. We'll populate the Territory, and when enough of us are there, apply for statehood. Without slaves and with enough land to make a living. And keep that country for America, snatched from British hands." He motioned to her to come and sit beside him on the bed.

"We have enough now." She stayed where she was and unwound her honey-colored braid. She began to brush at the kinks and curves, avoiding his eye in the mirror's reflection. Finished in silence, she tugged at the hairbrush and put the soft strands into the porcelain hair container. She planned to add it to her collection of Oliver's baby-fine hair, make a mourning weave she'd frame. But every time she set to work on it, her tears flowed, and instead she put the cover on the little pot, accumulating memories. Perhaps that was all she was capable of doing in grieving Oliver's death. She couldn't leave Oliver's grave. And her own grandmother was buried in Missouri too. More reasons to stay. She brushed at the throat ribbon on her cotton nightdress, then moved around the room, tidying this and that. It amazed her that her mother wanted to leave her mother's grave behind.

"Come to bed," Virgil told her. He lifted the light sheet so she could crawl in beside him. "We don't have to decide now."

She relented. Moisture beaded above her lip. "This heat." He lifted her hand and stroked it. "I didn't think you'd want to go. I . . . I've liked not having my brother around all the time. I adore him, but he's intense, driven, and he convinces people of things they don't really want to do. He seems to know everything and badgers others into his . . . sphere of influence. He intends well, I know, but—"

"He didn't badger me into investing in his journey."

"I wish you'd told me you'd done that." She moved to the bed.

"He's laid claim to a lot of land. There are hardly any people out there, and he says the ground is fresh and fertile and can grow anything. He planted a crop last year when he got there, and the grain grew all winter. No hard freeze at all."

"I heard all that." She tucked her gown around her knees, lifted the sheet to cover them both. "But Orus exaggerates too. He can make things sound better than they are."

"He didn't spread honey over his escape from the Arapaho."

"No. But it acted as fodder for telling Mother it would be too dangerous. And it ended with him as the hero. It always does. I've rarely heard him claim a mistake, so that makes me wonder if he learns from errors. And I wonder what Dr. White's version of the story might be. Did my brother make their escape worse rather than better as he tells it?"

"What matters is that he made it back."

A warm breeze brushed against the curtains. They lived well here, as well as her in-laws in early St. Charles had. Pherne had tried to emulate her mother-in-law by keeping a good house, being involved in St. Charles society, ensuring her children could read and write and make educated choices. This decision, to go to Oregon and leave her mother behind, wasn't an educated choice, and it surprised her that her husband would make it.

"And your brothers? What have they said, or didn't they know of your investment in Orus's trip either?"

"They understand. Might even venture out themselves if things get politically more strained here. Missouri is not the best place to be for someone opposed to slaving."

"Oregon might not be either. Half the group that left earlier this year were Missourians, some taking their slaves with them into the Oregon country."

"There are the children to think of." Virgil's voice purred low.

"My very thought." She sat up. "Virgilia is of courting age. She'll marry before long. What if her husband doesn't choose Oregon? We'll lose her if we leave them behind. I couldn't take another loss like that."

"You're bouncing ahead. For all we know, she'd like to go. You're the only hold-up."

Pherne felt herself stiffen. "I'm only holding up my part of the family, creating a good palette for them to paint good lives. You could do likewise instead of smudging a perfectly fine picture with strident hues." She brushed at a fly. "And if Mother doesn't go, someone needs to remain with her."

"Oh, she's not going. As you said, Orus said no to that and his is usually the last word. But Mrs. Brown's a good hand. She'll tend to herself just fine." He rubbed her back as she sat, knees to her chin, facing away from him. His voice softened. "Look, Phernie. It could be the new start we need. Oliver's dying—"

"I knew you'd bring that up." She threw the covers off and stood, shaking, her jaw clenched so she wouldn't say something she'd later regret.

"It's been years, Pherne. Life goes on."

"It wasn't my fault."

"I've never said it was."

"You've thought it, though."

He sighed and shook his head. "I have not. And I have grieved that you assume responsibility."

"I need to check the children."

He reached for her hand but she pulled free, separated herself, and wondered if that was what she'd be doing in the months ahead. It was what she'd been trying to do for three years.

What would they do, the Pringles? Virgilia had missed some of the conversation when she went for the cake. She'd taken a few minutes longer to rework the icing that the heat had begun to dribble down the sides like raindrops on a windowpane. She'd held the pewter icing knife her gramo had given her like one of her mother's paintbrushes, admiring the icing rescue and the swirls she could put onto the buttered icing. But when she returned, her grandmother was speaking in clipped tones, Sarelia jumped about to help her up, and her own parents dropped their eyes in silence. Only later did her brother Octavius tell her what her gramo had said.

"Gramo was upset," Sarelia said as she stood beside the washbasin. Virgilia wiped at the girl's eyes, forehead, neck, and cheeks. Her sisters stood in their chemises, wishing for a breeze to cool them but getting lazy, warm air instead. The tepid water could help. The scent of oleander drifted through the open window.

"Yes, she was upset. But grown-ups get that way sometimes. She'll be fine."

"Orus says Grandma can't go." Emma broke her usual silence. "I'll stay with her."

"We likely all will. I didn't hear Papa say we'd head west, did you?" Sarelia and Emma both shook their heads no. "Well then, let's not put our cart before the horse."

Emma frowned. "That won't work, Sister."

"Exactly. We'll wait to see what happens. Now climb into that bed and let's get some sleep despite this heat."

"I'm bedding down on the balcony," Sarelia told her. "It can't be as hot out there."

"Moths and bats will get you." Virgilia grinned as she said it. Her sisters hated bats and moths. Virgilia didn't mind flying things; it was slithering things that bothered her.

"Eeeeh." Sarelia instead crawled into the high bed, pushed her sister over, and made room for Virgilia. But as soon as soft snores came from her sisters, Virgilia eased her way to the balcony herself. She pulled her shawl around her slender shoulders. She could put up with the night flyers. She wanted time alone to think about what she wanted. If her parents didn't go, she still could. With her cousins. Aunt Lavina could use help with her many children. She'd be under the thumb of Orus, but she'd have the adventure. But could she leave her gramo? Her parents and those snoring sisters? She'd missed the nuances of what occurred while she was artfully saving her cake. She was always one step behind. Some people didn't know what they wanted, boys especially, that's what Gramo told her. "So you've got to know what you want." She guessed she'd have to answer that question first before trying to convince her parents or Judson Morrow of what he might want. This living was complicated. But here, on Hickory Farm, things were familiar, predictable—until Uncle Orus came back. Was that what she wanted though, unsurprising days? This had not been one of those. She wanted adventure. Oregon promised that. But St. Charles promised safety. What to do? She'd put her wishes to poetry in the morning, her special kind of prayer.

— 6 —
Considerations

"I behaved poorly," Tabby told Beatrice the next morning. "I've set a bad example for the children for when things didn't go my way. I acted like you during molting, being all cranky." The Rhode Island Red squatted in comfort with Tabby's strokes. One needed to find a new route rather than sulk and grumble. The thing to do was to trot as best she could right over to Orus and apologize. And then plan a trip to Vibbard and talk with Manthano. She couldn't see herself living on alone here.

Manthano lived over a hundred miles away. Well, if she couldn't make that trip, however would she make it all the way to Oregon?

"Pherne said almost nothing." Tabby continued chattering to Beatrice while she fixed her tea and stirred hot water into cornmeal she'd have for breakfast. "That surprised me. I thought she'd say for sure that I could go with them. I mean, I assume they're going." She stopped her stirring. Maybe they weren't. She tried to remember how Virgil had taken all the western news. Well, then, all this fuss about having to visit Manthano and lay herself open to that wife of his (who kept him from spending time with *his* family) might be letting the cat out of the bag before it even got put in. The thought lightened her mood.

Sarelia arrived at Tabby's cabin as though the girl had a sixth sense when Tabby was ready to head out, walking stick in hand. "What's your papa say about all this Oregon talk?"

"Nothing."

"He hasn't said a word?"

"He and Mama talked till late. We heard the rumblings rising up the stairs." She shrugged her narrow shoulders.

Again, she was asking a child something she shouldn't have. *Mercy me, what is wrong with me!* "This morning I'm headed over to Orus's. I think I'll walk. It always puts me in a better mood."

"Mama says to come by to break your fast."

"Already finished but I'll stick my head in and say hey."

Tabby loved soft, misty Missouri mornings. She could find a way to stay. If she wanted to. She made a quick stop at Pherne's, telling her she was going to apologize to Orus "for making such a fuss about not being asked along. Not a good example for the children."

"You were only expressing your upset, Mama."

"Yes, but a good example finds a way to move forward, not set her heels in and revert to childhood. Isn't that right, Sarelia?"

"What? I mean, excuse me? I don't understand, Gramo."

"Not necessary." Tabby tugged at the child's braid. "Anyway, I'll find a way to stay and I will make the best of it. I wouldn't want to hold any of you back worrying about an old woman."

"Maybe not all of us want to go." Pherne fingered her locket.

"Virgil having second thoughts, is he?"

Their conversation was interrupted by the arrival of hungry children as Pherne put porridge on the table, sliced slivers of brown sugar from the cone, and let each child stir until the sugar melted. "We'll talk later, Mama." Pherne turned back to her stove, a recent purchase Virgil made to ease her days. The stove wouldn't be easily taken west, nor would that dining room table and set of chairs they'd paid dearly to bring by steamship down the Ohio. Pherne did love nice things.

Tabby thought of what she might take with her—if she had a chance to go. It kept her quiet as she and Sarelia walked down the boardwalk streets toward Orus's farm on the outskirts of town. Tabby tugged at her crocheted collar. She had few things to take with her. She'd learned to live frugally. A widow with children had to. And besides, memories were easily packed.

Once at Orus and Lavina's, Tabby sought out her son, finding him at the edge of the field, tin cup in hand, surveying his crop.

"I've decided to apologize, Son. I'm so happy you're back and I confess I forgot to be grateful that you were safe and sound before I snapped my lips about your thinking me too old to go with you."

"The girls are out by the spring, Sarelia, if you want to find them." Sarelia skipped away. Then to Tabby, Orus said, "I'm glad to see you've come to your senses, Marm. Your staying really is for the best."

His easy acceptance stung, but she plodded on with her latest plan.

"I've decided I'll go visit Manthano and see if I can appease his wife into having me live with them. I really can be a helpful soul despite my foot lagging."

"And tongue wagging." Orus grinned.

"That too. The older I get, the more I realize I need to be more helpful." Visiting Manthano before the leaves turned would tell Tabby if she and her second son could set aside old irritations, smooth salve over old wounds, and live together. But more, it would interrupt the image she feared her children held of their mother and grandmother as an old, lame woman in her hickory chair, living through their lives rather than finding a purpose of her own. "But Catherine isn't so taken with me, I'm afraid."

"Not taken with many, I'd say. I can't take you this week." Orus scanned his fields. "September, I can go with you then."

"I can do it alone." He really did see her as a cripple. "I'm no little waif seeking refuge." She laughed when she said it.

"You're no waif, but harnessing a wagon and—"

"I've done it before, I can do it again. I didn't come to seek your permission, Orus. I came to say I was sorry for acting the child. I understand why you don't want me. I'd be a burden to you and I've never wanted that."

"It's for your safety, Marm. Wait until next month. I can go with you then."

She let him think she'd consider waiting.

They walked back into the house, where Lavina brought hot tea to the table. Tabby took a seat, breathing hard. Walking on the uneven ground of fields strained her foot more than she wanted to admit. Walking at all was a struggle, but she needed the motion to keep that limb limber. She mentioned her plan to visit Manthano.

"Orus said he and Dr. White stopped at Manthano's on the way back and Catherine was with child. She might welcome an extra pair of hands." Lavina removed the tea caddy, shaking it once over Tabby's cup. "A new mother always needs extra help."

"Yes. Midwifery is worthy work."

"It's settled then. We'll go next month." Orus pressed both hands on his thighs and stood.

"I go this month and without you, Orus. You

have things to tend to here, I know, so let me be on my own. Get used to the changes before they happen."

"Mama, I won't—"

"Let her, Husband. A woman needs to have some say in her direction, not always be a weather vane pushed by a son."

"I don't like it."

"We Browns have lots of things we don't like, but we make do," Tabby said. "And I will too, Orus Brown. There's a limit to your bossing your marm. I've just reached it."

With that she took her stick, lifted herself from the chair, and limped out, shouting for Sarelia as she made her way down the steps. She'd come with the best of intentions to hold her tongue, get her relationship with Orus back on track. Then in an instant she'd acted the child again. What was she trying to prove?

Virgilia liked the idea when Tabby broached the subject of taking Virgilia with her on her sojourn to Manthano's, but her mother said no. "But, Mama, I can be helpful to Gramo. And I haven't seen my cousins in forever."

"Surely you're not worried about me making the trek, are you, Pherne? You know I can go that far." Her grandmother held her arms out for the wrapping of yarn. Emma and Sarelia sat in the corner, reading a James Fenimore Cooper book, though they seemed young for such fare as *The Pathfinder*. Still, the subject was appropriate with all the talk of traveling.

"Oh, I suspect you can do whatever you set your mind to, Mother. It's a Brown trait. But, well, if you do talk Manthano into taking you in, I'll lose my last argument with Virgil about needing to stay here to care for you."

Her grandmother blinked. "You want to stay?"

"Mama doesn't want to go."

Pherne scowled at her daughter, sending Virgilia to check on a venison stew she'd put on while her mother and grandmother sat at the table tending yarn.

"And you know this because?"

"Because I heard you and Papa last evening, talking."

"Eavesdropping is—"

"You don't want to go to Oregon? Oh, Pherne, it'll be such an adventure." Tabby reached across and patted her daughter's hand, interrupting an eavesdropping lecture, something her grandmother did all the time. "Oh, the experiences of new places, new ways. Adapting. It keeps a person young, it does. And nimble."

"You'd leave your mama's grave? My Oliver's?" Pherne shook her head. "I can't."

"You can. I left your father's grave and my child's and my father's grave too. Their coffins are holding places, Pherne. Their spirits aren't

64

there. They live here." She tapped her heart. "We take them with us. If your husband wishes you to go, you must go."

"Our roots are deep here, Mother. Don't you feel that?"

Virgilia listened, stirred with a wooden spoon smooth in her hand.

"Roots spread. And we'll spread our family tree across the continent," her grandmother said. "Or rather, Orus will. And you and Virgil. Mine too, I suppose, through each of you. But I'd love to plant a few roots in Oregon country. Each time your father moved us, I wondered if I should stay, be separated. But then I realized that I left behind experiences only. Memories I took with me and I still have all of those, made sweeter through the years."

Virgilia could see tears welling up in her mother's eyes.

"Look, Sweet Pea, I know you have to make it your own choice, not do it because Virgil insists. If you go for him, when things get tough—and they will get tough—you could become spiteful and carry misery that'll last a lot longer than whatever is the current trouble. You'll blame him for the problems, and frankly, a blaming woman is not very attractive. It's harder to find fault in others if you've chosen a route for yourself. That's what I'm trying to do here, having Manthano take me in, though I'll keep making my own way too. I'll find something to do there. Start a school, maybe."

Pherne blew her nose in the handkerchief Virgilia handed her.

"It's only for a week or so, Mama. Gramo and I will have a fine time of it. Please can't I go?"

"I'll speak to your father. If he says yes, then all right."

"Maybe Judson would come with us." Virgilia slapped her hand over her mouth.

"Judson Morrow? Your beau, is he?" Her grandmother picked right up on things.

"Oh, no, ah. Never mind, Gramo." Virgilia could have kicked herself for her outburst. "I just thought we'd need a driver, wouldn't we?"

"Virgilia." Pherne clucked her tongue at the idea.

"He'll be a huge help, Gramo. We won't have to lift a finger."

"Or a foot, I'll wager. We'll have to talk, girl, about your beau," her gramo said, "but since we'll be taking the stage, I doubt his services will be needed."

"Feet or wings: My foot. I know you've asked before what happened to make me lame and it's a sad tale, Sarelia. I don't like dwelling on sad stories. It mixes up so much pain and later trials, now overcome. No need for it, but I suppose in a memoir one must write not only about the happy

66

things that turned out well but also about the harder things, failures."

"That's what I want to hear about, Gramo. The hard things."

"Hmm. Well, we'd gone skating. My papa had taken me along with Alvin, my brother. Mama came too, but she didn't skate. Alvin could swirl rings around me. Papa too. Papa was a fine figure of a man, standing on one foot and spinning to my applause. The lake had been swept as smooth as a baby's cheek, but still there were nubbins of ice that rose up to surprise, like pimples on a chin. It's not unlike life, Child, when things go smoothly for a time and then we stumble. There's nothing to do but get up, decide if we were wise to be on that lake in the first place, and maybe choose to never go there again. But often, life just happens to us, and it will, over and over again."

Sarelia blinked, keeping her attention like the dog's nose to a bird in the bush. "Did you break your leg, Gramo?"

"Here's what happened. On that December day, I wore my pair of wooden skates. They were made by a craftsman in exchange for money owed my father for a difficult delivery of the craftsman's twin sons. I wobbled and lurched, forward and back, until I got the rhythm of it. Lean to the right, then left and back again in order to go forward, hands flailing and then eased behind my back, elbows out. The cold bit my face and I loved it. My mouth froze open with the joy of the sensation and my smiling, smiling. I can feel that cold air sucked into my lungs even now. How does that sound, Sarelia? Can you picture the lake and me on it?"

The child nodded.

"Good. My father had shown me how to slow down by dragging my toe, and I did that as I approached what I knew to be a nubbin-infused part of the lake and pushed off to my left. Everything was a dance and I stopped myself as three skaters swished by. Then, watching them wing past me, while simply standing, I fell over."

Sarelia gasped.

"I heard the bone crack and wailed with the pain. Alvin had seen me fall and he shouted to my father, who skated over and swished to a stop, pushing up tiny beads of ice as he bent. 'Can you get up, Tabby? Where does it hurt?'

"I pointed to my ankle, and when he lifted me, the weight of the boot and skate felt like a horse pulled against it. 'It's worse, Papa,' I told him.

"He lifted my leg to bear the weight as he skated me to the warming house, where my mother sat beside a fire. I saw the look pass between them, and then she began to remove the skate, my foot already swelling tight against the bindings. 'This will hurt now. Be strong.' Papa eased the boot off as best he could, but I remember the pain as searing, almost causing me to swoon. Or maybe it was the smell of blood. Was this the biggest challenge of my life?

"My father proved to be my wings that day as he whisked me to the carriage and then his surgical office. I tried to see my foot, but my coat and my father's back as he bent over me severed my view. He would try to set the bone, the sharp one sticking out. I could view it with my stocking cut off and the blood washed away. The throbbing was like a woodpecker thumping on a tree. My mother administered the laudanum and I felt lifted away from the present moment as a leaf is levitated by a calming breeze." Tabby floated her fingers into the air to demonstrate. "I had momentary wings. The sensation kept me from the knowledge I would come to later, that my first experience with skates upon my feet would be my last."

"Oh, Gramo. That must have hurt soooo much."

"That it did. And the accident marked a turning point for my father. His usual demeanor of happiness and hope faded as red dye over time weeps into black." Tabby's fingertips brushed Sarelia's braids. "Perhaps seeing me every day and his not being able to fix me up as good as new proved torturous. Once I heard him tell my mother that he had 'botched the repair.' But I told him that broken things can be patched up, not as good as new, maybe. But useful. My father blamed himself. I had done that as well, thinking if only I had done something differently, the accident wouldn't have happened. But that's what accidents are, for the most part: unplanned. We can only imagine how to pick up the pieces and wing anew through the sky, reaching higher." She smiled at her grandchild. "Always reach higher, Sarelia Lucia, push yourself beyond what you think it is you are limited to and let God surprise you with the result."

"All right, Gramo. I'll keep reaching higher. Like to your cookie jar? It's too high on the shelf for me."

Tabby tweaked Sarelia's cheek, then pointed to a stool. "Sometimes we have to use tools to help us." Something she needed to remember herself.

— 7 —
The Reality of Things

Virgilia's enthusiasm began to wane the second day out. Holding Beatrice in her cage on her lap, being squeezed in the stuffy stage between her grandmother and an oversized man who fluffed out his suit coat as though it was a skirt, the dust and chicken smell all sucked at her usually positive spirit. The man snored as he snoozed (how anyone could was beyond her), often dropping his head onto her shoulder. He kept his vest and jacket unbuttoned. Well, it was pretty hot inside so maybe that made sense, but the women had to keep their corsets on and dress buttons all the way to their throats. She waved a handkerchief to stir the stale air, giving rise to an errant chicken feather. No summer dresses for this kind of travel. Across from her sat a young woman with a swaddled baby and a man who didn't talk to the woman but smiled at the infant now and then. Maybe her husband? A brother? Virgilia let her mind imagine scenarios about the others on the stage. Wanted for murder and they've hidden out in remote Missouri. Running from a domineering brother. Traveling to reunite with her husband, bringing their child. Virgilia liked that scenario best. She dozed, though rest was only tolerable. Her chin dropping onto the cage woke her with a start.

But there were lessons here. The way her grandmother made friends with everyone, for example. She complimented people, like how careful the mom was with her baby or how the fluffy man had so politely helped her grandmother up onto the stage and didn't mind that she had to lay her hickory walking stick down so their feet rolled across it while they rode along. She never complained about the stage conditions nor the food nor the tattered beds, though one night they did request a change, as Virgilia saw bugs crawling on the graying white sheet. They considered letting Beatrice from her cage to consume the problem. If complimenting people was all it took to warm them up, then maybe Virgilia herself could find a way to have reasonable conversations with strangers, boys included, and maybe one day she'd make a friend of someone new.

The second best part of the trip was anticipation, a foray into the future. She'd see Pherne, her cousin, once they arrived. She hadn't had a letter from her for a long time, but they were family, so Virgilia was certain they would fit together like hands to a glove. There'd be new routines, different paths to walk, and fresh ideas to ponder.

"I think we should arrive tomorrow at Vibbard," her grandmother told her as they settled into bed, their fifth night out.

"Will we have to rent a buggy to go to Uncle's farm?"

"Possibly. But maybe we can walk it. You know, if Manthano will have me, I'll likely not return to St. Charles."

"You won't?" That possibility had not occurred to her. "I'd . . . I'd go back alone?"

"You'll do fine. I've watched you. You're kind and gracious and smart and know when to be quiet."

"But I haven't ever, I mean, what if we're robbed? Or what if I miss the stage while I'm tending to my dailies? Or what if—"

"Living in the what-ifs is dangerous. Those are good questions to ask in the planning of a thing. I'm sure your uncle Orus asked himself, 'What if my mother was to join us?' He obviously didn't like the answer. But once you've decided, well then, you can't keep worrying about what lies ahead. It will rob you, Virgilia. You must take each moment, find the good in it, and be grateful."

Virgilia shook out her petticoat to be worn in the morning. "But bad things do happen, Gramo." She thought of Oliver and of her grandmother's foot that stumbled her so.

"They surely do. But worrying about them

73

doesn't stop them, now does it?" Her gramo squinted at her through round eyeglasses. "What is it you're afraid of?"

Virgilia looked at her shoes. "Snakes and loneliness and sickness and . . . snakes."

"Snakes? Well, facing that fear will only make you stronger. As for sickness and dying, they happen to us all. No sense worrying them sooner." She plumped her pillow. "And loneliness, well, that's where your imagination comes in. You have to build yourself a ladder to take yourself out of sadness or grief or fear. Each rung lifting into better light."

"Like Jacob's ladder?"

"Something like that. Now, Child, we best get some rest."

Virgilia lay quiet beside her grandmother, trying not to move or upset her sleep. *Imagination*. She hadn't considered it a rung of a ladder, something she could draw on to change the circumstances she found herself in. She'd build a ladder with courage as a rung. Maybe kindness would lift her higher too. It was the image she fell asleep pondering.

When they arrived at the stage stop in Ray County, there were no buggies to rent and the stage manager told them it wasn't a far walk to the "Brown Plantation." So walk they did, leaving their bags and Beatrice (with a fresh pan of water) at the stage stop until they could be sent for. Dust wisped over their shoes as they trekked along the boardwalk. Quail chattered. Virgilia slowed her pace to her grandmother's. It was nearly dusk when they saw the house on a hill described to them, scrub oak and cherry trees clustered in plots that Virgilia's uncle must have planted with an eye for design. He'd set the house within them, the white pillars like steamboat stacks announcing their importance. A winding drive led up the hill, where Virgilia helped her grandmother use the stile to climb over the fence. Dogs barked. Her grandmother's breathing sounded labored.

"Why don't I go on ahead, Gramo. You rest here."

"I'm good. I am." But the woman leaned against her walking stick. "Yes, you go ahead as you offered to. I'll be along."

Virgilia hesitated. "They have slaves, Papa said. Should I speak to them?"

"Of course, Child. They're people like us. Tell them we're kin and ask for your aunt and uncle." Her grandmother panted in the early-evening heat, and the soft breeze moving the cottonwood trees didn't cool even with the spring nearby. She adjusted her crocheted collar, brushing at the dust.

"I'll ask for Pherne if Aunt Catherine isn't about." Virgilia straightened her bonnet and admired the leafless path and white pillars on the porch. She could do this, meet strangers, introduce herself. She had courage.

The house wasn't on a high stone foundation the way St. Charles homes were. No fears of flooding here. The mansion looked south over a river, a tributary to the Missouri. As she approached, a dark-skinned man dressed in a fine suit of clothes stepped out on the porch. His presence and the imposing structure started to steal her confidence.

"Good evening, sir. You're looking very dapper this evening. What a fine suit."

"May I help you, miss?"

"Oh. Yes. I'm Virgilia Pringle, Mr. Manthano Brown's niece. That's his mother." She turned and pointed toward her grandmother, who had begun the slow trek up the driveway.

"I'll tell them you're here, miss." He bowed to her and started to walk inside.

Virgilia licked her dry lips, excitement growing as she anticipated seeing her relatives, sleeping in a comfortable bed, and best of all, giggling and sharing secrets with Pherne.

"Is Pherne here?" The words blurted out.

The porch man, or whatever he was, had already turned away but stopped and came back. "Mrs. Bain no longer lives here. She's married and lives in Camden. I'll tell the Browns that you are here."

"Married?"

"That's what that man said. Pherne's only sixteen, a year younger than me, Gramo. And she hadn't even written about it."

"Nor included any of us in her wedding festivities, either." Tabby wondered how Manthano's family had become so estranged. "Maybe there's a good reason they didn't invite the rest of the clan." Tabby had her own disappointment with that news, surprised at how the slight of not being included stung. She loved occasions and a granddaughter's wedding would have been one. "I'm sure there's a good reason."

A smallish black boy lit lanterns along the railing as dusk whispered in. Then a tall, handsome man with trimmed sideburns and a smooth face stepped onto the newly whitewashed porch. "A good reason for what, Mother?"

"A good reason why it's been so long since I've put my arms around my son."

He bent to help her up the steps, taking her hand, then motioned them inside without coming into the open arms she offered to hug him with. Moths flickered at the lights; tiny bugs alighted on her shoulder, then flitted away. Tabby straightened her back.

"Do you recognize your niece Virgilia?"

"I see resemblance to my sister now that you say it. That honey-colored hair and eyes as blue as cornflowers. Do you have dimples when you smile? How did you get here, Mother?"

"We walked. From the stage house." She caught her breath at the top of the stairs.

"You should have sent word instead of that hard walk. I'll send Tom to get your things."

"We're here now."

"We're finishing our supper. I assume you have not eaten?"

"We have not eaten."

"Come along then."

The welcome from Manthano had not been warm, but then she had expected nothing more. Somewhere along the journey of their lives this son had chosen to set himself away and apart. He liked making his own shadow rather than trying to shine within his brother's. Or his mother's. But it had been years since she'd seen him. She would have liked holding her son for a moment.

Five children looked up as Tabby and Virgilia entered the large room where Manthano's second wife, Catherine, sat at the head of the table, her chair pushed back to accommodate her pending childbirth. So many lanterns lit the room there were no shadows at all, even in the corners.

"You remember my wife, Catherine. And children, here are your grandmother and cousin Virgilia." Each of the children stood, said their name with a "Welcome," and the girls curtsied their respect.

"I'll have ham brought in and cheese." He motioned to the black woman who had begun clearing the table. "We have bread from today. Will that suffice?"

Catherine spoke then, her voice husky with fatigue. "We want you to have more than sufficient, Mother Brown." She scowled at her husband. "Sweets are in order, don't you think, children? To honor the occasion? Would you like peppermints, Virgilia?" The girl nodded and Catherine smiled. "You are welcome here. Forgive my not rising. I am . . . well, you see." She cast her eyes toward her stomach.

A few "yes, ma'am" and "Sweets!" rose up from the children, who eased their formality as they made room for Virgilia on the bench, and Manthano brought a chair for Tabby.

"What brings you, Mother?"

"Oh, our business can wait until morning, Son. Let's enjoy this family time, shall we? Catherine, I was sad to learn of your boy's passing last year. A great loss when a child cannot thrive."

Catherine nodded, and for a moment Tabby wondered if she should have mentioned the death of a child while another waited to enter this world. But Orus had said she expected, though grief still hovered from their baby not surviving a year. There'd been no letters telling of the birth or the death that followed, the news only coming because Orus had stopped at Manthano's on the way back.

"Thank you for the condolences. We should have written, but . . ."

"You had enough on your plate." Tabby patted Catherine's back, felt her slender shoulder bones. She said to her son, "*You* might have written, though. You haven't forgotten how, have you, Son?"

Why she jabbed at him she didn't know. He'd been a good student as a child, but he didn't like to either read or write. He had a head for numbers, which explained in part his present prosperity.

"I imagine Orus has told you of our plans to head to Oregon next year?" Manthano said then.

Tabby heard Virgilia gasp. She almost did herself. "You're going to Oregon too?"

"You know Orus. He convinces, says I can have a larger farm there and without the moral puzzle of keeping slaves. If you came hoping I'd encourage you to go as well, you are mistaken, Mother. You're frail, and from all I hear, the trip is so demanding you would likely not survive. For once, perhaps you should listen to others."

"Orus did not tell me you were thinking of leaving Missouri too."

"Perhaps he picked up on Catherine's reluctance, but we have worked that through."

Tabby watched a slight narrowing of Catherine's eyes as though she might object but kept silent. "I . . . I had no idea you would make such a large change. You have so much here. The farm. Your boot-making business in town."

"We have had words over it." Catherine passed honeyed butter to Virgilia.

"I imagine you have. Goodness, Manthano, if you're worrying about me not being able to make the trek, what of your wife? New mothers will have a challenge as well, I would think."

"She is willing and will be rested from the arrival of our next child due anytime. It will be a new start for us."

"Yes, yes it will."

His mind was made up. Unless Virgil listened to his wife's reluctance, by this time next year all Tabby's children would be on that trail west, all but "this old folk." The ache she'd been carrying grew deeper. They were all leaving. Why hadn't Orus told her that? Well, maybe it hadn't been decided when he'd come through. But now, well, she would be left with none of her children? Unless Virgil listened to Pherne and stayed behind.

"I see your shoe is in need of repair, Mother. I'll take it tomorrow and remake it myself."

"I'd be grateful." A small gesture of healing in this fractured relationship, even if it was just to fix a shoe.

Virgilia didn't know if her family had made that decision to go or stay, but she had hoped if they didn't, that Gramo would keep her small feet right under the table next door rather than at Uncle Manthano's, so far away. With her uncle's announcement that his family planned to join Orus, she didn't know what her gramo would do. She'd seen how surprised Gramo was when that branch of the Brown tree said they'd be heading west and that both her uncles now thought Gramo's old and broken limbs weren't up to the journey. Virgilia had listened at her uncle's office door later. He'd been adamant, saying his mother needed to learn to accept "the reality of things."

"The reality of things is that you are elderly. You are lame. You are frail, and your going would put your life at risk as well as others who might have to slow down for you. Don't be foolish, Mother."

"What life will I have if my entire family leaves me behind?"

"You can carry on in St. Charles as you have all these years now. You never wanted to join me here."

"I didn't know I was welcome."

"Marm," he'd said, using a word Virgilia had only heard her uncle Orus use for her gramo. Virgilia felt a bit uneasy listening at the door of her uncle's office, but she wanted to know, wanted to be able to comfort her gramo when this was all over and they headed back home. Which she hoped would be soon.

Virgilia didn't like the way her aunt Catherine looked, heavy with child, waddling, holding her back; nor the pinched looks on her face when Oregon was discussed. Her slaves worked hard so Catherine didn't have to during this waiting time, but Virgilia's cousin Pherne no longer lived there and Virgilia suspected that daughter had brought the greatest support to her stepmother, being the oldest. She hoped the baby wouldn't arrive before they left. But she also wished they could leave, because she thought that their being there was a strain Catherine didn't need.

She told Gramo as much as they crawled into the large featherbeds in the room they shared. The house was so large her cousins hadn't even had to give up their beds for guests. Manthano had a room just for visitors to use. Virgilia appreciated being treated as an adult and given the bed space, but she also knew how hard it was when visitors came—at least at her house it was hard. "I think we should leave tomorrow, Gramo."

"Why, whatever for? We've just arrived."

"Catherine looks so tired, and what if she has the baby early because of the stress of our being here?"

"Fiddlesticks. She's had three babies already."

"They get harder with each one though, isn't that true?"

"Is it? No one knows, Child." Tabby sighed, pressed the covers over her stomach, clasped her hands in prelude to her prayers. "That's kind thinking on your part and I admire you for it. We can't leave before I try to convince Manthano to let me travel with his family, but he's as stubborn as Orus. You help out as much as you can. We'll make our way and take the stage home in a few days. About the time we get our trunks delivered."

"They're here, Gramo. Tom brought them from the stage stop. I brought Beatrice's cage up." She pointed toward the veranda where the bird squatted in apparent comfort.

"Oh, I know. I was being cynical. Not a good thing to be at all."

In the morning, Virgilia performed the work she did at home, learning a few additions and subtractions from the way her aunt Catherine said to do a thing. They changed their aprons daily at this place, as their slaves washed laundry twice a week. Here the Browns didn't have to do the heavy laundering, heating all that water, using up the soap. The hams at Manthano's were cured differently too, with a hint of an herb she wasn't familiar with. Her cousins had a cyclone cellar where they kept dried foods and blankets, and water from a spring not far from where they had the house. Virgilia had never witnessed a cyclone and hoped she never would, but she liked the idea of having a safe place to go. Where they lived, the basement served as a cyclone cellar, not a separate stone house dug into the side of the hill. They had to worry about flooding in St. Charles; something the Manthano clan could forget, living on top of a high hill.

"Always check before you go in, looking for snakes," her cousin Mary had warned as she showed Virgilia the cellar. "They like the cool too. I usually have one of our slaves go in first." Mary spoke with authority even though she was younger, and Virgilia was startled by how Mary ordered adults around.

Snakes. She'd have to ask her uncle Orus about snakes in Oregon.

This Brown family was already busy preserving meat, drying foods, making sure they had sturdy wagons so they'd be ready in the spring. Virgilia supposed that if the decision for her family to leave Missouri was made while she and her gramo were at Vibbard, that her family, too, would be busy making preparations. She should get home to help them, but convincing her gramo to leave sooner than she intended was like pulling a bone from their dog Buddy. It just made him hang on tighter.

"Are you looking forward to going?" Virgilia asked Mary while the girls played Draughts that second evening. She moved the small colored bones across the board of black-and-red-colored blocks.

"I think so. I don't know."

She concentrated on the board. "I crossed over your bone so I get to have it, right?"

Mary nodded and picked up the board piece, handing it to Virgilia.

"I haven't played this game before."

"It's easy. I'm going to take it with me in the wagon."

"Will you be allowed to take playthings?" All the talk from her uncle Orus had been about essentials, necessities, requirements.

"I don't know if we're allowed, but I sure enough will."

"Spoken like a true Brown." Both girls laughed. "Then I will too. If we go." Though Virgilia had no idea what plaything she might take. She wasn't musical but wondered if someone would bring a violin. Her mother would bring her pencils and drawing papers—though she hadn't drawn anything since Oliver's death. Virgilia had so little time to herself she wasn't sure she knew how to be frivolous, but she liked the idea of trying to find something that mattered that she could take. She'd be sure to take the pewter icing knife. Surely she'd be able to bake cakes.

Virgil Pringle rode to Western House, the gathering tavern in St. Charles. Orus spoke there often, prodding people west. Even when Orus wasn't present, Virgil brought back news about consequences of bank failures of a few years previous, the current drop in hemp prices, dissension in Congress about slaves, and, of course, Oregon. When he arrived home, he had stars in his eyes and not just reflections from the heavens. He spoke of ordering a Peter Schuttler wagon from Chicago, delivered to St. Louis where he and Orus and sons could assemble the green box and attach the bright red wheels. He came home passionate —that was the only word Pherne Pringle could think of to describe the enthusiasm, the delight, the excitement he espoused. It was as though he'd fallen in love. It hadn't taken very long. Pherne wished her mother and Virgilia were back so she could talk with her mother about it, find out how Virgilia felt about heading west. She felt like an island in the Missouri with the river channels passing her by, carrying her family away.

"It's going to be extraordinary, Phernie. So much enthusiasm, even without Orus carrying on at Western House." He hung his hat on the rack by the door. The children were upstairs in their beds.

"It's been decided then?" Pherne sat at her spinning wheel, the threads warming her fingers.

Confusion narrowed his eyebrows. "We discussed it."

"We did discuss it and I gave out a number of reasons not to go."

"And I addressed them."

"I didn't hear myself convinced."

"Pherne, it's the greatest adventure of our lives. Can't you see that? Beginning anew."

"Where—" She tried to find the words that had escaped her as she'd watched her husband's interests turn west these weeks. "Where do I fit in to your . . . adventurous passions?"

He frowned. Moonlight shadowed his strong jaw. "Truth is, you don't fit in."

She felt herself sinking at hearing her greatest fear spoken aloud. Dear Lord, how would she go on alone?

He lifted her hands from her work then and took her in his arms. He stroked the back of her head as tears of loss seeped from her eyes. She smelled leather and sweat.

"You don't fit in, Phernie, because you *are* my everything, don't you know that? I'm doing this as I've done everything, for you. For our family."

She wasn't sure she believed that, but she believed that he did. She let him hold her, each with silent prayers upon their breaths. His assurance was enough to turn her face to his and take the next step toward accepting that they would go.

— 8 —
Choices

"John?"

"Hello, dear Tabitha." The tallish man tipped his bowler hat, clasped his age-spotted hands over his ivory-knobbed cane. "And you must be Virgilia. I'm your uncle John. No, your great-uncle, your grandfather's brother."

They'd just gotten off of the stage in St. Charles, returning from Manthano's. John could have tipped Tabby over with one of Beatrice's tail feathers, she was so discombobulated to find him standing there.

He turned to Tabby. "You look tidy and fit and, may I add, as beautiful as ever."

No one had called her beautiful in twenty-eight years. She knew it wasn't true, but the compliment washed over her like warm bathwater anyway.

"Tidy and fit? Well, my children don't see that. They see me as old and lame. What are you doing here?" She had not seen John for maybe . . . fifteen years. He'd visited once after she'd dragged her boys kicking and screaming from the sea John loved. She hadn't been all that happy to see him then, still holding him accountable for his stories luring her sons like Odysseus's sirens to the sea.

What was he, twelve years older than she was? Yes, she was born in 1780 and he was born in . . . 1768, making him seventy-seven—soon to be seventy-eight. If she remembered, his birthday was close to All Saints' Day. Despite his age, John cut a fine swath in the fall scene. Snow-white hair, a black suit with green tapestry vest, and a fine round-topped hat. When he smiled, his coal-black eyes smiled too. Tabby remembered that cane, the one he'd gotten in the Orient with an ivory handle. After his ship had wrecked and he'd been rescued by the French. She wasn't sure he needed it, but it added to his finished fashion.

"Old and lame? Nonsense. Children don't always see things as we elders do." He pointed his cane toward Virgilia and winked.

"You're an elder now," Tabby said.

His black eyes sparkled. "We must claim any advantage we can, Tabby. It is good to see you." He brushed his lips over the top of her gloved hands he'd lifted, then grinned down at her and held her gaze. He had Clark's eyes and even his deep voice, but he was more flamboyant than her husband had ever been, liked finer things, too, while Clark had eschewed pomp.

The clerk lifted their trunk onto the wagon that John had apparently driven. The horses stomped and swished at flies.

"What are you doing here? Have you been commissioned by my son to look after me while they desert me and head west?"

"It would be my pleasure to take care of you." He said it with a timbre that brought throat-clearing to Tabby.

"You must be between ships."

"I am. But I may be ready to start a new phase of my life—shipless but seeking a new mate, perhaps." He smiled as he said this and she could smell his cologne. The same kind Clark had worn. *Did he always share that choice? What is happening here?*

Beatrice clucked in the cage as Virgilia placed it on the wagon bed. "Gramo, Uncle . . ."

"Oh, yes, let's get us home and we can talk then," Tabby said. "So many stories you have to tell of your exploits, I'm sure." She pulled away from his fingers, gripped her walking stick with both hands.

John helped Tabby up, then Virgilia. "How did you find Manthano then?"

"Busy packing for Oregon. They're all going, John. Unless Virgil stays?"

John shook his head. "Arranging going on at the Pringles as well. That's where I'm abiding, by the way. It wouldn't be respectable to house with a single, attractive widow woman such as you."

"You're family, John. Goodness. And do my

children have you remaining with me while they head off to Oregon? You haven't really said."

He leaned toward her. "I did in fact receive a letter some weeks back suggesting such a thing. But I thought I might offer an alternative. Maybe it's time we considered making that family designation more formal."

Tabby's mouth went dry. She forced a laugh. "You always were a character, Brother Brown. Let's not distress the young mind of Virgilia here with such talk. She's managing enough change." She patted Virgilia's knee. She placed her walking stick between them on the seat. As good a barrier as she could imagine until she could make sense of this unexpected arrival.

On the ride home, Virgilia chattered with John, giving Tabby time to think about this man on the other side of her walking stick. The breeze picked up the ties from her cap and they tickled her neck. She hadn't had such a compliment about her person for years. Beautiful? At her age? With her crooked body and wrinkled face? There'd been a few suitors after Clark died, but most faded away with three children to tend and a strong-willed woman directing them and any potential stepparent. It made her miss Clark more. He'd known her faults and foibles and loved her anyway. Did John see her faults? She'd known him almost as long as she'd known

Clark. But he was so different than her husband. Still, given her years and miles? And his?

Once at her home, John helped her into her cabin, dragged the trunk in with Virgilia's pushing, then tipped his hat. He held her hand softly once more.

"Think about it, Tabby. We could start a whole new life together here. What an adventure."

She was thinking with more than a little trepidation.

Virgilia prattled on about her visit until her little sisters rolled their eyes and her brothers gestured as though they sewed threads through their lips. "I know you want me to be quiet, but it's going to be exciting. And now that Uncle John is staying behind with Gramo, I won't worry about her. I can get excited about the journey."

"Get excited with a little less noise," Albro told her.

"Doesn't bother me." Clark made a long reach with his fork to pick up the last sausage on the platter. "She can talk all she wants about Oregon, but it won't be what you think it will be. It never is. You set a goal, but the lessons, well, they happen while you're on the trail. Might even be the whole point of a journey, what happens along the way." He chewed and looked at her, used his fork to point then. "You have a tendency to have short-lived excitement, Sister. As soon as you hit a little barrier, you sink like a rock in the pond."

"I do not!"

"You do. This trip will require staying power, won't it, Papa."

"It will."

Virgilia pouted. Yes, she had once agreed to work at a neighbor's when the woman of the house took ill, and she'd only lasted three days. The children were demanding, the husband of no help, and they expected her to cook, clean, and tend the ill woman. Three days was all she could take. "You're very philosophical. Thank you, dear brother. But I am truthfully looking forward to all the new people I'll meet, viewing new land-scapes, baking cakes with different flour. And I won't have the daily drudgery. I mean daily chores. Sorry, Mama, I didn't mean to complain."

But Virgilia did see the daily work as drudgery, and the prospect of having to find new ways to do things living out of a wagon intrigued her, if it didn't her mother. They'd been incorporating new activities to get ready. Drying food, making tons and tons of bacon, preparing pemmican as Orus said to do it. Knitting extra socks, sewing wool dresses and wrappers, two for each girl, and new duck pants for the men or maybe pantaloons for summer months of travel. Candles. Candles and more candles and lanterns. All the excitement was perfect for Virgilia. Added to that was the hope that Judson Morrow would be hired to help manage one of the ox teams along with her brothers. That would be the perfect ending to a dream even before her journey began.

She would think, though, about what Clark had said. She might need to be cautious about hoping for too much. Still, she resented his assertion that she lacked the ability to continue to persevere in the face of trouble. Her gramo was her model. If she could endure through hard times and face the pain of being left behind, she, Virgilia, could surely face whatever life had to offer her ahead.

"It isn't decided yet," Pherne told them all then. Heads turned with shocked looks on her brothers' faces. "I may stay behind and insist that your father return to get me and the girls after he's built us a home and we'll have a proper place to live."

The general chorus of complaints came from the boys as much as the girls. After all, they'd have to do their own cooking and washing if the boys went on without their mother and the girls.

"Well," Virgilia told them, "it seems there might be a fly in your butter, boys. How will you adapt?"

Their voices rose toward their father to insist and plead with their mother. Virgilia was being smart, she knew, while her heart pounded at the possibility that her father and the boys might leave them behind.

Tabby served John her special pudding of plums with fresh cream slurried with sugar. He had a sweet tooth, had ever since he'd stopped consuming spirits. It had only been a few days since their return from Manthano's, and he'd come by each morning to tell stories and offer to chop wood or pound a loose nail to tighten the porch steps. She'd hardly had a chance to write in her memoir. He was good company though. She laughed more than she had since before Clark's death, and the idea of being left behind had eased into another possibility. Still, her mind made plans.

"I have a proposition for you, John."

"Good. What shall it be? A willingness to take me in at last? To see what the Lord might have in mind for these old Browns while the young ones plod west?"

"Not exactly. What would you think about our teaming up—"

"My thoughts exactly." He clapped his hands. "Wonderful, Tabby. Wonderful!" He stood and put his arms out as though opening his heart. "There is nothing more that I want at this point in my life than to team up and take care of you."

"Yes. Well. No, not exactly . . . that." She gripped her walking stick, held up her palm to stop him from moving toward her. "Eat your pudding and let me finish." The entire countenance of his face dropped. She meant to cheer him, not discourage. "What would you think about our teaming up with our own wagon and going west with the 'young ones,' as you call them." There, she'd said it. Out loud, it sounded a little hollow, but in her prayers it made perfect sense.

"I don't think Orus will allow it. Not likely Virgil either." He took another bite.

"But it doesn't matter what they think. We can do this on our own. We could use the journey to get our feet wet, so to speak. Figure out how we are together." She felt her face grow hot and she fiddled with the strings on her cap. She had to be firm. Strong. "We aren't past our prime yet, John."

He grunted.

"Maybe we are, a little. But we're still here so there must be a purpose for our lives. I've prayed about this and I can't see that staying behind without family is what God intends."

"Orus says it's a dangerous journey. That's why he doesn't want you to go, why he summoned me."

"But why did you come? Wasn't it for the possibilities?"

"I suppose." He brushed crumbs from his green tapestry vest.

"Then let's set up a united front. I'll sell what wares I have and buy a wagon. Could you furnish it?"

"Indeed. I have plenty of resources in that regard. I could even make the purchase if that would help. If we decide to do this." He pointed with his spoon.

"I'll pay my fair share. But I see no reason why we can't travel with our family, make the trek, and show them what we're capable of. If Manthano's wife can make it with a new baby— and probably she'll be pregnant with the next by the time we leave—then surely we are not too old to begin a new adventure."

"And you'd consider the . . . other? A marriage, perhaps?"

Tabby had known he would ask that and she didn't want to mislead him. "I will prayerfully consider it, John. And regardless of the prayer's answer I am humbled that after all these years and with all your world travels that you would find me . . . approachable in a . . ."

"Romantic form?"

"Yes. That's not a road I ever imagined I'd be taking at my age. But then I never imagined I'd be heading to Oregon either."

He rose, bowed as though to royalty. "My brother loved the delight, the enthusiasm you brought into his life, and now I see that too." Then, "To Oregon it is." He lifted his ivory-handled cane and tapped it against her walking stick, striking the deal that would change both their lives forever.

— 9 —
Sorting

Pherne Pringle shook her husband awake. "Virgil. There are coons after the chickens. The dogs are barking up a storm." Virgil rose, rubbing sleep from his face with his wide palms. "And will there be raccoons in your Oregon?"

"Of course there will." Virgil lit the lantern. Dawn threatened to make an appearance but shyly hid behind a crescent moon. "We're taking the dogs and the chickens and pray they'll keep laying eggs. That'll lure coons too, I imagine."

"We may have to live on eggs from what I hear."

"Orus says game is plentiful."

" 'Orus says. Orus says.' "

"Now Phernie, don't flummox yourself." His fingers lifted her chin. "I'll see if we can have coon patties for breakfast to go with those eggs you're so fond of." He grabbed the lantern and shouted up to their son Clark, whose reply said he already stood on the landing, holding his small-bore Kentucky rifle, twin to his father's.

She heard them thunder down the steps, watched them head toward the barking sounds. Darkness and rifles, a recipe for disaster.

Her brother and husband and sons had worn

her down about Oregon over the last few months. As had her mother. Oh what a ruckus there was when she announced that she and John were taking a wagon and would join the train that Orus and Virgil and Manthano were a part of. Orus had been livid, as though her mother was a child who had defied him. Pherne felt less so. She actually liked the idea that her mother would be with them. The thought of leaving her behind had been one of the reluctant steps she had to overcome in agreeing to join her husband. It was settled now and she was grateful.

The months had slipped away; Christmas came and went. The new year blasted in with a storm that sent them to the cellar, quite a way to spend the first day of 1846. And sometime during those weeks, after she saw her mother making preparations and pretending that no one could stop her from going, she decided she would step forward rather than let herself be dragged. She spent the next weeks drying beef, sewing socks and crinolines, curing hams and bacon. Now, here it was March. They'd be leaving in less than three weeks. She would mark their departure as a life-altering date.

Her mother's telling them that Manthano was going to Oregon too was the last holdout Pherne had. That and her mother's newfound confidence that she and Uncle John would be heading west, despite what "Orus says."

The stage trip had invigorated her mother, and her daughter. It had apparently proved to her mother that she could endure rough travel and found the presence of other travelers exciting rather than invasive as Pherne knew they would be for her. She'd wanted to gauge the effort of overland travel and had delighted, she said, in meeting new people and having time with Virgilia. Her mother had a way of simply ignoring the reality. Even Orus had stopped trying to talk her out of it.

Six months with strangers! But also with family in a new crucible composed of green wagons and red wheels. Could she and her mother become closer with so much time together? Still, she wasn't relishing the work that cooking over fires out on the prairie would be. Or bruising her knuckles on a washboard in a stream whenever they might find time. Or being out in the elements with nothing but a canvas to cover them when the infamous prairie storms hit. She wouldn't let herself think about the mountains or snow or the cold or sickness or Indians. She vacillated between wanting to hear more of Orus's stories so she could be prepared and yet hating to hear them. So many of his mentions swirled up a bile of fear that settled in her throat.

Her brother Orus had taken over Western House on more than one evening regaling locals with the stories, and now a great number of families were planning to join them on this journey. The man did have a way of convincing people.

At least Virgilia was going with them and appeared happy as a lark since Judson Morrow had been hired to drive Uncle John and her mother's wagon. That too had been a bit of an issue.

Her mother and John had joined them for supper, and Virgil had suggested his nephew Charles Fullerton, whose parents had died, drive her wagon.

"Take Charles. He'll do fine for you, Mrs. Brown."

"No, now, I've interviewed Judson Morrow. He's shy and has no kin anywhere to speak of, so this is an added bonus from my part. My dear Clark always said to care for widows and orphans as our first duty. Your Charles has you and your brothers. So I've decided on young Morrow."

Virgil narrowed his eyes, but Pherne couldn't tell if it was irritation or anger. She decided he was annoyed that her mother had opinions. But he knew that already. And she was financing her own wagon.

"You know very little about him and his ability with oxen. That concerns me. You don't want to lose that wagon because of poor handling." Virgil raised his eyebrows at Tabby.

"Believe it or not, John knows a thing or two about oxen, don't you, John?"

"I've managed a few now and then. Cargo on a ship, but you learn their ways."

It was one of the many details of John's life that surprised Pherne in the very best way, and it had silenced her husband with a final "humph."

Her sons were happy in the planning and her daughter excited that Gramo was going with them. And, truth be told, her mother wasn't dozing as often as she had before. It was as though she had a new mission, something to reach for. Her mother read all she could about the "pioneering" experience, reading out loud to Pherne as she and the girls practiced embroidery stitches. The newspaper ran letters now and then from people in Oregon country, and pilots placed ads to invite people to sign up with them. Pherne supposed they'd be as prepared as anyone could be, and there was the relief in knowing that once they arrived, a cabin awaited them in the midst of a grove of trees, one her brother had built. There'd be a crop of wheat to harvest as well. She would focus on the fact that others had gone this same way and made it and set aside all the unknowns floating between. She and Virgil had only one big thing left to decide: what furniture they would take with them and what would be left behind.

She was thinking of that when she heard the gunshot and she jumped. The barking stopped.

She waited for the men to return, lifted the lantern as she walked to the second-story porch. Virgilia joined her on the balcony.

"Raccoons."

"Sorry, Mama." It was Clark shouting up to them from below the porch. He held up a chicken. "Coon got a couple but we got him. And this one is fresh dead."

She hated losing chickens, hated the uncertainty of everything despite how much she planned. Her mother said that was what life was, living with interruptions and that no one really knows what lies ahead. *"Don't let events take you over,"* her mother had cautioned. *"Find a way through."*

"I guess we'll be having chicken for breakfast instead of eggs, boys."

"And coon." Albro stood beside his brother. "We kilt a coon too."

"Killed a coon," Virgilia said.

"Can you heat up water, Mama?" Octavius appeared below the balcony now. Had all her sons slipped out in the night? "We'll have to tend the dogs. A couple of bad bites on 'em."

"Mama?" Emma's soft voice floated out onto the balcony from the girls' room. "My legs hurt. Can you rub them like you do?"

"My tummy doesn't feel good," Sarelia now complained.

"Doesn't feel well," Virgilia corrected.

"That's what I said. Mama, make her stop acting like Gramo."

"I'll get breakfast started," Pherne told no one in particular. "Virgilia, see to Sarelia's upset and then rub dear Emma's legs. Her feet too."

"Yes, Mama."

Find a way through. That's all that Pherne could do.

Tabby sorted through the things she treasured, hobbling around her home, deciding what to take and what to leave behind. That silver teapot her mother gave her made by Paul Revere himself—or at least his silversmith. It sat on the sideboard, which was a beautiful piece of furniture but heavy. If she could take the teapot, she would, but the sideboard would need deeper considera-tion. She set the elegant silver item into the "Oregon trunk," then took it out. They might need to sell it to buy supplies. That was the truth. She rubbed the silver with her forearm. It would make someone in St. Charles happy.

The butter churn. She got her butter now from Virgil's herd. She guessed she could continue to purchase butter when they arrived in Oregon. She just needed things to get her through the journey. All would be well once they arrived. She'd seen a list of required items. She had already decided that she and John and their driver would be independent of the rest, not requiring anything from her children. That way Orus could keep his annoyance about her going with them a little more at bay. The butter churn would go. So would a brass school bell. She rang that bell in a New England school building after Clark died, and she'd supported herself and the children by teaching. That bell was a link to both her past and possibly her future if she had to teach again. She carried a bit of pride knowing she'd raised her children as a widow without having to marry for someone else's protection. God had provided. The wooden handle felt smooth as glycerin in her hand. It had been a splurge of her income to buy it those years back but a joy finding a way to blend practicality with fine workmanship.

She picked up a pair of gloves. Soft leather. Strictly sentimental. She'd worn them when she and Clark had married. She wouldn't need to use them on the journey, as she planned to purchase heavy gloves so she could help with harnessing, loading, leading a horse or ox to water. But the soft gloves would make her feel elegant once they arrived. Who knew in what condition they'd find that cabin Orus had built? They all might need a little something special, not even all that practical, but items to soothe the soul. She already had peach pits she intended to take and plant as soon as she could. And cherry pits too. The lilac starts came from her Maryland home, and while they hadn't thrived in Missouri, they did well enough. She hoped they'd take on better in Oregon soil. A wooden bucket with dirt would keep the roots moist.

Of course she'd take copies of Clark's sermons. And her small, black Bible with print so tiny her eyes had trouble at times reading the words despite her acquiring round-lens glasses. A book of Shakespeare's selected plays. She knew so many of them by heart. Knitting needles, yes, they had to come along. Yarn. And her scissors. Would someone out there in that country have a knife and scissor sharpener? What would women do without sharp scissors and knives?

Tabby opened the back door, shook a tin can with corn in it, and watched Beatrice run across the yard. A brisk March wind pushed the bird forward into the room, her reddish feathers ruffled by the breeze. Of course she'd take Beatrice. She already had a cage for her. That bird would swing from the side, or if that motion bothered her too much, she could ride on the seat next to her while Judson walked beside her ox team. Captain John announced he'd be riding his horse across the continent. Tabby thought a mule would be better, but when she proposed that, John had said he'd make his own choices, as Tabby had. John, too, would be sorting and stashing and tossing and selling. It was a good thing St. Charles had a sizable population who could purchase what the emigrants weren't taking with them. She wouldn't have much by the time they left but a few coins. The rest she'd need for bartering, at least that's what Orus had told his family to plan on.

Bedding. Lace-lined pillow-slips. Dresses, aprons, petticoats. She placed those in the "Oregon trunk." A pair of wooden skates. She held them for a time, knowing that her father's hands had been on them, had unlaced them when she had the terrible fall. Why on earth had she saved those? One thing about taking the steamship years before to St. Charles, families could bring quite a few belongings so long as they could pay the fare. Her family had gotten out of the boat business—at her instigation—and Tabby herself had taught school, earning small amounts that added up. Pherne wasn't married then and she helped at the school. St. Charles had a Catholic school already, the Academy of the Sacred Heart that still served children of all faiths. Her family had begun a new life in a faraway place. She could do it again, even if her sons didn't think she could. All these things were reminders not of sad times but of how they had persevered and started over, loved, and done good things.

Tabby had brought everything she really wanted to bring to Missouri. She ran her finger along the wooden blades, the touch taking her back. She felt an ache in her foot. "No sense dwelling on that, Beatrice. Old thoughts can apparently bring on new pain." Orus said there were lakes in Oregon, but Tabby didn't know if they froze over. Maybe she'd give the skates to Sarelia. Her feet were about that size. Then Pherne would have to decide about whether to take them or not. Tabby chuckled. "That's one way to get myself out of deciding, though into trouble with my daughter, no doubt." This would be a different trip from when they'd come to Missouri all those years ago, as Orus said. This would be a trip to test their resolve, and it began with letting things stay behind. Just not her.

— 10 —
Divers Seasons, Divers Climes

"Not the cradle." Virgil shook his head.

Pherne started to protest. "But it's where . . ."

"And reason enough to leave it behind."

She gathered herself. "The harp-back chairs, then. They have to come with us."

They'd finished breakfast and now the day's work included whittling down "the list" of what they'd take with them and finishing loading the rest. Spring rains dribbled across the fields, sometimes stopping before it ever hit the ground. "You can see how little room there is for furniture, especially wide-seated mahogany-heavy dining-room chairs. Be realistic, Pherne."

They'd been at the strain for more than two hours this time, and each day that passed Virgil, or Orus, vetoed something Pherne felt she must have in order to feel at home once they arrived in Oregon. Each choice felt like a time she'd fallen asleep in the hot sun without her hat on and her face peeled away for days after. She caressed her gold necklace.

"What's left for me to take? I like nice things,

Virgil. Is that a crime? I love the feel of polished wood on my hands." She rubbed the arms of the harp-back chair she sat on. "This fine cloth on the seat. Someone spent hours making this chair. It's a work of art."

"Take a piece of art with you. Buy something you like. That artist, Bingham, in St. Louis, who does portraits. He does them in a day. Have one made. It will take less room than the chairs, the table, the sideboard, the hutch, the . . ." He counted on his fingers all the items he'd forced her to say would stay.

"But that's not something that is a part of who I am, of my family. I wanted something for each child as a reminder of their babyhood. A silver rattle, the one your parents gave us when Virgilia was born. That leather ball that Octavius loved. My mother's yarn is wrapped inside that leather. She made that ball for him. Your mother gave Virgilia the toy doll."

"Those were given to us as blessings," he said. "But taking them with us will not bless us any longer. They will be burdens. Choose one item to represent all the others."

Tears came unbidden and she wiped at them as though they were bugs annoying her.

Virgil knelt beside her. "Phernie, please. It breaks my heart to see you suffer so. It's not like we are saying to our children that they can't go. These are things that have to stay, things with memories, yes, but they are not you. We're not leaving you behind."

"I believe you are leaving a part of me behind, Husband. Oliver—"

"Yes. Oliver." He ran his hands through his dark hair. "We are leaving him, but don't you think if he had lived he would have wanted us to live fully? To choose to go, to go forward, to go together. And we take his memory with us. That's all any of these things represent." He swung his arm wide. "There'll be new memories in Oregon."

"Yes, but—"

"No more buts." Virgil stood. "Orus says I indulge you."

She felt her face grow warm with the words "Orus says." "I imagine he does say such things of you, and I would hope that you counter his admonishments with facts. It is not indulging to work together to resolve painful issues. It is not indulging to give a person more time to decide going or staying. We don't all come to decisions as my brother does, gathering enough information to decide a thing without seeking all the facts— and feelings—others might have. He often comes up short and has to adapt later because he has not looked for information so he can decide. I prefer assessing so one doesn't have to make later changes."

"You're going into your head now, Pherne. But your heart is what's making the decisions." He took her hand. "Your heart and the great loss we both still feel. You are not leaving Oliver behind. We are taking him with us. Here." He tapped his chest. "Your sadness, your anger at Orus, at me, those are losses reaching out like the gnarled hands of Shakespeare's witches. They seek something to hold on to, but there is only air." He stood and pulled her to him. "Let's fill that air with newness, with the excitement of how our lives will change. Take your paints and pencils. Draw your way across the continent." Pherne flinched at their mention. He stroked her back. "You won't be tending a huge house, planting or harvesting a garden. For six months we'll all be together with a common goal. Making it to Oregon as a family. Think of the memories we'll make. Together, isn't that what matters? Not all the nice things. Us, our children."

"You're sounding like Orus now."

"Is that so bad?" He took her in his arms and she allowed herself to sink into his touch, his words. Maybe they would be enough to sustain her through this wrenching away of things.

"You haven't made the leap yet, Love." That's what Pherne's mother said when she told her of the conversation, or at least bits of it. Pherne had walked to her mother's, finding comfort in the woman's presence, her always hopeful spirit.

"The leap?"

"Onto a cloud of faith believing that we won't fall through."

"That's the unknown I'm to contend with?"

Her mother heated tea water. "Not only that we won't fall through but that we will thrive on that cloud of faith, draw new energy each time we need it, knowing that God is an unending source of hope no matter the trial. You and Virgil, each of us, have come so far together, Phernie." She patted her daughter's hand. "Let's not make the journey full of pain because we couldn't let things that needed to stay, stay. We have to make room for more treasures. In our hearts if nowhere else."

"Virgil says I should take something symbolic of all the children and our years here. I have no idea what that could be."

"What started the conversation?" She strained the tea into the porcelain cups. Pherne wondered if those fine cups would find their way to Oregon.

"This time? The harp-backed chairs from New England. The ones his parents gave us when we married. I love those chairs." Pherne leaned over the teacup to inhale the scent. Moisture beaded above her lip.

"Tell you what. If you're willing, let's take the legs off one of those chairs—"

"And ruin it?"

"Now hear me out. Take the legs off and we'll attach the chair and arms and back to the seat of my wagon. Put those legs in a bundle under the wagon floor. When we get to Oregon we'll reattach them."

"Virgil says it's because it's so heavy we can't take it. It'll be hard on your animals too."

"I've been pondering on how my back will manage sitting on that hard seat with no high backrest, and your harp-back chair will be perfect. Solves both our problems."

"It'll break up the set. People won't want to buy the table and chairs set if one is missing."

"It might lower the value of the set, but it might also give them a story to tell, about how one of those chairs went to Oregon to help an old lady. Stories are worth their weight in gold where commerce is concerned."

Pherne laughed. She pulled a piece of tea leaf from her tongue with her fingertips. "Mother, I do believe you can reconfigure any problem. I'll get the saw and we'll cut off those legs together."

April 15, 1846. The wagons constituting the Brown-Pringle party lined up outside of Hickory Grove, the name Virgilia's father had given their farm years before. Virgilia's eyes cast over the line of wagons and she tapped her foot at the newest delay. Orus pressed again for her cousin Charles to drive the ox team for her grandmother and Uncle John instead of Judson Morrow, criticizing an old decision already made.

"Gramo's made the arrangements, Uncle Orus.

I think she needs to decide. Can't we just go?"

Her uncle had turned on her, scowled. He was used to people skipping to his orders without letting their feet hit the ground.

"Learning to speak up for yourself, eh? Spending time with my mother will do that."

"She's speaking my thoughts," her grandmother said. She'd hobbled from around the wagon. "You aren't going to discourage me, Orus, by trying to make last-minute changes. No offense." She angled her walking stick toward Virgilia's cousin, who nodded, cast his eyes to the dirt. "John and I are packed and ready to go, and young Judson here is too."

"Mother, Orus says Judson lacks experience."

Now her mother had to intervene!

"Phernie, my dear daughter, stay out of this one."

"My daughter has an interest in Judson, so it's my business, Mother, it truly is."

The freckles dotting Judson's nose faded into the red of his face. Virgilia wanted to rush in and protect the boy . . . young man. He didn't stand up for himself.

"Stop, please." The bickering wore Virgilia out. "Whatever works best for you, Gramo. Please, Mama, don't let's argue." Her face felt hot as a riverbank stone in August. Talking about her "interest" in a boy in front of him. Goodness. Was everything open to discussion in this family?

When Orus made his pronouncements, a

disagreement always seemed to follow. At least from her gramo. The harp-back chair had caused a ruckus all right, but Virgilia was pleased her gramo and mother had won that debate. Her gramo sat on the wagon seat like a princess on a throne, with armrests and a pillowed seat. Best of all, when she rode in her gramo's wagon box looking forward, she'd see the beautiful harp design her gramo would lean against across the country. Emma had been sitting on the chair while they had this driver conversation, and she'd seen Orus and Lavina's younger ones running their hands along the arms before jumping down and heading to their own wagons. Each family had two wagons, and with her gramo's, that made five in their group. But once they reached Manthano's, there'd be at least two more. She wondered if any of the slaves would be coming along and if they'd have their own wagons too.

"Let's get rolling," her father called out. Her mother made the motion of washing her hands. "You're right, you're right. It's whatever you decide, Mother. It's your wagon. Your driver. Let it be, Orus."

"And I've decided on the Morrow boy," Tabby announced. "That settled? Let's get this wagon train on the trail." She looked at Orus. "As Orus I'm sure will say."

But Virgilia's mother had gone back inside the house, the home that had been theirs for all the years of Virgilia's growing up. Virgilia followed her inside and watched her mother with stooped shoulders stand by the cradle. She might have been praying, likely fiddling with her gold locket that had a lock of Oliver's hair inside. Then, like a hummingbird, her fingers feathered the headboard, ran across the sides and the stays that held the baby's bed at either end. She pushed it lightly and it swung, back and forth, back and forth. " 'Hush-a-by baby on the treetop.' " Her mother whispered the words.

" 'When the wind blows, the cradle will rock.' " Virgilia's clear voice sang the next line. "Let's not say the rest of it, Mama. Let's say good-bye. Let the memory of the bad time stay here and just bring the happy times with Oliver with us."

Her mother nodded. "You're right, I—" Her voice caught and tears came now uninterrupted. Virgilia let her cry on her shoulder, the daughter a comfort to the mother, until she stopped, wiped her eyes with the handkerchief she pulled from her sleeve. "Sorry, I don't know what came over me."

"Pherne! You're holding things up." The shout came from her father.

"Coming," Virgilia answered him. Her mother pasted a weak smile on her face. Whispered "thank you."

Virgilia walked outside, her arm wrapped inside

her mother's elbow. She saw her gramo and said, "Take Mama's other arm, Gramo. We're in this together." She could bring comfort to another. Love and do good in whatever way one can. Maybe this journey was her chance.

They'd made camp by a small creek, and everyone took an assessment of how things had jiggled or been jostled in their wagons, noting the amount of fine dust that filtered over everything, the shifting of barrels that needed a tighter rope. Virgilia's father would be keeping the diary of their journey, and she sat beside him as he made the initial entry at the end of their first day: *"April 15, 1846. Left Hickory Grove this day with my family for Oregon. Went seven miles. Stopped for more company."*

"You didn't say anything about the trouble we had with the ox, Papa, nor how much dust there is to contend with. I thought how Judson shod Ben—casting, he called it—was really something. That rope pulling around Ben's middle and how he plopped down on his side so the farrier could shoe him."

"When you don't have a shoeing stock, that's a pretty good way to take care of things." He closed the diary, rubbed a spot on the leather cover. "No sense including everything we know. There'll be more trouble and I won't want to take the time to write it all. You could, though."

"Write about the trouble?"

"The details, things I won't be covering, like the casting. The smell of the rain when we get it. The grit of dust in our mouths. How swift or slow the rivers flow. What the weather is like, how different or the same. Maybe write a poem or two."

"Oh Papa, I don't know how to write poetry."

"Don't you? Why did I think that?" He smiled at her.

"Because I recited Alfred Lord Tennyson's 'The Day-Dream' poem. It wasn't my poem. I like it, though, because he talks of 'titanic forces taking birth in divers season, divers climes.' " She exclaimed the words as she had for her school lessons a year before when she'd memorized the long poem.

" 'For we are ancients of the earth,' " her father continued. " 'And in the morning of the times.' "

"I would change it to the 'morning of *our* times,' even though I'm not sure I know what it means. But I do feel as though this journey is a titanic force, that none of us will be the same after it." She thought of her mother's sadness at the baby's cradle.

"In the morning of *our* times. A good addition," he said. "I doubt Tennyson would mind. Perhaps that speaks to why I wanted to go so much. Life is short. Remember that, Child. What more is yet to come for an old man like your papa and yet I seek the mornings."

"You're not old." Virgilia leaned in, whispered, "Gramo is old."

"And still she fights on, finding her own new climes and seasons."

"I'm glad she fought for Judson."

"I imagine you are." He pulled her into his side, his arm a comfort on her shoulder. "He's not much older than you are, Virgilia. Not ready to settle with a bride. I don't want you hurting, now."

She lowered her eyes to her hands folded in her lap. "I know that. We're just friends, really we are. I hope I make many friends on this trip. And I intend to imagine myself into a new life in Oregon." She surprised herself with that comment because, indeed, she had begun to daydream about a new life. This morning, she felt as she did just before she let loose the rope over their old swimming hole: anticipation, a trust that the water would be buoyant enough to hold her up once she plunged deep and didn't fight the natural rise to the surface. And she relished with just a shiver letting loose that rope, dropping through the air, and then the moment that would take her breath away. It was how she wanted the rest of her life to be. "I'll daydream my way into those new climes and seasons."

"Like the rest of us." He removed his arm, made another note in his diary that Virgilia could see:

"Tennyson: Day-Dream." He looked up at her and grinned. This journey was already memorable, as she'd never had such a moment with her father before, not ever.

She sauntered to the wagon and took out her own foolscap paper, writing not of the journey but of her mother during those last minutes before they left. For days she'd been putting the words together in her mind.

Empty now, the cradle stays
without a baby cooing.
Empty now, down feathers
without comfort
embrace the bottom of the child's cot
like the lining of a coffin.
Empty now, no laughter reaches
from the confines of its polished rails.
Left behind, it may cheer another
while memories travel
in a mother's
heart, her arms
so empty
now.

— 11 —
Last Arguments

Virgil rode beside Tabby's wagon for a time, chatting with Uncle John while Judson walked beside the oxen. Tabby's back felt sore, but she knew it was better than trying to walk.

"How are you doing, Captain?" Virgil asked.

"Still sailing high. Did I ever tell you about the time I—"

"I'm sure you did."

John laughed but kept on telling his story. Tabby lost the thread of conversation as she let her mind wander, heard the *clop-clop* of the oxen hooves, smelled the animals' sweat and droppings they deposited on the trail. She nodded off, then jerked awake with the wheels lurching over a rock. Tabby grabbed the arms of her harp-back chair. How she wished she could walk, but her lameness would slow them down. She'd have to settle for a little exercise when camp was made and she let Beatrice out of her cage to peck on the ground. *Ride or Walk.* Maybe that should be her next memoir entry, when she had time to write. She certainly couldn't write while sitting on that chair, luxurious as it was. Knitting would be her pastime. The wagon bounced and rocked from side to side. She had sat for a time with her legs hanging over the back opening of the wagon, watching the faithful oxen from whichever wagon had drawn the space behind theirs. Couldn't write there either.

The day before, Virgil had stopped and bid adieux to his brothers and sisters, none of whom were headed out with them except for the nephew, Charles. Maybe she should have hired him instead of Judson, but no, he had family; Judson didn't. Tabby saw Virgil's shoulders droop as he bear-hugged his brothers, wiped his sisters' eyes with his thumb. Her stomach tightened at how close she had come to waving good-bye to her family. *Oh please may I have done the right thing.* She recalled again the tension of the morning they headed out.

"We'll have to pace ourselves to the slowest wagon and that can be dangerous, Marm. Indians can see our weakness—in this case your wagon—with that ridiculous harp-back chair." Orus shook his head. "Makes us vulnerable to attack with slowed animals. You don't want that on your conscience, do you, Marm?"

"And you know our wagon will be the slowest one how? Have you put weights on our wheels? Tied a log to the back to drag behind? Found our oxen wanting in some way? Why, I picked out their shoes myself and we have extras along. Plus tar. Plus grease buckets aplenty. I've read the materials. I know what we need. And we don't need the extra weight of guilt that you're hoping to plop upon our backs."

"Facts are not guilt, Mother."

"I can assure you we will be of no trouble to you or the other wagons. Judson's a good boy, a strong young man. Uncle John can ride just fine, and if not, he can sit in the wagon with me. You just put us in the line wherever you wish and we'll keep up. If we don't, by the time we get to Manthano's, I'll reconsider going at all. How is that for a good understanding?"

Orus flicked his Green River knife into the dirt, pulled it out, wiped it on his duck pants, then flicked it again. Tabby waited for his response but watching him, couldn't resist a chide. "Did you weigh that knife? Does it put you over the limit? It best have other practical properties. After all, playing mumblety-peg is a frivolous thing."

Orus lifted his eyes to her. "It weighs less than that school bell of yours. Or John's violin. So don't lecture me about what's essential." He sighed then. "I'm sure I'll use this knife for practical things."

"I'll find a use for my school bell too. And music is a boon to any trail."

"I'll take you up on your offer, Marm. If you and Uncle John hold us back, you'll drop out at Manthano's and either head back or remain there. Agreed?"

"Agreed." She rang her school bell at him, and he shook his head. "We'll either be good to go or we'll agree to stay." She prayed she'd accept the outcome with dignity, and that Orus would too.

Virgilia had the ague. Pherne worried over giving her Champion pills. She'd heard they helped, but Pherne didn't like newfangled medicines inside bottles or capsules. She preferred cool cloths, mustard compresses, herbs and plants that she had dried herself for healing. But pills were easier and she had little time to mix up her potions during the day and was too tired at night. Her mother always was more open to new things, suggested the pills, and had brought extra along. Little of that enterprising spirit had rubbed off onto Pherne. Virgil noted their daughter's illness in his diary that day, that and the number of miles they'd made. "15."

"I think your temperature is going down." Pherne touched Virgilia's cheeks.

"I feel better walking than riding in this stuffy wagon."

"You need to stay out of the sun for now. You never have managed heat very well." Pherne tore a piece of her bottom petticoat off and dipped it into water she'd placed in a bowl. "It's not as cool as I'd like but it'll feel good." At least they had plenty of water following or crossing streams and always camping beside one.

They made fifteen miles almost every day, nothing holding them back, despite her mother's insistence that she and her wagon be left alone to tend to everything themselves. Still, Pherne watched over her mother while strolling beside their ox team or walking beside her mother's wagon when put into rotation behind theirs. Pherne scanned the actions of her young ones, watched with concern her boys working the teams. She looked at the sun when Virgil rode off, wondering how long it would be before she'd see him again. She lacked a word for the feeling of constant concern despite things going well. They had good milk cows along, and the milk and butter made while the churn hung from the side of her mother's wagon made their meals a blessing. The boys trailed sheep they'd need once they arrived in Oregon, her sons' laughter reaching her now and then. They often had milk enough to give away and did. Her mother expressed her indomitable happiness at offering up butter each evening.

Wagons from Georgia overtook them at one point, and while they chatted for a moment or two, mostly people kept their bonnets in a westerly direction. The Georgia group had been on the road since March. They looked tired already. Virgil had been right about one thing: there was a certain rhythm they'd gotten into. She had long hours when she wasn't cleaning or cooking. Sunrise to bedtime she walked, talked, watched how her children handled challenges. She witnessed sons and daughters growing in ways she hadn't had the time to notice before within the busy business of raising a family in one place.

She didn't like her family being sick, though. Illness wasn't easier to manage on this moving tidal wave sucking them out through prairie seas of grass and grit. As she left Virgilia sleeping in her wagon, she heard coughing from the wagon in front of her. *Mother.* Pherne hurried her pace until she was beside her mother's team. "How long has she been sick, Judson?"

"Just came on last evening, Mrs. Pringle." The boy nodded with his chin. She guessed she should think of him as a young man. He did look older with the bowl cut of rust-colored hair moved out of his eyes.

"I'm right here," Tabby shouted from the wagon back. "I'm fine."

Pherne lowered her voice. "I need for you to let me know whenever something like that happens, when she falls ill."

"She asked me not to tell."

"She would. But she doesn't always know what's best for her, so you need to come get me or Lavina Brown or Virgilia if anything changes for my mother. Agreed?"

"Yes, ma'am. Should I tell the Captain too? He rides off most days."

"Yes. But tell me first."

Her mother sneezed, then coughed again. "You're mumbling out there."

Pherne touched Judson's arm, his eyes affirming their agreement, then waited until the wagon moved past. She lifted her long skirts, measured the pace, then hiked herself up onto the backboard and crawled inside. "You don't sound good."

"Did you jump up with that wagon moving?"

"I did."

"Well, don't. That's a dangerous act, Daughter. A dress caught, toe stubbed, and we'll lose you."

"I hadn't thought."

Her mother waved her hand, dismissing. "All I've got's a little cold." Her voice came through a stuffed nose. A coughing fit took her with the effort. Finished, her mother flopped back on the feather mattress she'd pulled over the top of trunks. At least the weather had been perfect with no rain. They had clean water to wash one's hands with, even though the water had to be hauled from a distant stream or boiled first for safe drinking. The constant motion of the wagon may have added to her mother's pale face—except for the red around her nose, which she now blew.

"Get me my Perry Davis Vegetable Pain Killer, Daughter. This may be seasickness more than a cold that's got me down."

"Are you vomiting, Mother?"

"No, no, my guts are where they should be. I just feel dizzy when I sit up and the bows on this wagon float around when I lie down, if I keep my eyes open. So I won't. Thank you." She gave her mother the Perry Davis pill. "I hate to ask, but could you remind Judson to check Beatrice's water when we stop? I'm not sure I can sit up."

"I'll make certain. And John can do that, can't he? Does he have no daily duties?"

"Ha."

"Well, you need to rest."

"Ha," she said again.

Pherne laughed. "I know. It makes little sense that word, rest."

"Oh it's a good word all right. Just hard to manage here. But I will. I'm not complaining. You're not hearing me complain now, are you?" Pherne shook her head. "Don't you even let Virgil or Orus think that. Do you want to sit in your chair?"

Pherne shook her head. "No, I'll hop out and walk."

"You be careful."

Pherne patted her mother's folded hands. "I'll catch up with Clark. He's got the lead ox team. I did envy those Georgia wagons and their fine mules. They make better time, I think."

"We're steady and our oxen are faithful beasts. We'll do fine without mules, though I think John might wish he had a mule before this is over. His horse doesn't seem to like his daily workout."

"I guess we'll all adapt."

Her mother sneezed and blew her nose, then coughed, nearly barked.

"You sound like Buddy."

"That hound is a good companion for your brood." Her mother sighed. "I'm sad you couldn't bring all the hounds." She coughed. "Keep the children away from me."

"I'll have Virgilia bring something over to the wagon for your and John and Judson's suppers this evening."

"No, no, I'll get myself pulled together for the evening stop. I won't have anyone coddling me. I said we wouldn't be a burden."

"Mother, be reasonable."

Her mother closed her eyes. "Quiet-like, then."

"Orus won't notice that you are willing to accept a little help. That's being independent too, you know. Exercising good judgment."

Her mother lifted her chin. "You've made a point."

Pherne pressed her palm against her mother's forehead. It wasn't feverish, so that was good. She gathered her skirts and crinolines. She had donned seven at the start, knowing she'd be tearing strips of cloth from them as the weeks went on—for bandages, monthlies, face rags. She leapt out from the wagon as far afield from the wheel as she could so as not to get caught up in the turning. Dust rolled up to her face and she coughed too. Maybe it was trail dirt that affected her mother. She hoped, though, that it was something specific like a cold or food she'd eaten, because if dust was the cause, her mother would be sick the entire trip and there'd be nothing Pherne could do about it. One more thing to make her feel powerless: dust. Maybe that was the word that described her feelings: powerless.

The two sat outside the wagon, Virgilia's grand-mother in the hickory rocker, Virgilia picking at her skirt seams beside her on a quilt spread on the hard ground. They'd managed another two days and already "sameness" was the first word that came into her head when she awoke under her tent canvas each morning. The evening meal finished, someone played a harmonica in the distance. Uncle John and Judson had meandered to the menfolk gathered to discuss the day's journey, help with harness repairs, or just smoke their pipes. Her gramo felt a little better this evening, hadn't coughed hardly at all. Virgilia's ague had cleared, and she felt bad reading the night before in her father's diary *"Mrs. Brown complains of a cold."* That didn't seem fair. Her gramo never complained, about anything. She thought he should cross that out, but she didn't say anything. After all, she'd be distressed if someone read her diary and thought she should change words. And she didn't want her father to tell her she couldn't read what he wrote each day.

They'd crossed rivers and streams, some of the banks without timber of any kind. Her father had commented in his diary about how strange it was to see a timber mill a good two miles from trees, the mill operated by a stream that had no drop at all, just ran through a level prairie. That same evening they'd had to scrounge for firewood, picking up pieces left over from the great floods of 1844, or so Clark opined. The late sunset cast a rainbow glow of colors across the horizon. Crickets sang into the quiet.

"I sure haven't had much conversation with Judson, Gramo. I thought having him drive your wagon would give me time with him, but Mama has me rushing here and there, entertaining Emma and Sarelia and helping Aunt Lavina too. I suppose it'll even be worse when Manthano and Catherine join up, her with a new baby and all."

"Ever think your mother might be occupying your time on purpose?"

She hadn't thought of that. "She needn't worry." She leaned back on her elbows, staring up at her grandmother. "As soon as he's finished unyoking the oxen Judson waters them, then washes them down and heads for Orus's wagon, walks right past ours, talks with Albro or Clark if they're around." She knew she sounded pouty, but his behavior was a huge disappointment. How could she try out her efforts at complimenting him to see if that would bring him around if he was never, well, around?

"There will be other beaus to banter with before long. You'll see. Meanwhile, enjoy the time with your old gramo or, even better, with your mama. She's grieving all the changes."

"Why aren't you doing that?"

Her gramo sighed. "I've lived through my share of ups and downs, I guess. And great changes like we're having now, those always bring up the upheaval of previous ones we thought we'd put to rest. I've learned to prepare for that."

"Like what?"

Her grandmother cleared her throat, halted her rocking. "Your gramo had a baby brother who didn't live long. And then we had our own baby who gained his heavenly wings early, like your brother Oliver. It took time for me to forgive God for that. Eventually I learned to say 'thy will be done,' though my dear Clark always corrected me, telling me it was God's will that we spend eternity with him, not that he take little children to him." She began rocking again. "Those things were part of the human breath of in and out, the way of living on this earth. We're to do the best we can for each other while we're here, but he didn't want me blaming God for what's part of living, the saying yes or no, go or stay, up or down, in or out. Ultimately we really only have the choice of trusting that God's with us, willing ourselves to walk with him as we walk this earth, learning from the roads we take."

"I give things to God, but then I—"

"Take them back."

"Yes." She loved it that Gramo understood her.

"Don't I know it. That lesson took your old gramo a long time to figure out. We can't make room for the treasures we'll be given if we keep the trunk closed on all the old ones that are gathering dust and taking up room. We have to keep opening up our hearts, even in the disappointments." She leaned in. "Even when we're afraid."

"What treasures are you looking for in Oregon, Gramo?"

"The same ones I have right now." Her grandmother stroked Virgilia's hair, pushing the damp strands from her temples. "You being here, time with my other grandchildren, my children, even Uncle John. And the new friends I'll make. And a new purpose. Think of all the discoveries about life and living and myself that I'll enjoy. That's what journeys are about, you know. It's not just the destination. Don't waste your time not having happen what you want; make what you want to have happen, happen. As best you can."

"How do I happen to get Judson to notice me That's what I want."

"Is it? Or do you want to have a friend Because if that's the case, you might just tell M Morrow what your intentions are, put him ɛ ease. Then see what he does with that. Could t he's more nervous than you are. He's all alone o this trek without any family. Making a frien might be the best way to get noticed by a potenti: beau anyway."

Virgilia sat in the quiet. She could hear frog singing at the river. The air smelled cool, and there'd been a cloud in the sky, Virgilia mig have guessed that rain was on its way. "I thir tomorrow I'll bake a cake in the little ove May I set it beside you?"

"And torture your old gramo with th wonderful smell all day as it sun bakes?" Virgil laughed. "Yes, you may. But you have to save piece for me . . . after you've iced it using r pewter knife and given Mr. Morrow the large piece, of course."

Virgilia stood as though to kiss her gramo.

"No, no. I don't want you getting this cold."

"Is there anything I can do for you before head back?"

"I've enjoyed our little chat here. You cor back for more of that and I'll be happy." Virgi nodded. "Oh, and Beatrice laid an egg, at la Take that for your cake."

Time with her gramo always made her feel better. She hoped she could make Judson feel the same—after she gave him cake.

Tabby did not want to be a burden. Even asking Pherne to get her the vegetable pills bothered her. She had to be able to do those things herself, despite a cold. Now if John wanted to pull out hardtack and spread it with blackberry jam, chop off a hunk of dried meat for his and Judson's supper, that was fine. The three of them were a unit. But she didn't want anyone else having to lift a finger for them, especially while they were still anywhere near civilization. Orus at any point might throw up his hands and tell her she had to stay behind. This cough was a trial, but she'd get through it and be stronger for it, she was certain. She'd make sure she stifled any signs of weakness around Orus.

— 12 —
We Are Call'd

The storm came up in the night. Tabby felt the wagon shake. She still slept inside, not having taken to the ground on her feather tick while she suffered the cough. She didn't want to get her blankets and quilts wet from the dew. So she first pulled her quilt over her shoulder to try to get back to sleep, hoping the rain would wait until morning. A flash of lightning brightened the dark wagon. Maybe only heat lightning, she hoped. But then she heard John grunt. "I'm coming up, Tabby. Rain's started."

"Come along then." He'd need to sit on the bed too. It wasn't a big four-poster like Virgil and Pherne had left behind but a smaller, single-person bed with a rope mattress. She slid toward the headboard when John sat down at the opposite end, nearly falling before finding the solid edge.

Thunder cracked and she felt herself shudder, pulled the quilt around her like a cape. "Not liking the sounds of that." Flashes of lightning startled them and helped them see that the rain was in earnest. "Guess we'll find out if the linseed oil keeps us waterproof."

"Reminds me a little of being on the sea. Wind and salt spray on my face, challenging the elements."

"You're missing your boat. That figures. Is Judson in his tent?"

"Aye. This wagon rocks like one. Whoa, that was a goodly blast."

They huddled and could feel more than hear cattle moving, restless in the circled area. A couple of dogs barked. It was the first time they'd circled their evening stop. Someone must have sensed a storm and been wise about it so they wouldn't have to waste time looking for stock in the morning.

"I won't be much good out there or I'd put my slicker on and get out in that to help calm the cows." John stood to look out the back of the wagon opening. Then he pulled the thongs to narrow it, keeping the rain out as much as he could. He crawled over trunks and squeezed between barrels to tie the front cover closed as well. "Yours and Pherne's chair isn't going to weather this well."

"I never thought of that. I figured I'd keep it from the hot sun because I'd be sitting in it. But rain. Hmm."

"Want me to throw my slicker over it? Or have you got an old Hudson's Bay blanket?"

"In the trunk but it's a little late now. We'll hope the oil finish protects it, and I'll dig out my slicker in the morning. I wonder if we'll hear orders or any cries for help. That rain's really pelting the cover." She looked up. Everything was dry above. "An advantage of being one of the ancients is we don't have to be the first ones to the rescue."

"So true." In the pause of their making new settling spaces, Tabby put her walking stick on the floor. Their wagon was tight as a cabin. John said, "Kind of cozy here, Mrs. Brown."

"That it is. Can't let you sit out in the rain."

"I appreciate that you convinced me of this trip. I find myself invigorated. And already there are new people who haven't heard my stories."

Tabby laughed.

"I'm glad you made that visit to find out Manthano was going west too. Gave me good pause to consider what I wanted to do, and it became clear I wanted to be with all of you. But I couldn't have done it alone. I do have some aches and pains, not that I'll let on to Orus, and I sure didn't want to hold anyone else back. You're my only family, you know. You and your kin."

"You have a sister."

"I do, but I mean family who has stood by me and wanted me with them."

"I know." She patted his hand. "We're in it together, John. Happy to have a companion on the trail."

Rain pattered on the canvas. "Wouldn't my brother have loved being a part of this?"

"He is, in a way. I think of Dear Clark every day and ask him about things like will my wagon tongue last the journey or will we be able to fix it on the way?"

"And what does he say?"

"He's silent on the issue. He never was one to fix broken things. I wielded the hammer for repairs." She was aware of John's presence and found it peaceful in the midst of the storm.

"Thank you, Tabby. Whatever happens ahead. Thank you."

"You're a gift to me too, John."

Tabby wondered if the darkness made it safe for him to speak such words. It did for her.

Thunder cracked above them, booming so close Tabby grabbed at her ears.

"There won't be much sleeping tonight," John said.

" 'What hath night to do with sleep?' " Tabby quoted. "Milton."

"I didn't know the man took a wagon train west."

The rain stayed through that evening and then all day, off and on and then again when they reached Ray County where they made camp in the wet. The following morning the rain invited itself to stay for breakfast, drizzle interrupted by downpours. There'd been no cake-baking, that

141

was for certain. The men sweat beneath their drenched slickers by the time the animals were harnessed, and Orus gave the shout to head out. Tabby thought they should give a few more hours to let the ground soak up the rain—not that she offered this bit of wisdom. But a few miles later she could see that Orus had made a good decision to go rather than stay. This section of road was in good shape, and the air cool though cloudy, and no rain.

At least Judson managed the oxen well. John had told the boy that if the oxen ears were forward, to stand in front and glare, and if the oxen didn't push their ears back, to growl at them. The oxen were being argumentative if they didn't set their ears back and acknowledge who was boss. "If they still don't put their ears back, you hit them hard on the rump with the whip or the goad. Really hard. Otherwise they'll not listen to you when you gee and haw them forward." So far, Judson had only had to use the stick once.

Not far from Camden a wagon approached, the cover curled back to expose the bows like ribs. A young woman, pregnant, sat beside a man. She looked familiar. It had to be Young Pherne. She and David Bain had married last year. Virgilia had felt cheated not to have seen her cousin when they visited Manthano, yet here she was, on a wagon seat beside her husband. Tabby guessed Virgilia would be pleased.

There were howdys and hat-to-hearts all around, though Orus kept his wagons rolling and reminded the rest to do the same. "It's not easy getting these rigs moving, so do your talking along the way. Good to see you, Niece," he'd added, tapping the side of his hat when he replaced it over his flattened dark hair, but he didn't stop, instead reined his horse to the front of the line.

Virgilia and Young Pherne chattered like squirrels while her husband spoke with Virgil's sons, easily keeping up the pace, driving the wagon beside them as they urged the oxen onward. He had a fine mule team. Tabby wished she could walk a good enough speed to be a part of the conversation with Young Pherne, but she'd have to wait until they reached Manthano's. That wasn't far away.

As they started up the long driveway to her son's, Tabby expected to see wagons parked beside the house or barns, to watch activities of loading and slaves moving here and there getting everything ready. But all looked the way it had when she and Virgilia had made their way up to the house the autumn before. She guessed her son was well-packed and prepared, just waiting on them.

She heard a cry behind her.

"Broken tongue," Octavius shouted, and the wagon behind him stopped. It was Virgil's second wagon. Tabby's would have halted too if she hadn't directed Judson to pull out and move alongside to keep going before their wagon stalled. It would be a hard pull up the rest of the hill for Virgil's good wagon, now that they'd been stopped. And there would be repairs to consider.

They were but a few yards from Manthano's and Orus had already reached the house with his wagons. Tabby saw black men now directing where to park the wagons, where to lead the oxen for water. Tabby got off her harp-back chair when Judson had pulled them to a stop. Her foot always stiffened after long hours of sitting. She shook her leg out, brushed dust from her linen skirt as John began taking off the oxen yoke. She approached Orus and Young Pherne, who had pulled their buckboard up beside Orus's rigs. That was where she heard the latest news.

"Pregnant? My brother might have waited until we got to Oregon to have another."

"Mama's . . . well, Alonzo, our brother born in October after you left, Gramma." Young Pherne acknowledged Tabby's approach without breaking her speech. "He . . . he didn't make it. Buried the same day as he was born."

"Your poor mama," Tabby said. "And she's with child again?" Young Pherne nodded.

"I hope she's early and can make the trek all right. Where is my brother?" Orus looked around, fists straight beside his hips. "Wouldn't want any complications on the trip. For your stepmother's sake," Orus said to the raised eyebrows Tabby showed him.

"Why don't we wait to greet him before we get ahead worrying, Son." Tabby could see that irons were in a fire and she wanted to spread the coals to cool things down.

Young Pherne's next words were barely audible above the commotion of the broken tongue, animals being taken to water, people and children and dogs stretching and beginning the evening routines. "I don't think my parents are going to Oregon, Uncle Orus."

"What?" This from both Orus and Virgil, who had joined the little gathering. Behind them Virgil's boys began removing the heavy yokes so they could begin the tongue repair.

"Papa said it wasn't going to work, them heading west."

"I hope he sold some of his property to pay me back the money he owes me."

"Orus. No." Tabby shook her head.

Young Pherne's husband spoke up then. "If Pherne wasn't with child, we'd join you. Maybe next year. Got bit by the Oregon bug myself."

Tabby said, "We don't know the whole story, Orus. They may well be in need of our assistance. Poor Catherine. And they may have changed their minds and are still coming."

Her sons would have to work things out. She

was more concerned about Catherine, who came out onto the porch, looking washed out as an old rag, as tired as she had the year before, and equally as pregnant.

"Welcome. Manny is inside. Please, go on in. We're putting food together for you all."

Orus sidled past her, though he tapped his hat rim at her in acknowledgment. Virgil turned back at Octavius's call related to the wagon tongue. The tension lingered. Maybe she should follow Orus inside and act as a diffuser between her sons, but Catherine directed her to a table beneath a hickory tree where a black woman placed chunks of cheese and sliced pork. Hunger spoke louder than family dissension.

"Was it us being here?" Tabby asked Catherine. "Virgilia worried over the extra work we were for you. I should have listened."

"No, no. It wasn't having you and Virgilia here, Mother Brown. That wasn't what caused the complications of Alonzo's birth. I'd been so frail, through the whole pregnancy."

Slaves fanned their faces with sheets of cloth stretched onto circles of willow boughs. Tabby fidgeted. She didn't like having owned people adding to her comfort. "And now?" Pherne had taken a seat beside her mother.

"And now I feel a little stronger. But not so strong I want to test it by traveling in a wagon all that way. You understand, don't you?" Pherne

146

nodded. Tabby did too. "I couldn't risk losing another child."

"It's unfortunate that your dear husband—my son—didn't give your poor body a rest." Tabby knew she should keep her opinions to herself, but it was a habit hard to break.

"Why, I heard tell that the best way to deal with a stillbirth is to begin again. Like getting back onto a horse after a bad fall," Catherine said.

Pherne stiffened.

Tabby tapped her walking stick once on the ground beside her. "A woman's body needs a rest between pregnancies, good or bad. My dear father told me that and he was a physician, he should know. Losing a child isn't like a horse tumble. No, no. And there is nothing written that says a woman has to have a child every other year, or every year because she can. Goodness, that's why so many of us die young!"

Catherine blinked, changed the subject. "What we wonder about, Mother Brown, is you being able to make the trek, you and your brother-in-law, both of you, well, being . . . old. Older."

"I think we'll do fine. We've had a good test in this route so far. I've loved seeing the terrain, the change in seasons from last fall to spring. My wagon is sturdy. No broken tongue, at least. I like seeing change. The cornfields coming on. The taste of honey made from new flowers. Your honey, well, thank you for giving us a couple of tins to take with us last year. We'll appreciate a tin for Oregon if you have one."

"Manthano has not spoken to you?"

Tabby shook her head.

"Of course not. You haven't seen him yet, though I thought he would write."

"About the honey?"

"No. He wants you to stay here, with us. Won't you please consider it?" She touched Tabby's arm. Her fingers were cool. "I know you'd be a good help to me, and Manthano would appreciate your being here, he would."

"Stay here?"

She'd be with family. She would be useful. She wouldn't have to weather the long trip. She could end her life with ease, slaves fanning her face, washing her clothes, tending the fields. She could influence these grandchildren whom she'd had little time with. Help Young Pherne out; go west when they did in a few years, perhaps. And Catherine certainly could use the assistance. If nothing else, a stronger voice to tell her husband no more children for a while. Catherine may think herself stronger than she was last year, but the color of her skin was that of oatmeal and she was thin as egg noodles.

"Manthano may want that, but how would you feel, Catherine, about my remaining behind? Uncle John would need to stay too, you understand. If we're as old and useless as my sons think

148

we are, we could well add to your burden, not lessen it."

"John, too?" Catherine cocked her head and the breeze caught the crocheted square that crowned thick, black hair. She looked Spanish almost. Tabby hadn't noticed that before. "Oh. He'd be welcomed, of course. Manthano would wish both of you to remain."

"And you?"

"It would make Manthano happy, I know."

"If Manthano brings the invitation to me, I'll consider it." Was God telling her that this was the place where she could love and do good?

Manthano came to her after the supper pause, the heat of the day washed away by the shade as they sat on the veranda overlooking the river. To the side, black men busied themselves hefting hams from a cellar to the summer kitchen attached by a walkway to this big house. Beatrice pecked with Manthano's chickens, though keeping to the outside edge. Chickens weren't always accommodating to emigrants.

Tabby looked around. When would she want to live in a home with such luxury? Perhaps her old age deserved a slowing time with predictable shelter, good food, grandchildren to help raise up.

"Catherine said she'd made the invitation to you. And to John. You'd be welcome, Mother. What do you say about staying on?"

"I'm surprised, first of all. Truth is, I've never felt welcome in your home, Manthano. I know you wrote to me some years back, saying that I didn't understand, that you hadn't closed your doors to me and opened them only to your wife's kin. But you never came to see us. You left in a huff when you married Rebecca, and we never even knew when you took Catherine to be your wife. And truth be known, if you had really wanted John and I to stay, I think you would have written the invitation before we left St. Charles to give us proper time to consider."

"I was concerned you'd think it was too soon."

"It is. Catherine needs a rest between these babies."

"I meant my marrying her so soon after Rebecca's death."

"A man with four children, one of which is a wobbler, is fortunate to find a new wife after only seven months. And Catherine appears to have served you well, giving you four children in eight years."

"But who is keeping track, right, Mother?"

"It is not a criticism, merely an observation. There are ways to ease that. Catherine is wearing out, it appears to me."

"That isn't really your business though, is it, Mother."

She sighed. How did an invitation become an argument so quickly? "I suppose not." With her fingernail, she picked at a nubbin on her walking stick. "But I'd be hard pressed not to wear my opinions on my apron rather than stuff them in a purse if I stayed. Which is why I suspect you didn't write to ask." Manthano clasped his hands over his stomach and leaned back in his rocker, closed his eyes so she could no longer look into them. "Or maybe you didn't want to disappoint Orus in a letter. Maybe didn't want Orus to know you'd changed your mind. Now *that* I can understand."

Tabby had heard her sons' loud voices, though couldn't make out the words while she and Catherine and Pherne had sat beneath the hickory trees.

"I think the way you boys talk to each other, the way you spar when it's not intended, I suspect that is part of what drove you away from St. Charles and away from your brother and sister. And from me. And I fear it would happen again if I remained here with you."

He sat silent. "I loved the sea, Mother. You took us from that."

"You could have gone back. I did it so I wouldn't have to ever wonder again if you'd lived or died on a ship. One time of not knowing was enough. And you've done well for yourself here." She spread her arms around. "Harness making, breeding those mammoth mules, farming. All good business ventures, it appears.

With slaves to help, of course." She knew that last was spoken with a sharpness that wouldn't enhance her son's invitation.

"Think on it though, would you, Mother? Perhaps we need more time together, not less, to work out our differences."

"Familiarity breeds friendship?"

"Something like that." He leaned forward, elbows on his knees and hands clasped as though in prayer, head lowered. "I don't know how many years you have left, Mother. But I would like some of them to be spent with me and mine."

She heard an evening dove coo, suggesting a quieting of her tongue.

"I'll consider it, I will. And talk with John as well." She had Judson to think of too, though she suspected he could hire on as an extra. Orus would likely take him to herd their neat cows they planned to buy from Manthano. "Whatever I decide, know that I am grateful and humbled that you would ask me to remain. I am a person who can be difficult to live with. If your father were alive, I'm sure he'd concur. But some of that contrariness is what has gotten me through tough times. I'm not certain I could turn it around when I'm being offered luxury in my final days instead of trials. I think our character is shaped by the challenges, don't you?"

"Maybe that's why I want you to stay. So you

can continue to shape my character." He grinned and she saw his father's smile as she looked upon his face.

Go or Stay. Tabby wrote the title in her memoir, then about choices she had made in her life. Whether or not to leave Brimfield, Massachusetts, and marry, for one. She'd known her way around Brimfield, had her father's reputation to polish her own when she behaved indiscreetly. A model child she wasn't. After the accident, well, Brimfield became a safe place. Everyone knew her story. She never had to explain the walking stick. But leaving as a young wife would allow her to make her own history in a new place. She had vacillated, and that is the heart of the pain of a choice. *"Once decided, amazing things can happen. Somehow I had hoped there would be a right and perfect answer, but there was none. We pray for guidance, make a choice, and then we live with it, adapt. Make new climes,"* she wrote. Her husband's ministry was always being scrubbed between those who thought him too severe and those who thought him too relaxed in his theology. Just like on the washboard, clothes can get worn out with such scrubbing. They struggled: should they go to some new venture or stay and work through the consequences?

She would not want anything to interfere with her sons' and daughter's successes. But oh the hole in her heart when she thought of starting anew without family, left waiting for her death while the larger part of her legacy moved west.

She paced the room. She wasn't finished yet, not ready to ease away her days with Manthano's slaves breezing her face in the heat. Writing in her memoir felt like praying, and she needed to do that now.

She would go, keep her spirits up. As Tennyson would say, "We are call'd—we must go." And so she would ride in the morning of the times. *"The choice comes back to knowing what we're called to do and then doing it with all our hearts and minds and souls."* She had to go. As a young wife, she couldn't say "stay," and she couldn't say stay now either.

Part Two

— 13 —
To Choose

"This is a pretty comfortable place, it seems to me." John gazed and Tabby saw what he saw: the sheep-cropped lawns, the whitewashed pillars that set off the front porch, black-skinned people hoeing in the gardens. Orchards. Fields of hemp. Children's laughter serenading. "Unless you'd miss me." His eyes caught hers. She looked away.

"It is comfortable here, I agree." Tabby's palms became sweaty with his words. Without him along, her children would never consent to her heading west. She wouldn't entice him unfairly. "But would you want to miss out on the great migration to Oregon country? That's the pull, isn't it? Like the next shoreline you haven't encountered before. You're an old sea captain who must always take on the siren call of new seas, isn't that so?"

"Yes, yes, I know. But maybe as I'm approaching my eighth decade, maybe a warm bed each night and the sureness of a full stomach is a greater lure for me." He rubbed his belly as he talked. "Of course a pleasant bed warmer is nothing to sniff at." He wiggled his white eyebrows, making light, but his eyes spoke of the seriousness of his hope.

"Bed warmers. Yes, there's that. I don't know, John. I . . ." She tugged at the starched white collar at her throat.

"I'm not rushing you, Tabby. Truth is, I love taking care of you."

She tried to think of how he took care of her. She couldn't draw on a thing except his traveling to Missouri on her behalf, no small sacrifice. "We share an other-directed, self-sacrificing affection. I believe my dear Clark called that agape love. I do care about you, John, in that very way. Could it be more? I don't know. But time on the road would tell."

Tabby's heart beat a little faster. He didn't help all that much; Judson did most of the hard labor, but being "manless" on this journey would appear burdensome to Orus. She was more capable than John, but she knew that her abilities to persevere wouldn't count. Without John, Orus would insist she remain behind. Again. And Virgil Pringle hadn't exactly been excited about her hitching her wagon to the tail of his two, either. *Stay? Go?* Catherine had plenty of help and wouldn't really relish an old woman hovering. Emptiness formed in her stomach as she thought about remaining. No, the emptiness came from being left behind, being abandoned.

"It's my intention to go on. I can't stay here. But of us, I have to be honest in my uncertainty." There, she'd said it clear.

They walked over by the chickens, John a step behind her. In the shed beyond, Virgil and his sons and Orus and Manthano worked on replacing both of Virgil's wagon tongues. Manthano offered Virgil oak hardwood, so now they'd all have oak. It meant a delay of perhaps three or four days but was worth it if they didn't have to stop again for that kind of repair. Extra tongues would also be attached on two sides of Virgil's wagon bed to keep the load balanced. They loaded extra brakes. The best oxen would be given that wagon to pull.

"The road this far has been tougher than I thought," John said. "Maybe that's the Lord's way of telling me I've done my work and seen my last ocean."

Was this the Lord's way of telling her to stay too? A thought entered her head. "I'm not sure young Judson will want to go on without you. Then I will be in a pickle."

John looked at her sideways. He removed his hat and ran his hands through his white hair. With the sun behind him, it appeared that he wore a silver halo. Tabby blinked. *Would Clark have looked like him if he had lived?* "I didn't think the boy took much notice of me."

"He doesn't take much notice of anyone, much to Virgilia's chagrin. But I do see him looking to you when you're unyoking Do and Re, following your lead. He tends to your horse without your having to, doesn't he?"

"Yes, yes. Now that you say it." He replaced his hat. "I'll need to thank him for that, let him know I'm aware."

"Yes, you will. And at the campfire, he's attentive to your sea stories more than to mine, that's for certain."

"I hadn't noticed."

"His foster family wasn't all that kind to him, I've learned. We're a healing family for him, you and me and the rest of the clan. He startles when I tap him—lightly, mind you—on the shoulder with my stick. I've stopped doing it, using my voice to get his attention instead. Have you noticed that?"

"I have not. See, Tabby, I'm getting old. I'm past those little things that might be telling a story below the waterline. Another reason for me to remain right here and float into the Everlasting."

Tabby scoffed. "Don't try to put your foot into a grave before it's dug." But what if she did convince him to go and things turned sour? Would he blame her? Would she blame herself? She plunged ahead without an answer. "There are things happening beneath the draft here at Manthano's, John. Catherine's being gracious, but she really doesn't want one or two more old people here, I can tell."

"Invitation seemed genuine enough." A child's laughter rose, and Tabby saw her grandchildren rolling a hoop and chasing after it before it started down the long driveway.

"And Manthano, well, he's pretty opinioned himself. I can say that about my own son, as he comes by it fairly from his mother." She grinned. "But I could see the two of you butting heads. Me with him as well." She found a patch of shade and stood in it, leaning against her stick as she watched Beatrice and heard the sounds of men hammering against iron and wood. "And what about Judson?"

"What about him?"

"I'm paying him to take us. He'd be without work and be set adrift if we both stayed, and that might be what I'd have to do if you don't come along. Is that how you want to treat that poor boy?"

"No. No, that's not what I want."

Tabby wiggled her mouth, twitching it when she influenced in a disingenuous way. "How is he going to build up his character without you showing him how to make his way. Besides, he needs someone to look after. We all do."

"And who are you looking after, Tabby?"

"You. And that boy. My grandkids. Even my sons and daughter when they let me. A body just needs to have another body in their lives that matters. We take ourselves too seriously without that."

John fanned himself with his hat. His hair was matted like an old goat's.

"You promise me a safe trip if I go along, Sister Brown?"

"No, but I promise an eventful one. Well, the good Lord promises that, every day. And any trouble we run into, we won't be handling alone. Doesn't the unknown excite you even a little bit?"

"I'm not the kind of man who seeks uncertainty."

"Isn't that all there is with the oceans?"

He held up his palm to silence her. "Let me think."

Tabby knew when to keep quiet, though she sometimes didn't pay attention to the signs. This time, she did.

John tapped his fingers on the top of his ivory-topped cane. "I guess I'm still young enough to change. My bottom will have calluses upon calluses when I arrive in Oregon. Not exactly the change I had in mind, but there is that boy to consider. And you. Clark would want me to look after you."

"I'll trade you now and then and ride your horse, if you'd like. You can sit on my throne, as Sarelia calls it. It doesn't leave calluses."

Tabby watched John walk toward where the men worked on the wagon tongues. She thought about what she'd said to him, wondering at the truth in it and her own manipulation of his emotions. She could do that with people, she knew that. Was that why she'd pushed her way along on this western adventure and would now turn down Manthano's invitation? It was true; she did believe that people needed a cause to care about outside of them-selves. But if that was the only goal in life, she could stay with Manthano. She could convince herself that Catherine needed looking after, that she could lend wisdom in getting to know her grandchildren. She watched Judson as he lent a hand to the men.

Was it wrong to admit that it wasn't only family that drew her to move on west, to push John to it? It was the adventure of it, the idea that she wasn't so old she couldn't still learn new things about herself, her family, her world, and even about her faith. Clark always said that what we know about God is but a grain of sand on the world's shores and living meant being open to the new beaches he'd show us. Tabby didn't always like the lessons—loss being a great challenge—but she didn't want to be deceived by not accepting it.

At supper Tabby watched the faces of her grandchildren. She would likely never see Manthano again. Who knew what sort of future each of them faced, what lessons they'd learn. What wisdom she might miss from not sharing time with these children raised in luxury. Manthano's eyebrows had lifted ever so slightly earlier that evening when she'd told him she wasn't staying. They were in his office, an official-looking room. Books surrounded them, and for a moment she wavered. *I could spend the end of my days reading.*

"Your invitation is sweet and warm, but you've no need of extra people to upset the wagon of your ways here. John's heading with me."

"Don't go because you think we can't incorporate you, Mother. Leave only because you wish it above all else."

"Yes. Well. I choose to go."

"You're leaving me this time, Mother. So we're even. No more letters about how I left you and family behind in St. Charles." He shook his finger at her. "But I knew you wouldn't stay. You've always had a special place for Phernie. She's your favorite. Then Orus and then me. I'm glad Phernie will have her mother with her."

Tabby gaped. She tapped her walking stick. "That's fiddlesticks. I love each of you equally. That you would suggest otherwise grieves me, Manthano Brown. I have my own wagon. I'm hitching up with no one. Virgil has his crew. Orus has other duties to tend to, like keeping us following the correct path. But that I love you children like rungs of a ladder with one higher than the other, well, I never—"

" 'The lady doth protest too much, methinks.' "

"You quote *Hamlet* to your old mother?"

"Only because there's no need to explain. If you leave annoyed with me, it will perhaps make your leaving easier. But I will still miss you." He rose then and came from behind his desk and lifted her in a bear hug, the scent of his cologne heavy and distinctive.

"And I will miss you, my son. I will." She felt a fullness in her heart at the same time that tears threatened to empty it. Tears for the time she hadn't had with her son; tears for the unknown future that they would never share—because she chose not to.

It was perhaps the last time they would all be together as a family. They'd once rallied each other in a time of great loss. Together they had begun a journey from the East to Missouri. Now one peeled away, for good. She watched her children and their offspring laughing and sharing a meal together. John sat next to Judson where Virgilia had just brought those two biscuits slobbered in dandelion jelly. Were the boy's shoulders less hunched, his smile rising a bit higher to his eyes? He spoke to John as Virgilia sashayed away. John let out a belly laugh. Phernie leaned her head to listen to something Catherine told her. Tabby caught Orus looking at her and he winked. He'd know what she was thinking. *My family.* She hated the severing that would come tomorrow. Tonight she would savor these children feasting together. Oh, the lessons they'd learn on this journey, lessons of leaving, of family, and of love. She just didn't know who the teachers really were: those who had grown into their years, or those still making their way?

— 14 —
What Friends
We Make

The wagons got fixed and her gramo had a tight-lipped good-bye with her son and grandchildren and Catherine too. Virgilia wondered why her gramo didn't stay. But the time she had with her grandmother was all the more precious in this uncertain place they all traveled in now. It had surprised her that Uncle John had changed his mind, as he'd already told Virgilia's father that he was remaining. Something changed.

Virgilia held back as her gramo and mother and uncle said their last good-byes to her uncle Manthano. Aside from little Oliver, whom she'd known only a few short months, she'd never had to say good-bye to anyone who really mattered. Her chest ached imagining what it must be like for her gramo. She'd have to be extra caring of her this evening when they made that first camp. Just because a person chose a thing didn't relieve them of pain. She could see that in her gramo's eyes.

The wagons pulled out from her uncle's on May 2, 1846. Her father wrote that in his diary.

In Virgilia's diary she scribbled, *"Judson liked the cake I baked. He even said I could walk beside him some now that he was more accustomed to Do and Re. At supper, he practiced with the whip that Gramo bought for him and that Uncle Orus showed him how to use. I hope he doesn't have to. A goading stick is less painful. They are good oxen so maybe he can cajole them to keep them in line."*

She wondered how much of how she felt about this sojourn she should write about; maybe just keep to facts, about how the days wore into routine once they crossed the Missouri. Or how the skies carried wispy clouds that hawks sliced with their wings. Balmy weather, ample grass, and birdsong blessed their road by day; fiddle music often serenaded their evenings. She wrote of that.

And she did walk beside Judson, often, in the days ahead, the lazy journey following the Platte, giving ample time for conversation.

"Where're your people from?" Virgilia practiced getting people to talk about themselves. Gramo said that always helped a friendship.

Judson shrugged. "I guess Missouri. I don't know before that. Didn't matter."

"Oh, I think it does matter. The stories people tell about my grandfather or grandmother, they tell me how I might be one day. They're like a little map I can call up to help me in the unfamiliar places. It makes me less frightened to think that

Uncle Orus has already gone this way to Oregon. Doesn't it help you to know someone already walked this road we're on?"

Judson shook his head, rubbed at his freckled nose. "I haven't thought about such things."

"I think about that sort of thing all the time."

"Why?"

It was one of the longest conversations she'd ever had with Judson. "Why? Because . . . well, what do you think about as you're walking along?"

"I count steps. And I think about a deer I shot once. Maybe how I might improve upon that shot if I had the chance back."

Like her mother, he spent time in the past.

"Do you read books?"

Virgilia watched those freckles form into a solid block of pink across his nose and cheeks, making his blue eyes look even more like sky.

"Don't have time for such."

"If you'd like, I could loan you a few."

"I'm pretty tired at day's end. I've got the animals and Captain John and your grandmother to look after. Not much time for reading. Or talking, either."

Virgilia had kept pace with him, feeling the vibration of the heavy oxen plodding along and hearing the chain *clink-clink* as the animals pulled their cargo west. Silence wasn't such a bad thing, especially if it was the only option. Now and then, she included more about Judson in her diary and the changes that walking beside another along an unfamiliar road could bring.

Virgilia's father loaded flour purchased at good prices at Blue Mills, a cluster of cabins more than a town. Super-fine flour cost $2.00 and just lain fine was $1.75. This was wheat flour and not the interminable corn. Her father was pleased with the prices.

Other wagons joined them daily, catching up or arriving from the south. The first accident of the journey occurred for one such party newly arrived. Their wagon overturned on a river crossing and the lady of the family was injured. They had the same last name as her uncle and Gramo—Brown—but weren't related. Eventually the wagons, now sixteen strong with new recruits, left the Santa Fe road. The larger group stopped to choose captains and divide up under two separate leaders. Orus was chosen as pilot for both groups. That was no surprise. Her uncle took over a room, so of course he'd take over a wagon train.

The groups crossed rivers by driving oxen through the waters or took ferries set up by enterprising settlers. Virgilia told her mother that ferries meant others had gone before them and done well. She hoped it gave her mother reassurance. Some days they lost cattle or sheep, mules skittered at a rabbit on the trail and took off, making the rest of the train wait until they were under control and the torn harnesses repaired. Men shouted and grumbled about delays, her father one of them. One day they came to a stream with a high bank, and the first double-teaming occurred to manage the heavy loaded wagons, but at least there'd been no order of leaving things behind. Yet. Virgilia hadn't taken much with her, but what she had she didn't want to give up anytime soon—her pewter knife and her blue aster porcelain thimble the most important.

Sometimes Virgilia felt her steps light as she plodded behind her sisters, stitching quilt pieces. She wore a pincushion on her bodice with different needles threaded with color. She'd already broken one needle and would have to be careful not to lose any. Where would they ever get replacements? She could lift her eyes now and then to her sisters and the skyline, but then focus on the tiny stitches that brought her quilt block together. She felt safe surrounded by family, even though the landscape often threatened. But men helped each other; strangers became friends working together to hitch and unhitch, to bring a wagon from one point to another. They weren't alone in the trials, and that kept her hope stepping high as Uncle John's spirited horse. Most days the promise of the future seemed so palpable, she could touch it in the air.

Other times she carried trepidation about what lay ahead. It wasn't only the uncertainty of this trail but in her life. Her gramo said "nobody knows" what to expect. What would happen to her in Oregon? Or on this road? Who would she meet to marry and what if she never met anyone? Would she be relegated to looking after her sisters' families or her mother and father as they aged, having "friends" instead of potential mates? Maybe she'd end her life looking after Great-Uncle John and Gramo once they reached Oregon. Caring for Uncle John was like crawling through a fog sometimes, because he often rode too far ahead and then someone had to ride halfway back with him to find Gramo's wagon. She couldn't imagine him as a ship's captain. He repeated himself often. Schooner, his horse, acted prancy, and she worried that her uncle might not be able to handle him.

Virgilia lived in the future and it was both an adventure and a very scary place.

The girl walked right up to Virgilia, stepped into her reverie, and put her hand out like a man would. "Hi. I'm Nellie Louise Blodgett and I'm sixteen years old and I want to be your friend." Nellie Louise was shorter, rounder, and a year younger than Virgilia. She had hair the color of Buddy's nose, black and shiny, and she was round as a biscuit, but she could still touch the ground with the flat of her hands without bending her knees. Which she did.

Virgilia dropped her mouth open like a baby bird waiting to be fed. "I can't do that."

"It's one of my many talents." Nellie Louise's dark hair curled all over her head and her bonnet had bounced loosely on her back when she'd bent to touch the ground. "Sorry I startled you."

"How do you know you want me for a friend? I might be lazy or outspoken or maybe I tell tales."

"I have times I like to lie around." Nellie patted her lower lip with her finger and stood with pressure on one leg, the way a horse does when it's waiting. "That's the best thing about this trip so far: being a little lazy. I don't have to constantly work in the garden or churn butter or make candles. That's all been done or the oxen do it, churning butter as they plod along. Mostly I get to stitch as I walk, and after helping Mama with supper and all, I'm free to listen to the music or read—"

"You like to read?"

"Yes, I do!"

"Me too. It's the most important time a person can spend."

"Hmm, that sounds a little opinionated." Nellie's bonnet was made of scrap pieces stitched together in a hodgepodge design. Virgilia liked it. "My favorite book is *The Last of the Mohicans*."

"I like *The Crofton Boys*. Have you read that story? My grandparents started the library in

St. Charles. They loved books and literary things, and it was the best thing that ever happened to St. Charles, taking it from a simple town to one with lots of churches, schools, businesses."

"What did you say your name was?"

"Virgilia Pringle."

"I like it. Telling stories always makes the day pass faster. I think I chose wisely in seeking your friendship."

Virgilia laughed. "I've been looking for a chum, but I didn't know how to find her."

Nellie pushed her arm through Virgilia's and got in step beside her. "I always say you have to go after what you want or it'll slip away like a garter snake in the garden."

"I do not like snakes of any kind."

"Well, that's a pretty strong opinion. But one I share. I think we'll be fast friends indeed."

Nellie's hands were soft as velvet. "How do you get your hands so smooth?"

"I make a lotion." She leaned into Virgilia. "It's a secret. But now that we're friends, I'll share it. Glycerin and Dr. Atkinson's Bay Rum, when my papa has it."

"Does he know you use his cologne?"

"He hasn't said. And my mama likes the lotion too. It smells good." Nellie put her hand to Virgilia's nose. "I'll make you some."

A friend! Virgilia's view of the future turned as smooth as Nellie Louise's lotion.

— 15 —
To Keep from Falling

People were injured and recovered; babies arrived and survived. Pherne let the flicker of memory of Oliver's birth press its way forward, soft as dawn. It happened whenever she heard of a newborn on the trail. It had been such a happy time. Oliver had been healthy, learned to put weight on his little feet when she held his middle. She could still see his pink mouth open with a drop of moisture ready to fall as he concentrated until he bounced on her belly and they laughed together.

She pushed even pleasant memories aside when death appeared on the trail. The Henderson child drank a bottle of laudanum while evening fiddlers played and people danced Virginia reels and sang "Pop Goes the Weasel." Salita Jane was the girl's name. It was important to Pherne to learn and remember the names of the deceased along this trail. Later, that child couldn't be awakened. A child whose life was an unfinished drawing, a mere sketch, never to be added onto. Pherne ached for the family, especially two older sisters who said they'd tasted from the bottle while their little sister watched. "We told her not to touch it," they said through tears. But children do what they will. The child's sisters would live with the guilt, always wishing they'd done something differently. Pherne knew that such a palette of regret could fade but never be painted over.

When a child died of scarlet fever diagnosed before they left the States, Pherne told her mother, "They ought not to have started out until after the child had recovered. Now they've exposed everyone. My children." Pherne twisted a cotton wick and put it into the lantern.

"Now, Phernie. Maybe they thought she was healed enough. Maybe that poor mother had a husband who insisted they move out. You know how that can happen."

Pherne nodded.

"That poor mother is already suffering. Don't add future weights to an already-burdened soul."

Then Pherne felt guilty for having judged another.

"I'll pray you forgive yourself one day, Daughter." Her mother looked up at her from the rocker she sat in, chores already finished.

"Why would you say that?"

But her mother didn't answer. Did she doze? Then, "If you carry regrets into the future, the future won't be a safe place either."

Disjointed, that's what Pherne was. The past

claimed her like a web, sticky across her face, and blurred any clarity for viewing the future.

But there were signs of life and living on this road too. A Mrs. Richardson had an uneventful birthing, though the mother needed a tonic the day after. Pherne offered up a bit of whale oil in honey, and the woman thanked her, saying it had helped, and the party moved forward after the day's delay. Pherne had known people to take small amounts of whale oil daily and live to ripe old ages, but she thought caution made sense. And the honey from Manthano's supply sweetened the oil. She noticed a man from Ohio carried two hives of honeybees with him. Why hadn't she thought of that as a way to serve her family and maybe a new business venture once they arrived? If she forced her mind to think of the future, perhaps it would blot out the past. Like births, burials slowed them, but Pherne was grateful the men stopped a day to honor the beginnings and the ends of being, even if they didn't stop for the Sabbath.

A terrible storm hit them on May 25. Virgil wrote in his diary that it was a "hurricane" and maybe it was. In less than forty-five minutes, every wagon, man, woman, child, every animal and wagon box was soaked and every little river branch running full. They slept in wet beds that night and rounded up cattle for two days. She complained to herself of monotony and then moaned aloud at the next overturned barrel, hornet stings, or stampede. She hated every minute of this terrible road, each step taking her farther away from Oliver and into an uncertain future. She couldn't imagine the many more months they'd be traveling with such regret on her palette.

Smaller groups of blue-painted wagons passed them, and then sometime later, on a higher part of the prairie, Pherne looked down into a swale with wagons spread out like spokes of paths through a sea of yellow and purple wildflowers. She put her hand to her breast and blinked. It was beautiful. White wagon covers like ivory dominoes dotted the plains; dust billowed up behind brown sticks of mules or oxen, speckled white on red. Green wagons, red wheels breathing brown dust, a rainbow of colors. Tears formed in her eyes. It reminded her of a landscape painted with beauty in vastness, deepened with detail. "Hobbema's work," she said out loud.

"What, Mama?" Emma asked her. The child slipped her hand into Pherne's while Buddy trotted along beside them, his tongue hanging out in the heat.

"A Dutch painter of landscapes. They invented that word, did you know that?"

"You sound like Gramo."

"Do I? Well, the Dutch painted seascapes all the time and then wanted to paint the interior of their country so they called it 'landscapes.' What I see out there reminds me of a picture in that big book of painters that I had to leave behind."

"You didn't leave it if it's right in front of you, Mama."

She laughed, squeezed her daughter's hand. "You're so right, Emma." Maybe she was a part of something large—they all were. This train of covered wagons moved unwieldy yet with design. A verse from 2 Samuel came to her: "Thou has enlarged my steps under me; so that my feet did not slip." This vista had cracked that shell of memory, split her open at her breastbone. She did not need to fear falling—into her past. Even in the sameness interrupted by moments of sheer panic, her steps were being enlarged. And for that moment she looked forward, feeling solid and sure. Maybe she could capture that opening of her heart with her pencils.

No, not yet.

In early June the sand hills of the Platte rose like whipped cream peaks. Virgil said they were "romantic" and reminded him of snowdrifts. "Why don't you capture that, Phernie? Get your pencils out."

"I don't deserve to enjoy my sketching."

Buddy hobbled ahead, chasing who knew what. His leg swung out oddly, a residual of the raccoon attack. Wounded beings were everywhere on this trail.

Virgil dismounted and led his horse to walk beside her. "There was nothing you could do. Oliver simply slipped away. Whether you'd have been churning butter or hovering over him. He just went to sleep."

"The down comforter was too thick and he couldn't breathe. If I hadn't been drawing, I might have heard his choking."

Virgil shook his head. "There's no evidence he choked. He wouldn't want you to punish yourself by avoiding something that always brought you joy." How many times Virgil had heard her story and yet he never sounded frustrated with her, never dismissed the pain in her memory. "He was a character. Remember when he tried to learn to wink?"

Pherne smiled. "His face scrunched up like an old apple."

Virgil looked out and her eyes followed his.

The sand hills before them were beautiful. "See what you can capture. Draw it for Oliver." He bent inside her bonnet to kiss her cheek, laughed when the brim poked his forehead. He rode off and Pherne waited for the wagon to pass by, then pulled herself up onto the back, opened the trunk, and took out her pad and pencils. She made her way to the front and sat on the wagon seat. She drew to capture the beauty of this exotic place. She drew to find a new memory for Oliver, one that placed him on this road with them, inspiring her fingers to capture a moment, an interior landscape. She'd forgotten how soothing the lead in her hands could feel, how uplifting to her soul to be praying with pencils, enlarging her steps, keeping her feet from falling.

"They always squish," Sarelia complained. They'd stopped at the mouth of Ash Hollow after hours of a steep-slope passage. Virgilia and her siblings had been forced to carry things to lighten the load and save wear on the brakes. Once there, children gathered up chokecherries and currants while whiffs of wild roses scented the air.

"You're supposed to put them in the basket, not in your tummy," Virgilia told her. "How else can I make a tasty pudding tonight if you consume them all?"

"But I like to eat them." Sarelia popped another into her mouth, then held up her small palm speckled in red.

"I've an idea." Nellie Louise lifted her skirt and tore a small section from her third petticoat. "Would you give me your apron, Sarelia?"

Sarelia complied and Nellie pulled a threaded needle from her pincushion and sewed three sides of the patch onto the bodice of Sarelia's apron. "I call it an outside pocket. The top is left open so you can put berries inside and you don't have to push through your skirts to the under-skirt pocket."

"I could put all kinds of things in there." Sarelia pulled the apron back over her head, her hands leaving red berry stains. Then she dropped currants into the pocket. "Rocks I find will fit in here."

"Not at the same time as the berries," Virgilia told her. "You'll have jam."

"It's pretty. Thank you, Nellie." She fingered her outside pocket.

"Not too hard. You'll squish them!" The older girls laughed.

"I can share with Gramo." Sarelia ran ahead to the wagon where her gramo sat on the harp-back chair.

"Where'd you learn about an outside pocket?" Virgilia asked.

Nellie Louise shrugged. "It's a way to carry something small and keep it protected without having to find the skirt slit for the inside pocket. I should have put a little flap over the top, then it would look like a tiny saddlebag. That's where I got the idea. It's a way to carry something small and keep it protected."

"It was kind of you, but you shouldn't waste your petticoats on such as that. What if you need them for bandages or—"

"Are you a worry worm?"

Virgilia frowned. "You mean like a bookworm, only one who worries? That's not me. That's more my mama." *Wasn't it?*

"Would you like a pocket? I can sew one on your apron too."

"I wasn't asking for anything." Virgilia didn't know why she was now annoyed.

Nellie Louise had spent the previous night with them, her parents' wagons far ahead. Many children clustered in a cousin's wagon, moving back and forth. It was an advantage of families traveling together, Virgilia supposed. Her uncle Orus's wagons were several days ahead, as he piloted the faster-moving portion of the train.

"Sorry," Nellie Louise apologized. Her friend noticed Virgilia's moods better than anyone. "My mama is always looking for ways to fix things. I've stood too close and it's sprinkled on to me, I guess."

Virgilia liked that image. "I sprinkle my sisters with flour when I'm baking. And being a bit bossy. I'm pretty messy too."

"You plunge into what you love. Me too. We're passionate. That's what I'd call it. Messy is something to avoid, but being passionate, well, who doesn't want that?" Nellie Louise flailed her arms about like a stubby windmill, turning and turning, making Virgilia laugh out loud. Who indeed? Her new friend could bring on annoyance, but her passion whisked it away. Virgilia wished her friend would sprinkle more of that passion on her.

Another mouth of a stream. Pherne wondered that the men seemed to know the name of each of these bodies of water. That they did should be reassuring that they were on the right trail, that others had gone before them. The maps inside their heads were getting them where they needed to go and ought to be reducing her anxiety about the unknown. This stream was called Ash Creek. Not too far down the draw on a bad road, they came across a cabin with the title of "Ash Grove Hotel."

"Look at that," she told her mother. "Some hotel."

"Fanciful thinking," her mother said. "Nothing wrong with that, way out here. Thinking big. I can admire a man who does that."

Inside was a single plank bar and the men could order up warm beer if they chose. Fortunately, Virgil did not, even though the owner claimed the beer was "as good as a Bavarian brew." Uncle John began his speech about the evils of liquor to thirsty travelers as Virgil prodded him back outside.

The owner nodded toward a large ledger book sitting on the plank counter. "Go ahead, folks. Leave messages to let those behind know you've made it this far and are all right."

Pherne held it for her mother to read as she stood with both hands on her walking stick. "Look, there's Orus's loopy signature. And the date." Her brother had been through a week previous. He had made a notation next to his name. *Hurry along, Pringles and Tabitha Brown.*

"It's like Orus to rally us." Her mother grinned. "And not reference that I'm his mother."

Pherne didn't find it laughable. A twinge poked at her ribs looking at her brother's comment. He was ahead that far? What if they needed help? Or had a question about their direction? Would Virgil know the way without Orus? Did she have more confidence in her brother than in her husband? Orus had spent more time farther ahead and his wagons kept up a faster pace than Virgil's or her mother's and that concerned her. Maybe Virgil should push harder.

Her unsettledness didn't lessen as they passed new landscape markers, even when she sketched the jagged lines of Parker's Castle with its steep chimney that made the rock formation look like a castle in the middle of the continent. They plodded onward. The next week Orus sent a messenger back, telling them that in two days' time they'd find a Sioux Indian gathering of two hundred lodges. "You're to give 'em a feast, Pilot Brown says."

A feast? What was her brother thinking? Feeding their own families and two hundred lodges of Indians? No one else questioned her brother's orders and the women worked up a frenzy preparing corn patties and venison the men had bagged. Later, Pherne had tried to sketch the gathering, men and women sitting in clusters, horses swishing tails, nearly naked children rushing in and out of teepees while dozens of dogs scattered about. Her renditions of humans lacked skill, she decided, so she didn't attempt to draw the men with their feathers woven into their long black hair nor the big clay pipe that was passed around the circle. She focused on the landscape and how the hide teepees blended into the hills.

Her three sons were ecstatic with the pomp and circumstance, but the women sat back, exhausted from preparing the meat, using dried fruits and vegetables from home, turning that fine flour into breads and cakes for this feast rather than for their own families. The men traded lead and ammunition and in return got the promise of safe travel through the Sioux country. Pherne hoped the ammunition wouldn't be turned back on the seventy wagons that had joined up for the feast. They'd delayed more than a day and Virgil called it a "good investment." Prayer would be their best investment.

The following days, they wound the wagons through wide vistas of pink sand despite the meandering North Platte with water aplenty.

Pelicans landed on the islands. She hadn't seen those birds since the Chesapeake. Rock formations they could see for miles before approaching rose up out of the sand, with names like Independence and Split Rock. Pherne noticed she felt light-headed at times, even giddy, laughing overmuch at something Emma said or Buddy's antics. Virgil said it was the altitude. "But I can't feel any difference."

"We are climbing. Word is we'll be at South Pass soon—that's the divide when rivers start running west."

"Uncle John was . . . disoriented this morning. He even wanted to teach my mother how to play the violin."

"I didn't realize the altitude would make someone delusional," Virgil said. "Of course with some people it might be hard to tell." They had laughed together then, and Pherne remembered just how long it had been since they'd shared a lighter moment. She hoped for more of that.

— 16 —
Waiting on Guidance

They crossed the Continental Divide and had more basins and mountains to trek. Wagons broke down—not the Pringles' or Tabby's—and they suffered bug bites and sore feet, but it wasn't nearly as bad as Orus had said it would be. They resupplied as much as they could at Fort Hall on the Snake River. Currency was limited. Tabby had none left, so she hoped the bacon in the barrel and the cornmeal she carried would be enough. They were on the last leg of the journey, Virgil told them, and the rest would be easier than what they'd been through. Tabby thought they'd done well. One thing about that high altitude: anything seemed possible.

"So who is he, exactly?" Tabby asked. They'd passed America Falls when new men approached, riding fine horses and mules. It was Sunday, August 8. Virgil had not felt well, but the wagons had continued to roll, and he'd rallied, easing Pherne's concerns. "The stomach upset could be altitude sickness too," Tabby told her daughter. The news of such an effect had resolved a discomfort to Tabby as well. She had a little trouble breathing sometimes, especially as they'd made climbs into the shining mountains. And she'd been forgetful, letting Beatrice out of her cage but not tying her leg to a yarn tether. Judson had spent an hour looking for the bird while John walked beside the oxen. John had now ridden over toward the men and, along with Virgil, had chatted for some time. A large dark-skinned man joined them. They'd ridden in from the south, the direction of the Mexican and Texas violence. Were they escaping that?

"Mr. Applegate, he says he is," John told her when he came back to their wagon. "Judson, you need help there?"

"No sir. You take a rest. I'll get the oxen watered fine. Not much grass here along the river though for your horse." He patted Schooner's chestnut neck.

"Virgil called it 'indifferent grass.'" John giggled. "Sorry. Something about 'indifferent' just tickles me." He cleared his throat, put gravitas on the next words. "Those men are the Applegate brothers. Came out in '43."

"Are they now going to Oregon, again?" Tabby hobbled around to poke at the fire. A kettle of beans had soaked the day and now cooked in her black Dutch oven, sending aromas that gnawed at her stomach. She had quite an appetite in this country, but she didn't seem to put on an ounce. She stood barely taller than Sarelia and weighed less than two fifty-pound bags of flour. With her long-handled spoon, she lifted the cover, adding bits of bacon pieces to the steaming water. Her bacon supply had waned, but judging from what the men said, they were but two months from Oregon. She'd make corn pudding later, using Beatrice's eggs and milk from one of Pherne's Durham cows. It had been a long, hot day and her back ached, but they would eat well that evening —as they had most days.

"Applegate never went back to Missouri. Has a new southern trail staked out and wants us to go with him and a Captain Levi Scott into Oregon that way, instead of down the Columbia River. That big man with them they call Moses Harris. He's been trapping these parts and back and forth across the divide. They seem like reliable sailors for this sea we're on." John pulled the saddle off his mount. Even almost eighty, his arms showed good muscle. He stood the saddle on end so the breeze could dry the lamb's wool matted from the horse's sweat. Those oxen, those dear beasts, didn't sweat at all. Tabby wondered how they cooled themselves.

John reached for his ivory-handled cane and moved to the fire. He needed that cane less often, as far as Tabby could tell. This trail had invigorating side roads, it seemed. Judson returned, motioned he'd take Schooner to water next. "I'll bring him back and do the brushing."

"Applegate says that we'd head southwest

like we were going to California, then when the trail forks, we start north toward the Willamette Valley, they call it. Virgil seems interested. Not sure what Orus would say if he was here." John scratched at his beard, a combination of salt and pepper.

"Is it shorter, this route?"

"So they say. And we won't have to raft down that Columbia River, which even Orus said was fraught with danger. Applegate brothers each lost a child to that stream. One reason they want the alternate route for folks. And too, if we had to leave the country in case of warring, we'd have a way out that's not under the watchful eye of the British across the Columbia."

Tabby handed her brother-in-law a tin cup of hot grain coffee and a small piece of one of Virgilia's cakes. He smiled up at her and she smiled back, a tiny tingling on her skin she attributed to the thin air. He popped the cake into his mouth and chewed. In the distance she heard Judson shout after Schooner, and quick as a lamb's tail, the horse bolted toward them.

John pushed and stood, put both hands out, dropping the cane. "Whoa, whoa, now." He grabbed at the lead rope. "You rascal, you. High spirits, he has. Just like his owner." John rubbed at the animal's nose, kept him from Tabby's bean pot as the horse pranced. He waited for Judson to retrieve the horse from him. John was still in good physical form for a man of seventy-eight. Quick when necessary. He could be entertaining. Maybe . . .

John sat then, his cane on the ground before him.

She shook her head. "An unpredictable horse isn't the best traveling companion."

"But a quick-thinking man can be." He winked at Tabby.

Her face grew warm. She hadn't flirted for decades and wasn't sure she liked being the target of it either. "How's your dessert?"

"That girl is a cake-baker's dream." John smacked his lips. "I hear she's trying pies now with that new little friend cheering her on."

"I like that Nellie." Tabby was happy he moved on. "It's a pleasure to my heart to see Virgilia smiling and enjoying herself a little. And I notice Judson's paying a bit more of attention when she comes around. The lad is still so tongue-tied he hardly speaks to anything in skirts, including me."

"Oh, he'll do all right. He seems to fancy Nellie Louise—but don't tell Virgilia."

"At this point, with a good friend, I don't think she'd care." Tabby leaned against the wagon, seeking shade, then jerked away as though she'd been shot. She turned to look, stuck her hand out. "That shovel blade is as hot as the fire."

John walked over, removed the tool. "We'll

need it later anyway for our latrine duties. So you think her shine to young Judson is wearing off?"

"I think Virgilia's coming around to herself, finding another side of her she likes, and that makes trying to interest Judson less important. She can rely on herself to move forward and not have to wait for a young man to set her course. She'll act as her own pilot."

"Never worried about her setting a course. She's a Brown, though young ladies aren't meant to pilot."

Tabby scoffed. "I've directed my own way from day one with your brother and even before. Being headstrong's no crime. Serves one well. Look at Orus. He's out there guiding this massive body of wheel-carrying adventurers, selected by his peers. He's convinced a fair number of folks to come along on this trip. He has to have confidence in himself to do the job people elected him to do."

John groaned like Pherne's old hound as he leaned against the wagon wheel. He handed his coffee tin back to Tabby. "Orus. I do wonder what he'd say about that new way Applegate touts. They say while they're here recruiting us, men are working on the road. They're seeking single men not otherwise occupied to go ahead and help chop."

"What young man isn't occupied?"

Judson returned, washed up, and Tabby served her beans and coarse bread baked from the day before. "Pudding follows. What thoughts do you have about taking that new cutoff, Judson?"

"Don't have one. If that's the way you want to go, I'll take the oxen. No matter to me. Whatever you decide."

"You're a part of my family, Judson Morrow. Your opinion matters."

He nodded, ducked his head. With his finger he wiped a piece of bread stuck on his tooth.

"You're one of my essentials, young man."

And he was.

Here they were again, families making choices. Go with the new route or stay with the old. "We'll chat with Virgil, some of the others. See what people think. Nobody knows the best choice," Tabby said. "We gather facts, then listen to our hearts and live with the results." Wasn't that the way of life? Nobody knows what lies ahead. And if they did, truth be known, they might never have started out.

The girls scrubbed dishes while squatting at the stream they'd camped beside, decisions about the alternate route not yet finalized as grown-ups sealed the girls' fate. Dusk drifted over the water, turning the river to a shade almost as dark as Virgilia's school slate. "My parents have decided to take that southern route." Nellie's dark curls poked out from behind the bonnet she wore more often now, the sun hot as desert rocks.

"I don't know what my family will do yet." Virgilia had overheard little of the discussion between her parents, getting most of her information about the alternate trail from her grandmother, who hadn't yet decided either. But if Nellie Louise went and Virgilia's family didn't . . . "I hope we'll go that way if you are." Virgilia changed the subject toward something less painful. "I saw Judson watching you the other day."

"He's cute. He's easy to tease, but I have to be careful not to do that. Boys are intimidated by a girl's quick wit. How old do you think he is?"

"Maybe seventeen. Why don't you ask him?" Virgilia encouraged her, though she didn't know why.

"Because I want him to be older, so my pa will see him as someone ready to make his way in the world, with a wife. Preferably me."

Virgilia blinked. "A wife? But you hardly know him."

"Say, you aren't interested in him, are you? I mean, he acts more like a brother around you and like you're his big sis."

"Do you think so? But—"

"He's under the care of your family, so that gives him status. Besides, he's interested in being a blacksmith. That's a good trade. He could support me and the children with that occupation."

Virgilia laughed, surprised she felt no jealousy. Nellie Louise hoped for heights, and that meant if it didn't work out, she'd have farther to fall. Was that why Virgilia didn't push herself into risk? She was afraid of the fall? Virgilia stood and stretched her knees as she dried tin plates in her apron. "If you're planning a marriage, my gramo better choose the cutoff. I wouldn't want to miss it." They headed for the pale shade of the Pringle wagon. "But my uncle Orus didn't take the route, and he has a lot of influence on our family even when he's not present. He's still expecting we'll be a week or two behind him, heading down the Columbia before long. When will you pull out?"

"If we go, tomorrow."

"So this might be our last evening together. We should do something special."

"Like what?"

Virgilia was thoughtful. "Let's write a letter to ourselves as though we were living in our future after we've arrived in Oregon. We can speculate five years ahead and give ourselves advice from our youth." She giggled with that term, "youth." "Then I'll give my letter to you and you give yours to me. When we're settled, we'll mail them. We can see how close we came to predicting our futures."

"How will we know where we each are? mail them, I mean."

Virgilia hadn't thought of that. "We'll s them to Oregon City, that's the main town in country, my father says. Surely after we've t in the territory for a time, we'd both have a rea to go there and we'll pick up our letters. But shouldn't only send *those* letters. Wherever end up, we'll send word so we can write al our everyday. I think it would be fun to get a le from myself when I'm twenty or twenty-one."

"Don't tell me what you put in yours an won't tell you what I put in mine. We w read them . . . will we?" Nellie's eyes he pleading look.

"It's okay with me if you know what I hope life will be like and whether I give myself a advice or not."

"I guess I can share my secrets with you. Yo my best friend."

"All right." Virgilia hugged her. "Let's daydreaming. Even if your family does take cutoff, we'll still have wisdom from our mouths to look forward to." This was what ha a good friend meant, someone to help f imagination into the future. Virgilia grab foolscap to share with Nellie Louise.

Tabby, John, and Judson made their way to Pringle fire later that evening. Someone play

196

harmonica in a wagon across the circle. Sarelia and Emma ran out to meet her, and Tabby let Sarelia take Beatrice's cage from her. When they arrived, she handed the yarn attached to the bird's foot to Emma. "You let her peck."

Tabby noticed Virgilia and Nellie Louise writing away on thin paper. The girls stopped when the company arrived. Virgilia moved over on the wagon tongue so Judson could sit between the girls, which he did after shaking Octavius's and Clark's hands. Both boys drank from tin cups. Judson tipped his hat to Albro too. Those boys leaned against the sideboard, drinking ginseng tea, Tabby supposed, from the spicy scent.

"Are you still writing your stories down for me, Gramo?" Sarelia's cheery voice called to her as Emma handed her the chicken's tether.

"Not as I should be. I have to keep making up schoolwork for you children." Tabby had taken to teaching "feet classes," she called them. She prepared questions on history and mathematics and gave them spelling words that each child learned as they walked along, trying to create sentences for each new word. They recited back to Tabby the following day. Some days she read to them from the few books she'd brought along as they hopped up to sit beside her while the wagon rolled. Tabby even planned a spelling bee, and several children from other wagons wanted to take part. She'd found good use already for her brass school bell. Her class would change, depending on the decision about whether to go on the new trail or stay on their chosen route following Orus.

"Guess we're going to have a confabulation." Tabby let John help her to the milk stool that Virgil pulled from the wagon bed for her. Her son-in-law looked tired, not yet recovered from that illness he'd had. She was sure glad she'd whipped her cold.

"I guess so, Mrs. Brown. Your daughter and I have had a few confabs ourselves about this new route."

"It's almost as important as the decision to come in the first place." Pherne bit her words.

"And you've decided?"

Virgil shrugged. "It's a tough one." He ran his hand through his hair, his floppy hat stuck on the end of the shovel handle at the side of the wagon. "It would be good to make headway, maybe even beat Orus and the other wagons into the Willamette Valley."

"This is not a competition." Pherne sounded as she did when she scolded Buddy, who lifted his head to her even though she hadn't used the dog's name.

"You know what I meant. I don't want to come in weeks later than he expects."

"We'd likely never hear the end of that," Pherne said.

"But on the new trail, we wouldn't be traveling in the dust of so many others. Might find better feed for our animals that way too."

"Which is why we shouldn't take such a chance. What if there isn't good feed? What if there are Indian tribes that Orus hasn't already encountered, that we didn't feed for our security."

"Life's full of chances."

"And some should not be taken."

"Nellie's parents are going." Virgilia raised her voice. She wiggled her bare feet stretched out before her.

"But we don't know if these men can be trusted. Is not our first obligation to make wise, safe choices for our children?" Pherne wasn't knitting or stitching or drawing, her hands instead wringing worries out of each other. "Orus, I'm certain, would want us to follow his lead. It's the route that's proven. Why take an unknown one?"

"Because we have new information. The cutoff could help Oregon become a state one day."

"We'd take it for a patriotic reason?"

Tabby heard fear rising in her daughter's voice. "It is always good to think larger than oneself, Daughter." Pherne brushed her hands toward her mother's supportive comment.

"The wilderness has a lure to it, Phernie. It can test a man's mettle." Virgil put his arm around Pherne's shoulder, pulled her closer, but she stood stiff as a long-handled spoon.

"Test your mettle at your own expense, not that of your family's safety. I'd think you've had enough testing anyway. Double-teams? Lost animals? Indian gatherings? Illness."

"And a frosty wife," he mumbled.

"What do you think, Gramo?" Clark asked.

"What do I think? I'll go wherever you Pringles decide to roam. I'm not leaving any of you." Sarelia sat now with her knees pulled up to her nose. Her new pocket held a wilted wildflower. "I like thinking we might be helping out by proving that a new route shortens the trip. And I feel that mettle pull too. It's not just for men, Virgil Pringle."

"Mrs. Brown, I didn't mean to suggest it was."

"So you think it's worth the risk, Gramo?"

Tabby nodded. "I figure Orus has his ways and I have mine. I've been known to start a long journey before and didn't always do what my firstborn wanted. He got over it."

"But you knew there was a safe route from New England to St. Charles, Mother."

"Yes. And I had both my boys and you with me and Uncle John's knowledge of the waterways." She nodded to her brother-in-law. "But things can happen on a steamboat. Or on the trail Orus picked for us. Danger is everywhere, but fear, that's a choice we make." She lifted her finger to the air to make her point. "It's a shorter route and no river floating. I like those odds."

A chorus of dogs barking in the distance raised Buddy's head and broke the silence. Albro patted the dog.

Then Tabby said, "I'd feel better though if I could have talked to those fellows myself rather than hearing what they said second ear, so to speak. Not that you're not a good reporter, Virgil. You are. And you've got more at stake than I do, old as I am with no young children. Judson there is my young man to worry over. And Nellie Louise too, for the time being." The girl grinned. "I'd like to get them to that so-called Promised Land Orus spoke of, sooner rather than later."

"You boys? What about you?" Virgil asked.

"We've talked, but we'll do whatever you say, Pa." Clark spoke for his brothers. Judson nodded. John did as well. He'd get no argument from them. If Virgil turned southwest, of course they'd go.

The truth was, Tabby needed to arrive in the Willamette Valley sooner rather than later. Even though she put on a cheery face, her supplies were low and she would not ask the others to resupply them. She didn't want to ask John for assistance either. She would need whatever she had left to trade for goods once they reached their destination. Her "things" would be as currency, that and what labor she might have to offer, which wouldn't be much given her age and her "foot." Oh, she'd prayed and asked for guidance but didn't see the clarity she would have liked. Some choices were like that. God left her to step into uncertainty. She guessed that's where faith grew strongest.

"You boys are acting like you don't care one way or the other. Have opinions." Tabby nodded to her grandsons.

"It's a matter of trusting Pa. We can cut limbs out of the way, we've got axes. Our oxen are sound." Clark summarized for his brothers, and Octavius added, "We've plenty of grease and we replaced the brakes again. Others have gone ahead to build that Applegate road. Somehow we're pretty far behind Uncle Orus, but we're not as far behind as a lot of other folks."

"That we are." Virgil chewed on his lip. Tabby wished he'd pray for guidance, but she had and still didn't have an inkling of an answer. Sometimes you had to jump into the pool and pray it wasn't too deep.

Virgil wrapped his whip into a loop, the slow process giving him time to think. He took a deep breath. "All right. We go south. We'll gather up with the others and start following tomorrow."

"Uncle Orus won't like it." Virgilia whispered the words.

Virgil frowned. "We'll beat him to the valley and he'll have nothing to say about it. I'll let Mr. Scott know we're in. We'll get an early start in the morning."

Virgil hadn't asked Tabby's opinion—her grandsons had. That was the "polity" of this wagon train: men decided. But the next generation at least considered a woman's way of seeing. She was grateful for that.

Back at their wagon, Tabby busied herself taking the yarn from Beatrice's leg and settling her into her cage. The activity gave her time to think, to put aside her niggling fears of what lay ahead on this new cutoff they'd take in the morning. She heard Judson's laugh coming from the Pringle compound, grateful he was making friends with her grandsons, if not her granddaughter.

"You really are a remarkable woman, Tabitha Moffat Brown." John sat on the stool, his violin strings having danced beneath his fingers. He set the end pin on his knee, leaned his bearded chin against the scroll.

He looked . . . lovesick. *Oh no!* She had to keep this conversation philosophical, not let it deteriorate into some romantic pause. She wasn't prepared to explore anything deeper than a friendship, at least not on the eve of this major change in their plans.

"Fiddlesticks." She skipped the word into the night.

John raised the bow in salute.

"I mean I'm no more remarkable than any other woman on this trail." She poured water over her hands, rubbed them with the soap she'd made herself with a hint of citrus from an orange she'd splurged on last Christmas.

"You don't take compliments well, Tabby, but you should. I watch you be with your grand-children, your children, and their mates, and you treat everyone as though they'll make wise choices."

"They will. They have." She pulled her knitting needles out to work on socks for Judson.

"But there's an aura of wisdom in your efforts, in the way you've lived your life that acts as a beacon for them, for us all. You have a hopeful spirit."

"Well, I do have that. But hope doesn't mean everything will go as planned, you know. But I try to encourage others that they'll endure. Why don't you play a tune there instead of gabbing?"

"You set your sights on a purpose that matters, and even if there are floods, you wade through them."

"I suspect everyone on this journey, you included, does exactly the same thing."

"They don't though. They get despairing or cynical. Some even turn back. You step over those boulders and keep going. Look at your foot."

Tabby lifted her skirt, raised her lame foot, and wiggled it as best she could.

"Yes, that foot. It's your symbol of that indomitable spirit."

"Oh no, that would be my walking stick. I lean on that and it also humbles me. I know I need others to get me through and I need the Lord's guidance. That's what keeps me from falling into despair."

"Whatever it is, it is a shining light in the darkness. I'm pleased to be sitting for a time in your reflected light."

"Oh pshaw." She dismissed his words but let them warm her, too, as he picked the violin back up and played a quiet tune.

When he finished, he said, "I'll teach you, if you'd like. It's something I can do."

"To play the violin? At my age?" Then, "I'd like that," Tabby said. "We're none of us too old to learn new tunes."

— 17 —
A Fork in the Road

August 10 was a Monday. It was the day they took the fork in the road. Pherne made herself think of it that way, not as a new challenge. She refused to stain the future. At the nooning time, they said good-bye to the wagon groups heading on to Oregon. Applegate and ten men had gone ahead, and his man would lead several wagons south-west toward the California route. Her family and others would then branch north onto the new cutoff. At least they weren't alone in their folly, and that's what Pherne thought it was. No, she must not call it a folly. *A fork in the road to Oregon.* The presence of others did give Pherne cold comfort, though noting that added to her sense of disloyalty to her husband. Wasn't his good judgment comfort enough? No. It wasn't.

At least the first many miles would be well-worn by others who had headed to California before. She'd heard chatter that land wasn't free in California as it was supposed to be in Oregon, so that might have kept some from taking that route and heading on to Oregon down the Columbia. She'd also heard that California had declared independence from Mexico but that US soldiers now occupied it, so it wasn't independent after all. Wouldn't that be something if they arrived in Oregon country and all the rumors about free land weren't true. She chastised herself. "You're getting cynical."

"Did you say something, Mama?" Eight-year-old Emma tugged on her apron. Pherne had forgotten the child walked beside her.

"Talking to myself." Pherne smiled.

"No you're not."

"I'm not?"

"You're talking to me." Emma tapped her small chest when she said "me," her dimpled cheeks showing a higher pink when the child grinned so wide.

"Let's get some glycerin on those cheeks of yours. Have you been taking your bonnet off? I thought so. You mustn't, not when the sun is out. You'll get berry cheeks." She touched her child's face. "Why, your cheeks are soft."

"Nellie has a potion."

"A potion or a lotion?"

Emma shrugged.

"I'll have to see what's in it."

The day they started on the California route, Virgil wrote *"1439 miles"* as their current separation from home. *Home.* He didn't want her to bring up home or how much she missed it. And he didn't want her speculating about the potential problems that lay ahead. He wanted her to fix his meals, tend his children, warm his bed, and agree with him. Well, that's what she wanted from him too. The agreement part. They were taking an unnecessary risk. She'd been afraid of that. She didn't really mind that the bed had been "frosty," as Virgil had said. The temperature in the air was too hot for intimacy anyway. It was a fork in the road, all right—and their relationship.

The child was in tears. It was the first day after the parting and Nellie Louise cried while Virgilia patted her back at Tabby's wagon. "Gramo, she can't find her family. We've looked all day, walked on ahead as far as we dared and checked behind us too."

"A few wagons moved out early yesterday. Could your family have gone with that group?" Tabby found a handkerchief and handed it to the girl.

"Maybe. I spent the night with the Pringles. I've done that before and my mama has said it was fine. This morning we got up early and Virgilia and I finished our letters and then we talked and walked. I figured I'd catch up with them at noon, but I didn't. And now, it's almost suppertime and we've walked the wagons pretty far."

"We'll find them. You're sure they took the new route?"

"That's what they said."

Tabby didn't think there were that many wagons involved, but she might have been mistaken.

"Well, for now you sup with us. I've got corn pone and there were a few blackberries, so I made a little spread to cut the crumbly taste of mine. I'm no baker like Virgilia is."

"She can join us, Gramo," Virgilia offered. "And maybe my brothers will help her look."

"I can too. After supper. If you won't need me, Mrs. Brown." This from Judson, volunteering.

Tabby nodded. "I hate to see you so distressed, Nellie. I'm sure they're here somewhere."

"I was certain then they'd be ahead. The wagon rotations really can confuse."

Her family might have been struggling and chattering about what to do same as the Pringle/Brown clan had. Maybe Nellie didn't hear the final word.

"We've quite a few miles to make before folks head into California, Nellie Louise, at least that's what Mr. Pringle said." Judson's Adam's apple bobbed. "I bet they'll wait to let you catch up. We'll find your family before then. Maybe Captain John can ride ahead tomorrow, ask around."

"Well, that's quite a long speech for you, Judson," Tabby said. "Why don't the two of you talk with John? He's putting Schooner in the rope corral—if that mount will behave, that is."

A mule hee-hawed from the same direction. "We might have been better off with a mule or two."

Judson's offer seemed to settle Nellie, and Virgilia and Judson walked away with the girl. Tabby hated to see a child distressed. And even though Nellie was sixteen, she was still a child. Didn't matter how old you were, really. When your mama and daddy weren't where you expected them to be, it was like swirling in circles in a wooden boat without a paddle to get you slowed or righted.

She did wonder why she was so moved by children's distresses. Her own childhood had been charmed, all but for the ankle episode. Her father lived to see her second son born. And she'd had her mother with her all the way to Missouri, living with them while Tabby continued to raise her three in a new place. They'd buried her mother three years before, right next to Oliver's little grave. There were a number of generations on this road, babies adding to it, old folks passing on.

"We're literally a little town right here on wheels," Tabby told Beatrice as she carried the bird back to her wagon and cuddled her for a time, stroking the smooth feathers right out to the tail. Maybe with her own children grown and them responsible for their offspring, she migrated to bereft children. "Well, Dear Clark, you put that care into my soul. I guess I'll always be looking after changelings."

That night she dreamed of when they'd had a newspaper, *The Vermont Precursor*. Typeface rattled across her dream, chaos and confusion woke her with a start. Clark had left the ministry to write words, to publish the Constitution, the Declaration of Independence, and even the farewell address of dear George Washington, a friend of her mother's. The dream had words and looks of shame from people saying they were foolish to leave ministry.

She untangled the covers, her bad foot aching.

It hadn't been a mistake all those years before, even though others thought it was. It had started a new life for them. Clark preached at independent places, his sermons requested over and over. She hated to see him traveling so much, but their choice had confirmed God's presence. Sometimes one had to take a leap and trust, not let other voices be louder than the Lord's.

She had worried overmuch about money and how they would support three children. But Clark admonished her to trust and that so long as a heart is not alienated from God, well, then, there is naught to worry over. Maybe the dream was a reminder of that wisdom she once knew. She'd write about the dream in her memoir, let it comfort if old worries pushed away faith.

Nellie acted like she didn't care what happened to her, no matter how much Virgilia comforted. Her friend had gone from crying almost nonstop to sitting in a stupor as a second and then a third day passed. Though Uncle John rode forward that first day, he did not find Nellie's parents either, nor was there any word sent back along the line. Her father told her uncle not to tire his horse. "He'll need all his strength to finish this race."

"All my things are in my parents' wagon. I haven't even—" she halted, making sure none of the boys were around—"got my monthly rags. How could they abandon me and my things like that?"

Virgilia looked to her mother, who walked beside the lead Pringle wagon. She pleaded with her eyes until her mother spoke. "I'm certain they didn't intend that, Nellie. This is a set of unfortunate circumstances put into motion by the chaos of these last few days. Once they discovered you weren't with them, they probably could not turn around. Those captains don't allow it."

"Seems like a horrible rule, Mama."

"A lone wagon is vulnerable and might lead others with ill intentions to attack not only them but other wagons too. We don't make the rules. The men do and we have to decide whether to follow them or not. You'll stay with us, Nellie, our wagon or my mother's. I have lots of crinoline left to rip up for what you need if you're still separated from your things by that time. And we'll put the word out when we reach Oregon. I'm sure someone will know your Blodgett family name and we can find them."

"At least you don't have a name like Brown or Smith that are as common as corn." Nellie didn't even smile at Virgilia's efforts. "Gramo says we have to find the secret door God puts inside every problem."

"I don't want a secret door," Nellie said. "I want one that opens into my mother's arms." Her lower lip trembled.

Virgilia had to do something. "Look. We're going a lot slower, I can tell. There's a river we'll be nooning at, Papa says. The Humboldt. There'll be a little time there, so if we fall behind the wagons, we can keep them in sight and still catch up. Let's you and me put our bare feet in the water, keeping our ankles covered, of course, Mama. Modesty is everything." She tickled her friend's rib cage and Nellie clamped her arms down to stop her but moved her lips into a smile as limp as an elm leaf after a late-summer storm. "Won't that be fun?"

"I guess."

This last passage had been brutal, the oxe pulling through an area the men called Hot Spring Valley, with a steaming spring awaiting them at dusk. The women washed clothes in the naturally heated pool, though the water was too hot to stick a foot into. Still, after buckets of water cooled enough, they could wash hair and scrape foot dirt off, and they crawled clean onto their mats, exhausted. Tabby wrote in her memoir and had remained awake long after. John slept under the wagon, his snores like baby snorts punctuating the quiet night. Once she thought she heard Virgil and Pherne with raised voices but only for a moment. How she wished she had Dear Clark to spar with. She missed that almost as much as his tender touch. Was John a suitable replacement? That wasn't a good way to think of him. No man wants to be a spare wheel, they want to be a new version taking a wife forward.

They headed back out in the morning, and as the sun reached its zenith, she noticed Virgilia and Nellie whispering, then watched as they slipped away through the willows. Curiosity made her follow.

"What are you girls up to?" Both girls squealed in surprise. "We're getting our feet wet, Gramo. Come join us."

The girls splashed their slender limbs in what folks said was Mary's River. They often stopped midday to give the animals a rest and nap themselves. Leaving at 5:00 a.m. made for a long day. Now here they splashed their feet in cool waters, away from the others.

"Get my feet wet?" Tabby harrumphed. "Let's go full bore, as the men would say. Strip down to our chemise and underdrawers and get a real cool bath."

"Gramo!"

"Oh, don't be a prude now, Virgilia." Tabby checked around for snakes. They liked cool mud too. John had warned her about snakes seeking shade beneath wagons. All clear, Tabby used her walking stick to work hand over hand down until she sat on the grassy bank. She began untying the moccasins she'd purchased back at Fort Laramie. The leather formed to her bad foot and left her feet smelling like wood smoke from the tanned leather. Once in Oregon she hoped to trade for necessities with knitted socks. She didn't mind going barefoot as the girls did sometimes, but she preferred to keep her deformed foot under socks.

Moccasins off, she removed her apron, then her wrapper, then her madder-red linsey-woolsey dress and her four petticoats, leaving her standing with pantaloons and a chemise. Her bonnet she tossed on the ground, leaving her white doily pinned on her head. The girls stared with open mouths. "What? Why carry the extra weight of a corset?"

"Gramo, you're so skinny!"

"Watch your tongue, Child. I still weigh a hundred pounds dripping wet."

Virgilia and Nellie both scrambled up the bank

and began stripping off their clothes too—Virgilia folding hers in a neat pile; Nellie leaving apron, shirt, and gathered gingham skirt like a pile of corn husks. Then on either side of Tabby, the girls lifted her arms and carried her down the bank, all three walking into the river. They splashed each other and sank down to their necks, feeling squishy mud between their toes and disturbing pebbles that had rested in the waters for eons. Their squeals would surely bring others but Tabby didn't care. In fact, she wished Pherne was with them. She found that sometimes writing her memoir brought nostalgia to the surface. But the memories also reminded her that she still had a life to live. Plunging into living wasn't all that unlike plunging into a river. Maybe that's why the old Negro spiritual of "Take Me to the River" often rang through her head, even in the midst of making sassafras tea or grinding corn. Life sources: food and water. And playing a little with grandchildren.

She inhaled a deep breath, pinched her nose, and closed her eyes and sank beneath the surface. Whatever lay ahead, she would keep plunging into life.

— 18 —
Moon in Morning Milk

They'd struggled through August, some days making only four miles, finding rivers with no water in them, seeking springs in a desert land. The moon displayed her phases. Pherne sat up in the night, her shawl wrapped around her. The desert could cool in the evening, then burn hot as ash in the daylight. She worked to keep her regrets at bay, didn't want to trouble Virgil further. But they were turning into foreboding like a bad storm coming that kept her from sleep. Nightmares of people without facial features begging for help woke her, the longing staying through the day, making her irritable when she held her skirts out as protection so her mother and girls could modestly tend their personal needs.

September found them at another juncture, another fork in the road. Some wagons would rumble toward California and the rest head on toward the Scott-Applegate cutoff. Pherne had hoped for Nellie's sake her parents would be there, waiting. Or at least had left a note scratched out on a precious piece of paper and stuck under a rock or on an old skull left along the road in this unusual and barren terrain.

While there were notes left for others coming behind, none were from the Blodgetts. Nothing there but the caw of a disturbed raven flying high overhead and heat rising from the sand that burned their feet. Dust devils swirled in the hot air.

"It'll be all right, Nellie Louise." Pherne spoke to the girl's fears as much as to her own, for even she could see the starkness of the route they were obliged to take by virtue of following after Applegate and his road builders. If they had kept up a little more, they might have missed seeing that man and missed learning of this alternate route as well. A desert awaited them as a desert of uncertainty awaited Nellie—awaited them all. Pherne regretted not arguing stronger to follow Orus and the more established route, but it was too late now. Regrets must be treated like wounds, remembered only for how well they healed. Or didn't. "You're safe with us. We'll look after you." She reached out to touch the girl's dark strand of hair that stuck to tears—or maybe sweat—on her cheek.

"Thank you, Mrs. Pringle. I never wished to be a burden."

She took the girl into her arms. "Ah, Nellie, that's the wish of us all and why we were given into families. You're no burden. Come on, let's go find Gramo, girls. Maybe she needs a little company. Old people get lonesome."

As they approached, they watched Judson clear mucous from the oxen's noses. Virgil had told the boys how critical it was to keep the dust from their nostrils or they'd overheat in the desert. The animals could get by with less water than a horse or a mule, but they couldn't abide the dust. "You're doing good work, Judson." Pherne encouraged the boy, who lowered his head in shyness, still.

"I wonder if my lotion would help keep the dust from their noses," Nellie Louise offered.

"More likely it would hold it and make it harder to breathe," Judson told her as they slowed their walk to watch.

"I suppose."

Pherne's mother sat in the shade, eyes closed.

"We came to visit, Mother."

"You brought your calling cards, did you?"

She snapped her eyes open. Buddy panted beside her, nuzzling his nose beneath her hand.

"Will we need calling cards in Oregon?" Virgilia joined her grandmother in the wagon shade, watching where she sat. Snakes liked shade too.

"I doubt that. The rules of civil living will be different. And we'll help make those rules. That's something to look forward to, isn't it, girls?"

Her mother was right. Yes, circumstances were

setting their responses now, but wouldn't they be able to control what happened to them once they arrived? This was a transitional time, like being on the steamboat that took them to Missouri all those years before. What happened these months wouldn't define the future. Being in Oregon would. She had to remember that and assure Nellie Louise of the same.

The Scott-Applegate wagons, as Virgil called them, pulled out and Pherne stepped more quickly as Virgil approached, their two wagons already creaking across the flat with her sons managing the teams. Her bonnet shaded her eyes. Beyond him, a malevolent black mountain like a nightmare formed a dark wall across the landscape, calling them deeper into their choice. "It's fifty-five miles across with only one spring, Captain Scott tells us. We'll have to keep on through the night. How's Nellie doing?" He nodded toward the girl who Virgilia had her arm around, bent in quiet talking as they walked.

"Disappointed. Feels abandoned. I can't imagine that they wouldn't have left a message for her here. I hope they didn't go on toward California. It could be months, maybe years before they reestablish their ties."

"Maybe they're counting on her independent spirit to take her on through."

"Which it will, but that doesn't mean it isn't

being tested, poor thing." Pherne took a deep breath. "Fifty-five miles."

Virgil nodded and pointed. "Scott calls this the Black Rock Desert. It'll be grueling with the stock already stretched and not much promise of water or feed."

"I baked extra bread with the cornmeal."

"They'll likely need it. Thank you." Virgil led his horse as they followed the line of wagons whose occupants occasionally waved or tipped their hats. Virgil's face was drawn and caked with dust.

"I really do want us to succeed. I'm not being contrary when I bring up issues that concern me," Pherne said.

Virgil nodded. "I know, I know. Sorry about the other evening. I didn't mean to raise my voice."

"Nor did I. I just felt so bereft, that's the only way to say it. Like we're floating forward without a real sense of where we're going or even why. I miss—" Her voice broke and she fought back tears.

"I know." He stopped then, took her hand, his fingers rubbing the back of her palm. "I know what you miss: safety. Scott says this route is essential to protection of the Territory, now that our joint treaty with the British is expiring. The British could easily block the Columbia River and settlers would have no way in or out. The Scott-Applegate route is for the self-defense of us all. Troops and supplies can come this way without fear of British engagement. Our war with them isn't that far back in history." She stumbled on a rock and he held her upright. "We take this route as a duty, not only a risk."

Pherne raised her eyebrows to him. "You raise the idea of war and think I'll feel safer?"

"The possibility of war is always present. Scott says Indian trouble on this route isn't likely. It's the British we have to be wary of. Here we don't have the Columbia River danger and we can reach the Willamette Valley quicker than Orus will. Support those settlers already there in the southern regions. We're helping answer the Oregon Question, Phernie—will it be British or kept for America? Those in Congress may argue, but we act. We know what we want."

"You know what I want?"

"Excruciating predictability."

She swallowed a laugh then, his using a phrase she'd often said when he teased her need to have order and design and safety. He stopped and held her shoulders, lifted her chin. Wagons continued to roll on by them, and someone hooted. Buddy rubbed his nose to go between them. Virgil's horse lowered his head, waiting. The earth was crust beneath their feet. Weeds like popped corn stuck out of deep earth splits in the desert. Yet there was a kind of beauty she had not noticed until her husband took her into his arms.

"We're making a scene."

His shirt against her cheek mixed sweat and the pungent scent from the hot spring where she'd washed it. She felt herself drifting to another place and time, when life had ease and she knew her role in the world.

His voice caught. "Phernie, stay with me now."

"Where would I go?"

"Away in your mind. Don't do that, please. I need you beside me, I do. The children do."

She inhaled, pushed back against his chest, her fingers to her cheek to wipe at the wetness.

" 'See how she leans her cheek upon her hand. O, that I were a glove upon that hand, that I might touch that cheek.' "

"You quote *Romeo and Juliet* to me in the midst of this?" Pherne spread her hand out to take in the vast flat with ground so hard and broken it looked like crumbling cobblestones all the way to that black mountain wall.

"What better bard to share my thoughts. I only wish I'd said it in the moonlight." He gave her a quick kiss. "I love you, Phernie. You believe that."

"I won't say 'I love you too,' because that's too predictable for an adventurer like you, Virgil Pringle." She smiled. "I will ponder on your patriotism and whether or not we do a thing beyond our own adventuring." She inhaled. "But know that you are the glove to my cheek and you mean more to me than breath itself. So let us breathe together and get through this desert."

"John? What's wrong?" Tabby heard a grunt from behind the wagon. She'd gone to the back to stabilize the butter churn. The cows weren't giving much milk and the churn bumped in the dark. She rumbled and shifted in the wagon, working toward the back. They'd reached the first spring in the early afternoon, took their supper, and filled buckets for oxen and horses to drink. They'd headed toward that black rock soon after and had been traveling through the night across hot, dusty ground. In places, the dust looked like soda, and Mr. Scott said the saleratus could help raise bread, so the women gathered some. The heat weighed on everyone and caused perspiration to gather beneath Tabby's arms. That's when she'd heard the grunt from John.

He led Schooner, not riding him as did most of the men, saving their mounts. The animal offered up no antics. In front, Judson goaded the oxen with his stick, the whip retired to the wagon box. They would have stopped, so weary were they, yet they plodded like ants to a hill, steady and determined.

"Oh, I'm all right." Disgust laced John's words. "Tripped over my dang feet and Schooner here clipped the back of my heel. I expect it's bleeding some. Moccasins don't protect like my brogans. Not your fault."

Tabby could tell he spoke to the horse with that last, not her, but part of her did wonder if the problems they faced right now were indeed her fault.

They had fallen behind Orus and now on this trail too. First it was pounding wooden wedges to fill in the spaces where the wood had shrunk away from the iron band of the wheels. They were all shriveling in the dry heat, but the wagon wheels at least had a remedy. Virgil's wagons had slowed for them, helping out. Then her oxen had resisted. Well, who could blame them? Judson did well with the yoke, but they paced slower than others with the boy lacking confidence in how to manage them through the different terrains. The oxen knew it. Still, despite their noses clogging in the heat, they plodded on, though not as fast as Virgil's well-trained teams.

Thank the Lord, the moon was full, and even though it was a Sunday, they were rolling through the night, crushing over sage and greasewood, the broken stalks sending up a pungent smell as they scraped the wagon bottoms. John wasn't leading his horse directly behind them. He didn't want to risk the next sage popping up and striking the animal in surprise as their wagon spit out the garbled brush that stood taller than she was. It was the same reason he hadn't tied the horse to the box. He led Schooner around the sage, but Tabby had warned about getting too far aside so that he couldn't keep track of them in the night, especially in that darkest hour before the dawn. And to not get overtired.

"Get up in here," Tabby told him. "I've got my medicines."

"Should I have Judson stop the team?"

Why is he asking me? "Not if you can hoist yourself up."

"Come on, Schooner." The horse barely lifted its head as John attached the reins. No resistance, that was sure.

They were both in the wagon now, being jostled like loose potatoes in a bag. "How much farther you figure we've got?" John asked the question after she administered a poultice to his heel, using a little of their precious water. Beatrice clucked in her cage. She knew what to do in the night.

"Kids count the white rotations on the wheel, but they don't do it at night so I don't really know. Virgil said it's fifty-five miles across."

"Judging by the moon location, I'd say we should reach that second spring hole around four in the morning. Sure hope we don't have another burial like we did yesterday."

"This country takes its toll."

"I hope there's water when we get there. Thank you, Tabby." He held her hand. "I'm sorry to trouble you."

226

"Nonsense. What is family for?"

"Not to take care of an old man. I never intended that."

"Oh, I know. But what kind of kin would I be if I didn't do what I could? After all, I wouldn't have been able to come without you."

"You'd have found a way. You always did."

The cooling evening chilled. John moved closer to her.

Tabby cleared her throat. "It's finally dawned on me that we're the first *wagons* through here. Other travelers have been on horses and mules. But the Applegates have surely marked the trail a wagon needs, don't you think?"

"Nice diversion, Mrs. Brown."

"What? Well, no. I was just—I wish I'd had Orus to confer with before taking this route. What if wagons can't get through?"

John shook his head and patted her thin shoulder, his hand warm against the calico. "Don't search for bad seas, Tabby. It is what it is. We're here now."

Virgilia thought of another exaggeration. "It's so hot, a planted seed would grow two feet a minute."

"It's so hot . . . the devil would need a freighter of snow to cool things down."

"That's a good one, Nellie. Let's see, it's so hot . . . the johnnycakes rolled off the desert looking for a griddle to cool down on."

Nellie laughed out loud and Virgilia breathed a hot sigh of relief. They walked through the night, giving respite to the animals. The little girls stayed in the wagon. Virgilia's mama walked on the far side. Her father hitched his horse to a wagon and moved on foot up and down the line, speaking encouraging words, making sure everyone was doing all right.

"I wish the moon wasn't so bright, though," Nellie said. "Then we could see the stars."

"They'll pop out eventually. I'm glad we can see as well as we can. Some of this brush is taller than we are. How does it even grow with no water? It makes my arms tingle thinking we might walk right off avoiding the sage and end up wandering away from the wagons."

"Wouldn't we hear them?"

"I guess. But the sounds are funny here. Sometimes I can hear Papa talking way up the line and then other times I have trouble hearing Mama from the other side of the wagon."

"It's the vastness. I think this is what my father left home for, the bigness and open spaces, all the new experiences. I . . . I still can't believe I'm not with them."

Virgilia put her arm through Nellie's. "I know you can't but you will." She wasn't sure why it mattered so much that the people around her be encouraged. Maybe it was good to lament. There was a whole chapter in the Bible called

Lamentations, wasn't there? And yet, having her friend be sad was like a pebble stuck in the finger of a glove; it worked on her in an annoying way, causing her to want to interrupt it. "Let's try . . . as cold as, you know, 'She was as cold as an icicle' or 'It was so cold her toes turned as blue as her lips.' "

Nellie shook her head, no. "I don't want to play anymore."

Nellie's words left Virgilia feeling as cold as a bummer lamb's breath. What was a friend to do?

When they reached the first spring around four in the morning, an ox bellowed its complaint while jerking ahead for water. The sounds awoke Tabby from her doze on the harp-back chair. She caught her breath. The moon floated over the Black Rock in a morning milk of clouds spilled across the sky. The desert itself looked like a beach before them. She spoke a prayer of gratitude, then called out to John lying in the wagon. "You don't want to miss this, John."

He grunted, then joined her, poking his head through the opening.

"Magnificent. Like low tide."

She turned to him. "My very thoughts."

He kissed her, on her capped head first, then lifted her chin to brush her cracked lips with his. "We see the world the same. Surely that's a step toward love."

She hadn't planned to, but she leaned into him and sighed.

A kiss had not been a part of her life since the day she had pressed her lips to Clark's, not long before he died. She didn't encourage John and she didn't discourage him. In fact, his action had startled her into silence. It was pleasant to be desired, to have his warm blue eyes catch hers over the fire. Having someone help her up and down without having to ask, even if at times it annoyed her that she needed assistance, was an unexpected comfort. But it also complicated things. What would that kiss mean when they arrived? She hadn't even thought about whether John or Judson would continue on with her. She'd always lived alone. And Nellie Louise. What of her? Did Tabby want a new family at her age? Oh, why did he have to kiss her? And what did it really mean?

— 19 —
The Form of
Things Unknown

In the heat of the day, exhausted men and women fell into a restless sleep inside wagons or under them. Mules scraped their front hoofs against the wagon wheels, *thump, thump,* demanding water.

Pherne tossed in and out of strained sleep. She dreamed of water, flowing water, flooding over them. She awoke with a start, breathing hard. She looked around. All younger children were accounted for. The boys would have slept beside the other wagon and no sounds came from her mother's wagon where Virgilia and Nellie had bedded down. None of them had bothered with a tent, just rolled bedding out onto the hot desert floor beneath the shade of the wagon.

Animals bellowed. *Thirsty.* Virgil said they were at the halfway point, having come about twenty-five miles. Would the next thirty be as strained?

Virgilia heard Nellie get up and relieve herself, leaving Virgilia beneath the wagon in the heat. She hadn't been able to sleep much. She made up poems in her mind, hoping she'd remember them to write down later. It helped pass the time.

"Virgilia?" Nellie's soft voice sounded strained.

"What?"

"Don't move."

"Why?"

"It's . . . a . . . snake. It's . . . it's moving toward you. Right where I was laying."

Virgilia whispered, "Can it . . . can it hear my heart pound?"

"I don't think so. Oh, Virgie . . ."

Don't move, don't move. Virgilia lay as still as death. Her worst nightmare, snakes, this one seeking shade. *Please keep me still. Don't let me hiccup or sneeze. Make it go around the wagon and be gone.* "Can you see it?"

"Shhh," Nellie whispered.

Virgilia stayed as quiet as a sloughed-off snakeskin. She felt something near her hair, the roots grabbing at her scalp.

"It's . . . it's stretching out. Right above your head, Virgie." Nellie's voice harbored panic.

"Not coiling?"

"No. It's like it's going to sleep. Don't move. I'll get your pa."

There was nothing to be done but wait. Could she smell the snake? No, that was her fear. Would the snake smell her? Her body wanted to shiver, but she willed it still. She heard Nellie move beyond, whispering to Gramo, maybe her mother.

Buddy was with her brothers. That was good. The dog would have barked and jabbed back and forth at it, making it mad. Virgilia heard rustling and could sense her father whispering. She knew he couldn't shoot it where it was.

"Keep still, Virgie." Her mother's voice. "It senses you're not prey. Night will come and the ground will cool and it'll get sluggish. They don't like vibrations. Be at ease, as though you're floating on a pond." *How did her mother know so much about snakes?*

The ground cooled beneath her or did fear cool her skin? She must not shiver. She imagined the snake asleep, restful, just being what a snake is supposed to be. *I'm too big to eat.* She willed the snake to know.

A pink-tinted sunset marked the chill. Virgilia shivered. No, she must not move.

How could it be so hot in the day yet cool at night? She must have slept, fear forcing her mind away. Her fingers felt like frozen sticks. Was the snake still there? Her hair tingled at the roots.

"Virgilia." Her father had kept watch over her, her mother too. "It's cool enough. Move away, slowly. Inch toward me."

With her heels, she tugged the earth with tiny steps, still lying flat as a paddle until she could no longer feel the presence of the snake against her hair. The reptile would be sluggish with the desert cold. "Far enough. Roll to your right."

She did, her father pulling her up and holding her to him.

She twisted around. The snake lay stretched beneath the wagon, its triangular head facing the wagon tongue. "Five feet if it's an inch," her father said.

Now Virgilia cried and her gramo hugged her and Nellie and her mother, all of them together.

"You were delivered, Child," her gramo said. "Now let's do it in and have it for supper."

Her gramo gave her walking stick to Virgilia's father, who lifted the snake to get it out from under the wagon. In its cooling stupor, it draped over the stick like a candlewick over a finger.

Her father took it a distance, dropped it, then whacked it with a shovel, announcing, "Orus says rattlesnake tastes like chicken."

The word went up and down the line that Virgilia Pringle had slept with a rattler and lived to tell. A brave girl," people said. "Amazing," spoke others. "How did you stay so quiet?" Virgilia knew it was a distraction, something to think about besides the desert ahead and that's why people carried on so about it. Albro, her animal-loving brother, wondered why it had to die. "Couldn't Pa have tossed it in the desert and let it be? We're the invaders."

Virgilia didn't feel much pity for the snake and she didn't feel brave. Fear had immobilized her.

She couldn't have moved before she did, even if she had wanted to. What looked to others like something noble, well, it wasn't, not even close. It bothered her, though, that she was afraid of snakes and that's what had shown up. Would her life be made up of having to face the very things she feared the most? If so, she'd better stop naming other scary things, like being without family, being alone.

They traveled again through the night. Pherne's body wanted water but they had little to spare. They all complained of a dry mouth. One trouble with the hours of boredom was one had time to brood, to indulge in self-pity. She pulled her shawl around her. It was cooler to move at night but not by much. A pink-tinted dawn spread across the landscape palette. Pherne watched as the light struck the black rock toward which they moved. When they reached it and the teams were unyoked to rest, she found her pencils and sketched the landmark bathed in light, not letting go of the miracle that had kept Virgilia safe and was getting them through the desert. The snake incident had taken her mind through a million terrors, but her mother had been right: Virgili had been delivered and she had to believe that they would all be allowed to live through this valley of the shadow of death. Sketching it reduced the fear to size.

At least that cursed black rock offered shade, and there was water (and gravel) for Beatrice and people. Tabby watched the antics of the children with her chicken. They'd reached the rock a little after eight o'clock in the morning, having traveled through the night again. They each found ways to find respite. John hobbled over and leaned against the black basalt that rose sixty feet above them. He looked down to check for snakes. They were all doing that now.

"Not much cooler in the shade," John shouted.

Levi Scott had led them this far and they would rest the day and that night to give the stock reprieve. One of Scott's companions had remained behind at the fork to make sure another group of wagons who had said they'd follow would be able to find the route. And there were men ahead cutting the trail through the timber when they got that far. Here, a good spring with grass around it welcomed them. This was truly the oasis in the desert, like the kind Tabby had read about existing in Palestine and Persia.

After nooning, she and Pherne and the children and some of the other women explored a cave, not very deep, but still intriguing. Looking out, the cave opening framed the desert they'd crossed, making it a picture small enough to grasp, the vastness diminished. It was something Pherne might like to draw. Tabby wandered over to Pherne and Virgil's wagon, carrying Beatrice. Her grandchildren lounged, though there was little ease in their motions. Pherne held her lead, and Tabby was pleased to see her daughter return to something she'd liked to do as a girl, something else she was good at.

"We've nothing to do, Mama." Sarelia laid her head on her mother's shoulder.

Pherne put her sketch pad away, patted her daughter's thin shoulders.

"Not bored, are you? There's a remedy for that," Tabby said.

"Imagination. I remember." The child sighed.

"How about this. Pherne, do you have a few scraps of cloth to spare? Your gramo has a doily or two she's not wearing."

"What for?" Emma sat up, interested.

Beatrice cluck-clucked in Tabby's arms as she buried her head in the bird's reddish neck feathers. The tips of her red comb looped over in the heat. Then, "I think it's time to see how Beatrice looks in proper clothes."

Pherne laughed out loud. "We used to dress up the kittens and the chickens when we lived at the glebe, I remember that."

"Maybe we can get Buddy to let Beatrice ride on his back." This from Virgilia. "Make a little riding outfit for her." Emma laughed.

"The possibilities are endless, though that may be a little more than I have doilies for. But doesn't doing something fun put a little spirit to our steps?"

"I just hope Beatrice feels the same way," Albro said. He tossed his knife into the dirt, retrieved it, tossed it again.

"You're the keeper of the animals, my grandson," Tabby said. "We'll expect you to step in if Buddy complains or Beatrice loses her riding habit."

Pherne shook her head. "Mother, you have the ability to turn sour into sweet. I wish I had half of that imaginative stew."

"You do. With your pencils and paper. See if you can capture a bit of Beatrice's experience in the Black Rock Desert. You'll preserve some of ours when you do." It was good to see her daughter smile and the children hustle about with purpose.

At suppertime, Virgilia and Nellie and Sarelia joined Judson, John, and her.

John started it in between a stroke of his bow on the violin strings. "I'm hungry for dandelion greens and potatoes, that's what I'd like." He gave the bow a bounce. "How about you, Judson?"

"Oh, maybe a nice piece of ham with apples and potatoes. A little molasses to sweeten the sauce." Another musical punctuation.

"Sweet potato pudding, like Gramo makes." This from Sarelia. "Or fried peaches."

"You have a sweet tooth, little sister." Sarelia

gripped her front teeth, grown back in now, and Virgilia laughed. "What about you, Gramo, what are you hungry for?"

Before she could answer, Nellie Louise spoke with sadness in her voice. "I'm not so sure it's a good idea to be longing for what we can't have."

Tabby missed that sweet giggle and confidence she'd displayed on those early days. Family nurturing close by had a way of being humus for good growth. The child was missing that now. "It might not be, Nellie, but it's a better alternative than lamenting our present circumstances. That kind of grieving robs us of the very energy we need to keep going through this endless desert. So me, hmm. Persimmon pudding with a foamy hard sauce." John played a short jig to Tabby's offering. "A little of the Pringle cow's cream and Beatrice's egg—if she ever lays again—and a couple of spoonfuls of butter, all whipped up with a scrap of brown sugar from the cone."

"I see where you get your sweet tooth from, Sarelia." John took the violin from beneath his chin. "Your very own gramo."

Tabby patted the ground next to her and Sarelia moved over to cuddle beneath her armpit.

"Forget food. I'd like a good cigar."

"I didn't know you smoked, Captain," Judson said.

"I don't. It keeps my mouth happy just chewing."

"You can't eat that, Uncle John." Sarelia shook her finger at him.

"No, I can't, but it would make me forget how hungry I am."

"At least we have provisions and it's only the heat making us weary. Mr. Scott says we should be in the Willamette Valley by the first of October. That's less than a month away." Tabby counted on her fingers. "We can all surely make a couple more weeks. We might not have to ration our supplies at all."

"And we never have to ration our imaginations, right, Gramo?"

"Right you are, Sarelia. Right you are."

Tabby hadn't considered imagination as an essential on this journey, but the girl was right. They could imagine their way through a desert and imagine a better life. Whatever did people do who took this trek because they felt compelled to? Or who escaped something in their past? Or who failed to put imagination into their trunks? One needed dreaming for the grand adventures, to spread one's wings and one day fly.

— 20 —
It Comes to This

In the morning, the wagons rolled out, leaving some stock behind, too weakened to continue. Pherne expressed gratitude that morning that their oxen still dragged their vehicles along. They squeezed one wagon at a time through an opening in the black rock that was so narrow the wheels on either side scraped the massive walls. Pherne sat on the wagon seat with Emma beside her, holding her breath that they would not get stuck there. She marveled how she found little comfort in knowing others had already done this—but not in wagons.

Once through, a new line of mountains, not so black, broke the horizon. The desert continued until a slow rise began that strained the weakened oxen. They plodded up the side of the barren ridge, a diagonal line of white covers against the brown landscape. Everyone walked to lighten the loads, and one of the emigrants tugged at a heavy sideboard and abandoned it beside the trail. It looked a lot like the one Pherne had left behind in Missouri.

On the other side of the grade, a grassy section offered promise, but the road was dusty and the clouds in the distance loomed dark, seething of snow. Someone rode up to tell them an ox had been killed with arrows. Had they gotten too far ahead of the herd of sheep and cows and relief stock? Where had the Indians come from? Mr. Scott had said the Indians along here fought with each other rather than poking at emigrants, but the arrows proved him wrong. Grumbling began against Mr. Scott, but since he was the only person who knew where they were headed, the complaints moved through the camp like low smoke waiting to stir up flames.

By mid-September more grass appeared and they were through the mountains and making fifteen miles a day again. They must be getting close, Virgilia thought, because it was nearing the end of the month. On the twenty-seventh, her father had written about a pretty lake they camped beside called Goose. Hundreds of geese called above them, chattering and blackening the sky. She'd heard Uncle John say that Mr. Scott thought they'd be in the Willamette Valley by October. A bit of an extension to the time, but still within reason. The drudgery of the trip would soon be over.

Then, a few days later, they caught up with the other group that had left Fort Hall before them. Fifty wagons now teamed up together, following the Klamath River, her father called it. The thing that bothered her was that when they caught up with the forward party, Mr. Applegate was not with them.

Neither was Nellie's family.

"They, they must have gone into California." Nellie choked back tears. "I was counting on catching up and finding them."

What kind of comfort could Virgilia offer?

"Letters. We can write letters and send them to the mission or forts or whatever they have in California. Let's go do that."

"No. I don't want to write them a letter. They left me, Virgilia. They didn't even think about me or come to look for me. It wasn't a mistake. They did it on purpose."

"That doesn't make any sense. Remember when my cousin Charles traveled with us for a couple of weeks? I think that's what happened. They thought you were with their group." What else could she say that was reassuring? "You helped a lot with your brothers and sisters. Your mama would be missing you terribly."

"For the work I might do." Nellie Louise clenched her jaw, pushed her bonnet back off her head, the ribbon ties pulling against her throat. "I'm surprised they didn't try to marry me off to someone, for a price." She yanked her shawl around her, tied the ends in a knot over her breast.

So trying to convince Nellie with words wasn't helpful. Maybe she needed better words. She prayed for that, to ease the terrible distress her friend carried now like burning fire, every attempt at Virgilia's calming just flaming it further. *Give me healing words, please.*

What she received was silence. Maybe that was the best thing she could offer.

In the night, Pherne had heard the commotion and so had Virgil. He cursed as he grabbed for his gun, but it was too late. Mr. Scott had ordered guards to watch the cattle while he looked for the trail signs ahead but no guard had been posted, the men being weary. Or perhaps the small rations had begun to affect their judgment. Indians came and drove off stock. They'd have to spend the day trying to get some of the animals back.

Uncle John had hobbled Schooner, keeping him close to her mother's wagon, and this had saved that animal from being taken.

"I told you," Mr. Scott scolded when he returned. "I will not be your captain if you don't do what I order." Her husband nodded and told Pherne later how foolish they'd been. Weariness taxed their thinking. And Virgil's cough grew worse.

Pherne planned to wash clothes while the men hunted stock, keeping her eyes scanning in case of their own Indian trouble while the men were away. She stopped at her mother's wagon and asked for her underdrawers and her alternate dress, the one she wore every other day.

"I can do it myself, Phernie. You have enough laundry to do. But if you'll help me down from here, that's good." She stood at the back of the wagon and grabbed her walking stick as her daughter reached for her hand. "There. We can go together. Where are your girls?"

"Sarelia and Emma are pushing beetles around a little maze they built with sticks, and Nellie and Virgilia are baking a cake with some of the fine flour, hoping to cheer Nellie up. Oh." Pherne clutched her mother's arm. "Look. Is Beatrice . . . is she . . . ?" The bird lay beneath the wagon, flattened.

"No. She's just hot. Chickens do that in the heat. She does look dead, though, doesn't she? But no, just an optical illusion."

"Nothing is as it seems." Pherne shook her head while Tabby gave a gentle poke to Beatrice with her walking stick. The bird cackled and Tabby let her be.

"I'm not sure what those parents were thinking, not making some effort to get a message to Nellie Louise. She's gone from feeling responsible and feeling guilty to sadness, and now she's just plain mad. Poor child."

"That's how loss shows up, all right." Pherne heard the resignation in her own voice. "A whole range of tones up and down the music scale."

Pherne stopped herself from saying more, not wanting to upset her mother. But she knew some of that song. Their supplies were very low. They had meat, as Clark had shot a large jackrabbit. Somehow they'd miscalculated and she supposed she ought not to have let Virgilia use the last of the fine flour for a cake. Was that her fault? They had paltry food she had to serve, and October had arrived and this so-called Willamette Valley nowhere in sight. Supposedly when they reached a single cabin built by a man named Skinner at the base of a high butte, then they'd know they'd reached the Valley. Mr. Skinner better have a lot of supplies because he'd be descended upon by over fifty wagons full of desperate people.

"I'm glad we're almost there."

"Is that what Virgil says? Good. I have no bacon left and only corn flour. My precious school bell is fully visible in the barrel. Much longer and it won't be riding in the comfort of corn."

"I'm keeping Grandma's porcelain rolling pin in my corn flour bin and it's not long for comfort either. I'd hate to have it break. One more loss if it does."

"It has done its duty, Phernie. It's only a thing."

The women worked the washboard. Tabby twisted her skirt to get the water out, then snapped it and laid it on the nearby bush. "So long as we each survive, that'll mark it a treasured trip."

She knew her mother was right, but Pherne still

liked her "things" and, like Nellie, she wasn't ready to give up her mad yet.

They walked back to the wagons. A certain pleasure came from clean clothes in one's arms and quiet moments with her mother. She sent her mother to rest while she hung pants and dresses on a line stretched between wagons. She basked in the everyday moment of grace. She reached to finger her gold locket. Where was it? Her fingers grabbed at her throat. Had she removed it and put it away? Had the chain broken? She turned back to the river, rushing before the dusk took her searching light. Nothing. Maybe she hadn't even lost it there. *How could I have been so careless?* Oliver's little curl, gone. As soon as she let her guard down, pain came piercing in. What else was left to lose?

The Siskiyou Mountains rose before them, patches of snow in the crevices up high. Cooler air woke them to a road rough, rocky, and steep. To look ahead was daunting for even Tabby, who wondered how any wagons could possibly make that grade. But on the other side surely there'd be the valley as promised. Soon.

Mr. Scott went on ahead to secure the next leg as the group harnessed and moved out. Tabby wondered how he felt about the trail hazards. Had he been aware of the difficulties the wagons would face? Did he delude himself into thinking that wherever a horse could go, oxen and wagons could too? Or had he counted on the Applegates and the young "unencumbered men" who had left Fort Hall before them to cut the trail, make more progress? They hadn't ever caught up to them. She thought of Orus, how he'd led them safely to Fort Hall, sending messages back, keeping in touch. Was he already in Oregon country? Waiting for them near his forest grove?

Tabby sighed and looked up the mountain-side. Like Pharaoh's slaves, they plodded up the precipitous trail. The peaks had snow on them and wind lifted bursts of snow that swirled and disappeared. Then Mr. Scott returned from where he'd been scouting ahead.

He shouted, "You've taken up the wrong path. Go back. You need to go around!" He swung his arms, his horse prancing close to the rocky edge.

The wrong trail? We're on the wrong road?

But so many wagons had already started up they didn't want to—or couldn't—turn back. They trudged ahead, ignoring Scott's shouts, until Tabby heard a crunching, grating sound: a large Conestoga-style wagon snapped its king bolt. The wagon bed began rolling back down the hill, threatening to crash into other wagons, women, and children, tumbling the oxen with them.

"My baby's in there!" a woman screamed.

Fear paralyzed Tabby as she grabbed at her

walking stick, shouted to Judson to hold the team.

Tabby prayed as the mother grabbed a rock and slammed it beneath the wagon wheel, causing the vehicle to twist and stop, tipping toward the steep side like a box of precious jewels that could settle back to safety or spill its treasures over the side. The mother leapt into the wagon box, grabbed her child, and jumped back out, sinking to her knees, crying, her child in her arms. Safe. Her treasure, secured.

Then began the arduous task of backing up, unhitching teams, reorganizing to shouts of blame and accusation, crying children, oxen bellowing their dislike. They would begin again. On the right road. It was all they could do.

As the reconstituting wore on, Tabby thought about that mother's actions. She'd always thought she would be good in an emergency like that mother, be able to act quickly. It gave her no comfort that no one else had moved either, to throw a rock beneath a wheel, no one except the mother. Children needed someone to look out for them. She made a vow to reach out a little more to Nellie Louise and thanked God they hadn't all been overturned by the loose wagon.

The broken wagon had been dismantled, everything taken out. The family would walk the rest of the way with what they could carry. *And there, but for the grace of God, go I.* They camped that evening without water or grass and little for their supper. It was already October 7.

Once over the high Siskiyous, they passed through timbered country, crossing streams, stopping often as men went ahead to help clear the trail of downed trees, boulders, and tangled vines. Each day Tabby wondered if the rise of mountains and their arrival through a canyon marked the beginning of the Willamette Valley, but Mr. Scott shook his head when she spoke to him over an evening fire, his eyes carrying the weight of growing disappointment.

The Rogue River with its sparkling rushes offered up a good ford, or so Virgil claimed. But no game. And the flour spoon now scraped the bottom of her barrel. Hunger gnawed. She had to take her needle and thread and sew up the waist of her skirt or it would have fallen to the ground.

"You're not in any position to help road build, John." Tabby sounded cross even to herself as they made camp that October evening. They'd buried a girl not much younger than Nellie earlier that day. Tabby had given up boards from her wagon for the coffin. Her granddaughters were no longer interested in spelling bees or discovering new words or facts. Being tired and hungry sure affected a child's learning spirit.

"It's hard work, Captain John." Judson handed John a tin of tea as John sat on the wagon tongue. "I'm not sure you'd be up to it or should be. Don't want to lose you like the Crowleys lost their daughter."

"That's exactly why all men who can work are needed to do so, young man. You're doing well with the oxen, so no need for you to feel pressure to do more. But what do I do all day but tire my horse and eat Tabby's cooking?"

"My scraps I have to offer."

John took a sip. "Those burns and old scorched timbers fallen across the trail make poor going. Our axes don't do much. Who would have thought to bring long cross-cut saws? Orus sure didn't think we'd need such things. Our little carpenter saws are nearly useless in that tangle ahead."

"Didn't the road builders bring equipment from Fort Hall or from their valley when they came this way?"

"Apparently not. So, Tabitha, here is what I hear." He lowered his voice. "Mr. Scott is alone in this. Applegate's road builders ahead have done nothing. Blazed a tree here and there, but otherwise they pulled the anchor and left us adrift. The men aren't talking much about it so as not to alarm you women, but that Umpqua Mountain they call it, even an old sailor like me can see it's going to be the worst of our trip. Add to that, Scott says there is another beyond called the Calapooia. Nearly impassable with wagons." He stared into his tea. "We've been snookered."

Tabby's stomach clenched. "Snookered?"

They arrived the next day at the foot of Umpqua Mountain. Walls of rock and timber. Fallen trees the size of ridge lines for a hotel splayed like children's sticks across a path more narrow than a game trail. Thickets of tangling shrubs and vines lured like witches' fingers.

"Nearly impassable," Virgil said in a voice Tabby hoped not too many had heard.

The physical work of chopping at logs, dragging them aside, managing restless stock, then moving wagons forward a few feet at a time took its toll on tempers. They made camps and prepared what food they had while stalled on narrow strips of land beside rushing streams. Sleep escaped on rocky beds beneath the wagons. How could rivers look so inviting, sparkling with rocky bottoms, then be such challenges to cross? The streams in this Cow Creek, Umpqua, and Rogue country were slashed by trees whose leaves were washed away by high water and wind, leaving river trash caught in the tree crotches that once held hawk and eagle nests. The plan had been to drive beside the rivers all flowing toward the Willamette. But the entanglements . . . Tabby thought it like warring factions, wooden wagons against rivers; hunger against dwindling rations.

"Is it true, Mother Brown? Are we going to die?" Nellie's dark eyes pleaded for the right answer. It was morning, though daylight acted too frightened to present herself fully, shrouded instead in rainy mist. They'd be entering another canyon with a creek, this one said to be the most difficult so far.

Tabby poked at the fire. She shivered. "We're all going to die, Child. That's a given."

"I know, but I mean today, when we try to get through that canyon."

"We've had rough spots before." She patted the girl's cold hands. "Let's not borrow trouble, Nellie. Just pray we'll have the stamina to make it."

"I'll look after you, Nellie." Judson rubbed his fingers across the brim of his hat, not removing it as he would have if the drizzle wasn't so steady. Water dribbled off the brim. Manners didn't matter much in these circumstances. Tabby was grateful for her wool, but the cold seeped through to her bones.

Nellie dropped her eyes and pulled her shawl tighter around her shoulders. The wooden brim of her bonnet kept the rain from her eyes. "Thank you."

"We'll do it together," Tabby told her. The girl had been spending more time in Tabby's company. Maybe the girls had had a falling out. The conditions strained marriages, so why not friendships too? Virgil sent word back that they'd be starting out. Tabby was beginning to hate these "canyons." Cow Creek a few days before had seen the oxen with water up to the animals' bellies. They slogged through mud once they reached the other side. At a place the men called Canyon Creek, Virgil told them they would have to get out of the wagons and carry whatever they cared about on top of their heads to keep their treasures dry as they crossed the creek. Grumbling shared their sloshing through the cold current.

"Never thought I'd see the day," Pherne said when she reached the other side carrying her grandmother's rolling pin. She didn't need to explain what she meant as they stood in the chill, wet beneath large trees dripping rain off their faded reds and browns while the men fed warming fires.

A few days before, several emigrants and a few women whose wagons had already been lost had been dispatched by Mr. Scott to take the stock—the sheep and milk cows—and their families and walk on ahead of the wagons. That meant no milk, not that the cows would give it up anyway. Tabby missed the pale offering. Milk never seemed so precious. Life never seemed so precious.

The Rogue River had a perfect name in Tabby's mind: rough and unpredictable with its rapids surging over boulders and running high from fall rains. Tabby had remained in her wagon and her faithful oxen brought them across, though her trunks were soaked. Now here they were at yet another canyon with a creek running along the bottom as narrow as a house gutter.

Virgil's wagons were at the front of both parties. One of his would lead, followed by Tabby's, then the second Pringle wagon. They had already lightened the loads as much as they could. Tabby had fought for and retained the school bell, but heavy trunks were discarded, clothing left to lie in the wagon bed along with anything else deemed essential. She'd carry it herself as she walked. There'd be no sitting on that harp-back chair, which so far hadn't been stripped and abandoned, probably because no one had the energy. Tabby would hobble or ride John's horse. Virgil's cough deepened and they could hear him approaching before they saw him. He didn't join the men cutting the road ahead to make even one revolution of the wheels. At the end of the first day, they had gone a mile, having tried to go around boulders big as a buckboard. Discussions about how to take the boulder or maneuver the wagons delayed them more, but those shared minds meant a better chance of success. They tried to make the creek bed into a road, and once Mr. Scott said, "If only we had more gunpowder," but of course that was in scant supply.

She'd heard of three children behind them catching mice in fallen logs and roasting them, hunger creeping like a pox upon them. At least they weren't that destitute, yet. But spending more time at the Pringle wagons made her wonder. They lacked flour too, and unless they killed a deer, oxen would be their only meat. No salt or fat or sugar in the larder either.

Tabby heard the sickening sounds of wood splitting when wagons toppled behind them, breaking on the boulders they had to squeeze around, or worse, tried to go over. The animals protested through their bellowing. At night they chained the poor oxen to trees, as there was nowhere to either graze or circle up. At least dust did not clog their noses.

The next day found Tabby in the wagon as John needed to rest his foot. He used his cane less for show now, but because he, too, limped. Tabby's foot hurt too, and she'd been the day in the drizzle, sitting in her harp-back chair.

"You'll have to get off, Mrs. Brown," Judson shouted to her. "Captain John too. Maybe rest aside here while Octavius and I bring the wagon through this pile of boulders. If I can follow where Mr. Pringle took his. We'll be all right, but it ain't safe for you up there."

"Isn't safe."

She heard John moan as he made his way out the back of the wagon that was pitched uphill on a bank above the stream. She pushed against the arms of the chair to stand.

Maybe it was the movement of John in the

wagon bed, or Tabby's clambering to the side. Maybe it was the fatigue of days, weariness of hunger and exhaustion, or perhaps it was the animals being asked to trudge yet another day over impossible trails. Whatever it was, the oxen bolted, yanked forward, bellowed, and shook their big heads.

The movement pitched Tabby forward as the wagon wheels rolled up against a boulder as steep as a cow's face. She shouted, grabbed the dashboard, her walking stick gaining wings.

"Grandma Brown!"

In slow motion, she watched the world turn topsy-turvy. Nellie's scream. Her heart pounded in her ears. Judson shouted—at her, at the oxen, she didn't know which. *So it comes to this, Lord? Well, you're in charge.*

— 21 —
Great Acts of Loving

She felt strong arms snatch her from the leaning wagon as it pitched. Wood tore. Oxen bellowed, forced as they were against the wagon tongue that splintered, allowing the bolster and wagon bed to topple. Chains snapped, men shouted, Judson jumped with her and they watched bow tip over box. Beatrice squawked somewhere in the distance, and Tabby watched as her wagon rolled up the side of the boulder, then over, landing upside down beside the creek bed, what had been left in her wagon now scattered like chicken feed down the side of the bank. Tabby's fall on the ice had been like this: one moment fine—the next, her world askew.

John! Had he gotten out? Tabby caught her breath, her arm against young Judson's chest. He handed her over to Nellie, and by then Virgil and Clark had made their way back and supported John, staring at the wounded wagon. Thank goodness she'd taken Beatrice off earlier and Sarelia had been carrying the bird. Several other men looked the situation over, their faces drawn in hunger and defeat.

"Never saw a wagon fly before," John said. His voice shook.

"Mrs. B, you almost . . ."

"But I didn't. And now here I am. I'm all right. With a wrecked wagon is all. Fiddlesticks."

She looked where the wagon lay like a beetle with wheels on its back, partway down the bank. Buddy barked at the commotion, and behind them Octavius brought the Pringle wagon up and moved into the space her wagon had left.

"I'll go get your walking stick, Gramo." Albro stepped forward.

"No, no, you help Judson with the oxen there. They're pretty flummoxed. Good thing the chains broke or they'd have . . . I . . . I can go there and—"

"I'll go." Nellie scrambled toward the wagon.

"Be careful," Judson shouted. "It could pitch on over."

Pherne and Virgilia joined Tabby, her granddaughter hugging her tight. "Are you hurt, Mother?"

"No, nothing wrong. Judson there caught me before I went over with it, or worse, got pitched under the oxen's feet. My, my, what a day and it's only begun." She put her hands to her chest, took a deep breath. Her cap strings fluttered at her neck. "Oh, I see the walking stick. There." She pointed. "It's leaned itself up against a rock like I put it there myself." Her eyes searched like a lighthouse beam. "Can you find my school bell?"

"We'll see what we can salvage, Mrs. Brown," Virgil said. "A lost wagon. It had to happen sometime." He coughed.

"There's room for you in our wagon, Gramo."

"Thank you." But she knew there wasn't. "We'll not be a burden, will we, John? Bring up the tents."

John shook his head. "Did my violin survive?"

Kitchen utensils remained behind. Tabby would wear a couple sets of clothes. She could use the warmth. Their bedrolls were salvaged. She had to discard all her books except one, the Bible. Nellie gave her the small book, and she turned it over in her hand. "If I have only one, this is the one to have." Then, "You go back down there, will you, Judson? And see if you can also get my Shakespeare and John's violin. I hardly think we'll live a civilized life if we don't have music, Bible, and bard."

Tabby tried not to think about what Orus would say. She was holding the others back now with her lost wagon, she and John having to be tended by Virgil's family. She still had Beatrice and the layers of clothes on her back, and Pherne had rescued extra shawls, those gloves she'd worn at her wedding, her knitting needles. Paltry little to claim after sixty-six years.

"I'm pleased you're all right, Tabby." John eased himself beside her as they stood at the end of one of the Pringle wagons. "I'm not much of a knight in shining armor, am I?"

Tabby patted his coat lapel. "It was one of those things. Judson was closer for my rescue. Doesn't say one thing about your abilities. Don't you even think that."

John nodded. "We haven't spoken of my little advance back in the desert. I didn't mean to scare you off."

"If a rattlesnake doesn't scare me, I doubt you do."

"Tabby. I'm serious."

"I know you are. But, John, I, it's not a good time to explore . . . emotions. Right now, I . . . I've lived alone a long time. I'm not sure I can adapt to—"

"Oh, don't say that yet, Tabby. Aye, these are highly unusual times, you're correct. It's not good to make major decisions when the ship's running aground." He wiped his forehead with his arm. "Still, a discombobulated time is also a time to consider new ways."

She thought of challenges in her life. "So it can be."

"We'll speak of it when we have smoother seas, all right?"

Tabby nodded, repeated his "Aye."

She didn't want to have a major discussion about love when life hung in the balance. But perhaps that's when the subject mattered most.

Two more days and four miles passed in this tangle of river and broken trees. Word came from behind them of more deaths from starvation, accidents, illness. Virgil kept his voice low speaking to Pherne, even though everyone else had distributed themselves in the wagons and wouldn't hear them. Virgil was too ill to help much, so Pherne and the boys had set their tents right in the middle of the high-water bank to the side of the stream bed. It was rocky but flatter than anywhere else, and the river had abandoned that portion of the bank, she hoped until spring. They'd surely not still be here in May!

"Mrs. Brown can take my horse," Virgil said. "Hasn't had a woman ride him, but he's a calm gelding. John can take Schooner. Let's look at what provisions we can send with them."

"Is that really the best thing?" Her husband had mentioned this before and she'd shook her head. But now, with their supplies gone and her mother's wagon demolished . . . "What are they supposed to do if they get through? Did I just say 'if'? Oh, Virgil, what's happening?" She clutched his arms.

Raindrops *pit-pit-pitted* against the cloth. Virgil kept his voice low. "They have a better chance of catching up with the forward party driving the stock than staying here. And when they do . . ." He inhaled, breathing difficult for him.

"Not if, mind you, when they do they'll have beef at least. And Scott's certain there'll be a relief party coming this way. We were expected early October in the Valley and it's already November the second. Surely they'll send out flour and hopefully men to hack this road out." He scoffed. "It's no road at all." His voice cracked. "Oh, Phernie, I've made such a mess of it."

The ache in her husband's voice made her chest hurt. "It's not your fault. Nobody knew it would be this bad. We all chose to take the shortcut. As my mother says, he was a 'rascally fellow,' but Mr. Scott's been a godsend. We have to hang on to that. And we are surely getting close."

"Scott's as disgusted as the rest of us. At least now he has the full confidence of the party." Virgil had a coughing fit. Then, "It's the hardships, Phernie. People dying, hopes dying with them. Seeing you and the girls suffer like this. Hungry. And your mother."

"We can survive on the little bacon we have. Butchering Mother's oxen didn't go far with so many wagons behind us to share it with. There's plenty of water, so thirst isn't our bane."

Virgil grunted. "Drenching, that's what we're getting. I wish we had flour. Never should have wasted it on that Sioux feast. What were we thinking, feeding two hundred families?"

"The past belongs where it is, Virgil. Don't

bring it here. We've done the best we could."
She couldn't believe she was saying that.

He stroked her arm. They had plenty of water,
all right, but no one had bathed for days, the
copper tubs discarded weeks ago. He kissed the
top of her head. "You've the heart of an angel,
Phernie."

"Too bad I don't have wings to fly us over all
this."

He squeezed her.

"But how will Mother and Uncle John even
find the road or trail or whatever it is that the
stock party took?"

"They'll follow the cow pies. They can make
better time on horseback so should catch up in a
couple of days. They can keep riding with the
cattle group."

"A couple of days? They'll be out there alone
at night?" Pherne swallowed. "I'm not sure
she'll agree to this."

"We'll have to convince them that it's the best
decision—for all of us."

"And pray it's the right choice. I'm so tired
of making choices."

Tabby did not like this conversation, no indeed,
and yet she could see the wisdom in their
suggestion. They'd posed it as a suggestion. It
wasn't an order. A morning river mist rose up to
mingle with the treetops. "Fly, everyone who can,

from starvation? Reach those driving the sheep and cattle? That's what you're suggesting?"

"It is, Mrs. Brown. You and Uncle John must go ahead." His words carried tenderness, fatigue. "They'll butcher a cow or sheep, but we've nothing left here but oxen we still sorely need. We've seen no Indians for several days, so I trust you'll be safe. You'll ride my Caesar. He's a good mount. Move as fast as you can but don't over push them. They're weakened and exhausted too."

"We've divided the provisions." Pherne handed her the food wrapped in a wide section of cloth. Tabby didn't take it.

"Your petticoat doing duty, Daughter?"

"Yes, Mother." She leaned in to her and whispered. "None of the girls or me either has had a monthly. Everything is confused. I'm so sorry." Pherne's eyes pleaded with her. Louder she said, "What food we have is wrapped in love."

Wrapped in love. They were sending them to their deaths, weren't they? No, she mustn't think that. She looked at the sunken eyes of her grandchildren, of Judson and Nellie, skin and bones. On little Emma's face she could see eye sockets so sunken the child looked already dead. "What about . . . What will happen to Nellie Louise and Judson? Each of you? What if we make it and you . . . ?"

"You and Uncle John, you save yourselves.

Live to tell what happened." Virgil coughed through the words.

Tears pooled in Judson's eyes. "Maybe you can reach a settlement and send back help."

Going meant what was left here could be divided among two less mouths. It was a good decision. Tabby took a deep breath. Maybe they could ride on ahead to that Skinner place and bring back food. "Did you leave enough for yourselves? John and I, we're old. We've had a life. It's your lives that matter now."

"I don't need much." John spoke up. "Keep most for the children."

"Three slices of bacon and a cupful of tea leaves. That's all that's here, Mother." Pherne looked like she'd cry. "No flour."

"That's more than I had in my wagon. We were plumb out. The bacon—" she patted the bag— "that'll be good."

Tabby made her voice sound light and full of enthusiasm. Inside, trepidation as she had never known it settled like a rock in her stomach. She could make it on her own, but John, well, could he with that foot? And his weakened age? She wanted to bury her nose in Beatrice's neck feathers, let the bird bring her comfort.

"Maybe John should stay. His injury and all."

"We thought of that," Virgil said. "But he can't ride in the wagons, none of us can. And he can't walk well. If he's going to ride, he should ride toward the possibility of food and maybe reaching a settlement sooner rather than later."

"They discussed it with me, Tabby. I've got to go to look after you."

"Look after me?" She pursed her lips. "You talked with John before you talked with me?" She frowned at Pherne.

"It just worked out that way, Mother. We're talking to you now." Her voice cracked.

Tabby would not let herself believe that this was the last time she would see her children. Dear God, could she leave them all, emaciated, skin stretched across skulls, rain soaked and weary?

"We never wanted to be a burden."

"And you haven't been." Pherne held the cloth packet out to her mother again. "Take it. Go. Save yourselves. Please."

Tabby hugged the soft package. "Look after Beatrice for me, will you, Nellie? She'll come to corn in a tin, you know."

"Yes, ma'am." The girl rushed her in a hug, almost pushing Tabby over. The child's bones felt like her walking stick.

"It's my fault the wagon wrecked." Judson looked like the waif he'd been when this trip began, all confidence lost.

She gentled Nellie to one side. "You listen to me, Judson Morrow. You caught me before I toppled over with that wagon. And you can't have seen all the dead oxen, pieces of lives littered since we left St. Charles and imagine that you alone made a terrible mistake. You didn't. Things happen. You center your sights on what you've done well, which is much indeed. And you'll continue to help build that road and look after Nellie. You hear me?"

"Yes, Mrs. Brown."

"Good." She looked around. She refused to hug each of them, fearful she'd frighten them more than comfort through her threadbare shawl. "It's not like we have to wait until after breakfast before beginning our day, right, children? John, are you ready?" Her brother-in-law nodded, stepped up on the stirrup, missed, tried again. Judson assisted and John mounted, reached for his cane from Virgil, and laid it across the pommel. Virgil put the bundle of food into Tabby's saddlebag, patted Caesar's neck.

Tabby stroked the horse's mane. "Let's be off then." Pherne's eyes glistened. "The Lord goes with us, I know he does. Put me on old Caesar, Virgil."

Tabby reached for Pherne's hand then, squeezed it. Buddy rubbed up against Tabby's leg. She patted him, then tugged on her wedding gloves. She felt a tiny stone in one finger, a small irritation considering their plight. "We'll make it then, Virgil, God willing. And I suspect he is or we wouldn't have come this far." She leaned into Virgil then, and whispered to him, "Cook

268

Beatrice before you let the children starve, promise me." He jerked his head back. "I mean it."

He nodded, his lip quivering.

She looked one last time at her family. Perhaps leaving them so she and John would not be a burden would be the last great act of loving and doing good that she would perform upon this earth. It just might be her greatest challenge and she couldn't even write about it in her memoir.

Virgilia borrowed one of her mother's pencils and wrote the words that preceded her most fervent prayers.

No One Knows

No one knows
what trail is best
challenging fat boulders,
over streams,
across deserts,
around trees.
No one knows
where they'll find food
to keep them walking.
No one knows
what's best to do
with those beloved
needing tender care.
Make them go

or stay.
A wagon overturns,
a boy cries out;
cuts infect,
a baby breathes too soon.
Still
they live.
Gramo leaves us all behind.
No one knows
if she'll come back.
Will we see her once again
this side of heaven?
No one knows.

— 22 —
Doing Good

It had been years since Tabby had ridden a horse, but it all came back to her: the roll of the animal's back; the ears twitching forward or straight up, catching sounds, wary of disaster. Caesar's mane was straggly as shattered silk, though Virgil's boys rubbed him down each night. She rode astride, the only saddle Virgil brought. If she'd been a more accomplished rider, they could have left the saddle at the side of the trail to save the weight, but she didn't trust herself to not slide off. Caesar was a sure-footed mount who didn't resist stepping over fallen limbs or rocks, and he didn't shy at strangeness, including a woman on his back. A good, solid horse. She hoped Schooner's former personality of antics and testing limits had been wiped away by the trip's demands. She wasn't sure what she'd do if the horse bucked John off, or worse, ran off. Oh, they said horses were herd bound and never traveled far, but any distance would be too much for them.

John plodded behind her. She wasn't sure how they decided that, maybe the strength of the horses they rode. Caesar proved the better trail horse under Virgil's tutelage. Schooner was more of a follower than a lead horse. But Tabby also knew she liked being in front, seeing what lay ahead, relaying information to John instead of the other way around.

The day was filled with mists and branches low enough to wipe them off without constant guarding. They did not dismount all day, letting the animals drink at the stream with them on their backs. At sunset they were startled by the sounds of voices. Had they already caught up with the stock handlers?

Three families. Small children cried like young kittens, clinging to their mother's threadbare shawls. *Hunger.* They'd fallen behind those moving cattle and sheep and felt they could go no farther.

"Poor little things," she told John as he helped her dismount, her knees stiff as old leather. They made camp together beneath oak trees, bedding down with her shawl and John's coat pushed in together with the families. Tabby said to their sleep mates, "I know you don't have vittles."

"No, ma'am, we're out or we'd have offered."

Tabby looked at John. Her children had sacrificed so they'd get through, have enough to survive until they met up with the others. But these people were destitute. He nodded.

"We have a little." She gave them the three pieces of bacon and the tea, along with the tin cup Pherne had packed.

"May God bless you for your generosity." One mother sliced the bacon into small pieces they gave to the children. "We'll wait here, no more willingness to move on. Surely a relief party will come for us."

"We can pray for that." One of the babies tugged on Tabby's cap strings. They bedded down to a restless sleep.

In the morning, Tabby drank rainwater collected through the night in the tin cup. Tea would have revived them, but these people were in greater need. One of the men helped Tabby mount. John pulled himself up onto Schooner, fell back. Another man assisted.

They would push onward to reach the group with cattle, and if Tabby had her way, she'd send food back. If they made it. They said good-bye and received a weak wave in return.

"It looks like the trail leaves the stream and heads up that ridge."

John nodded, squinted at the broken branches and manure that marked the path. "Seems better to stay at the stream."

"I filled the canteen. We'd best follow where they've gone and pray they know what they're doing." But really, no one knew.

Riding higher on the ridge, where wagons couldn't go, she saw the beauty of this country: valleys wide and deep with dots of forests, the quiet broken only by bird calls and the crunch of broken twigs, their horses picking their way around the natural barriers. Some fall colors still clung to branches, and Tabby had a lapse to Connecticut and Vermont. They rode up and over a mountain, seeing meadows that surprised them with their grasses greening beneath brown and halted at the sight of open vistas. Would Virgil's party follow creeks? Would they ever meet up with them again? Hunger pushed against her ribs. Tabby's knees ached; hurt, really. She hoped she wouldn't fall off, because she couldn't imagine getting back on.

They followed the cattle signs through the trees, ducking under moss-covered limbs, brushing twigs from their clothing. Tabby noticed John shivering with the cold and damp air. In silence, they rode into dense foliage where larger tree branches threatened to knock them from their mounts. Out in the open again, above a canyon, John shouted, "Look!"

Tabby turned to see what he called about.

He pointed. "Indians."

Tabby squinted. "They're too far to worry over, John."

"Still got my eyesight though."

"That you do."

They were bottles on a fence post if Indians were closer and had mal-intent. They'd die right there, old bones all they'd leave behind. They rode on in silence as the afternoon beckoned them forward, grateful that the drizzle had let up hovering beneath clouds. It was better doing this with someone else rather than alone, Tabby decided. There was that goodness to consider. She twisted around to smile at John.

Instead of smiling back, John groaned. Tabby pulled up the reins, heading toward him.

"I'm not feeling so well, Tabby. I think I'll walk a bit, lead old Schooner here."

It will slow us down.

"My stomach aches." He rubbed his belly. "You'd think I had seasickness the way my head's swimming."

"We can't stop, John."

"No, I know. We need to keep going. It's—" He wobbled in his saddle.

"Stay on."

He jerked, nodded, and gripped the reins.

Tabby turned often after that, the trail too narrow to ride side by side. She considered trailing behind him, but he wasn't reining Schooner. His horse plodded along, following hers.

"There's land ahead. I see it. Starboard. Make way. Aye! Make way!"

Schooner startled Tabby's horse as the animal surged past her. John slid from his mount, staggered, his weight yanking his animal to a stop, his cane falling with him. There John sat, legs out in front of him, while Schooner twisted his head up and down in protest. Tabby pressed her knees, urging Caesar ahead. She leaned over to grab Schooner's reins. The last thing they needed was that horse galloping off or stomping all over John.

"You have to get back on. John?"

"Ship's on the right course. No need to sound the alarm."

"Captain Brown. Listen to me. Get up!" She felt her heart beating at her temples, the scent of troubled horse ripe in her nose.

John squinted. "It's so nice and warm here in the barn. Can't you smell the hay?" *Delirium.* He frowned. "Why are you here, Tabby?"

"You need to get back on your horse, John. Back on Schooner."

His cane had fallen with him and he pushed at it in the half-frozen ground while Schooner pranced. If that horse chose to bolt and run, there'd be nothing she could do but let loose the reins. She prayed that the horse was too tired to act the scamp.

She fumbled at her saddlebag. "Captain. Drink this." She leaned over, handed him the canteen, her own hands trembling. *Lack of food?* He took it, started talking without drinking. "Drink, John." He looked up at her, dazed, then swallowed, lifting the canteen back to her waiting hands. She stretched to get it, nearly tumbling forward. She hooked it over her saddle horn. It was still half full. "Now, use your cane." John looked at the object, then back at her. "Give it to me." His

brown eyes held a glassy stare. "Yes. Your cane."
Snow began to fall.

He handed it up and she grabbed for it. *If I fall off this horse, I'll never get back on. John won't be able to help me. I'm alone in this.*

She leaned over farther than she should have but grabbed the cane, then jammed it into the ground beside him. "Take hold. Use it as a climbing stick."

Miraculously, he understood and, hand over hand, pulled himself to standing, falling, then rising again.

She yanked the cane from the ground, poked it toward him so he'd take it, wishing she had her own walking stick. It was longer. "Now let's move a little, John. A step at a time. I've got Schooner's rein. He'll follow. You walk beside us. Hang on to the stirrup."

Caesar's ears twitched, but he plodded forward. Schooner sidestepped away, wanted to be behind, not with this man on the ground, unpredictable. John held on to the stirrup. He took a few more steps, then collapsed. Schooner yanked against the rein, his head high, eyes wild. Tabby held firm.

"Whoa, whoa, whoa," she said in a voice to calm both him and herself. Schooner settled. She had to get John back into the saddle. "Give me some guidance here." She spoke her prayer aloud.

In answer, she noticed a depression in the ground. Maybe a bear wallow. "John. Starboard. I want you to go toward that sinkhole." John wobbled. "Crawl if you have to." His eyes held hers, then he started toward the wallow. "Good. Now I'm going to lead Schooner and he will stand in that sink and you'll be able to step onto the stirrup and get on."

"I don't think I—"

"You can and you will, John Brown, or I will personally come there and smack you on the head with your cane."

The badgering seemed to work, as he watched her rein in Schooner and her own horse into the depression. "Come along."

John did as he was told, shoulders hunched over like a recalcitrant child. Schooner sidestepped as John reached for the stirrup. John tried again, and on the third try, he grunted, then sat his horse.

Tabby breathed a sigh of gratitude. "All right, now look at me. You hang on to the mane and the saddle. Just keep yourself on that horse. I'll lead him and we'll go forward. All right? John! All right?"

He nodded, his face as pale as the snowflakes now collecting on his coat.

The horses' hooves grabbed at the dirt on the sides of the sink, surging them out. She wouldn't let herself think of what might have happened if she hadn't gotten him back on the horse. She should have made him drink from the canteen sooner. She'd do that when they rested ahead.

Maybe the combination of starvation and exhaustion without consuming water had turned the man toward confusion. If so, she could find herself there without even knowing. She stopped a moment and drank, offered him another swallow.

They rode through the afternoon light, Tabby leading. Ahead, another timber-shrouded mountain loomed, cold air settling around them. This journey was like life, all mountains and valleys and challenge. But if one persisted, they'd be led to green pastures, beside clear water, their souls restored. She hoped.

"We'll have to go into the timber. It's where the trail leads." John nodded. "Are you up to taking the bridle reins yourself?" He nodded again. She reined her horse back toward him, had him drink again from the canteen. "Rainwater is good for something." He nodded. "Are you ready?"

"Aye." He trembled as he handed back the water. "I'm better."

They rode in silence up the mountainside, patchy with bare spots, then dotted with clusters of oaks and farther up, fir trees. A late-afternoon wind picked up, carrying rain that misted the distant hills. Once over, a valley opened up. A solitary place. No cattle or sheep in sight. They were alone.

Poor me! Perhaps this staying alive was the

greatest challenge of her life, the one she hoped to write down when she finished her memoir. If she lived to finish it.

Hunger created images of puddings and creams and steaming roasts and peach cobblers and— she stopped herself. They pressed on, seeing where three mountain spurs met together. Shrubs and rocks broke their path, acting as sentries to the ravines they had to meander through, racing the dark now, dusk having appeared like fatigue, unnoticed until it overtook a soul. With the steady rain, signs of tracks disappeared. As long as she had a next step, they could keep going.

"Here, John." She told him to dismount and hang on to Schooner, but he stared at her. "We'll spend the night here." She slid from her horse at the edge of a meadow, her knees a jolt of pain. Steadying herself, she loosened the cinch, pulled the saddle, and tied Caesar to a tree. Then she grabbed the wagon sheet from beneath the saddle blanket and hobbled over to a low-hanging branch. The canvas billowed out like laundry on a bush.

"What are you doing?"

"Making camp for the night."

John groaned and slid from his horse. Tabby tied and unsaddled his horse, then hobbling, dragged the tack and blankets under the cover, motioning John farther back under the tarp, his cane beside him.

"Whose barn is this?"

She frowned. "It's ours. For the night." She covered him with the saddle blanket and wrapped the bedroll around her shoulders. His eyes glazed again. His breathing changed. "Try to rest, John."

He leaned into her and she motioned for him to put his head on her lap. Hunger clutched at her. Leather and horse scents assaulted her nose, but none could mask the smell of the valley of the shadow of death.

— 23 —
Grief and Guilt

Pherne feared they'd call the man "Rolling Pin Roberts" ever after because he argued so hard about giving up the rolling pin that had been his mother's. Since her mother and John had gone, the way had gotten worse, and each was being asked to lighten their loads further. Ahead, shovel handles broke and wagons behind them split apart. Animals died from exertion. People sat beside their wagons and cried when they were told to leave more beside this god-forsaken road. And it did feel god-forsaken. In the evening when word of road progress came back with everyone being told to go through their things one more time and discard any nonessentials, Pherne had cried. She'd thought she couldn't cry any more. She vowed to keep her mother's memoir she'd worked on and that little book of sermons that had been her father's. Judson had gone back down for both of those. But when even forks weren't essential anymore—there being no food to eat—they would probably have to go too. And no one should hoard a bar of soap either. "Every ounce counts," they were all told. A tall man with clothes hanging from his shoulders like a thread-bare quilt over a rack exclaimed so much that he could not leave yet another thing and prayed that lightning would strike him dead on that spot rather than be forced to disgorge yet more of his few possessions.

At that very moment he dropped to his knees. Dead.

They delayed roadwork for his burial, fatigued from digging yet another grave and the sadness of watching the poor widow and seven children grieve.

"Did that man cause his death, Mama?" Virgilia stumbled beside her when they started in the morning.

"In a way. He let himself get so worked up, his heart couldn't take it, and over what? A little of this or that? Only things." She reached for her missing locket, a habit not yet replaced. "In the end, things don't really matter. We think they do, but they don't. What matters is keeping those we love alive."

"That's what Gramo always said."

"Says. She'll say it again."

She wished she could have brought that school bell, but they never found it in the wreckage. It had likely bounced or pitched on down as far as the creek and that's where it would stay.

They plodded along, taking refuge inside the wagons while the men double-teamed to pull a forward wagon through the muck and mud. She tried to busy herself with knitting or mending, but her mind kept going to her mother's fate and Uncle John's and when, if ever, they'd see them again. Even though she told Virgil not to visit the past, she was doing that. Again. Should they have sent them ahead? At least they had bacon. A slice a day and strong tea would get them through to the cattle herders and, hopefully, a relief party. And there was nothing for them here.

She took out her lead. She still had that. She began to draw what she could see out the wagon opening while listening to Virgilia make up tories for the children. At least someone was able to do something good.

"Mama, she broke it!"

"Broke what, Virgilia?"

"My icing knife. Look at it. Snapped in two."

"I didn't mean to." Emma dropped her eyes.

"Why did you even have it?" Virgilia accused.

"I couldn't find a spoon and I was trying to dig out a pretty rock."

"A rock. How stupid."

"Virgilia, that's no way to speak to your sister. Give me the pieces. I'll see if they can be soldered when we arrive."

"I'll take both pieces, Mama. If it had broken at the handle, it could be resoldered but not snapped in the middle."

"Clean it with kerosene and maybe you'll still be able to use the longest piece."

"Don't tell Gramo. She'll think I didn't take good care of a gift she gave me."

Broken things littered their lives. Oliver's little face came to Pherne. She'd been given the gift of a child and she had not taken good care of him; that was the core of her guilt and her grief. It had never been so clear.

Virgilia's papa had wished out loud that he could take the spare parts from her gramo's wagon and even the harp-back chair and somehow bring them along. She was glad he still spoke of the future. "Maybe we'll come back this way one day, Papa, and pick up the pieces."

"I can't imagine it, Child. Once we're out of here, I hope to never return. These canyons, ravines, raging rivers. I've never experienced anything like this before and never hope to again." The speech tired him. Whiskers like moth-eaten cloth covered his chin. So frail.

In the morning Virgilia watched Nellie and Judson with their heads bent close to each other under a wagon cover. Sadness tugged at her heart. Those two had become best friends and Virgilia was once again alone. This trip sure hadn't turned out as she thought it would. She had met a few other boys at the dances during early days of the journey, but none had caught her eye. The more time she spent with Judson, the younger he seemed, and she even wondered what had made her heart pitter-patter when she'd seen him at church. Nellie had brought him out of his shell. And he brought comfort to her. She guessed she was grateful that she had a family when neither Judson nor Nellie did right now. What Virgilia had were younger sisters who broke her things. Her brothers were like men already, working as hard as Papa. She'd thought maybe a place of trial would bring people closer together. It happened that way in novels she read.

Sarelia stepped up beside her in the second wagon where Virgilia sat alone. Emma followed.

"I've got Gramo's mem-o-are. Want to see it?" Sarelia held the leather-bound book out.

"It's a memoir, not mem-o-are. Why do you have it?"

"See where she writes about her and Grand-father leaving a church they'd loved and then becoming newspaper publishers."

"Let me see." Virgilia read to herself. "Gramo set type and wrote stories."

"What's type?" Emma leaned over, squinting.

The script was tiny and a couple of lines were smudged from the wet, making it hard for Virgilia to decipher.

"Type is little pieces of iron or lead shaped like letters of the alphabet. They put them in boxes and then run ink over them and then they press the paper onto the wet pieces." Virgilia motioned with her hands. "When the paper pulls off, there are words printed onto the paper." Emma scowled. "As in a book," Virgilia clarified. Then to her sister's confusion, "It doesn't matter." Her grandmother had written for a newspaper. Maybe Virgilia could get a job like that in Oregon.

"Gramo always writes there is a really big challenge she'll tell me about, but she hasn't yet."

"Tell *you* about? Why not all of us?"

"She wrote it for me. She reads it out loud to me. You're always too busy."

"I'm never busy," Emma said.

"She writes for everyone. It's not just for you." Why Sarelia's possessiveness annoyed Virgilia she couldn't say.

"My name is right in there, see?" Sarelia pointed.

"Only because you pestered her to do it and she agreed so you wouldn't bother her anymore."

"That's not true." Sarelia crossed her arms, thought again, then reached for the book.

Virgilia held it above her head.

"But the rest of us want to know what happened to her too," Emma said. "Did she write about her foot? I always wondered about that."

Sarelia grabbed the leather book from Virgilia's hand and clasped it to her chest. "I'm taking care of it."

"You share!" Emma said.

"Girls! I can hear you all the way in the other

wagon. Everyone's nerves are on edge. Please." Her mother rubbed her temple, leaving a smudge of lead on her forehead.

"Sarelia is hoarding Gramo's memoir."

Her mother sighed. "Give it to me. I'll keep it."

"Noooooo."

"Go put Beatrice out to peck," her mother told Sarelia as she took the book. "Maybe we'll have an egg for our supper."

"I get to eat it if we do." Sarelia pouted.

"It's my turn!"

Virgilia shook her head. This journey could never bring her friends and family closer together. All they did was bicker and try to quell their growing hunger.

Wolves howled in the distance. Tabby heard the horses move about, restless outside the make-shift tent. Had there been wolves before? John's breathing turned shallow. "I may well be alone here in the morning, Lord. Except for your presence. 'Though I walk through the valley of the shadow of death, I will fear no evil, for thou art with me.' I will not be afraid. I will not be afraid." She lied to herself, for she was frightened, perhaps for the first time in her life.

She had tried to build a fire but couldn't, rain and spitting snow seeping through even deep piles of leaves, keeping dry duff from her flint. Her fingers felt stiff and thick as sticks. John's breathing rattled, slow and heavy. She pulled the blanket over him, stroked his cheek, his earlobe. They'd argued on this road west. She'd gotten irritated with his stubbornness; he with her bossiness, as he'd called it. Both of them were strong-willed people, but at this moment, she was the stronger. Whether she could stay that way without food, as each day brought them no closer to a destination, that was the mystery.

She remembered those first days after Clark's death. She had called upon Providence and God had answered. Friends helped. She'd taught school to keep them alive. She'd taken in laundry for extras until they had enough and her sons had decided to go off to the sea, under John's influence.

"I'm sorry I got you into this, I am." She stroked John's cheek. Other-directed, self-sacrificing affection, that's what she felt for him. It wasn't enough for a marriage, she knew that now.

Tabby dozed. Her legs grew numb with John's head resting on them, her cold bones ached with the weight. She didn't want to move him. Animal sounds startled the night. The sky was as black as her Dutch oven. Yet at the darkest of the morning chill, she moved slightly and witnessed through the tent opening a spattering of stars, giving reassurance that the heavens still ruled.

Surely if they survived, there would be a reason. There would be some task that awaited her, some hope, healing, or purpose to fill her days. And then, as it had one morning a few weeks after Clark had died, a peacefulness came to her like a butterfly settling over a bud. There was nothing more to do but trust, and await the metamorphosis.

— 24 —
The Wisdom of Bones

Virgil tried to shoot the wolf. Pherne could see his arms tremble, his shoulders dropped as he realized he'd missed the shot. They'd been dealing with broken wheels and wagon tongues. Double teaming. Oxen dead from exhaustion and then the work of moving the animal aside, butchering, sending food behind them, then putting young, untrained, weakened stock to harness, men shouting, women crying. Then the rains came, sheets as pale as pewter. Still they slogged on, grateful it wasn't snow.

Tabby didn't think she even slept, but soft light filtered into the tent and she knew that dawn had replaced the night. She watched to see if John breathed. The slow rising of his chest brought comfort. She spoke an ancient morning prayer out loud. "All praise to Thee who safe hast kept, and has refresh'd me whilst I slept. Grant, Lord, when I from Death shall wake, I may of endless light partake." It was part of a long prayer her father taught her ending with the praise of the Doxology. Tabby moved John's head aside, waited for her leg to tingle back into feeling. She hobbled outside into morning mist and tipped the flap of their tent cover like a funnel. Melted snow and accumulated rainwater ran into the canteen she held in shivering hands. She roused John then, helped him sit up, sip. He blinked his eyes.

"Do you know where you are?"

He looked around. "Under a leaky tent, Tabitha Brown."

"So it is." She inhaled relief. "Let's see if we can get the horses water."

Outside she found a rock where rain pooled. Dragging her foot, using John's cane, she led the horses to drink. Not their fill, but enough. They'd be crossing streams again, no doubt. She thought they should return to the canyon below, follow the rivers out now that the cattle trail was gone. She returned, checked John's heel. It no longer oozed, a good sign.

She saddled their mounts, no easy task from her short perch of a person. Their backs were wet. As she reached for the reins to lead the animals toward John, she heard the rustle in the trees and her skin prickled.

"John." She kept her voice low.

"I hear it." He crouched, motioned her to do the same.

To have survived the night and then die in the morning from a bear? A wolf?

Then a voice. "Aren't you Mrs. Brown, from the Pringle crowd?"

Tabby blinked at the man who emerged from the trees. "I am. Are . . . are you the relief party?"

"No, ma'am. I'm with the stock group. We've stopped to hunt." His accent said New Englander. "The rest are only a half mile ahead." He helped her mount, then John. "You keep on that way. You'll come upon them." They'd pressed their reins against their horses' necks when he whistled. "Lookee here."

"What?" John said.

"Moccasin tracks. Looks like you had company in the night passing right in front of your shelter." He scratched at his beard. "Didn't want to alarm you, but Mr. Newton was killed in his sleep last night. Indians stole a cow. Newton left a widow and kids. You're lucky."

"Not luck," Tabby said. "Praise God from whom all blessings flow." She sang the ending to that earlier morning prayer.

A mile ahead they found the cattle and sheep drivers in the process of burying Mr. Newton. Later, they roasted venison, the smell like frankincense, the finest gift a body could want. They had survived another day. John acted stronger. This had not been the greatest challenge of her life. Not yet.

Pherne's family plus two wagons arrived at the end of the canyon five days later, wet, and exhausted. They'd only gone five miles. "A mile a day," Virgil told Virgilia. "Hardly worth writing in the journal." It rained the next day, washing them into November.

"I think we need to send Octavius ahead, over the Calapooia Mountains, to get provisions." Virgil had gathered them together after a meeting with Mr. Scott, slickers on, with water dripping from the men's hats. Pherne and the girls all wrapped themselves in the wool shawls they had, the wooden brims of their bonnets soaked and drooping. Octavius leaned against the wagon, pushing aside the grease bucket. Judson joined them, standing close to Nellie, his freckles faded as old rose petals in this incessant rain turned every now and then to snowflakes as large as a man's thumb.

Pherne felt ashamed that it had come to this, that they had not properly prepared and that she had not rationed well. If they were going to send a son off, why not do it before sending her mother and John off? But her mother could not have walked; the wagons couldn't be ridden in either. And there was hope she and John would reach the stock party. Octavius would have to go farther. "Octavius, you're so young."

"I'm old enough, Mama."

"He'll borrow one of the emigrant horses and we'll share the supplies that he brings back. Assuming he can get some. You and the girls will need to move the oxen along," Virgil said. "There's no other help for it."

Virgil wore a dejected expression and Pherne wished she could erase it. It was always difficult to see someone you loved in pain; even worse than tending to her own suffering. Emma cried softly and she heard Virgilia tell her to "Shoo, shoo. Everyone's hungry." But she held the girl in comfort, rubbed her arms to warm her. Pherne missed her mother.

"I'll be building road while Clark, Albro, and Judson handle the other wagon," Virgil continued. "I'm sorry it's come to this. I've stomped up and down the ridges, being angry with myself and Applegate. Octavius might be able to find supplies and secure help to bring men with decent tools back this way. I would go myself but—"

Pherne touched his arm. It was a long speech even for her husband. "No. You're needed here." He nodded agreement, his eyes holding a mixture of embarrassment and resolve.

Octavius left in the morning, heading some forty miles distant was what Mr. Scott projected.

"You be careful, now." Pherne looked up at him. Fourteen was incredibly young.

"Mama, don't you worry. You'll be along before I can even get back, is my guess."

"You always were my little optimist." She patted his arm. *So thin.*

They moved the wagons out across wretchedness through trees so tall she could barely see their tops without falling over backward. At times, it felt as though the wagons would roll over from the side hills they traversed. Scott would halt them in line and they'd have to wait while he rode on ahead to scope out a trail of some sort, the men chop a route, return to drag the wagons. Waiting added to their hunger.

The next day, November 3, it rained steadily as she and the girls walked on either side of the oxen, all their heads bowed nearly as low as the stock. They ate the last of the tripe they'd gotten when another emigrant's ox died and they butchered it, pulling a canvas out from a tree like a lean-to where they worked in weakened states, then ate with a little protection from the rain, cold, wind, and gnawing hunger the unsatisfying sauce.

It went on like this for a week. *Feed me with the food I find convenient.* That's what the Proverb said. "Give me neither poverty nor riches; feed me with the food convenient for me." Proverbs 30:8. Her mother quoted that verse. Weren't they like the Hebrews in the wilderness? Where was their manna?

On the ninth, Pherne heard Virgil cry out. He shouted to her, "Convenient food, Mrs. Pringle." *What's he talking about?*

Indians. Friendly. They gave them six venison hams. Pherne cried as she took one, thanking them, hoping they understood. The tallest lifted his chin in recognition, then left with his friends disappearing into the mist. Pherne sent Albro with the hams to wagons with young children, keeping only one. How more convenient could food arrive than already harvested and given as a gift? These tall men with long black hair and eyes as kind as Virgil's were angels, even if they didn't know it.

Pherne prepared a smoky fire to roast the ham. She sliced thin pieces for each of the children and told them to "eat like little mice," that their stomachs would be anxious and might have forgotten what to do with food.

"Oh Mama, our stomachs can't forget the only thing they're supposed to do." Sarelia looked at her.

"You might be right. Still, eat slowly."

The drizzle of rain and snow hovered like a wet spiderweb. Nellie and Judson sat with them, savoring the meat. Pherne wished she had fat to give her family. Venison had proven to be a lean meat. Only fat would really stave the hunger. She wished her mother and uncle and dear Octavius could be there for this convenient feast. *Oh please may they have found food, shelter, safety.*

The stream they followed had places with water as smooth as a mirror, then within the length of a wagon, it frothed with wild white. Trees with

branches wearing gossamer moss leaned o
the river, snapped when a wagon bow brush
against them as they drove beneath. The hea
pewter sky magnified the sounds of strain.
mind could lose itself with such deman
moment by moment praying for her childre
survival and her mother's success finding oth
to help. God would tend to the future; the p
was no more. Into the present she poured
hopes.

In the morning they began again. Pherne
strengthened by swatches of sleep and a turn
her trust.

They scaled a mountain they should ha
gone around. The morning wore on, leach
hope, until on the other side of the ridge th
saw a group of people.

Virgilia squinted as she moved beside
mother. "I think that's Gramo?"

"Is it?" Nellie stepped out, started ahe
"That's Schooner. Uncle John's there!"

The girls ran ahead and Pherne watched
mother slide from the horse and hobble forwa
her arms out wide. "Oh the pleasure of reunio
Pherne clapped her hands. " 'The joys of
mornings, in the mornings of our times.' "

"Gramo, Gramo, I was so afraid." Virgilia hugg
her grandmother. "I wasn't certain we'd see y
again. I mean I—"

"There, there. I had not a doubt. Not one."
Maybe one.

"Tabby tells me I was in the delirium pen, thinking I was sailing one time and the next looking for the hay barn." Uncle John laughed. "She kept me alive, she did."

Virgilia's relief had caused her to overlook the deepening wrinkles flowing from Gramo's eyes. How feather-light her body was when she hugged her. She was safe, that's all that mattered. But her cheekbones looked sharper, and she shivered as Virgilia held her.

Then, before Virgilia could bring her elbow through her mother's and her gramo's, she heard another cry. "Mama!"

Her brother? Octavius? *Back already.* He bent as he rode beneath the trees, a hand on his hat.

"I've got a bushel of peas and forty pounds of flour, Mama. We'll have full bellies tonight."

Virgilia was so happy she could dance! She grabbed Judson's hand, then reached for Nellie's and began to circle. Emma and Sarelia found a dirty palm, and with shawls wrapped over forearms, her sisters reached for others to join in. Virgilia began to sing, "Praise God from whom all blessings flow. Praise him all creatures here below . . ." On they sang, circling. Virgilia hoped that dancing to a prayer of gratitude wouldn't offend. How quickly fortunes could change in this place. It was all that they needed, those peas and flour—and their family, all together in one place, again.

They camped in a grassy, flat area. Virgilia thought it was at the top of a mountain and maybe it was. She could see beyond, though, that more timbered hills awaited them. For three whole days they worked on repairing oxen shoes, and soaking peas, baking bread. Each family got a pound of flour and two cups of peas. It wouldn't go far. Judson shot a deer and Uncle John whooped when he brought the carcass into camp. If they'd had the strength, Gramo said they should save the hide, but few cared. Listlessness caught her like a virus, Nellie too. She had no interest in baking cakes. Besides, Beatrice hadn't laid an egg for weeks. More friendly Indians brought in salmon, and Virgilia watched her mother trade one of her father's shirts for the wide-bodied fish. "Good for belly," one of them said, motioning over his stomach as though the fish would leave them sated and full—which it did.

Despite the fact that they had a little food now, each family getting a small portion, a woman died, the rescue coming too late. They stopped building roads to bury her. Her mother tried to comfort the woman's husband, but what could one say? People got sick and died. Nothing anyone could do could stop that. She watched her family like a hawk watches field mice, but for very different reasons.

There were still no major relief parties. Snow now slowed their way. They crossed the Calapooia Mountains with as much consternation and challenge as along the Umpqua River, finding themselves at what Levi Scott said was the headwaters of the Willamette, a north-flowing river. Virgil told them it was November 22.

"We should not try to make the settlements until spring," Scott said. "I'll ride north for provisions."

Virgil agreed. "Our boys will build cabins here, manage our tents. It makes no sense to go—"

"But we've come so far," Pherne interrupted.

"And no farther without provisions."

Pherne stood beside her mother, arms wrapped across her chest.

Virgil mounted Caesar. "It'll be all right," he said. "Tell her, Mrs. Brown." He reined the horse, and with very little additional preparation or good-byes, he rode away.

"This is . . ." Pherne started to cry.

"Crying gives up nothing but wastes precious fluid that your body needs. So stop now. You're setting a bad example for the children." Her mother hugged her shoulder to her side.

Pherne tensed. "Don't you ever just want to

sit down and cry? Didn't you ever?" She wiped at her eyes.

"I keep going. Indomitable, that's what you said when you sent us away. We made it. He will too. I have no doubt that we will reach the settlements yet this winter." She took her daughter in her arms. "Hush now. God goes with him. He'll be back."

"We never sent you away, Mother." Pherne sighed. "It was to save you both."

"Oh, I know, I know." She patted her daughter's back. "We chose to go. It made sense. You know me and my sharp tongue. You'd think I'd learn to dull it, wouldn't you? Let's just speak prayers for Virgil."

But the days wore on and Virgil did not come back. After a week with only water once again to fill their bellies, Pherne ordered Clark to shoot Virgil's favorite ox.

"Mama, no."

"It must be done, Clark. It's the right thing to do now. Please don't challenge me."

Clark hung his head. He lifted the gun from the wagon bed, loaded it with powder and lead. He patted the ox, who twisted its big head and licked Clark's face. Clark stepped back and did what had to be done.

Not an ounce of fat on the animal, that's what they found. But the meat kept them alive.

"One day of gratitude at a time," Tabby

said to them as they chewed the stringy meat.

"Do you really believe that, Mother? Really? What has the Lord provided so far?"

"Each other. Food when we've been desperate. We're all still here."

"Except for Virgil."

"Except for Virgil. But he'll be back. I feel it in my bones and they are very old, as you know. Old bones are also very wise."

Pherne didn't often recall her dreams, but she did remember the one that came to her that night. She dreamed not of food or of Virgil nor broken wagons littering the trail but of Hickory Farm and the home she'd left behind. There was a room she had never seen before, and it was cluttered with a crib, shelves with a silver tea set, a pewter tray. The new owners stood frowning beside the fireplace.

"I forgot to clean this room out," she said. They seemed unhappy with her lingering. They told her she needed to leave but that she could remove items she had meant to take. She looked around the room. Should she take the crib? Her eye caught a silver bird lying in the corner. A breeze once moved that bird and a ring of others, entertaining Oliver when they'd hung above his bed. Only one remained. "I'll take this bird." She put the cool silver object in the palm of her hand.

The people asked her to leave, but then she couldn't find her shoes. She looked around, frantic. Where were her shoes? Then she saw them: the woman wore them. How could Pherne walk away without her own shoes? Small stings of anxiety pushed their way into her dream. *I have to go. My family needs me.* Then, beside the door, she spied a pair of moccasins, white as snow. She slipped them on. They fit perfectly. With bird in hand, she tiptoed out, allowing the new people to walk in her shoes while she walked on in another's.

Part Three

— 25 —
Orus Says

"Orus? Orus Brown, is that really you?" Behind this burly man with brown eyes peeking out through long hair, carrying a throat-covering beard with streaks of gray, rode her son. Tabby's face hurt with grinning, tears spilled down her weathered cheeks. Behind him rode Virgil Pringle and three other men, each leading a mule loaded with tools and food and utensils to cook them with. Tabby recognized the dark-skinned Moses Harris who had been with Mr. Applegate all those months earlier. He wore leathers and a wolf-fur coat, the raw side out. She wanted to have words with him but was too weak.

Virgil dismounted and opened his arms to Pherne, pulled her close. "No need to cry. I'm back. I made it. We made it. Surprised by your brother. I'd made a canoe to cross the Long Tom when Orus and friends showed up. It was the best December day of my life. Aside from this day, getting food back to all of you."

Pherne clung to him like a woman drowning, not yet certain she was saved.

Orus nodded to acknowledge his mother and sister, dismounted, tied his horse to a tree far enough away that the other animals and their pack strings also being tied wouldn't tangle with each other. Tabby closed in behind him.

"There you are, Mother. What are *you* crying about?" Orus picked her up in a bear hug, the wolf-fur of his coat tickling her cheek. "I don't believe I've ever seen that before, you with tears." He set her down, straightened the strings on her cap. "The worst is over now."

"I'm so happy to see you. We've had our trials, we surely have."

. "Some of your own making, I hear tell."

She nodded agreement. "But let's not go backwards into those decisions made with good intentions at the time. Truth is, no one knows how things will end when we begin, isn't that so."

"I could have told you it wasn't a good cutoff." They headed toward the others, Tabby leaning on Orus. "If you had asked."

"You were too far ahead." This from Pherne, who overheard the conversation.

Orus patted his sister's back.

Moses Harris interjected, "The men who returned to build the road were fewer than needed. The cutoff can be taken, as you've shown with your courage and perseverance, and it will serve the country if war comes." He crossed his arms over the pommel, leaned forward. "The road crew who were supposed to cut and clear figured you'd have enough people to carve out the road yourselves, with a good pilot, as Mr. Scott is. So they didn't do it."

"Without tools? I'm not sure what Applegate was thinking," Orus said. "Newspaper articles suggested those on the trail were lounging about, taking their time, not starving at all."

"You can see that's not true."

"You're right, Marm." His brown eyes softened. "I can see you've suffered. And who knows if I'd have taken the cutoff if I'd been there." He clapped his gloved hands together, raised his voice. "It's done and what matters is that you are alive. There are still a few more rough spots before we get you to decent shelter at my forest grove. Moses will take supplies to the groups behind you. For now, let's distribute this flour, dried meat and molasses, salt, pemmican, and a little sugar for the children." He moved to his saddlebags and returned with a cone of maple sugar, taking his big knife from a sheath on his leg and scraping flakes into the open palms of Emma and Sarelia, Virgilia and Nellie. Orus raised his eyes at the girl. "Gained a child, did you, Pringle?"

"She's Nellie Louise Blodgett. Does that name have any recognition?" Tabby told him that her family had taken a different route.

"There was a route toward Sutter's Fort," Moses Harris said as he held his hand out for sugar too, his palm pale. "I believe a group from Illinois—Donner, Breen, Foster—went that way. Don't know if Blodgett did."

"I remember Donner, yes. Hope they made it through." Orus scraped a sugar flake into John Brown's open hand. The Captain dipped his head, touched his tongue to the sugary flake. "The snows were deep in the Sierras. All we've gotten is cold rain and wind. And a spit of white stuff now and then. Octavius, don't you want a little sugar?"

"It's for the children."

"We all need a little sugar," Tabby said.

Orus took a shaving himself, licking from the side of the blade. Octavius put his palm out then, and so did Clark and Judson, Pherne and Virgil. And then Tabby.

"I knew you'd want sugar, Mother. You're like one of the children."

"Am I? That's good. I don't ever want to stop playing and being hopeful." She felt a peace she hadn't felt for weeks.

After they'd eaten pemmican, Virgilia heated water and strained tea into tin cups.

Virgil said, "I thought we'd winter right here, wait it out until spring, now that we have supplies. Skinner has a cabin at the base of that butte. We could add to his settlement."

"No, no, that won't do." Orus put his knife back in the sheath. "We'll head to my forest grove, follow the Willamette, and you'll see this remarkable valley but also the lushness of the Tualatin Plains. My cabin is there and a few others. We can take you in. Lavina's waiting on you. Wintering here is not a good idea with Indians about and nothing else."

"The Indians gave us venison," Virgilia defended.

Orus shook his head. "Can't count on friendliness. Skinner doesn't even stay this season. Besides, by the time you built shelters enough, you could be home with me and mine."

"We're depleted, Brother. You can see that." Pherne spoke up in defense of Virgil's plan. "We need to rest."

"And rest you shall for a day or two. No more." He raised his finger as though in warning. "Any longer and you'll eat up your provisions and then what?"

"We'll build huts and hunt," Clark said.

"We'll discuss it after we've eaten," Orus announced. "Sister Phernie, let's get these vittles into stomachs. You'll feel more invigorated once we've had sustenance. Right, Mother?" Orus swirled her around again. "You're light as an eggshell."

"Starvation will do that to you."

"At least we haven't had to eat a skunk," Clark said. "If I remember right, that was your first meal, Uncle Orus, after a long hiatus from the Arapaho and food."

"It was indeed."

"And this time we'll bless the food proper," Tabby said.

Pherne and her mother and girls prepared their first real meal in weeks. They began with corn biscuits baked on the top of the Dutch oven Virgil brought back with him, theirs having been left behind. Inside, beans cooked. A second skillet steamed peas. Virgilia brought dried berries back to life, soaked in water made into a pudding with wheat flour, a luxury. The smells teased. Each person was also given a hunk of pemmican to chew on while they waited, the mixture thick with nuts and berries and meat and seasonings that lasted savory long minutes. The main course, venison backstrap taken from a deer Moses Harris had shot along the way, melted in their mouths after a quick fry on the skillet seasoned with salt.

"What day is it?" Tabby asked.

"December 6," Virgil told her.

"A late harvest feast," she said. "The Lord is good, isn't that so?"

Nellie nodded as she wiped her mouth. At least no one's teeth had fallen out. Tabby knew starvation could do that to a person too, take the teeth right out of hope.

Despite the drizzle, good food and laughter helped warm them, along with dry blankets, part of the provisions the men brought. But hopefulness was the greatest supply the relief party carried with them. Pherne could see her family surviving now. The evening brought Pherne comfort knowing that even in the wilds, word spread, people reached out to help each other, to care for strangers and family. Orus could have easily ignored the stories of destitute emigrants creating a road to defeat the British should war come or ignored the rumors that all was well. He could have figured that the Pringles came down the Columbia and had settled somewhere else, but he acted. They would make a new life now. She wished Virgil could have gotten back before Orus, so the glory would have gone to her husband bringing relief and without having to share the glory with her brother. She chastised herself. She should be grateful no matter who arrived first.

Still, the tenor of things changed with Orus's presence. His big, blustery voice rang out giving orders, telling other emigrants how to divvy up the flour, which wagons looked sound enough to continue on and which should be left behind. He told Pherne's son Clark where to move his tent to avoid the wind as though the boy hadn't been doing a man's work since May and making good choices too. Orus cut a new walking stick for her mother with his big knife. The rest of them hadn't had time or strength. He had words about

Mr. Scott too, though Virgil calmed him down with, "He was our savior. Don't give him bad words meant for others."

Pherne whispered to her husband later that night, nestled with a full stomach beneath the tent, lying safely in the crook of his shoulder. "We don't have to do what Orus says. If you think it's best to stay here, that's what we'll do."

"I've thought it through. I'd be a fool to argue with a man who's wintered over and who had the good sense to come looking for us when we didn't follow him."

"I've liked having the two of us and our family make decisions."

"Even bad as they were?"

"You did the best you could with the information you had. What more can you ask yourself to do?" Pherne fluffed the fresh, dry blanket up over them, patted the wool. "And you talked with me about it. Some men don't involve their wives in choices, but you do and I love you for that, Virgil Pringle."

"But here's the thing, Phernie." He stroked her forehead, his fingers gentle against her skin, onto her hair. *My hair is filthy.* "He's a good man and he knows things we need to know. And he's generous. Word got to him about the cutoff and the troubles we were having and he showed up."

"Did he chastise you, about our following Applegate's advice?"

"Only that little jab at supper. Oh, I think he thinks we should have continued down the Columbia, but he knew we had your mother with us and she can be pretty persuasive." Virgil chuckled at the thought. Laughing seemed to bring on his cough. "He may well think she suggested we make that trek, so as not to hold anyone back."

"She didn't hold us back." Pherne's voice grew soft.

"I know. And it was brave of her to go on ahead."

"We sent her off. That's what she thinks."

He lay thoughtful. "Yes, we did send them off, for their benefit, to survive when we might not have."

She changed the subject, the memory of sending her mother and John to their possible death, their own destitute state still raw. "I'm sorry I had Clark kill your favorite ox but we had nothing."

"I know." The scent of wet leaves and earth and the sounds of the river rushing could be heard through the night. Pherne longed for familiar, for safety once again.

"I thought we would all die. When you didn't come back . . . the days and nights were interminably long."

He paused, his hand still. The silence spoke a thousand words and feelings before Virgil said, "Orus is who we need to follow now."

She accepted his avoidance of her expression of fear. Who did want to consider how close they'd come to dying? She heard Beatrice cackle. "I don't like how he barrels into our lives."

"He barreled in when we needed him, Phernie. Let's let him set the pace now. We'll be fine." He kissed her forehead. "We're not planning to live with him."

"I should hope not."

She told him then of her dream. "It was so strange. They wanted me to leave. I wasn't welcome there and then with bird in hand I left, walking in someone else's shoes. And I was . . . happy. Isn't that odd?"

" 'A byrd in hand is worth ten flye at large' from the *Boke of Nurture*," Virgil said.

"I've never paid much attention to birds, but a dove is of special significance. And a sparrow. Yes, a sparrow. I think my silver bird was a sparrow." She smiled as she curled closer to her husband, relished his presence. "There's an ancient custom of bringing a bird into a new house to sanctify it. Isn't that lovely?"

"I wish I could give you a silver sparrow."

"Fiddlesticks."

"You sound like your mother," Virgil teased.

Pherne laughed. "You're back in my arms and we're almost where we were headed. We have each other. That's worth so much more than a silver bird."

• • •

After two days of rest, taking in bread and peas, checking on wagon repairs, looking at the oxen's shoes, replacing yet another set of brakes, they headed out. The day before, Mr. Scott had taken some of the supplies and, along with Moses Harris, rode back up the Applegate cutoff. There were others, starving, behind them, still trying to bring wagons through.

The animals plodded along, with Tabby's sole ox yoked to Virgil's. Mud, still their companion, sucked at the wagon wheels. A few days north, they met another relief party headed south. Tabby sent up a prayer of thanksgiving that those behind them would get help. Not long after, they fell in with French-speaking trappers and their Indian wives and children. The trappers from the British Hudson's Bay Company traveled with a large group of horses heading south to California for the winter. Virgil and Orus negotiated with them and hired six of the horses, arranging for them to be returned in the spring when the trappers moved back north. They pushed on ahead, but Tabby, Pherne, and the girls could ride now.

"Is this journey the biggest challenge you've ever had, Gramo?" Sarelia rode beside her, her short legs sticking straight out. The Indian ponies were well broken and familiar with women and girls on their bare backs. Sarelia's was a chestnut-colored mount she'd fallen in love with.

"It might be."

"You didn't finish your mem-o-are so I don't know which is your bi-i-i-i-g trial." She spread her arms out, her hands tugging on the reins in opposite directions, and the horse jerked his head up and down. "Oops," she said.

"I'll finish it one day. Not much time to write, though you'd think there would be with us doing nothing all day but staying alive and sitting on our bottoms."

"Virgilia says she gets to read it too."

"Of course she does. I'm glad your mama kept it safe while I rode ahead. As for reading it, any who want to can." The corners of Sarelia's mouth dropped. "But you are the inspiration for it, remember."

The child's dark eyebrows lifted right up, framing her square face. "Am I? Does that mean I'll know first what your greatest challenge was?"

"You'll know second."

"Who gets to know first? Virgilia? Emma? You said I was the inspiration!"

"Me. Your old gramo. I get to find out first. I won't really know what my greatest challenge was until I write again and the words will tell me." *Or until I reach heaven.*

"Oh, Gramo. You're silly."

But she'd never been more truthful.

— 26 —
Tired of Choosing

They were near a fork in the big river when the wagon her brother Clark walked beside broke an axle. Virgilia knew they had nothing to repair it with.

"It's too much for these animals." Virgil's voice was one long sigh. "Take only what you can put in your saddlebags. We're leaving the wagons here."

"But Papa, that means room for almost nothing."

"Virgilia, hear me about this." Papa's left eyebrow rose in that expression Virgilia knew meant *don't argue.* "All we'll have is the oxen and our Durham cows and our few sheep." He sounded so tired. He'd worked so hard. "You children don't know of such things, but we have no currency. We'll have to work for our suppers, everyone. Maybe make butter and trade for flour. Hopefully we can come back when the roads are less muddy and bring the wagons in, but now, with provisions rationed, we need to leave more behind."

"Sorting again?" Virgilia leaned against the broken wagon.

"Be grateful you have your life, Daughter."

"Yes, Papa."

319

"We must put on our creative hats, Virgilia, and see how much we can get into that bundle." Her mother rubbed a smudge of dirt from Virgilia's cheek as she spoke.

Creative hat? Who had time for being imaginative? She'd been doing everything asked of her without complaint. She'd cooked and carried and crafted solutions to problems with neither praise nor notice. What did she have left to sort? A dress she hadn't worn. Her hair combs. Her pewter knife. Both pieces? Why bother?

"If you look around, you can always find someone with less than you. Remember that." Her father raised that eyebrow again.

"I guess you're sorted to the nubbins too." Virgilia approached Nellie, who sat lump-like on a log, though her roundness had long ago faded into angles and ridges. "What I have on. And the pincushion your mama made for me, though none of us have needles now." She touched the stuffed cloth square over her heart. "Nothing more." She lifted her hands to the skies that at that moment broke open with a splutter of mist while a shaft of sun made the grass glisten like gems. "Makes it easier to follow your father's direction."

"I guess. I'm down to the book of sermons that my grandfather wrote years ago. I'll keep that. I like reading them now and then, but I can't seem to concentrate. My mind wanders to thoughts of food."

"I only have what I'm wearing, and what's left of my lotion." Nellie plopped on the ground. "I'll ask Judson if I can help him decide what to leave or take, but he doesn't have much either. He's a real orphan. I'm a . . . forged one."

Virgilia pondered. "Forged can mean counterfeit and you're real, Nellie. You'll find your parents one day."

"I'm forged by being pounded out of something else and fired."

Virgilia changed the subject when she saw the grief of her words flash across Nellie's face. "What will you do when we reach my uncle Orus's place?"

"I don't know. Judson wants to apprentice with a blacksmith or farrier in exchange for his room and board. When he can go out on his own, then we'll see if there's a future for us. Like your papa said, he's pretty young, but he's my best friend. After you."

"I guess it's pretty lucky to fall in love with your best friend."

Nellie looked up at her. "I know you mean well, Virgilia, but you don't have to try to make me feel better nor always find something good everywhere."

"I only want to help."

"And you do. But sometimes, a person just needs to sit and make sense of a thing herself."

Virgilia nodded, but she swallowed back tears.

All she wanted to do was relieve suffering and cheer people up.

After a pause, Nellie added, "Lucky, yes I am. To have Judson and to have you. A forged orphan has to find luck somewhere." Nellie grinned then. Virgilia smiled back. "It's nice to have a friend with great dimples. Starvation almost stole them."

Virgilia touched her cheeks. It had been months since she'd seen herself in a mirror or a reflection in a still pool. She started to compliment Nellie but then decided she didn't need to. She could love and do good just by sitting beside her.

"Why that's generous of you, Child. Thank you." Virgilia had offered to carry anything her gramo might want. "My memoir. Funny that I'd say that was so important to me. John's violin, though how you'll manage that on your horse with whatever else you have is beyond me. But you'll find a way, no doubt. I've watched you, Virgilia, and been so pleased to see you help me and your mama. You look after your sisters good too and take such close care of Nellie, even when she stole your beau."

"Oh Gramo, he was never really my beau. I wanted it to be so, but that didn't make it real." They knelt beside Pherne's trunk that had been salvaged. It would have to stay behind now.

"Food seems to be the most important thing to take with us."

Tabby wondered if for years to come the youngest boys would stuff bread—whenever they had it—into their waistband pockets so they'd never again be without.

"What about these?" Virgilia held up that pair of wedding gloves in the softest white leather.

Tabby put them on. "I wore them when I married and when we went off on our own, John and I." A little stone or a button nestled at the tip of her ring finger. She'd have to remove that. "I doubt these are essential."

"But they're full of memories. Happy ones."

"They are that." She turned her palms over, remembering. "I may as well keep them."

"Maybe when I marry I can wear them."

Tabby leaned over and squeezed her cheek.

"But let John carry his own violin. He can tie the case onto his saddle. He needs to start taking care of himself."

They moved out, on horseback or walking, driving the oxen and cows forward. The end of the scattering train dragged behind them. Before long, small cabins appeared through the timbers, set at the edge of great meadows of green, dusted in the morning with frost. The freshness of the air invigorated. No one was home at the cabins; no provisions had been left either. Fir trees rose three hundred feet into the sky and oaks kept mist from the animals as they dozed beneath branches. Despite how destitute they were, Tabby felt her spirits lift. She found joy with the changing landscape, joy at seeing evidence of civilization. Joy at the way people offered help. Why, several days forward, while crossing a little creek called Soap, they'd passed by a cabin and a black-skinned woman came out to greet them. She offered up a hunk of cheese, the first they'd had since leaving Missouri. A baby sat on the woman's hip, a quilt wrapped around her. Orus and Virgil spoke to her man—he couldn't have been her husband, she didn't suppose, as he was white—and conferred about any kin the Pringles and Browns might have known back in Missouri. The cheese providers were from there too. Orus said slavery wasn't allowed, though there were laws against free blacks being in the territory. It was a strange blend of people in this Oregon country.

The rain continued, wind and sleet its constant companions. Nellie's laugh hadn't been heard for days. Tabby wondered if she might have overheard words about the snow being heavy in the Sierras and feared her parents were there. But they might have joined a train going to the Columbia and stopped at the Whitman Mission for the winter. Many settlers did, Orus said. She'd have a talk with her. No sense brooding over what the girl couldn't control. She had to keep her focus on what she had now and what she might want for her future.

John, in the cold and wind, had renewed moments of strange thinking. One night they'd made camp and Judson had to go find him because he'd wandered off "looking for his ship." Tabby remembered getting him water and believing that had helped his scattered ramblings. She insisted he drink more. They really needed to get to permanent shelter, and she guessed he might still need her help. She would assume responsibility for John whatever their relationship. She'd talked him into this whole affair. Judson, too.

Nearing what she thought must be close to Christmas Day, Orus told her they were a day or two away from his forest grove. The creak of his saddle leather as they rode beside each other broke the silence. "Scott will lead you. Keep on this trail and you'll be fine. I'm going on ahead to alert Lavina and others to your arrival."

"Isn't there a settlement closer?" Tabby asked him. "Those trappers we got the horses from mentioned Salem. They said there's a mission school started by the Methodists, even a sawmill. The Methodists will have a church. Does your place in that grove have a church?"

"Congregational. Quite a few independent missionaries there, in fact."

"Hmm." She straightened her bonnet. She was

ready to stop. Here. Now. "There's a ferry for the crossing into Salem."

"Dr. White served in Salem." Orus stared ahead before speaking again. "I thought you might want to see Lavina and the children. Wasn't your coming all about being with me and mine?"

"My coming was about not being left behind."

Orus stiffened.

Was that true? Sometimes she wondered why she said such things, words that asked for affirmation but that she tossed aside like so much old bread. And after discovering how precious old bread could be too. Maybe now that Orus could see she had the same nine lives as a cat, he wanted her close by. The thought warmed her. But not enough to take the chill off his next words.

"I should have figured you'd head wherever Pherne went. It was always about her."

"That's not so. I love you all equally. And I haven't decided about whether to go to Salem or not. Do you feel that strongly about my coming to your forest place?"

"Not really." He looked away as though the timbers needed his attention.

She deserved that. "Oh. I thought when you said—"

"I'd have to build you a cabin. Takes a lot of work. There's no room in mine." His eyes never met hers.

"Right. And John . . . well, you saw him. His bouts of delirium are unpredictable. I think getting him to shelter must be our most important task." Deciding whether to stay with Pherne's family or go with Orus was really about John's health.

"Pringle suggesting Salem, is he?"

"There might have been some words about it, yes, but you know I make up my own mind."

"You always have." He pulled his horse up beside her. "I want you on the Tualatin Plains, in my grove. Just so you know, Marm. But not if you come because you're pretending affection for me and mine. Just one time I'd like to see the real Tabitha Moffat Brown and not this 'I always care for everyone the same' when I know for a fact you don't." His horse startled at Orus's kick and lurched forward, taking her son and any retort out of Tabby's range.

Had she been so difficult for her sons to be around? Manthano had invited her to stay back in Missouri, hadn't he? But early on, he'd moved away and seemed more attached to Catherine's family than the Browns. Why else had he changed his mind about even going to Oregon as a family? Maybe because she was going along?

Since the birth of her children, she'd kept her chicks together. They'd lived like peas in a pod—except for Manthano those later years—and

327

she assumed it was because they liked being together: one big extended family. Pherne had discussed crossing the river to Salem. But Orus wanted them all near him. What did she want surrounding her as she made her new way? To go with Orus or stay close to Pherne? Or be with John? She was so tired of choosing.

"Go or stay." They halted close to the ferry, and Tabby and Sarelia sat on a blanket under a spreading oak while they waited for the decision about following Orus or heading to Salem. Sun warmed their faces. "Do I set my feet on Salem's ground or wing my way to the forest grove? That's my dilemma."

"What's a dilem-i-mina, Gramo?"

"It's a choice, a troubled one. And I'll wait for a time to write about it. A memoir needs reflection, a time between the deed and what it might mean. I'm still too close to write about being sent ahead with your uncle John and what that meant to everyone's survival. Go or stay? That one was a tough one."

"I didn't want you to go."

She patted Sarelia's arm, the material so thin she could almost see the child's veins through it. She pulled her closer. "I went because that was what I could still give to my family: one less mouth to feed. One less burden for your parents to carry. It was a sacrifice we could make in our declining years, and truth be known, it might have been the last loving thing that I could do."

"Gramo, I'm getting cold."

Tabby pulled the quilt around them tighter as she thought of what they'd been through and what came next.

"We had a good life in St. Charles. And so we will again in Oregon. I feel it in my bones, Sarelia —bones that have not yet faced their greatest challenge."

Sarelia responded with a snore.

— 27 —
Resting Place

An afternoon of balm with shafts of sunlight through a pewter-colored sky greeted them. The world here looked green and the Willamette River ran blue, unlike the brown Platte and Missouri they'd left behind. Every shade of green covered the ground around them: fields, riverbanks, the centers of the trails they rode marked by sturdy grass. Even tree trunks had moss, as did the shingles of the ferryman's shelter. The landscape promised spring even in December and with a sky as gray as the bottom of a duck.

"Orus is right." Judson's voice held firm. "It'll be easier to find a place for Uncle John and you and Nellie if I'm not with you." Judson used his penknife, one of his few possessions, to scrape at his fingernails, though the dirt beneath them appeared permanently attached. The activity kept his eyes from meeting Tabby's. "Besides, Nellie will need to look after Beatrice, won't she, Mrs. Brown?"

She could look after her own chicken. But she could see the boy needed a bridge to say good-bye to Nellie. "We'll find ourselves a place, don't you worry. I lived in a glebe long enough to know that people don't hesitate to ask the pastor for all levels of assistance, including a roof over their heads and food for their bellies. And with Beatrice, I'm bringing eggs." She looked at him with reassuring eyes. "You can learn a trade in Salem, Judson. You don't have to go with Orus."

"Not that I'm not grateful for all you've done for me, Mrs. Brown. I am. But Orus says I can blacksmith with him and learn harness-making too. I think it's best I go with Mr. Brown."

"You said 'I.' Does that mean you're not taking me with you?" Nellie's question came as she, Tabby, and Judson stood by the ferry that would take the Pringles across to Salem. They had discussed this and Tabby thought it was all decided. Nellie and Judson and John would go with her and the Pringles into Salem and Orus on to the plains to his forest grove. Why couldn't people just stick with what they'd said?

Orus and Pherne and the rest of the Pringle clan stood off to the side, talking with the ferryman with no signs of animosity. Tabby was grateful for that. She didn't want her children feuding with each other—or with her. They no longer had their rented horses, as Orus would take them to the rendezvous spot where the Frenchmen and their Indian wives would pick them up. John still rode Schooner, the old horse as faithful as a dog. And Tabby rode Virgil's horse while he walked with his sons loading the oxen and "American cows," as the ferryman called them, onto the wooden craft. A light breeze picked up her horse's mane as Tabby listened to Judson and Nellie separate.

Tabby wasn't certain she'd even heard Orus say those things earlier that spoke to his feelings of rejection or jealousy or just plain not understanding what it was like for a mother to be forced to choose between her children's wishes. Maybe their emaciated states affected her brain.

Pherne didn't need her and hadn't asked her to trail to Salem with them. Neither did Orus require what little Tabby had to offer in her aging and now pecuniary state. He'd always managed without her. Her family looked exhausted except for Orus. Eyes sunken in, shoulders stooped, and each had lost more than twenty pounds. How were they even paying the ferryman? Hadn't she come west to be her own keeper, not to burden either of her children? But beyond that, what? It probably was best for Judson to leave them here and go with Orus. With her he'd be sailing without a good rudder.

"Mrs. Brown." Nellie touched her arm.

"My mind's been taking a trip, I'm afraid."

She hoped Nellie could see the value in deciding for herself too—after prayer and consultation, of course. She said as much to both Judson and Nellie as Virgilia approached.

"I'll come for you, I really will," Judson told

Nellie. "But I need to make a place for myself and then you."

Nellie's eyes watered. The girl held her hand to her chest, fingers at her throat. She did that when she pondered, worried.

"You can live with us," Virgilia told her. "Papa's talked with the ferryman and he knows of some people willing to take us." That child could be so quick to rescue.

Tabby moved her walking stick to her other hand, then linked Virgilia's arm through hers. "Let's let them talk alone. Nellie knows where we'll be."

"I'm getting tired of these good-byes, Gramo," Virgilia said as they walked toward the ferry.

"Good-byes are the bookends to hellos. There's always a little space between them we hope is filled with wisdom. Let's think about that as we get ready for whatever awaits us in Salem."

She'd miss Judson. He was a good companion for John. She hadn't even conferred with the Captain, but it would be best if he came with her. They'd started out together and would finish that way, though not as husband and wife. Hopefully with regular food and warmth, John would return to his old story-telling self. Judson needed to make his new start, become independent. Why, he could claim free land here on his own when he came of age. Each of the men could. The future held promise so long as one could stay alive for it.

Wasn't that the Oregon draw, getting a new start —and keeping the territory for the grateful government who gave them free land to do it?

They sauntered toward the Pringles, Virgilia's arm around her. Orus tapped his hat at Tabby and his niece as they approached. "Marm, Virgilia. Looks like you're set. I wish you all safe travel."

"More, we'll need a roof," Virgil said. "We're grateful to you, Orus." The men shook hands.

Tabby stomped her walking stick, then held it up in one hand. "I'll think of you every step I take, Son." Orus grunted. "I'm headed to the nearest church. They'll take us in."

"And wonder forever why they did." Orus laughed as he spoke.

Nellie ran toward her then and Tabby opened her arms to the girl, her face wet with tears. She had work to do, Tabby decided. Maybe not far in her future, but right now she knew her Oregon promise would be met in comforting this child.

Tabby had chosen neither the Pringles nor Orus, though she doubted Orus would see it that way. She had chosen those who needed her most, Nellie and John. She would trust the Lord in the details of just how that would all work out.

The ferry lurched forward, animals and people huddled between the rails. They could see where they headed, but the fast-flowing Willamette took them, jolting them downstream. Tabby held her breath until the chain caught, and the oxen on the far side strained to bring the loaded craft back upriver and onto the opposite shore. They didn't approach shore directly, but the ferryman and his animals worked as a team. Maybe that was like any step forward. A choice, then uncertainty, then a momentary fear of all being lost, and finally, with the aid of others, a place to land safely ashore.

Tabby and John mounted up while Nellie walked with Virgilia ahead. She carried Beatrice in her cage. Buddy, skinny and limping, made his way too. The boys drove the sheep and Durhams as the women rode toward a livery sign. The horse's hooves sucked mud. At least it wasn't raining and the air smelled of leaves and wet earth and carried a freshness with it. Tabby felt that tinge of excitement that comes with a decision made and needing implementation.

Once in the settlement they could see that the streets were deserted. Was it a Sunday? She had forgotten to ask Virgil, who kept the diary with the dates. As they made their way through the muddy street, milled-lumber buildings stood on either side. From the sawmill, or were those old wagon boards put to new and better use?

Maybe no one would take them in, as bedraggled and trail-worn as they looked. Virgil got to the livery before them and went inside. Tabby looked about for a cross on a building.

"Over there, John. Let's put our heels into our horses and see if we can find the glebe."

She rode in that direction, calling after Nellie and John to follow. "If nothing else, we'll thank God for giving us life to arrive here." Nellie nodded but she still sniffled. Tabby sniffled a bit herself, wiped her nose with the back of her glove. *That button stuck in there.* She'd have to get it out.

As she started to pull her glove off, John raised his voice. "Visitor, starboard."

A short gentleman with graying hair and bushy eyebrows black as night approached down the boardwalk. A red vest winked from beneath his suit. His face was shaved, no beard but a mustache, and he wore a bowler-type hat.

"You look lost, if I might say so."

"We've just arrived from Missouri," Tabby said.

"You're part of the southern-route party that received relief? My little flock provided some of that food."

"We are, sir. And we thank you. We're seeking the glebe."

He grinned; the mustache ends curled up and widened the smile. "Haven't heard that term for a pastor's home in years. You must be from New England?"

"By way of Missouri," John answered and Tabby turned to him. He was alert.

To the stranger, she said, "And you would be?"

"Reverend Roberts. Methodist. You and your wife and child looking for shelter, are you?"

"He's my brother-in-law. And Nellie is our little changeling. And I'm a widow of a pastor myself. We do indeed seek shelter. Can you recommend a place that might take us? In exchange for work. We have nothing left but what's on our backs here and our willing hands." She held out her gloved palms.

He scratched at his chin, thinking.

Into his silence Tabby said, "So this is Salem. It isn't much, now is it?"

"The Indians call it *Chemeketa*, a resting place, but the man who founded it called it Salem. It means—"

"Place of peace. I'm familiar with that name," Tabby said. "We have one in Massachusetts too. Looks like the history of the East is being rewritten in the West."

"And we transplants will keep on writing."

"There are no people about," Nellie said. "Where is everyone?"

"It's Christmas Day, Child. They gathered last evening and will do so again this night."

"Christmas Day." Tabby sighed. "How good the Lord is to us to bring us out of the wilderness to be here on this day."

"You're welcome to board with me and mine until the Lord brings better things for you."

"I think he already has."

— 28 —

The Hearth of Her Heart

Pherne hated not having her own things. She hated feeling weak and strained bringing her family into the mix of others who were less prosperous than the Pringles had been when they left Missouri. They'd arrived like babes, with nothing to offer but a willingness to work for food. Clark, nearly seventeen, along with Octavius and Albro, slept at the livery. The boys would help muck out stalls and oil harnesses in return for food. Pherne, Virgil, and the girls had been taken in by a kindly couple with four children of their own. Pherne helped prepare meager meals, though having bread at each one felt like a feast twice a day. On top of feeling her own strain, she worried over Virgil, who carried the weight of it all on his shoulders and still suffered from the ague. Thank goodness they had the cows. They could trade something for the kindnesses of strangers now that the animals could graze on the abundant grasses that swept like a green skirt toward the copse of trees beyond the town.

Her mother's party had found help from the Methodist minister, just as she'd said she would. The woman never ceased to amaze Pherne in how she put out her prayers, precise and certain. And good things appeared. It was one reason why she'd finally relented in sending her and Uncle John ahead those days. Her mother seemed indestructible. Pherne wished she was.

"First thing I'll ride to Oregon City and file on a claim." Virgil spoke from the loft bed they'd been given by a family named Matthews. Virgilia, Sarelia, and Emma slept on the floor. "When we rode out yesterday, Matthews showed me parcels of good ground not yet claimed. Extraordinary ground." Virgil went silent as he dressed, then chuckled. "I bet we could plant your mother's walking stick in the ground in this country and it would grow into a tree."

"That fertile?"

"That fertile." He finished pulling on his brogans, sat and caught his breath, then twisted back to her as she leaned against the headboard, her hair brushing the ceiling angle. She could see her breath, it was so cold, but the loft was dry, and being dry counted for everything. "I know this isn't what you hoped for. Me neither. But it'll get better. I promise you that."

"I'm not blaming you, Virgil. I know you've done the best you can."

"And so have you. Oh, Phernie, I hate seeing

you like this. The boys and I will get a cabin built as soon as we can."

"I know you will."

Virgil stood. "Promise me you'll try to see your mother today. I know she can be a trial, but you always seem cheered after you've been with her."

Cheered? Maybe so. "Right after I feel terrible that I'm so woeful while she who has less than anyone can be so stalwart." She whispered then, "I actually sometimes resent her."

He laughed. "Envy takes its toll. But think of it this way: some of her undaunted courage rubbed off on you, Pherne Pringle. Or you wouldn't have carried your finest possessions on your head slogging through Canyon Creek. And you wouldn't have raised good, strong boys who will help build up our land and get their own when they turn twenty-one." She sank back down under the feather comforter. "Nor given us girls who will one day make wives as good as their mother, looking after children of their own."

"You make me sound like a saint."

"And so you are."

"I don't feel like one. I don't feel much at all except sadness. And I should feel grateful that we all survived when so many didn't. I feel guilty a bit."

He bent to kiss her then. "See your mother. I doubt she ever does."

· · ·

Tabby began a new chapter in her memoir. They'd survived, arrived, and now had to discover what God intended next.

The glebe—or parsonage, as the reverend called it—consisted of a moss-covered cabin with a shake roof, a small outbuilding to house the reverend's horse and a pig that one of his parishioners had given him for providing a marriage service. Wood stacked against it fed the fireplace. A young man wielded an ax against the chopping block while Captain John watched. He leaned against his cane.

Nellie carried an armful of split wood inside, laying each log from her arms beside the open hearth. "I never thought I'd be so happy to see a fireplace inside a house." Nellie brushed her arms of the bark and bit of green moss that stuck to her shawl. She stood with her palms against the coals that Tabby poked with the iron before she added one of the logs.

"Dry firewood. What a luxury." Flames danced before Tabby's eyes. The reverend and his wife slept in the loft, having given their bed to Tabby and Nellie, and made a pallet for John on the ground floor. The reverend, perhaps in his forties, feared Tabby couldn't make the ladder. And she couldn't. Still, putting a man and his wife out of their bed gave Tabby pause.

The young man who'd chopped the wood,

Fabritus Smith, slept in that small barn and took his meals, such as they were, with them. He was from New York and nearly twenty-one when he could claim land. He'd arrived by wagon along the Columbia, and Reverend Roberts had taken him in as well. There were many mouths to feed. Perhaps this was to be her purpose in this new land: to find ways to return the favor of the reverend in giving them shelter, maybe even passing such generosity along.

One early January morning, Tabby set praying hands across her chest and announced to Nellie before leaving their bed, "We need to find a way to return our room and board. I have a plan."

Nellie rolled toward Tabby and whispered, "Mrs. Roberts isn't much of a cook or house-keeper, is she, Mrs. Brown?"

"How about you call me 'Mother Brown.' I think we're close enough, don't you." Nellie giggled. "This is a new chapter in our lives. We're truly family now." Then returning to Nellie's earlier remark, she said, "But we mustn't criticize the reverend's wife, Child."

Still, Tabby had thought the same thing in less-kind words. Mary was a pitiful thing. *"Ignorant and useless as a heathen goddess."* She'd have to scratch that out in her memoir. The story she told herself should never malign another. Still, she had evidence daily of the woman's failings. The mahogany table fine enough for a governor's house was caked with bits of food Mary had failed to wipe up after eating. Mary served sparse fare. Porridge, stuck to the tabletop, as that was what they'd been served at each meal along with pieces of pemmican. No dried fruit, yet Tabby had seen bushes along the way that promised berries. No milk, as they had no cows. From their first days there, Tabby realized the floor wasn't daily swept. Mice droppings clustered in the corners. The feather tick lay matted and dusty with old grass. Tabby hoped when spring came and Virgil returned to the wagons that her own bedding would be salvageable. Meanwhile she had offered to wash the ticking and see if they could find dry hay or something better to stuff the bedding with. The reverend had clasped her hand with both of his, eyes shining in gratitude. "You are a gift."

Tabby didn't feel like a gift, taking and not giving back, at least as much as she wanted and felt was required of a guest. Maybe it was time to behave as someone different than a guest.

"How long have you been here?" Tabby asked as she swept the floor before breaking their fast.

"My mother cried when I married and came here on the vessel *Lausanne*," Mary said. "We were part of the Great Reinforcement to the Methodist Mission to the Indians. It wasn't far from here." Mary pointed. "She was certain the wilds would consume me. The mission closed three years later and our little school for the missionary children closed with it. I came to teach and now I have nothing to do." She sighed. "Now we live off the goodness of our neighbors, the gods of misfortune pounding on our heads." She wiped her eyes with her apron, something she did frequently, whether from habit or truly from her misery.

"You have a good home." Self-pity bothered Tabby, whether in another or herself. The morning prayer she had added was "Help me to be what you would have me be, do what you would have me do." She spoke that now in silence.

"May I?" Tabby asked Mary later that morning as they stood before the larder. "I've a great desire for fresh bread."

"We have none of that. I wouldn't know what to do with flour."

Tabby shook her head. At least Beatrice had a feast with worms and bugs aplenty.

They'd been at the parsonage for a week. The reverend would soon be leaving to serve his people up and down the river, he'd told her, and she and Nellie and John were welcome to stay for as long as they needed. But staying with them felt like being caught in a river eddy, moving but not going anywhere. Was this God's purpose for having kept her alive? *The Lord knows my lot. He makes my boundaries fall on pleasant places.* The psalm came to her and she savored it.

"I found this, Mother Brown." Nellie had returned to the barn, spent a little time talking with the boarder Fabritus Smith, then came inside and handed her an egg. "Beatrice is laying eggs again."

"Excellent! Where are my gloves? I'm going to take that egg and find us some cornmeal. You stay here and mix up the porridge. Young Smith will need something after his wood chopping."

"He's a handsome young man."

Tabby stopped her activity and squinted, hearing a new tone in Nellie's voice. "So he is."

It hadn't been long since Judson left. Maybe Nellie had found a path to her future without him—and without Tabby's help at all. All the more reason for Tabby to take the next step toward the independence she was sure God intended for her.

Virgilia rose early and walked. She walked down the narrow boardwalk into town. She stepped out of the way of passing carts and walked down an alley marked by potato peels and watermelon rinds rotting in the wet. She made her way toward the river and watched it rush by. She didn't know where she was going. She felt as adrift as a tree branch floating by, bouncing off the shoreline as though hoping it would stick somewhere, then back out into the current rushing into the unknown. Gramo had said she should pray for her future, that God listened. But what to pray for? They'd survived, all of them, fortunate indeed to have been one of the first wagons through the canyon, as there were still people stuck out there. Destitute, with new relief parties heading their way. She had no way to help, nothing to send to those still struggling. She'd heard that Mr. Scott had met up with the Applegates and expressed "words" with the brothers about having deserted them. The Applegates were surprised, as they thought enough men would have been able to cut through the worst of it and assumed Scott knew the way, having been through there. Yes, they might have marked the trail better, but the emigrants ought to have had little trouble, they surmised.

Little trouble. Virgilia rarely allowed herself to remember the horrors, the deaths and burials, the injuries, cuts that infected and them with no salves for cures. Her brother sent off alone to find food. Her father doing the same. Cattle lost to Indian arrows. Buddy weak. And the fear that shivered her the day her gramo and Uncle John rode off. Their leaving so the others would have more food was a sacrifice, and it helped her see how precious life was and that her family had a pattern of giving of themselves for others.

The more recent parting also saddened her. Judson had gone with her uncle Orus, and only then had she allowed herself to be upset with Nellie. It wasn't jealousy of Nellie and Judson having found love, she knew that now. Once she had shamefully confessed to her gramo that she was envious. Her gramo's reply was, "Envy is the crumb that falls from the feast of a table God has prepared for us, Child. You don't want to waste time with crumbs—seek the feast." Judson had been an infatuation, a word found in one of her novels. He'd been more like a younger brother than a beau. She could see that now. But she had enjoyed talking with him, being his friend—until Nellie came along. She had admired Nellie's boldness and asking for what she wanted, for setting her own sails, as Uncle John would call it. But after Nellie was separated from her family, Virgilia found herself taking care of Nellie. It had seemed right to do that; it had also been hard, something Virgilia had failed to acknowledge until now. Feeling what others felt, hoping to cheer them, well, that proved tiring. Maybe she could sympathize, care, assist others in expressing their sadness, but not take the sorrow of others into herself. "Give sorrow words," Shakespeare had written. That was a better action for comforting others: help them find healing words. Nellie would need that now too, Virgilia imagined, with Judson having left her behind.

Her feet had taken her to the glebe or parsonage, Gramo called it, reminding her that they would all find a new way to call things here in the West. She said it was next to the church.

"Your gramo isn't back from the mercantile yet." Nellie greeted her with a warm embrace. "I've missed you."

"How are things here?" Virgilia looked around. "You seem cheered."

"I am." Nellie returned to the fireplace where she stirred the large black pot. "I'm making porridge for Mr. Smith."

"I thought the reverend's name was Roberts?"

"It is. But he has another boarder. Fabritus Smith. Isn't that an odd name?"

"He'd fit right in with my family. I've often wondered why Gramo named her children with such unique names or spellings. I mean, why not Fern, spelling it like the plant instead of *P-h-e-r-n-e*? And Uncle Orus? Manthano?"

"Octavius. Albro. Sarelia."

"Virgilia." Virgilia giggled. "I have to meet this Fabritus. I bet there's a story to tell there with that kind of name."

"Carel Fabritius." A baritone voice spoke. "He was considered one of Rembrandt's most promising pupils." Virgilia swirled to face the voice that would change her life forever. He held an armful of wood. "That's the story of my name. And my mother's misspelling of his name for mine, leaving out an *i*. And the fact that Carel Fabritius died quite young in an explosion of a Dutch gunpowder magazine that burned down half of Delft and consumed nearly all of his paintings, the *Raising of Lazarus* being one of his best known." He nodded and she saw the wet drops of moisture on his dark hair. He wore a smile that sent the promise of a feast straight to her heart. "Happy to make your acquaintance, Miss—"

"Pringle. Virgilia Pringle. I didn't mean to make fun of your name. I—"

"If I had a farthing for every time someone has commented on my name, I'd be a wealthy man." He smiled at her and she felt filled in the way eating bread after those days of famine had restored her hope. "Virgilia? That's a unique name." The deepness of his voice and his brown eyes warmed Virgilia to her toes.

"I'm named after my father, and he was named after Virgil, the poet who celebrated the founder of Rome, among other great works."

"In the *Aeneid*. I've read it." He squatted and placed the wood next to the hearth. Leaning toward the cooking pot, he inhaled. "Smells good, Nellie."

"Mr. Smith is looking for land," Nellie said. "I might ride out with him if your gramo approves. And if he asks me to, of course." She winked at Virgilia behind Fabritus's back.

"That's why I came out here from New York, for the free land where a man can let nature be his foundation."

"My mother is an artist. Fabritius painted

The Goldfinch, didn't he? It survived that fire."

"You know about that?" Fabritus looked up at Virgilia. "It was painted the year he died, 1654." His gaze meant a squeezing of her heart.

"I think your Fabritius the painter would be pleased you find nurture in rivers and trees."

He rose from the hearth, brushed wood debris from his duck pants. His comfort at the fireplace caused her to speak without thinking. "Did you know that we receive the English word *focus* from the first-century word for *hearth*. Because it's the center of the home." She blushed.

"Where people were fed, shared their lives, all things of import happened there."

"You love the meaning of words too."

He nodded. "And it's where the heat is, at the hearth. The farther you get from the heat, the colder things get. I intend to keep fires burning in my life."

Virgilia swallowed. Nellie had faded into the logs, only she and Fabritus filled the room. "The hearth is the center, the focus."

"Hey, I'm still here." Nellie shook her hand between the two.

A log crackled. Then, "Where is your father, Virgilia Pringle? I want to ask his permission to take you along on my search for property. If you'd like to go."

Go or stay?

She remembered Nellie's earlier admission, the

importance of sacrificing for others. But a voice inside her told her it was all right to pluck this plum from the tree. "Nellie, would you mind?"

"Well, two's a company and—"

"Three's a crowd. I'm so glad you understand, Nellie. Thank you." She curtsied to Mr. Smith. "Let's find my gramo. She can give consent. Nellie has to finish her porridge-making."

Fabritus opened the door and touched his hand to the small of her back as she passed before him, a touch as brief yet pleasant as the watching of a falling star. She didn't want the sensation to ever end. She had found her focus, the hearth of her heart, and Fabritus Smith stood at the warming fire beside her.

Six and One-Quarter Cents

So what could Tabby do in this Salem town to keep John and Nellie and herself from returning to starvation, or worse, dependence? The question never left her, not while she scrubbed the Robertses' floor or brushed out Nellie's long hair or listened to John play the violin. Today these thoughts came as she headed toward a cabin that Reverend Roberts said acted as a mercantile, "though he has little on his shelves." She liked to walk along the river and had learned not to hunch her shoulders against the soft rain. It only gave one a sore neck and didn't keep her from getting wet. Funny, this Oregon mist. It mostly beaded up on fur hats she saw men wear or on her own wool shawl. This February morning, rain stayed at bay while wildflowers small as baby tongues pushed up through black soil. She passed by a group of round-faced Indian women working hides near the river. Beyond, ducks quacked at their intrusion. She wondered if any of the women had been part of the group who had rented them horses after they left the Pringle wagons behind. Virgil and his sons had gone back to retrieve those wagons. She looked at each face, smiled, but she couldn't distinguish their round faces, one from another. She'd need more time with them to see the uniqueness of each. It wasn't the noblest thought, but strangers were like chickens to her: they all looked alike until you got to know them.

What were the occupations available to a woman who would turn sixty-seven years old on May first? A newspaper called the *Spectator* fed the territory, and she might talk with the publisher about setting type or even writing a piece now and then. But newspapers operated on the edge, as she well knew, and would have little for payment to their workers. Besides, it was published in a town farther away, and she didn't plan to move to another city again, having found this resting place. She might teach, in the spring, but there were plenty of younger men and women, former missionaries, trained for that as well. Her prayers held a constant plea for what she was supposed to do. The story of the Hebrews and their manna being provided daily always rose in her mind. They'd had just enough. If one hoarded, it spoiled. They were given sustenance for one day, meant to put their trust in God. She sighed. She'd already posed the idea of keeping the Roberts household running, cooking and cleaning, in return for their room and board, but she needed something that might bring in currency so she could move forward into . . . what? She didn't know.

At the trading post she waited for the owner to exchange the cornmeal that Reverend Roberts had received as payment for wheat flour. Then they'd barter about how much each was worth. She didn't like that part of commerce here in this Oregon country. Very annoying and time consuming. The trader seemed to take especially long this morning getting himself ready for commerce, tying his apron around his back, wiping off the plank counter.

Patience. Patience was the voice of reason in that classic poem of John Milton, "When I Consider How My Light Is Spent." She had not thought of that poem for years. Clark had liked it. Milton had the full confidence of his employer, making his way up the social ladder. Then he'd lost his sight and wondered about his worth in serving both his employer and God. In the poem, Patience reminded Milton, "Who best bear His mild yoke, they serve Him best." Patience finished with "They serve who only stand and wait." Tabby guessed that she was fortunate to stand at all. She needed to remember Patience.

She tapped her gloved finger on the counter, patience having stepped aside. She again felt that object stuck in the tip of her ring finger. It needed to come out. This was as good a time as any to turn that glove inside out and free the pebble or button or whatever it was. As though kneading a tiny roll of dough, she massaged the irritant down the glove finger, niggling at its resistance. Weren't we all like that? Resisting old habits, not wanting to be pushed out old channels and into the wide unknown world?

The irritant dropped on the wooden counter with a *ping*. Tabby adjusted her round glasses. *A coin?* Yes, it was! A six-and-a-quarter-cent piece, so tiny and worn she couldn't make out the image pressed into the copper. Currency. How long had it been there? Years? It might have somehow gotten in there even before she married Clark. Oh, wouldn't he laugh to know that she'd carried something of her former life—lives—into this new land that everyone touted as full of hope and opportunity. A gift from the past, but also, a gift from Providence.

"Is that a coin?" The trader leaned over. "See so few of these. Our coinage here is trade for salmon, wheat, horses, occasional gold dust, and beaver hides. Soft gold we call it. And cornmeal for wheat. But here 'tis this." He motioned, asking if he could pick it up. "Here is coinage. One day I'll hope to see such in this neck of the woods. I tire of the constant haggling over value."

"Can I buy six needles with it?"

He blinked. "Six? Hmm. What about one?"

"Five?" Tabby offered.

"Two."

"Four."

He pulled on his beard. "Three."

"Done."

Tabby left the shop with her needles and wheat flour. She stopped where the Indian women worked their hides and there had a moment of insight. They must have other buckskins, already soft and ready to sew. She hurried back to the parsonage. "Nellie, let's find what old clothes we might rid ourselves of."

"You don't have much, Mother Brown." But they found two calico dresses, faded and worn. A lace collar, a knitted shawl, and her finest black dress she'd refused to part with back on the trail. She'd worn it after Clark had died. Now was the time to put it into better service. They put the clothes into one of Mary's baskets.

"Come with me."

It was amazing how the mind worked. From darkness, light.

She had no idea what the hides were worth but wanted to be fair. And then there was the matter of being able to negotiate to get what one really wanted. "Does anyone here speak English?"

"A-mer-i-can." A round-faced woman spoke. When Tabby nodded, she touched her chest. Her dark eyes shone clear as fine crystal.

"Would you consider trading these clothes for three of your tanned hides?" She motioned toward the basket Nellie held, then the buckskins they worked on.

The woman shook her head. Tabby paused. She held up two fingers. "Two?"

The woman said something to the others, who rose and huddled around the clothing, pulling from the basket, holding the items up to their chins, giggling. "Two."

"Done!"

Tabby collected her precious purchases, her mind full of possibilities, wondering if she'd see that black dress torn into strips to decorate a horse's mane or sewn onto a child's dress, ribbons fluttering in the breeze. Nellie carried the hides, soft as butter, in the basket. Trust in the manna. Why did she ever doubt?

Homes had to be protected from threats, Pherne knew, weeds and vines cut back often or they'd creep in and take over. Living inside someone else's space proved daunting. Little adjustments she might make in her own home would be intrusive inside someone else's. Oh, the Matthews family was kind indeed, and Pherne and the girls worked hard to assist, but Sarelia dropped and broke a gold-rimmed teacup and Emma ate the last of a chunk of biscuit that Mrs. Matthews said she'd planned to use for stuffing the chicken they'd have for supper. "I'll have to bake more," Mrs. Matthews said through gritted teeth. They used up the Matthewses' soap doing laundry, had nothing to share to lighten the load. A person given shelter and sustenance needed a way to repay it, to carry her own weight. Preparing meals and watching over young ones was hardly a fair exchange.

And there were other threats to creating a home: the long wait in getting to where they had intended all those months ago, the delay moving toward the new lives of prosperity that Virgil had touted before they left. Yes, she'd made her peace with leaving all behind in Missouri, but she felt like one foot was stuck in tar and all she could do was twist in circles, keeping her in one place. She watched Virgilia fall in love, heard her boys make plans to claim their own boundaries. Even Albro, who at thirteen didn't always ride out with his father and brothers, rather spending more time at the livery. He traded his labor not only for his place to sleep but for his brothers' bed and board until he could come home. Except that they had no home.

Spring came early at this Salem place. Pherne watched while Virgil, Captain John, and the boys left in the mornings, still identifying the exact acreage they wanted to claim. Six hundred and forty acres was much to manage and Virgil hoped to find land that had a mix of both timber and prairie. The former would be cut for buildings or for sale; the latter, tilled for crops or to act as grazing for their cows and sheep. He'd traded the wagon they'd gone back for, for seed, and wanted to get it in "their ground" as soon as he could.

It was late March and the weather perfection. It had rained only at night and the days were filled with clouds that dotted like white notes across a sketching pad of blue. Virgilia looked after the younger girls, and her sons all rode off with their father, so Pherne had time to explore, praying as she walked. This day, Buddy trotted beside her. His bad leg kept him closer to her more now, his hound ears nearly dragging the ground as he sniffed in this new land. She was glad for the company.

She'd missed that old cabin at first, buried as it was in a thicket of brambles and brush on the outskirts of town. Buddy had startled after a rabbit and she'd left the path to follow him and found an area with foliage like a rock wall that ran for several hundred yards. It must mean a stream wasn't far away, or a spring. She'd called Buddy back, then pulled the twigs and dead leaves off his furry back while he panted. A few brambles later, blackberry canes torn aside, there stood the cabin.

She'd sketched the house the next time, drawing the perimeter as she could see it tangled as it was with blackberry vines. She rubbed with her finger to make the foliage of the oak tree that shaded over it. She'd looked at the drawing now and then, wondering about the cabin's history. Over a meal she helped serve one evening, she asked Mr. Matthews if he knew of the house, and he nodded, said the people had come and gone before his time, though he'd only come out in '43. No one owned it, he thought. "Might have been someone with Hudson's Bay had it built for wintering over. Or maybe one of the Methodist missionaries who came by ship and they've returned home."

The next day she brought with her a big knife that Mr. Matthews kept out in his barn. She began to hack and pull and tear while Buddy's tail wagged, his nose stuck into vines.

The hard work broke a sweat in her and she realized it felt good to have her body engaged in physical effort. Not that there wasn't work in doing laundry or making soap. She hadn't given that activity much value. But there was mystery in this work, wondering what she'd uncover. Perhaps that was why Virgil took so much pleasure in looking for "their land." He was careful to always include her in the outcome, saying "we" and "our" with frequency. She was grateful for that. It would be "their land" when he made the claim, but this discovery felt different. He liked exploring, and she found she did too, though this was "her" cabin, at least for now.

She wiped her forehead with her forearm. Leather gloves would be a welcome protection as she pulled and chopped, but gloves were a premium in this country and expensive if one could find them at all. Was that the doorway? She'd thought it was a window. Branches brushed her cheeks as she stepped inside.

It was dark and smelled of animal scat, dead leaves, and dirt. Her eyes adjusted to the pale light slipping past foliage that blocked the two windows, warbled glass still intact. The puncheon floor creaked as she crossed it. The wood meant someone had taken great care. She wondered if the people who had built it had become too ill to keep back the growth or if they'd lost hope and left. Nothing hung on the walls. They hadn't departed in haste, as the cabin was bare . . . except for a canvas covering objects in the center. Her eyes adjusted to the light, she moved toward the covered pile. She pulled at the tarp, hoping she wouldn't hear mice scattering or uncover a snake. As the canvas slipped to the floor, she stepped back and gasped, her hands reached for the absent locket.

"It's meant for us," she told Virgil that evening. "You have to come and see."

"We'll soon have land, Phernie. Can't you be

patient at the Matthewses'? I hate to move us from there to a place, what, at the edge of the village with nothing in it?"

"That's what I want you to see. I know I can make it into a home. It will free you up to work the land, not worry over a structure for us. It's meant to be ours, it is."

"How can you be so certain?"

"Come with me tomorrow and I'll show you."

"Don't get the children's hopes up. The land I want is a good ride from here. We'd be better to build on that."

"Yes. But that won't happen this season and won't need to. Trust me. You'll see."

In the end, they took the children too.

"Close your eyes, Virgil. You children wait outside."

She led her husband through the doorway she'd cleared even further of tangles and vines. She brought him to the center of the room where she'd replaced the wagon cover over the objects that had taken her breath away. "Ready?" Virgil nodded. She whisked away the cover. "Open| your eyes." He blinked, then opened his mouth in an *O* of surprise. "Do you have any doubt that this house is to be in our lives?"

Before them stood four harp-back chairs set around a Federalist table. Twins to the very chairs and table they'd had to leave behind.

···

Gramo sewed gloves. Whenever Virgilia and her sisters and mother went to visit, her gramo was hunched over, cutting or stitching. When Virgilia thought of it, she couldn't remember a time when her gramo wasn't engaged in some pursuit. She was never idle except when she napped. Here in Oregon, she'd seen little of such napping as she had back in Missouri. None of them had much time for idle dreaming.

"Got some sinew from one of the deer hides your father shot and it works as thread," her gramo told her. "Tough and a little rough for seams but men like having watertight gloves. The trader says he'll take all I can make. Here, you sit, you can help. I've got several laid out. It's my route toward independence. When I sell these, I'll have made thirty dollars above my board. Imagine that. Thirty dollars."

"I thought you were looking after the Roberts house in exchange for board?" Virgilia's mother picked up one of the needles.

Gramo pursed her lips. "We all thought it better that we remain friends and that would be best by my finding a boardinghouse. It was a mutual parting of the ways, though my leaving Beatrice behind was no small matter. The boardinghouse wasn't interested in a chicken kept in the room." She cheered herself and changed the subject. "We are planning a trip together, to the ocean, me and the Robertses. Nellie and Beatrice too. Besides, it takes so much of my time making gloves, I hardly had time to do the necessary cleaning and cooking for the reverend." She shook her head. "My, my, but Mary does need help. I'm not the one to give it forever. John's off looking for land, though how he'll ever farm it I can't imagine. He's better off resting at the boardinghouse or telling his sailing tales to new listeners at the saloon, where he assures me he drinks only the good water of this Oregon country."

"Where's Nellie?" Virgilia looked around.

"She's washing dishes, hoping Judson comes back for her before too long. She's had no letters, but I'm not sure the boy is literate. A lapse on my part, not knowing that. I could have taught him on the trail. And how are you and Mr. Smith getting on?"

"She's in lo-o-o-ve," Emma crooned. Sarelia giggled.

Virgilia felt her face grow hot. "You two go outside." They giggled more but followed their big sister's order.

She didn't want to talk about Fabritus in front of her sisters or her mother or grandmother either. And yet she wanted to tell the world. This was the strangest time she'd ever known. Whether she spoke of him or not, everyone seemed to see how much he meant to her and teased, as Emma did.

"Her father and I approve," her mother said. "He has a plan, that young man. Anyone named for a painter can't be bad." She patted Virgilia's hand.

Virgilia decided that the glove she stitched needed her full attention. Emma and Sarelia spoke loudly about slugs, as locals called the slimy fat worms who appeared from the soil like bees to a swarm. The girls sat on stumps used for chairs outside the boardinghouse door. Her mother and grandmother chatted on about Gramo's pending trip to the sea.

Yes, Fabritus did have a plan. He'd gone that very week to register his claim in Oregon City and told her he'd begin as soon as he could to clear the ground. Planting must precede everything else so he could one day support her. He had apple starts to nurture.

He hadn't actually proposed, just told her about his plans and then that promise to "one day support her." Until this journey west, she hadn't thought much about what it took to support another, to keep alive, find ways to sustain a family, and perhaps one day prosper beyond what her own family had done. She couldn't help but remember their comfortable life back in Missouri where they wanted for nothing, where books could be loaned out, read and returned, and necessities and luxuries purchased off supply ships sent down the Missouri from the East.

Dwelling in the past wasn't helpful. Her grandmother had taught her that too. She poked her finger, sucked at the blood. At least her mother had rescued the porcelain thimble painted with tiny blue asters. She used it to push her needle through the leather. She'd have to keep pushing through this time of waiting, hoping that Fabritus had friends to help him plant so he could begin working on that cabin. *Friends?* Of course the man had friends to help, but why not her? She brightened. It would take some convincing, as Fabritus preferred to treat her like fine china. He'd held her bare hand once and frowned, saying a cared-for woman ought not to have calluses nor lift anything heavier than a child. *I need more of Nellie's lotion.* She'd show him how sturdy she was. Hadn't she survived the Applegate trail disaster? Hadn't she slept with a rattler and lived? She helped raise her younger siblings. Maybe her mother didn't go out and till behind a mule or an ox, but that didn't mean Virgilia couldn't.

"Gramo, could I buy a pair of these gloves?"

"Of course. But you don't have to pay me. Let's call them an early wedding present."

"Oh, Gramo, Mr. Smith hasn't proposed."

"He will. I've seen the way he looks at you."

"You already have a wedding present for me. I get to wear the gloves you wore, the gloves that gave up your six-and-one-quarter-cent piece."

"A farthing that set me on my way." Her grandmother smiled, showing yellowing teeth, while her leatherwork rested in her lap. "It's a good lesson for me to trust in the Lord's plan and not my own."

"You said once that it's easier to change the direction of an oxcart that's moving than it is to get one started in the first place."

"I did say that. Good you remembered, Child. But I'm learning too that it's all right to be still. For if one's always busy, busy—"

"It's hard to hear that voice moving through the vines and brambles of our lives, harder to let light in," her mother interrupted. Was that a new sparkle to her mother's eyes? Probably. Her father had moved them into that abandoned cabin and named the creek behind it "Pringle."

"I am so fortunate." Virgilia rose to kiss her mother's cheek and leaned over to hug her grandmother's narrow shoulders. "Two strong women to show me the way forward." She lifted the gloves. "I have plans for these, but I'll keep listening, Gramo. I promise."

She had the discussion Tabby had been putting off, not wanting to hurt John's feelings. But when she told him that she adored him, wanted him as a brother but that she didn't think they'd make a marriage match, he'd nodded, already aware. "No need to saddle yourself with an old man," he'd said. But he had a twinkle in his eye and told her he might find himself a ship and head back east. "Wouldn't have missed this Oregon journey for the world, though." They sat in the parlor, such as it was at the boardinghouse.

She had wondered what he'd use for currency and considered asking him, when he unscrewed the top of his ivory-handled cane. "A few gold coins," he said, flipping them in his palm.

Tabby's eyes grew large. "Saving them for a rainy day, were you?"

"I'd have pulled them out if we'd have needed them, dear Tabby, but I knew we didn't. You took care of things, like always." He winked.

She shook her head, but a part of her was pleased he hadn't offered to rescue her. She liked knowing she'd made her way, almost alone.

— 30 —
New Trails

They sailed to the Pacific, Tabby, the Robertses, and Nellie, deciding at the last to leave Beatrice behind. Tabby had turned her glove money into a place on a ship heading first north on the Willamette, then on the Columbia, the river they'd avoided by taking that fateful Applegate road two years before.

The trip proved lovely. This was such beautiful country, August dressing in fading wild rose and vines sporting blue berries. She'd walked on the flat beach and seen where Lewis and Clark had their salt works, stuck her toes in the cold Pacific. Still she wondered what next for herself, what of her spent light? They stayed a month and then decided to head back toward Salem. But Reverend Roberts made some comment about them passing through Tualatin Plains and a forest grove being a mere twenty miles south where several indepen-dent missionaries settled.

"A forest grove? Where Orus Brown has a cabin?"

"Indeed."

How could she not go there and see how her son and grandchildren fared? And Judson.

"Nellie? Shall we take a side trip to that forest place? We're close."

"Are we? Oh, yes, please." She chewed on her lip. "I don't know what awaits me there, but—"

"Time we both faced fractures and see if we can chink them tight."

They boarded an open boat upriver again, but this time the wind and the tides were against them. They were thirteen days getting to Oregon City. There, she hired a wagon from a man who it turned out was a neighbor to Orus. She paid two dollars for their passage and vowed to stay but two weeks with Orus and then return to her "resting place" in Salem before the winter rains set in.

Anticipation wrapped around her like a cape and she inhaled the landscape, different yet the same as Salem. Copses of trees dotted prairie browned by summer sun but promising green, come winter rains nurturing grasses tall. Land flat as a tabletop brought forth crops without the effort of clearing ground of trees. Trails crisscrossed the area. Their driver said they were Indian crossings, people of friendly souls he assured them, the Atfalati people. Wild strawberries grew unfettered, their fruit now gone to birds. Geese called overhead, reminding them that winter waited. Nellie chewed her lip.

"It may be he wanted to write," Tabby suggested.

"I know." The girl wore a straw hat Tabby had purchased for her and a new frock she'd sewn herself from material Tabby had purchased for her.

The little village had few buildings, small, not as prosperous-appearing as Salem. But each cabin had a view of the spectacular Mt. Hood, snow-capped and splendid. They rode uphill.

"Orus has the best sections of land," the driver said, "above any flooding and with pretty nice views."

He pulled his team up in front of a cabin with wheat in sheaves dotting a vast field behind it. Outbuildings nestled amidst blackberry vines and hollyhocks. Orus came out to greet them.

"Marm? Well, well. Wonders arrive in wagons. I never expected you'd ever make it."

"I have to say your forest grove isn't . . . as large as I thought it would be." She knew the minute she said it, she'd erred, criticizing before commenting on the magnificent views and worse, not speaking at all on her happiness at seeing her son.

"Out of the abundance of the heart, the mouth speaks, Marm."

Oh, that tongue of mine. "And 'whoever keeps his mouth and his tongue keeps himself out of trouble.' You quote me Scripture, Son. I am humbled. Let me try again."

She alighted the wagon using her walking stick

to balance. "Come here and let me hold you, Orus. It has been too long."

Orus hesitated, but only for a moment. Then he lifted her and swayed her like a metronome, the movement swinging the ties from her bonnet. It was enough to bring them back toward a synchronized rhythm.

"The girls will be pleased to see their grandmother, and Lavina too. She is with child again. Nellie." He put his fingers to his hat and nodded. The girl curtsied.

Tabby held her tongue about Lavina's state and entered the cabin. She felt the warmth of this place, children helping each other. Lavina greeted her with a hug. The cabin itself was tightly chinked. The men of her family were good providers in addition to being dreamers. They kept their feet on the ground, but they fluffed their wings as well. Orus told of selling part of what he'd claimed in land those years before to a Mr. Clark, for a school "for missionary children mostly" and church ground too. Orus may not attend, but something of his pastor-father's influence continued.

His cabin housed her many grandchildren, and Tabby could see that staying even two weeks with them would be a burden. What to do? She did not know, not wanting to offend again, suggesting his home was insufficient for their stay.

Nellie looked about and Orus said, "You'll be seeking Judson." He cleared his throat. "Nellie . . . there was an accident."

The color drained from the girl's face, faded from cheery cheeks to white. "Is he . . . ?"

"In his room, at the barn behind."

On Sunday, Orus and his family headed to a Presbyterian meeting. He introduced Tabby to the Clarks, Harvey and Emeline, formerly of th East. They had purchased land while Orus had made his claim three years before.

"Will you stay with us?" Emeline said. "We have room, and Orus and Lavina have a houseful." Tabby looked at Orus. She thought she saw relief on her son's face as he nodded. Still, she had lasted one night with him and his. And she hadn't been asked to leave.

"Nellie too?" Tabby asked.

"Of course, if she'd like."

"I'm needed elsewhere, Mother Brown." And from what she'd told her, Nellie was.

Nellie Louise surprised Judson in the Brown barn where she'd climbed up the short ladder. In a moment she would see Judson again after all this time. She spoke his name, then popped her head up over the floor opening. She thought she heard a groan before his voice called out, "Don't come in, Nellie Louise."

"I have to."

He'd made a spot in the loft with a mattress. A canteen of water sat on the loft floor beside his bedding. Her eyes scanned the space. A humming-bird paused at the small window opening before flitting away, finding nothing sweet at this spot.

He stood to the side, shoulders hunched.

"Oh." Nellie hoped he couldn't hear the gasp escape.

"Yes, oh."

"What . . . what happened?"

"I'd rather not have words about it, if you don't mind."

"I don't mind. I mean, I'm sorry it happened and that you don't want to talk about it, Judson, but I don't really see—"

"You can't see that I'm maimed?" He held his arm up, elbow accusing her for not seeing.

"I do see that you've been wounded. Was there a skirmish?" She stared at the empty space below his left elbow.

"What are you doing here, Nellie?"

"Why, I came with Mother Brown. We were at the ocean and then on the way back there were terrible storms that stalled us so here we are, a side trip. I'm sorry if I'm intruding." But she wasn't sorry, not really.

"You saw me, so now you can go on back to Salem."

"Is that what you want?"

He sat on his mat, his legs crossed. "Oh, Nellie, everything has turned out poorly. I can't ask you to come into this. I'll never be a blacksmith. You don't need a . . . broken man."

"What if I choose it?"

"A life of looking after someone else?"

"I saw veterans of the wars when I was in Illinois, some without limbs. They carried on and more easily if they had someone to walk beside them, holding them up—in their hearts. That's what I can do. Hold you in my heart where you've been these many months."

"You had a whole person in your hopes."

"I'll adjust. I'm learning how to do that with a little less disruption." She hoped he'd smile.

He didn't. "Go on back to Salem. Make a new life for yourself."

"I'll decide what sort of life I want and where I want to live it." He was being pitiful but telling him so wouldn't help. No, the way to walk beside Judson Morrow was not to use words to convince him of anything but to be generous in her spirit, continue on as though his injury was just another boulder on the road, one they'd have to go around or climb over. "I'll see you at supper. I'm helping Lavina at least until the baby comes." He looked up at her. "Yes, I'm staying. I'm not sure if Mother Brown is, but I came here for a reason and I don't see that that has changed. Don't nap too long. You'll miss Lavina's fixings."

• • •

Tabby's life took on a new rhythm with the Clarks. A shipment of religious books arrived from Fort Vancouver and the Clarks relished turning the thin pages. With Tabby they read until the evening light faded. There were others staying with the Clarks too while working on homes they built, and it seemed emigrants coming down the Columbia often made their way to the kindnesses of these hearts. Mr. Clark had built their two-story home himself, made the furniture, shaped the doors, and used a pocket knife to trim the windows. He had a skill he put to service.

Tabby thought they missed their families and she brought something of the East Coast to their hearth. She saw the young couple as an extension of her own family. She hoped she wasn't betraying her sons and daughter in broadening family that way.

"How did it happen, Judson?" Tabby looked at the sleeve tied up at his elbow.

"I'd rather you not know, Mrs. Brown. Just that it did. A foolish mistake on my part, though I had the best of intentions."

They were at the trading post where Judson had been hired on as a clerk. He'd grown taller and the strain of the injury had put creases in his forehead and around his eyes. Freckles still dotted his nose and his red hair looked healthy again. "I can manage the till here and Orus spoke kind words about my character to the owner."

"It must be good to have Nellie close by too."

He looked away. "Can I get you something from the shelf? I made this stick that works like fingers to reach high for packages." He showed her.

"Why, that would be right handy for the likes of me and Nellie Louise too, short as we are. You just pull this little rope and the ends open up like a forked tongue. Aren't you clever."

"Necessity."

"Plato wrote that a need or problem encourages creative efforts to solve the problem."

"Who's Plato?"

"A wise old man. You've proven him a prophet." She smiled. "I'm sorry this happened to you, Judson, and I've been remiss in not keeping you closer. You were my responsibility. I should have fought harder to have you stay in Salem. Maybe this wouldn't have happened—whatever it was that happened."

Judson's freckles had faded, but his face flushed pink. "A man has to make up his own mind, Mrs. Brown. You didn't interfere with that and I'm grateful."

"I am pleased to see your good spirit has kept you above the sorrow. Now, how do you and Nellie Louise fare?"

He swallowed and his Adam's apple bobbed up and down. "I can't be a burden unto her, Mrs.

Brown. A man with one arm? I've told her as much."

"Fiddlesticks. How can an inventive young man like you not see the love that girl has for you?"

"She'll find another, just as she'll find her folks one day."

Tabby thought less than a moment before blurting out, "Why don't the two of you go to California before winter sets in and see if you can find her folks, together. People check in at the posts along the way. If you haven't heard of any Blodgetts in Oregon country by now, why not set your sails for California?" She could finance the trip, use what few coins she had left. Start making more gloves, if need be. "It would be a good task for the two of you. Of course, for appearance's sake, you'd want to marry."

Judson laughed, but bitterness tinted the sound. "Orus told me that you were a woman of many inventions."

"Did he, now? So I am. But this invention is to help you see beyond that missing limb and to what a future with the right young lady can mean. I believe that Nellie Louise Blodgett, for you, is a necessity."

Her grandmother had promised to return to Salem before September, but she detoured to Forest Grove instead. "She'll miss the wedding," Virgilia pouted.

"You could wait," her mother said. "There's no need to rush."

Virgilia shook her head. "One less mouth for you and Papa to feed and one less person taking up a mat."

"Oh, you're marrying to help us out?"

Virgilia laughed. Her fingers embroidered a red rose onto the bodice of her yellow flower-printed dress, material she'd swept the trading-post floors and stocked shelves for in order to trade for the cloth. She bunched the material onto her lap. "Gramo wouldn't want me to delay nor let her absence ruin the day. She'd say, 'Decide if you're going or staying—I'm going.'"

"You've done your part for us, Daughter. I'll miss you."

"Don't cry, Mama. We're less than a day's ride distant."

Fabritus had asked for Virgilia's hand in marriage in July, and they'd set the date for August 15, expecting her gramo to be back by then. Nellie too. But her grandmother hadn't returned, and finally, Virgilia decided it was her wedding and Gramo would simply have to hear about it from others. At least Uncle John was there to play the violin.

Nellie would miss the nuptials too, but maybe she would have preferred that. Virgilia's boldness on the day she'd met Fabritus still amazed her. Had she been selfish, thinking only of her interests? No, it was all right to recognize a desire. It didn't mean she'd forget how to care for others' feelings. Nellie's interest in Fabritus Smith had faded in Virgilia's glow, and she'd remembered that Judson was somewhere on the Tualatin Plains and planned to return for her. That he hadn't yet concerned them all, but Nellie had stepped off the craft on the way back from the ocean and hope-fully found her way to him.

The rest of Virgilia's family would celebrate the nuptials with her, and she had the gloves Gramo had worn when she married Grandpa Brown, a man Virgilia had never met. Still, the soft leather on her hands reminded her of that long devotion cut short by death, but a devotion that remained for her gramo. Virgilia hoped for that kind of love and marriage too.

Reverend Roberts officiated at the Salem Methodist Church on a sun-drenched day. No humidity, a light breeze to lift tendrils of her hair. Her mother had wrapped greens and both purple salal and white snowberries among the braids that crowned Virgilia's head. She'd dry those winding vines and put them in the book of sermons of her grandfather's. Her little sisters spread wildflowers before her as she and Fabritus walked down the aisle together, her parents preceding them, then standing on either side. Fabritus's voice boomed as he repeated the vows, and Virgilia heard twitters of laughter from the audience delighted by his exuberance.

It was Wednesday, September 1, 1847, the middle of the week, a day that took on new meaning for her. Afterward they consumed gallons of sassafras tea, steak and onion pie, cold sliced potatoes, cornmeal bread, and one of Virgilia's own wheat flour cakes. They finished the meal with raspberry flummery, a dish her gramo said was a New England staple. Virgilia had simmered the berries herself, adding just a touch of salt. The flummery needed no sugar, as the wild berries in this Oregon Territory grew small but sweet. Her sisters had whipped the cream until their arms hurt. In the heat of the afternoon, the white peaks draped over the fruit served in tin cups that Fabritus's friends had given them as wedding gifts.

Fabritus chatted with their guests and Virgilia watched his easy way with people. It had taken some persuasion to convince him that she was strong enough to walk behind a mule, to peel logs and chink them with a mixture of mud and straw, that she would be a helpmate and not only a "mate needing help." He had relented and she had participated in the building of their home. Seeing how he remembered people's names and how his attention made them smile. When people spoke, he listened as though no one else in the world mattered, his articulateness about politics and Oregon's future, subjects he warmed to. Admiring him among the guests, she saw a bit of her future. She would have to share him with a larger world. Her life would take new twists and turns. Had it been only the year before that they'd taken the fateful last turn and begun to cross the Black Rock Desert? How life had changed and would again.

"Mrs. Smith, are you ready to sleep your first night in your new home?" Fabritus spoke the words directly into her ear, his arm slipped around her waist. Uncle John played his violin and guests danced on the wagon boards laid down for them as they once had on the better days of the crossing. Hands clapped and feet stomped, but she heard her husband's words and nodded to his invitation. The future beckoned with welcoming hands.

"I'm ready whenever you are."

Fabritus and Virgilia moved into a cabin that her brothers and Fabritus's friends had built—and Virgilia had labored over too. They had little to furnish it with, but her father and brothers made a table for them. Her mother gave her two of the harp-backed chairs she'd found in the cabin the Pringles now stayed in. And Albro, the brother with a heart for animals, had gifted them with a hound puppy he assured them was from Buddy's line.

As she lay within her husband's arms, Virgilia could see that her eddying in an unknown stream that had been their journey west now spit them out to flow into the fast-moving current of life. Each day forward, Virgilia would look upon her hearth with gratitude, and promised to do all she could to make her home a welcome place for her husband, children, and for others. One couldn't think of their circumstances now without remembering those who had lost their lives on the trail, and some who had not reached settlements until February of that very year. She remembered the families in the Sierras caught in the same early winter storms that had confounded the Applegate travelers. She hoped Nellie's parents had not been among them. The Donner party, as people called it, had been so destitute it was said they'd resorted to cannibalism. Virgilia shivered. Not a pleasant thought on her wedding night. If her father had made other choices for them, if Octavius had been unsuccessful in bringing peas and flour back, if her uncle Orus had not sought them out, if total strangers had not funded their relief, they too might have ended up having to make such grisly choices.

Gramo always asked her to find the wisdom in a trial. For that time along the Applegate road, she would say, "A tragedy tears away a hope; a kindness brings it back." She would make kindness another rung on her ladder toward light.

— 31 —
Reconciled

The thing is, Tabby decided, we are never finished while we breathe air, never totally broken without hope of repair. *What's left for me to do?* Clear the air with her oldest son. Was there still a fracture there?

On a Tuesday in October she rode one of the Clarks' horses to Orus's home and asked to speak to him alone. "I have come to talk with you about . . . things."

Orus loaded bales of hides he'd take for trade at the Hudson's Bay fort in Vancouver. His back was to her, then he faced her to retrieve another hide, fur side tucked inward, exposing the salted beaver skin. "How have I disappointed you now, Marm?"

"You have not. But it's that very expression, leading out, that suggests I frequently find fault with you, that makes me want to speak." She touched his arm. "Do you truly believe I find no merit in you?"

"If you find it, you keep it well hidden."

"My tongue is sharp, I know that." She gripped her walking stick with both hands. "And we differ on things of a theological nature." He frowned, but she rushed ahead. "I adore that you live as though you have Christ within you, your generous spirit speaks well of you." She cleared her throat. "These things of the heart and soul mattered to your father, you know, how his children walked. I committed to carrying on his legacy as best I could."

"Is this where you tell me I've failed his test?"

"No. You have never failed him or me. I do wish that things might be different, but what I wish more than anything and wonder if my steps have not been directed to bring me here for this purpose, is that you would know . . . how much I do love you, Orus Brown. How proud I am of you for dreaming large and yet keeping your feet on the ground and your ear to the wind so that you learned of a wagon train struggling. You brought supplies to us. You saved us and many more."

"And you decided not to let me continue to look after you."

"I . . . that's true. I do want to do things myself. I don't ever wish to be a burden. But I went to Salem not because Pherne means more to me than you do. You suggested that. I went because I really thought John needed shelter quickly. And because I knew your house would be full."

"There was room for you." He'd stopped loading, took out his penknife, and cleaned his nails with it as he leaned against the wagon, crossed his ankles. Geese honked overhead.

"I appreciate that. And I hope you don't hold it against me that I accepted to remain longer here in your forest grove but staying with the Clarks."

"I do not." He looked up. "Likely you'd have been gone within a week with my brood." He grinned then. "I understand. But sometimes allowing others to help you is giving them a gift too. One you can't ever repay, of course, but you can pass it on. Allowing others to assist brings you to their equal instead of above."

She furrowed her narrow brow, the tie beneath her chin pulling at her. She tugged at it. "I've never felt myself above anyone." Tabby squirmed remembering what she'd said about Mary Roberts and her housekeeping. She did feel above that woman, that was certain, but that was a minor point to be prayed about later.

"Refusing help of others can be seen as stoic and stubborn, and condescending too. And sometimes makes the life of those who would help you more difficult. You could ease their days by letting them make sure you're thriving."

"Do you worry that I'm not?"

"I have. But not while you're with the Clarks. And besides, I can ride over there if I've need to reassure myself that you're well."

Warmth flooded through Tabby. Her son cared about what happened to her. She wasn't sure how to reconcile that with a man who didn't want her coming to Oregon in the first place. But now that she remembered, she was to stay with Manthano after she refused to remain in St. Charles. Orus did have a plan for her safety. She'd thwarted it.

"Our slate is clear, Marm. I like you being close . . . but not too close. But when that time comes, there will be room and care for you."

She exhaled. "This means much to me, Orus."

He put his arm around her shoulder. "Come inside. The little ones are always anxious to see their gramo and I'm sure Nellie would like to pour a cup of tea for you and Lavina."

She let him help her in, surprised at how his words had lifted her footsteps. Now to find what she was supposed to do with the rest of her days.

Those first months of Virgilia's marriage brought hours of joy. Loneliness, too, as Fabritus worked for others in exchange for a pig and cow, seeds he'd plant in the spring, kitchen supplies, rope to frame their bed. Virgilia traded a lap quilt she'd stitched, giving it to Mary Roberts in exchange for Beatrice's return to the Brown and Pringle clan. "I never knew what to do with the eggs anyway," Mary had told her. She hoped to surprise her gramo with the bird's clucking presence, and oddly enough, the puppy they'd named Rembrandt and had shortened to "Rem" got along with the bird. Maybe she'd train Beatrice to ride Rem. Buddy had resisted.

Winter rains began in November, but this season they were sheltered and she vowed not to let the heavy skies remind her of the tragic winter of the year before. This working and conversing and reading together was what contentment was and Virgilia savored it. Yes, there would be new trials, but she was ready. She'd remember past ones and how they made it through. God was in the world and in the small details of her life. Nothing else mattered.

One week led to two, then three. Tabby visited, reacquainted herself with her grandchildren, and reminisced with her son. It seemed a good metamorphosis of a mother finding a new way to be with a child. She considered returning to Salem but then weather set in, making Tabby's next choice: they'd be in Orus's grove for the winter.

And harsh it was, not so much the weather, but from strange tragedies farther east, the casualty of which drifted to them like ashes from a fire. First one, then two, then many orphans and displaced people arrived. Something would have to be done for them. Maybe she was the one to do it.

"What is it?"

Fabritus had returned from Oregon City before Christmas Day. He placed a copy of the *Spectator* on the table. He pointed to the paper, then opened and closed his fists as he paced. Rem jumped at his legs, but he brushed him aside with his foot. "What's happened?"

"There's been a terrible killing of emigrants and others at the Whitman Mission, east. We stopped there when we crossed the trail. Hostages have been taken and the Cayuse are gathering other tribes to come against us. We're raising an army, though we have no government funds to do it, the territorial government so averse to taxing we're left vulnerable." He scoffed. "Someone's proposed approaching the British, hoping they'll make a loan to pay a ransom—if that can be worked out—and others are railing against the American government for not offering us soldiers when they deemed we'd be a territory."

She read the paper. A letter signed by twelve Oregon City single women also ran stating they'd marry no man who had not gone to war in defense of their honor and their country.

"What do you intend to do?"

"Join up with Lee and Gilliam. They're leading the charge against the Indians."

Her heart pounded faster. "Turn to war so quickly? Can't they send emissaries to negotiate?"

"They're considering it, but they're relying on the Nez Perce people to do the talking. That's the tribe who suggested a parley."

"That's good then. Things can wait until we know if they succeed or not."

"Can any Indian be trusted?"

She thought of the Indians who had given them the venison hams when they were so desperate; of those who had loaned them horses; of women who had bargained with her gramo for buckskins and how that had changed her gramo's life. And they'd sat with all those two hundred Sioux on the trail . . . they had been trustworthy. She reminded him of that, then added, "How many captives are there?"

"We don't know. We'll send reports back for the *Spectator*, but I have to go, Virgilia. You understand." He took both of her hands in his. "If they aren't brought to justice, they'll come here too, join up with other tribes to assault us."

"I haven't seen many hostile Indians here." She could feel the perspiration seeping under her arms, down her back. She pulled her hands free, then grabbed the poker from the fire. She used her apron to hold the handle and pour hot water over tea leaves into cups. "Let's think about this, Fabritus. There'll be others who—"

"We have to stop them before they come here."

How could it be that safety and serenity could dissipate like river mist?

"What will I do while you're gone?"

"Stay with your family. I'll take you there myself."

How quickly she had wanted a refuge around her own life, didn't want her husband risking their safety on behalf of others. Yet if others hadn't done so, she and her family would have starved to death. Her face felt warm with shame and yet she did not want her husband to die, didn't want to be alone.

"We have to fight for what matters, Virgilia. You understand. The captives have to know that they're not forgotten."

"And what do we do here?"

" 'They also serve who only stand and wait.' Milton."

"I know the poem," she snapped at him. "It's about tragedy in the life of a young man who held great promise."

Fabritus kissed her forehead, held her to him. "And Milton went on to write his greatest works after that tragedy. It's the challenges that define us, Virgilia."

"I want you defined as alive."

Pherne's sons felt called to this war effort too. But forming an army stalled. The governor wanted Mr. Applegate to go to California to enlist the aid of the governor there. He tried, but was turned back by the winter storms in the Siskiyou Mountains. Then the legislative assembly hoped to send a letter to the American emissary in Honolulu, but the ship that might take it never came up the Columbia. Their isolation from the east, dependence on the British settlement in

Vancouver and an independent company— Hudson's Bay—reminded them all of how vulnerable they were in this Oregon Territory. At least they had a land route back east on Applegate's trail that didn't take them through the Columbia River regions where the uprising had occurred.

Five hundred men volunteered. Pherne was amazed that so many willingly chose to leave home and hearth. She was grateful, yes, and humbled how the trials of others were woven always into lives unknown. Emigrant trains who had come through before the tragedy now sought homes to stay in, telling tales of their ordeals across the shining mountains and thanking God they'd missed the killings.

Virgil rode to different cabins, seeking whatever could be spared for the riflemen. "It's how I can best help, by raising supplies."

"Have we really come all this way, survived the trail, and then what, lose sons in war?"

"We are all at risk."

"I know, I know." She struck the butter churn with new vigor. "I understand. Strangers did for us and we must do for them. I know this, but I don't have to like it." Nor did she like her reluctance, so full of selfishness and worry. *Give my effort to the present, let God handle the future.*

"I've offered what little we have, a meager

wheat harvest, a cow. That's what most are giving. Hams, if people have them."

"We have blankets."

"And ammunition to spare."

"Just feeding five hundred men will be an effort." She stopped her churning. "And the wives and children they'll leave behind, what's to become of them?" Virgil remained silent. "I'll speak with Virgilia. We'll bake bread and share it. Look after our neighbors. That's what we can do."

After forty-seven days, negotiations were successful and the Hudson's Bay Company sent both an emissary to the Cayuse and paid the ransom of ammunition and other items in exchange for the hostages. In the forest grove where Tabby stayed, the influx of missionaries and their families flooded the few homes able to take people in. Building went on with frenzy, making shelters for refugees from The Dalles, Lapwai, Kamiah, places east. They came for safety and to be among others who had come west years before as missionaries. Tabby had heard of the Spaldings, and now, she met them, arriving with their children, one of whom had been a captive, ten-year-old Eliza. With them came Matilda Sager, orphaned on the trail, then orphaned again when Mrs. Whitman lost her life. Tabby thought her a sad little elfin child.

Two of her sisters arrived with other families, older girls. Pretty. One named Catherine. Tabby felt an affinity with Catherine, whose leg had been badly damaged when she'd jumped from her parents' wagon. Her dress caught on an axe handle and the wheels had crushed over her limb. Tabby could also look the girl in the eye—they were the same five-foot height. Catherine had made most of her 1844 journey like Tabby, jostled about in a wagon because she couldn't walk. And now, she too limped.

The brothers had both been killed in the massacre. The Spaldings stayed with the Smiths, but other missionaries and their families were welcomed by the Clarks, and Tabby shared her bed. With little more than the clothes on their backs, these refugees needed comfort. And with them came children from the wagon trains. Children whose parents had died of fevers and ague, or whose parents had met their deaths at the hands of the Indians that the Territory now armed against. Tabby was surrounded by widows and children. "Fly to their aid," her husband had preached. But how to do that?

Tabby and Emeline Clark prepared porridge and wheat bread for the newcomers, brought hams from the smokehouse, made puddings sweetened with molasses, and served them to the refugees, for that was how Tabby thought of them. She calmed as she could, speaking in a soft voice, making no quick movements that might startle. The children whimpered from their hunger and from fear, staring, their tongues silent as the Sphinx. Tabby put the last of her glove-making currency into use buying blankets and bed-clothes, sugar and treats for these latest changelings.

Several days into the rescue, Tabby crawled into her bed at the Clarks', shared now with a parentless child. She tucked the child in, then lay awake awhile. She was destitute again, as poor as she'd been when Orus had rescued them, having given everything she'd earned away. Those troubled times she'd wanted to lie down and sleep: when her foot was damaged, when they had barely a widow's mite to care for their family, when Clark breathed his last, when her sons went missing at sea, when Orus threatened to leave her behind, when her wagon tumbled down the canyon shadowed by rock walls rising 1,300 feet above. And when she shivered alone with John, her stomach empty as a pudding dish, not certain her family had sent her away for her own good or for theirs, when she had nothing. Then a six-and-one-quarter-cent piece. During all those trials God had seen to it that she kept breathing. But he had also kept her with an amount of money to face each day. Manna, was she supposed to trust in the manna again?

She had taught her children and grandchildren that God orchestrated both the composition and the single notes to make the music of a life, but had she failed to hear the notes herself?

She sat up in bed. She knew what must be done.

"Mr. Clark," Tabby ventured to her host the next morning, "I'd like a word with you. As a confidant and man of the cloth."

"Oh, sounds serious." He had the kindest eyes, reminding her so much of her husband Clark. "Where shall we go? No privacy, I fear."

"I thought we might walk beneath the umbrella. It's chilly, but the sun breaks are lasting longer."

"The barn. It's dry and the crunch of horses chewing will be a comfort." Tabby loved the way he said certain words like "crunch" that came out "cranch," so reminiscent of Vermont. She'd lost her accent to Missouri. "Now, what's on your mind?" Harvey Clark closed the heavy door behind them, the action settling them into semi-darkness, window light flickering against the threads of dust rising floor to rafter. Birds chattered in the loft and Tabby wiped a floating cobweb from her face.

"I wonder what I can do for these hurting children? I have no resources anymore. I gave them all away." *Where is the manna for them?* "I wonder why Providence has left me both longing to care for them and yet destitute to do so?"

Harvey Clark shook the umbrella free of its

moisture. "And if you had means, what would you do?"

"I would establish myself in a comfortable house and receive all the poor children, and be a mother to them." She wasn't sure where those words had come from, but hearing them rang the bell of truth. "They need a mother's love now more than ever."

Clark narrowed his eyes at her.

"You needn't look at me as though I've lost my senses."

"Are you in earnest?"

"Yes, I am." She had never been more certain of anything than she was right then; and she'd had a great many certain moments in her long life.

He raised his eyes, stood silent for a time.

Is he praying?

"Then I will tell you of something we have tossed about long before you came. And that was to establish a school here on the plains and an orphanage if needed. Many of my colleagues came to the Territory in order to reach the Indian children, but they were few, disease taking them back in the '30s. There are still a few, but clearly, this influx of families from the States and now our missionary friends bring us many children in need of safe harbor and education."

"I've taught. But these children need security, food, consistency, and love before they can begin to learn again."

"Yes, I see the trauma on their weary faces."

"Necessities first."

"If you are indeed serious, Mrs. Brown, I'll speak with Alvin Smith and some of the others." He rubbed the nose of a horse that had put its head over the half door of the stall, the action soothing the animal but also giving Harvey Clark time to think. "We could move you into the meetinghouse and receive all the children there, rich and poor. Those parents able to pay a dollar a week for their board, tuition to a school, washing and all, we'll charge. The others will be free." He turned to her. "What would you need for your labor?"

"Nothing, for a year. If you and the others can provide provisions for us all, I will live there and give all they need, the money going to supplies and sustenance for their keep. Most of all, I'll give them love from a never-ending supply."

— 32 —
The Varieties
of Manna

Tabby stepped into the log meetinghouse where all awaited her to "cluck up her chickens," as she thought of them. A hodge-podge of dishes, broken knives and forks, feather ticks (needing airing), and fireplace utensils furnished the log cabin Harvey Clark and others had commissioned. It had been the Congregational meetinghouse that would now be used all week long and not just on Sunday, at least until they could build a larger structure. For now, this was Tabby's orphanage and a school. Thirty children, ages four to twenty-one, lived between the logs. Many were true orphans, but others had no mother but a father off fighting Indians or working far away or heading to the streams of California where it was rumored gold had been found. She had day students as well, not only boarders.

Judson was one of those.

All Tabby needed now was a teacher and Mr. Clark had promised her they'd take care of that. Tabby's job was to devote herself to her charges, to give them what they'd missed: tender, loving care. The day students would be taught too, but only Tabby's cluck of chickens would live there, have a home again.

"It's a dandy," she told the assembly. "You've done well."

"With so many educated missionary wives clustered here on Dairy Creek, we didn't have a problem finding our children a strong instructor either," Harvey assured her. "You'll meet her later in the morning. For now, I'll give the tour."

Tabby chuckled. "Not a lot to tour—not that I'm complaining."

"We have a few surprises," Emeline Clark told her.

Orus and Harvey had made benches for the students to sit on in the school and brought in long planks for the table where the children would eat, in a separate room. They'd sleep in that room as well, in rope beds attached to the logs. A dozen of them and a real rope bed with headboard for Tabby.

"My bed's not much bigger than the children's." Tabby laughed, as did the others.

"And see these. From your first group." Judson had cut two barrels into chairs and Nellie made pillows stuffed with bedstraw plants to soften the seats. The cloth had come from a neighbor on the plains. Each child also had a pillow to call their own, thanks to Nellie's hand.

"We've ordered slates but they'll be arriving

by ship," one of the organizers assured her. Boards, slanted outward, had been nailed to the wall to serve as writing surfaces. "Peach pits began your orchard, Mrs. Brown." She looked out through one of the 8x10 windows. "Apple and pear trees too. Someone donated a Durham milk cow."

"Orus," Tabby said under her breath.

"We'll have a little farm going here for you, Grandma Brown."

"And my little chicks will help make it run. They'll see what good they can do in helping each other." The log cabin was more than what she could have hoped for and it was hers to use. Along with two dozen children, of course.

Not long after, while Tabby busied herself with making a pot of beef stew, Harvey Clark introduced Tabby to the new teacher. "Eliza Spalding, meet the indomitable Mrs. Brown. Eliza's the mother of one of the captive children."

"You are the indomitable one."

Mrs. Spalding lowered her head to the compliment. "I've heard about your journey keeping your brother-in-law alive on the Applegate cutoff. We've both had our trials."

"So we have. Perhaps we'll talk sometime."

"I'd like that."

Tabby knew she'd find encouragement listening to other stories of resilience, love, and doing good.

· · ·

Tabby was still without personal financial resources, but her heart felt full. If only she could hang on to that contentment, that absolute abandonment to worry, trusting that even without coins, God would provide all that was needed, including purpose in a later life.

"Grandma Brown, may I have that last cookie?"

Tabby nodded her consent to little Jessica, a parentless child from an 1846 overland trail. A stranger had brought her from the Portland village where he'd found her sleeping in an overturned barrel on the dock. Next to her stood a small boy, a survivor of the Southern Route. His family had been in a wagon behind theirs by several weeks. She watched him pack bread in his pockets, even though she'd put plenty on the table. It would take time for him to trust again. She'd be there until he did.

Judson helped her plant the garden of cabbage, potatoes, and carrots. Wild greens supplemented their harvests. Judson still worked days at the mercantile and with one arm pulled sides of beef from the wagons the settlers brought to feed Tabby's growing family. He hefted the beef onto his shoulder and later helped Tabby slice and boil or make jerky. The youngest children collected wild strawberries in teacups they had for dessert. Tabby began to instruct Judson at night.

"I was remiss in not teaching you on the trail," she told him.

"Aw, who had time then, Mrs. B? But I heard you give words to the girls and remembered them. I didn't know about spelling and whatnot. I can recognize certain words at the store but can't figure out the new ones."

"We'll start with the alphabet." The boarders had been fed and were asleep, the older children helping the younger ones. Tabby did all the cooking but not laundry. She was grateful for the older boys who heated the water and the older girls like Catherine Sager who swirled the sheets and underdrawers in the lye soap water.

For her class with Judson, she used the half-barrel chairs. "I see you were able to make these." She gestured for him to sit. "And with but one arm." He'd still never said how the accident had happened, but thank goodness he must have been near a doctor who could make the amputation with skill. Through the open door, she watched robins bring in spring, perched on budding branches. Beyond, the forest floor gave up pink blooms of rhododendrons.

"My stump does some good. And a vise holds things for me."

"They're very nice chairs. And Nellie made the pillows?"

"Yes, ma'am, she did."

"So you two are still talking?"

"Oh, we always kept our friendship, Mrs. B. But I wouldn't hold her back from having a good life. Mine's meant to be alone. I see that now."

"Judson, dear boy, we may find we're by ourselves at times, but I'm convinced that we are never really alone."

"I've got to make it by myself, like you did leaving Missouri without Orus thinking it a good idea for you."

"I may have pushed a bit more than I should have. But I wasn't alone. I had you driving my oxen and I had the Captain to look after too. But I know about being a burden on others. Still, you have to respect Nellie's choices too. She wants to be with you. You have to consider that."

"She doesn't know what she's getting into with the likes of me." He raised his stump.

"We all have stumps of some kind, Judson. Things that stumble us, get in our way, make us need another now and then. We're all broken a little bit. Yours is visible." She touched his shoulder. "Does it hurt?" He shook his head no. "But for the rest of us," Tabby continued, "we try to keep our 'stumps' hidden. They trip us anyway." She thought of her sharp tongue and her pushy ways that sometimes got her what she wanted . . . and sometimes left her standing in an empty place, her children slipped away. "No, we can't let our stumps stumble us."

• • •

Tabby heard the horses whinny. What now? She had this bread to finish, a stew steaming on the fireplace irons, and butter to churn. The children did their part, but they needed their studies. She didn't mean to be a disgruntled hostess, but visitors stopped often and took her from her toil.

When she stepped outside, her annoyance changed to surprise. She recognized that horse. Schooner, but the Captain wasn't on it. She watched her grandson Clark dismount and saunter back to assist his mother and his sister from the buckboard. She'd been longing to see them, trying to figure out when she might make a trip back to Salem but coming up with no options that didn't mean abandoning her charges. She would not do that, even for a few weeks. She had older helpers, Catherine Sager, for one. But her orphans depended on Tabby's presence, and she vowed that while she breathed, she would not disappoint them by leaving them in another's care, not even for a fortnight.

Tabby stepped outside, her hands dusting flour onto her apron. "What are you doing here? Oh, what a terrible greeting. It doesn't matter why you're here. Welcome." She opened her arms. "What a joy!"

"You wouldn't come to us, so we came to you." Virgil stepped off the far side of the wagon and walked around behind to help Emma and Sarelia, who ran to their gramo and hugged her, the pressure of them warm against her belly.

She heard a cluck-clucking like a chicken celebrating the laying of an egg. *Beatrice!* The bird ran to her when Clark released her from her cage. Tabby lifted her up and buried her face in the chicken's feathers. "My friend, my friend. How I've missed you." The bird cooed her contentment.

"We are together at last, Mother. All your little chickens here in Orus's little grove of trees."

Tabby stroked the bird. "Except for John. Where is he?"

They turned toward Pherne. "He passed on, Mother. From this life to more life. Last February. He sailed on a ship to the Sandwich Islands one last trip, then came back. Ending his life here."

The news hit her like a brass bell thumped against her breast. He was gone. She tugged Beatrice a bit tighter.

"No suffering?"

"He didn't, Mother. He said this journey to Oregon was one he wouldn't have missed for the world. And then he did this most surprising thing. He took his cane apart and he gave the coins inside to his grandnieces and nephews. And he left a few for Judson and Nellie Louise too."

"A good thing."

"He helped us plant fruit trees," Virgilia added.

"I'll miss him. He had money for you too, Gramo."

"Did he? I know just what use I'll make of it. Come on in. No wait, it's balmy. We can sit outside. The privy is there." She pointed. "I'm fixing to make bread. Do you know that I've kneaded more than two thousand pounds of flour this summer? I can't imagine how many loaves I'll make come next year."

"So many, Gramo?" Sarelia said.

"Yes." She patted the child's back, set Beatrice to peck, then brushed flour from her hair and moved both girls to her sides. "I have almost thirty children I'm looking after and they do like their bread."

"Are you still writing your mem-o-are?"

"I haven't forgotten, but I've been a little busy living."

Virgil surveyed the cluster of buildings Tabby had badgered the missionaries into adding to the single log house. Two smaller structures were linked with roofs over the walkways between them.

"Looks like you've got a pretty good setup here, Mrs. Brown."

"I do. But it's too small. I've got to get another structure put up before winter for the next phase of my plan."

"You and your plans." Virgil smiled as Clark lifted his grandmother in a bear hug.

"Now you put me down." Tabby laughed. She

turned as Catherine came outside. "Catherine, this is my family from Salem. Would you bring out some sassafras tea? It's lovely out here. Autumn in this country is beyond compare." Catherine nodded to Tabby and then limped back inside to get the tea.

"I'll help you," Clark said, following her.

Tabby had noticed the glance Catherine gave to her grandson, one he returned. "A young man's fancy turns to tea." Tabby then opened her arms to her daughter.

"He's considering becoming a minister," Pherne told her. "A Methodist."

"His grandfather would be so proud. And you, Virgilia. You are—"

"Married, and yes, with child."

"Now that I can see."

"Oh, Gramo. Fabritus and I wed last September. We thought you'd come back but you didn't."

"I got myself occupied. I should have written. Where is young Smith then?"

"He's . . . away. The war."

Tabby nodded.

"I hope he arrives home in time for his child," Pherne added.

"I'll be all right. I'm an independent woman, like Gramo."

"Of course you'll be fine, but it's always good to have that man beside you, if you can." Tabby clucked at them as though they were chickens needing the comfort of the night shed. She hobbled without her walking stick for such a short trip. Fir trees and oaks shaded splotches of grass greening back up from their summer dryness with scattered fall rains. Pherne spread quilts Virgil brought from the wagon.

Pherne helped Virgilia sit. She leaned her back against the trunk of a tree, her eyes searching. "Is Nellie with you?"

"With Orus. She helps Lavina for her board. She's become quite a seamstress and I suspect that before long she'll be able to make her own way."

"With Judson."

"That remains to be seen. She'll be pleased to see you, Virgilia. All of you. Now fill me in. Have you seen Orus and Lavina yet? Oh, of course not or you'd know where Nellie was. I'm chattering."

She sat back, her hands folded in her lap. "Now, I'll listen." And she did, astounding her children, she suspected, as she waited patiently to hear each one, not interrupting as she was prone to do. Her thoughts turned to John. He would have loved this gathering. Had she missed out by not seeing him as a suitor instead of a friend? No, he had gone on to do those things that filled his life and she had tended to hers. She'd mended fences with Orus and she'd found a new path. Like John, she wouldn't have missed this Oregon adventure for the world either. Savoring, that was what her life was like here; savoring the unexpected, the many varieties of manna.

The following day, the family held a final gathering at Orus's home with food and laughter and music. She heard Virgil say, "This is a fine land, Orus. I see why you settled it and am grateful you came back to Missouri to tout its virtue. Otherwise we might not have had our farm along Pringle Creek."

"Nor family within wagon distance either," Orus said.

"You certainly captured Mama," Pherne told him. "I don't think she'll ever come back to Salem, will you?" Tabby sat in a rocker out on the grass close by.

"The orphans captured Marm. As one might capture young Clark, there too." Orus nodded toward his nephew and Catherine Sager, who had come along to help serve the food that Tabby contributed. The closeness of their faces, and the smiles, told stories.

"You'd think in her old age Mrs. Brown would like to bask on the throne of a harp-backed chair," Virgil said, "instead of kneading dough."

"I'll take my throne in heaven, if I'm so fortunate," Tabby told them. "There's too much to be done here on earth before my light is spent."

"Did Uncle John teach you how to play the violin?" Virgilia said.

"He did. At the boardinghouse, though my screeching the gut strings seemed to put his ears in pain." The group laughed. "What happened to his violin?"

Pherne said, "He wanted you to have it. Virgil drew it from the buckboard." Her husband grinned. "John said you'd proved that there was always time to learn something new."

Tabby clutched the violin, ran her hands on the smooth wood as she listened with a new ear to her family's sharing. She'd heard many of the stories before and understood that was how family culture was passed on from one generation to the next. From Orus and Pherne to her grandchildren. She missed Manthano, but he was a part of the story too, the one who stayed behind, who chose not to go.

Nellie and Judson had joined the gathering. Tabby thought a tension between the two had lessened as an old wagon spring does over time. So a part of her was not as surprised as the others seemed to be when Judson made his announcement.

"We're heading to California, me and Nellie."

"To the gold fields?" Virgil put a slice of ham on a half loaf of Tabby's bread, buttered the other half. Ham and jams and jellies and sliced cucumbers and even a green-striped melon with a pink center covered the planks set up as a table. Beatrice clucked beneath the boards.

"No. To see if we can find Nellie's parents. Someone suggested that might be a good occupation, awhile back." He looked at Tabby.

"Will you get married first?" Sarelia asked the question the others had likely wished to but had kept their peace.

"No. We'll travel as brother and sister. Good friends helping each other along the way. Like you and Captain John did, Mrs. B."

Tabby wondered if Nellie saw things quite the same, but time would tell whether a friendship could become a love affair even without that moment of being smitten that marked so many marriage stories. She thought Clark and Catherine would have one of the latter to tell.

But none would be as hers and Dear Clark's had been, resisting his proposals twice before she agreed on the third time. She was a stubborn soul. Had been, she corrected herself.

The men explored various aspects of the journey, and Nellie Louise and Virgilia exchanged pleasantries, walking arm in arm. The girls had renewed their friendship in these days of visiting, a value in simply chatting and listening, one Tabby didn't always give merit to.

She wished she could paint this picture of her family, wished she'd had Pherne sketch one when they left Missouri. It would be fun to compare it to now, at Forest Grove. She'd begun thinking of this cluster of houses as Forest Grove. In two short years their lives had sprung wings that took them to wonderful places. How life had startled her along the way. And could yet again, she imagined.

"I . . . I think, Mama . . ." Virgilia reached out to Nellie Louise's arm, her face white. "I . . . my water . . ." Her eyes were as startled as a deer's. "The baby . . ."

And there it was, another story for the telling, offered when she least expected.

— 33 —
Frontiers

"Gentlemen, it is time to build another structure. That way these buildings we've been sharing with the school can go strictly to boarding the children." Tabby met monthly with the former missionaries, now pastors and teachers, to discuss issues of the boardinghouse and school. Children came and left, swept the floor around them. It was after teaching hours, and older girls watched the venison roast Tabby had steaming while the boys milked the two cows. A constant influx of children came into her care—those whose parents had died or who scattered to find work or sought their fortunes somewhere else, being shaped for a time without their kin. People from across the territory had heard of the woman who took children in and gave them love and sustenance. Some days, Tabby felt like she'd stepped into a nursery rhyme as an old woman in a shoe with so many children she didn't know what to do. Except that Tabby did know what to do. "The new structure should be set aside for a dedicated school."

"Dedicated." There were mumblings among the men.

"Yes, with trustees to bring education to a new level."

"We've had a school here off and on for some time, Tabby. Is there a need for such formal action?"

"I think there is. Here's my story, gentlemen. Years ago, I moved my family from Maryland to the fledgling town of St. Charles, Missouri, in part because of the Catholic Sisters academy there. Yes, it was a burgeoning hub on the Santa Fe Trail and a grand blend of French and Spanish and frontier activity. Yes, it was close to St. Louis, that jumping-off place of new beginnings in the West. But I knew that an education was what truly mattered. A city that sees the importance of feeding minds, as well as bodies, is a lure. Your Methodist missionaries thought the same when they began the Oregon Institute, I suspect."

"But they had to close it," one of the missionaries reminded her. "It was too ambitious, the idea of it."

"I heard that you ran out of students back in the '30s, that there weren't that many Indian children and the missionaries weren't populating well."

"Are we so likely to attract that many students in our little grove here? I mean, if Salem couldn't sustain it." This from another of the group.

"They had to move the mission because of the Willamette flooding and the ague, that's how I remember it," Harvey Clark said. "And it may reopen one day. It's still chartered, I believe, and—"

"You're thinking of a university?" Emeline Clark expressed her surprise. Tabby was surprised she'd interrupted her husband.

"Yes, a university built in a climate of both educated citizenry and mild winters, with no flooding. It's the perfect place." Tabby's heart hesitated, but she knew this was her next frontier. "More people will come when they hear of a good institution of learning." If she couldn't convince these men and women so close to all their efforts, how would they ever convince a legislature to accept a charter? "Let's see if I can get you to think with wings and not just your feet."

Emeline frowned.

"Institutes of higher learning are essential for a thriving society," Tabby said. "They attract dreamers, people with bigger ideas for the betterment of all. Oregon will be a state one day, and what better way to support that effort than to show that we are committed to that factor of civilization that best prepares our children and our nation for a prosperous future: building up a university." She inhaled. "Such a long speech." She folded her hands and leaned forward on the table. "It begins with us in our little school. We'll call it the Tualatin Academy and name trustees."

"Oh, for heaven's sake," Abigail Smith chimed

in, and Tabby couldn't tell if she supported the idea or found it wanting.

"For heaven's sake, yes," Tabby said. "And for our children."

"The building I can see," Harvey Clark told her. "But let's pray about the university."

"Fine with me. The Lord's familiar with the subject."

A few days later, the community rallied, and before the first dusting of snow sifted across the grove, Tabby had her boardinghouse only—and the new log structure became a school and church. Eight men agreed to serve as trustees. Tualatin Academy had begun.

Tabby found herself singing to the children, grateful her voice still held despite her age. She improved on John's violin, in her humble opinion. The children loved Beatrice, who tolerated their pets. Daily, Tabby thanked God for this joy in her "spent light." She remembered with embarrass-ment her expression that day to Harvey Clark wondering why "Providence had frowned" upon her, leaving her poor. She'd been rich as a queen all along and hadn't noticed.

Judson and Nellie prepared for California shortly after the new building had been chinked.

"I wish you'd wait until spring," Tabby said. "The mountains, snow and all."

"We've talked with trappers," Judson said. "The

passes are open still. We can cross them and be in the Sacramento Valley before the weather sets in." He paused. "Maybe we should stay longer, to get the kinks out of the new structure for you." Defeat came easily from his tongue.

"I understand." She patted his shoulder, rose from the table they sat at to get him more hot water for his tea. She refilled Nellie's cup too. "You have a way to make. Taking horses or a wagon?"

"We'll each ride a horse, and Judson's going to let me lead the pack mule." Nellie's eyes sparkled at the possibility.

"I can't handle reins and a pack line both, now can I?"

Nellie stepped right over his retort. "I'm glad you'll let me do it. The mule we have is big with friendly eyes. It's a grand adventure we're undertaking. I'm so grateful for Judson's planning for all this. I would never imagine trying to find my parents alone."

Judson grunted. Tabby hoped Nellie knew what she was getting into. This trip could tax her generous heart but might be the mirror Judson needed to see his own capabilities. Nellie loved him whole, even if he didn't see himself that way.

Tabby saw them off in the morning. She waved, pulled her shawl tighter around her, then loosened the strings holding her hair covering. They tickled on her neck. A light mist filtered over her. People came. People left. They couldn't be kept, not if they paid attention to both their feet and their wings.

Clark pulled the wagon up before Virgilia and Fabritus's cabin. Albro opened the cabin door and Rem bounded off the porch, tail wagging. But before Clark could step down to help his sister and her child, Virgilia gasped. Fabritus followed Albro out of the house. He was at her side in an instant.

"Fabritus! Oh, oh, I'm so glad you're—"

"Here. So am I, I've—" He stopped when he saw her hand Clark the bundle from her arms. Fabritus helped her down, his strong arms held her close, and then released her as she reached for the bundle that wiggled and cooed.

"A baby?" Fabritus's voice sounded hoarse, even deeper than it had been.

"I didn't know before you left, at least for certain. And he came a little early."

"He?"

"I named him Virgil, after my father. I hope that's all right. And it's a distinctive name for our widely used Smith."

"Virgil's a great name." He took both mother and son into his arms, wrapping his bigness around them. The scent of her husband, the brush of his beard on her cheek, the feel of his hands on her back through her shawl and her dress, felt like wings fluttering out from her heart.

She sighed deeper into his arms, tears moving down her cheeks. She felt Virgil squirm ever so little. "Oh, we might be crushing our baby here." She laughed and pulled back, but Fabritus put both of his hands on either side of her cheeks and gazed at her, then bent to kiss her lips.

"How I have missed you, Missus Smith."

"And I you, Mister Smith. Now, meet your son."

Virgilia loved seeing her husband hold his child for the first time. She hadn't thought of mothering as also giving a gift, but it felt like that. She offered up this precious life that both had promised to care for when he was only an idea in their hearts, nothing more.

"Now there are three of us." She pushed the blanket back away from the tiny face no larger than her palm.

"Five," Clark said. "There are five here right now, but Albro and I are leaving. Welcome back, Fabritus." Her brother shook her husband's hand. "And congratulations. You had quite a few proxies for you during the delivery of your child a few months back."

"I had him at Uncle Orus's house. We'd all gathered for a picnic, getting ready to return, when Virgil . . . happened."

"He was born into a crowd. Maybe he'll be a politician," Albro teased.

"I think that's Fabritus's future, but we'll see," Clark said.

That evening Virgilia said, "Will you tell me of your war?" She nursed her son. Candles danced shadows on the walls.

Fabritus stayed silent, drinking his mug of coffee. "It is not the conversation for a lady to hear."

"I've witnessed death and destruction."

"Maybe one day," he said. "But I don't want those days to hover over this one, the day I met my son."

"I wish you could have been a part of his arrival."

Fabritus put his mug down, reached for the baby. "No apologies. We begin this new chapter of our lives with neither of us carrying regrets. Agreed?"

"I'm going to bake a cake," she told her husband. "And frost it using Gramo's pewter knife, broken as it is. In honor of our new son."

"Excellent."

Virgilia thought about her words, then to Fabritus she said, "Out here, people call icing 'frosting.' Even our words are changing."

"Along with us."

Virgilia wondered what regrets her husband had from his days of warring. But she would not press him. Her gramo always said it was the story keeper's right to share or not and when to tell his tale.

— 34 —
As Vast as the Pacific

What money Tabby made above the costs of boarding her charges, the trustees decided she could keep. And so she invested the dollar-a-week some families could afford to pay. She put her coins into land, into milk cows, bought small houses she rented to emigrants. And she gave back to the school to help cover teacher salaries. Being generous, Tabby decided, changed everything.

"The legislature is in session," Tabby told Harvey Clark one morning in 1851. "You've so generously given over a quarter section of ground for the higher school. The trustees have served two years already so they're seasoned. It's now or never to seek a university charter."

"So much business before them, Tabby. People have to sign up now for the land they claimed when they first came. Three hundred twenty acres they get instead of that 640 they'd been working. Unless they're married. But there is disgruntlement. The legislature is allowing women to have land in their own name. I'm not sure that's such a good idea."

"I've managed my money as well as many men."

"That you have." He was quick to calm her. "And the trustees are grateful you've given some of that good management back to the academy. But maybe this isn't the best time to press for more, is all I meant. The Yakima wars are costing the Territory plenty. The push to become a state takes revenue."

"I don't want to hear all the reasons we can't. I want to hear when you're going to take the request. Even crusty old legislators need to have something hopeful to focus on. A university will appeal to their higher natures. I'd present our case myself, but they won't let women, you know. Not proper." Tabby pursed her lips, mocking some unknown gentleman responding to the very idea of a woman having a head for money management, let alone legislation.

Harvey Clark chuckled. "I wish you could take the request. Second best, you ought to come with us if I can cajole the others."

"I'll convince the trustees, don't you wonder about that."

"I suspect you will. You can sit outside the chambers and cheer us on, if nothing else. But first, we need to get the trustees on board. That won't be easy, despite your . . . persuasive skills. The idea of a university is pie in the sky for many, even learned men of the cloth. They may not be up to the risk."

"Are you?"

"If we don't dream big, we'll sleep small."

" 'We are such stuff as dreams are made of, and our little life is rounded with a sleep,' " Tabby quoted. "The *Tempest*. I have no time to snooze."

Pherne sang as she put her sketch pad away. In the three years since she'd found the hidden cabin, they'd added to it, plastered an inside wall, hung a bolt of cloth on others. Her home reflected warm light. The table and chairs shone with the polish she'd put on them. They'd given two harp-back chairs to Virgilia and Fabritus, but they still had three, the third a special gift.

Virgil read beside the oil lamp as she wiped her hands and put some of Nellie's lotion on them. She inhaled. Spring 1851. She'd be forty-six this month of March. Clark and Catherine Sager planned nuptials for the fall. But before then, Pherne would be a new mother. The question was whether the babe would arrive before her birthday or after.

Virgil had been pleased when she'd told him. "Now it seems that you have truly forgiven me for taking you away from all you loved in Missouri, our Oliver's grave especially."

"I needed to discover more awaited in my life. I spent too much time ruminating about the past." Buddy groaned as he slept on the floor. "I even let the dog stay inside now, I've become so lax." Virgil laughed. "All that time and I didn't

424

realize that the richness of a life comes with being generous."

"You're claiming Judson and Nellie Louise?"

"A little. Nellie, especially. Our family took her in. She found her own strength there, I think. It's quite remarkable that they returned from California and made a foray into Canyon Creek on their way." She looked at the additional chair. "It must have been quite a time getting what was left of that seat off Mother's wagon."

"I think they wanted to show that they could do it, revisit a spot of tragedy and take something away from it to remind them of their . . ." Virgil sought for words.

"Resilience."

"Yes. Resilience. And maybe repair."

Judson's former good cheer had returned with them. Nellie's patience and loving had built Judson up, convincing him that he had a life ahead, the missing limb strengthening who he was rather than taking something from him. Could there be a better outcome for an orphan than to believe himself both capable and part of a larger family, whether he had parents on this earth, alive or not?

"Are you feeling well?" Virgil had always been an attentive man.

"I'm just full of reminiscence. Pregnancy will do that to you."

"I wouldn't know."

Pherne smiled. How fortunate she was to have this man in her life. Even with the trials of the Scott-Applegate Trail, he had not become embittered or blameful. He accepted his decisions in the matter. He had come into his own in this Salem country, well out from under the shadow of her brother. He chose good farmland away from spring-flooding streams. His wheat and fruit trees flourished. He acted as an advisor to Fabritus and Virgilia, who had already named their place with future hopes as "Smith Fruit Farms." They'd planted apple starts bought from a man named Luelling who had put dirt in the floor of his wagon and brought trees across the plains. Fabritus brought peach pits. The young man had a future in mind, one that Virgil participated in without being a father-in-law's hovering shadow.

Pherne sat at her writing desk, a small table Virgil had constructed. Her hearth was as warm and complete as she could ever have dreamed, though simply furnished but for the table and chairs. The baby's arrival would mark yet another confidence in the future. She folded the drawing to send to her mother.

Virgil came to her.

"What's this?"

Virgil handed her a cloth-wrapped object. "It isn't silver but I thought, well, I remembered that dream you had so long ago. About the bird and walking in another's shoes."

She opened the wrapping, revealing a tiny wooden sparrow with delicate feathers carved with care. They'd never discovered the story of where the harp-back furniture that Pherne had found in the cabin came from. They accepted it as a detail in the miracle of life. " 'A byrd in hand—' "

" '—is worth ten flye at large,' " Virgil finished.

"It's beautiful." She thumbed the carving in her palm. "A bird doesn't only represent the cleansing of a house, you know. It says to me that I am being held in the hands of someone who cares. And in the psalm, a bird represents the soul."

"We found it, Mrs. B." Judson's grin encompassed his entire face. He pushed aside his red-rock hair. "It fell out when the wagon rolled down the hill. Nellie Louise pawed her way down the side and, halfway there, found it stuck in the dirt."

"I almost missed it. The bell was the same color as the ground, all tarnished. Judson put it into a vise he built at the back of the wagon we bought, and he polished and polished it with kerosene."

"It looks better than it did new, except for that dent there." Tabby turned the refurbished school bell in her hand. Shook it to hear that familiar *clang*. "Why would you undertake such a dangerous trip?"

"Because it was a small thing we could return to you."

"And we got the chair back too." Nellie Louise gazed at Judson with such admiration it made Tabby's heart sing.

"Aren't you clever! Did you bring my throne to me, then?"

"We gave it to the Pringles." Nellie Louise blinked. "Maybe we should have—"

"No, no, you did exactly right. It was Pherne's to begin with. She'll like having that extra chair. And that it's from her own Missouri collection, well, that'll mean even more. It's nice to have something from home." She held up the bell, clanged it once again. "Thank you."

Nellie Louise hugged her.

Tabby didn't know whether to ask the obvious or wait until they offered. She couldn't wait. "Did you find your parents then?"

"We failed at that." Judson dropped his eyes and Tabby chastened herself for not waiting yet again, for pushing young Judson back toward a place it looked as though he'd left behind— until she stuck her impatience into it.

"But the destination wasn't as important as we thought it would be," Nellie Louise said. "People will always be enticed by the possibility. Didn't you tell me that once, Mother Brown?"

"I doubt I said anything as elegant as you just did. And you can call me Gramma Brown. All my little charges do."

"Trying to find them was a good reason to go,"

Nellie Louise continued. "But as we made stop after stop asking, inquiring, leaving notes, I understood at last that I might never find them. They might look for me in Oregon, but we didn't have any evidence of that either. When I wrote the notes to contact me, I realized they couldn't. I didn't have a home or a way for them to find us."

"That made us think about the 'us' part." Judson's blue eyes took on a sheen.

"Where did I want to be in case my trying to reach my parents proved successful? I decided I wanted to come back here, to this family, the one I already had."

Judson said, "Then one thing led to another and—"

"You decided she couldn't make it back all alone."

"No, I decided I wanted to marry my best friend." He tugged her to him with his good arm. "Nellie Louise will open a shop and sew dresses and whatnots. And I'm going to build her a house to do it in. Or have it built. We didn't find Nellie's parents. And we didn't get rich in the gold fields. But we found something even better."

"Each other." Nellie beamed.

Oh, they are so sick with love.

"I've gotten my old job back and we'll make it, like you said we could, Mrs. B. We'll make it."

"We want to get married in the log church here

429

at Forest Grove. Do you think we can do that?"

"I don't see why not. You go talk to Reverend Clark. Do it quick. I'm making him go to the legislature and he's taking me with him."

At times, Tabby could not believe her prosperous life in the second half of her being. It had begun with that coin in the tip of her glove. No, she thought further. She had spent all that she'd earned from those gloves she'd sewn. Her prosperity began when she had given everything away, when she had nothing left and when she'd prayed to understand what her poverty was meant to teach her. From that day forward, God had opened doors of service and she kept walking through them.

She'd purchased a new hat for the trip to the legislature meeting in Salem in a downtown building. She looked out through the wavy glass windows onto the bustle of a city. So much activity in so short a time. She tapped her walking stick. This waiting in the wings for a performance she couldn't even participate in was enough to make an old woman's heart beat harder. The men had been discussing the charter now for hours. It was not enough that those in charge approved the town's incorporation of the school. They must also fund it. Nothing said "I support this idea" more than an infusion of coinage. Local supporters would have to raise more money, she knew, selling things. Virgilia would bake a dozen cakes for a cake walk, Nellie Louise would make a batch of lotion and sew up a storm. Pherne would paint a scene of old Salem some would buy, and the men would donate beef and fruit, with all the proceeds going to the college. Her college. But their good intentions needed the seed that could only come from a collective commitment of "resources" toward the end of advancing education.

Tabby tapped her walking stick. This had gone on long enough. She stood, rapped on the meeting room door. Harvey Clark came out.

"How's it going in there?"

"We're making progress, Mrs. Brown. I think. The stickler now seems to be that if they allocate funds for it, they want to name it."

"After themselves?" He shushed her to keep her voice down. She imagined with disgust a major university carrying the name of some legislator or big donor. That would never do. This university must welcome and speak for every child and not the privileged few.

"No, they just want the naming privilege."

"They don't like the name Tualatin Academy?"

"That'll stay, as the school for younger scholars. They want a name that says something larger than the Tualatin Plains or even Forest Grove. More like the Oregon Institute, a name with a wider vista."

"As long as they fund it and don't call it Governor Curry University, we can live with it, can't we?"

"We can. I've got to get back in there."

He closed the door, but then opened it an inch or so, so she could hear the discussion. She wasn't sure why this had become so important to her. She'd had so many successes in her life. Even if they refused this time she'd be back for as long as she had breath. *What are they arguing about in there now?* She pushed the door open a little farther with her walking stick. They still haggled over the idea of it? No, they were exploring other sites. Well, that could work, she supposed. But Reverend Clark had donated the land for it, so no purchase from legislative funds was necessary. Without thinking she said as much, out loud with one foot inside the room. The men turned to her. "It's true. You won't have to fund a purchase, you can put public funds into the construction and operation, invest in minds. As it should be."

She thought afterward that no one asked who she was, nor did they chastise her boldness. Instead, they took a vote and it passed. They chose the name "Pacific University." She liked that name. What could be grander than the call of a western ocean that stretched across to the Orient, the very seas that John had once sailed upon?

"I approve," Tabby said.

The men chuckled but indulged her interruption. She could have mothered every one of them, she was that old. They'd been taught good manners by their mothers.

"Now, the funding," Tabby said.

Harvey Clark's eyes grew big as fists and he shook his head, put his finger to his lip to silence her. *Have I pushed this too far?*

"I believe the woman is correct, gentlemen. How does $50,000 sound to the little lady?"

Tabby nearly fainted. But she gripped her walking stick instead and said out loud, "As the patriot Benjamin Franklin wrote, 'An investment in knowledge pays the best interest.' You gentlemen have worked wisely. The children of Forest Grove and the future scholars from around the world thank you for giving their dreams wings through Pacific University."

1858. Virgilia opened the sealed envelope addressed in her own hand all those years before. She'd forgotten the letters she and Nellie Louise had written the evening before they took that fateful cutoff trail. When Fabritus brought the letter in from Oregon City, it all came back. She'd have to send Nellie's to Forest Grove right away. It was years past the time they'd promised to send them. She opened the letter as greedily as her son took to her breast.

Dear Virgilia of my future,

I know I'm supposed to write a letter about my hopes and dreams of where I'll be in 1851 but instead I think I'll write a poem.

Your friend, Virgilia

Virgilia laughed at the youthfulness of the introductory words. And then she read.

What I Wish For
A pewter knife.
A reason to bake cakes to give away.
To envy no one.
To like the person
I've become with both warts
and winsome ways.
When broken
To find tools to make repairs.
I want my family safe and sound
all around
close enough to call upon
in danger, times of trial
and celebrations, too.
A good husband, one who loves
me and is guided by his faith.
But if that mate should fail to wing
my way then I wish
to have a say
in how I face my days.

Most of all I hope
to create steps
of imagination, courage, kindness, hope;
rungs of a ladder
that take me ever
out of fear and darkness
into light
I share with others.
Virgilia Pringle
written on August 9th, 1846

— 35 —
Feet or Wings

Dear Sarelia, as this memoir is the story about myself I'm telling myself, let me say thatyou, too, will learn things through the years, things to remind yourself about. I ponder, for example, how once I wrote that I was born with feet, as are we all, but without wings. Now, I see we have both. You may correct your old gramo by pointing out that she has none of those fluttering feathers (as does Beatrice) growing out from her shoulders, but wings take many shapes. God gives us wings we cannot see but can feel as he lifts us through the air to ascend to heights we never imagined, heights he has in store for us because of his great love for us and because we are willing to fly.

This will be my last entry, Sarelia. I suspect you may be happy about that, such a busy young woman you've become at twenty-two years of age. You have little time to read the meanderings of an old woman. Especially as you prepare for your wedding to that young Charles Northup. Reverend Northrup. Your grandfather would be so proud. And still you have time to help your mother with your baby sister. Mary Ella is right now nearly the same age as you were when you asked me to write my mem-o-are. But I did once say I would tell you of the greatest challenge of my life, and I would be remiss if I failed to finish what I started.

You may have guessed by now my greatest challenge, and I confess, it has been only in the telling of my tales that I could find the words to describe it. I had thought it would be that old foot of mine, lame with my walking stick, my companion all my life. I imagined it might be family squabbles and repairs. Or the terrible loss of loved ones held so dear. Your brother Oliver for one and my son John and Dear Clark and Captain John. Or the demands of the Scott-Applegate Trail and our near deaths, your great-uncle John's and mine. Even those times of pecuniary struggles when I lacked resources—God soon provided. His manna we are taught we must not hoard but use only what we need and give the rest away. Trusting in that has been a rocky road for me.

Now, my greatest challenge . . . did you know, Sarelia, that Webster tells us a challenge is a call to engage in a contest, or a claim to question truth or fact? But here is an oddity: the word comes from the Latin word *calvi*, meaning "to deceive." I've thought often of that word root, to deceive. I've decided that to refuse to accept a challenge is the deception. To let one's heart hesitate so long the challenge is missed, that forms the trickery. To resist our calling, whatever that may be, to keep our feet planted in one place rather than use them to go forward, or from fear, to fail to spread our wings—that perhaps is the greatest cheating of any of our lives. What a deception it would be to turn our backs on what we're called to do, discovering that purpose. For within that action of acceptance of our worthi-ness for service comes our greatest joy.

Did I tell you that three years ago, the trustees of the university asked me to consider going back to Missouri and to Maryland and Vermont and Massachusetts to raise funds for our dear Pacific University? But I declined. Oh, I would have loved to have seen my son Manthano and held my grand-babies once again, but comes a time when one must recog-nize one's limits and I could not have made the trip alone. I did not wish to be a burden to others. There are younger folks with honeyed tongues who can raise money for our cause.

This spring I will accept your dear mother's invitation to live with her and your father beside Pringle Creek in Salem. Perhaps that is the greatest challenge, to accept the kindnesses of others, to live to be "worthy of the calling," as the apostle Paul would say, adapt to change; more, to let the joy that comes from those commitments, whether we succeed or fail, wash over us. Agree to go, dear Sarelia. We cannot stay. And there it is, my greatest challenge: to face the uncertainty of each day, trusting that there will be enough —enough to meet our needs and enough to give away. We must keep both our feet and wings in good repair to face the uncertain road that is our life. I hope my mem-o-are has told that story most of all.

With love, your gramo,
Tabitha Moffat Brown

Author's Notes and Acknowledgments

The Oregon State Capitol honors 158 people with their names engraved throughout the rotunda or in legislative chambers. Only six names honor women. One of those is Tabitha Moffat Brown. In 1987, the Oregon legislature named her "The Mother of Oregon," writing that she "represents the distinctive pioneer heritage, and the charitable and compassionate nature, of Oregon's people." I learned of this designation following a P.E.O. presentation in Forest Grove some years back. Members took me to Old College Hall and told me of Tabitha's journey. Years later, I found her story "A Brimfield Heroine" in *Covered Wagon Women Diaries and Letters from the Western Trail 1840–1849*.[1] But it wasn't until the spring of 2013 when Lisa Amato, a Friend of Historic Forest Grove, approached me at a book signing that Tabby's story caught my imagination. "You should write about Tabitha Moffat Brown," Lisa Amato told me. And as I always do, I suggested that *she* should write the story. "Oh, I have, in a way." She'd coauthored a book with Mary Jo Morelli and Friends of Historic Forest Grove called *Forest Grove* (Arcadia Publishing, 2010). "But that's not really about her and we think her story needs a novel to explore who she was and how she came to be known as the Mother of Oregon." The idea percolated. I talked with my editor Andrea Doering at Baker/Revell and we decided that discovering Tabby would make a fascinating story. And so you have before you *his Road We Traveled.*

Another Forest Grove citizen and volunteer extraordinaire Mary Jo Morelli gave countless hours and made arrangements so I could immerse myself in Forest Grove and Tabby's life and I am grateful. With the help of Friends of Historic Forest Grove; Eva R. Guggemos, the librarian at Pacific University; George Williams, a descendant of an early university trustee; the docents at Old College Hall; and descendant, historian, and author Stafford J. Hazelett, I've had the privilege of these many months getting to know this remarkable woman, Tabitha Moffat Brown. I am indebted to each of these fine people for whom history beats inside them "like a second heart." I thank them for meeting with me, answering questions, giving me tours of Historic Forest Grove, private showings of artifacts held in Old College Hall, family photographs, archival information at Pacific University, and for sharing their genuine love for this Mother of Oregon. Whatever is good about this story belongs to them; whatever pales is my failing to capture Tabby's remarkable character.

A point of clarification in my use of "forest grove" and Tualatin Plains. Forest Grove as a town did not exist until 1872, years after Tabby died. For most of her life, Tualatin Plains referred to large sections of land west of Portland (which also didn't exist as an incorporated city until 1851). I use the terms interchangeably in part to anchor the place where Orus established his claims and Tabby began the orphanage (Forest Grove). That settlement consisted of small cabins on large tracts of land where forest groves brought shelter and building materials that later allowed clusters of cabins to form the eventual town. Perhaps the fact that there was no town when Tabby began her orphanage and school speaks to her vision and commitment to meeting a need even in the midst of nowhere, believing that one day it would be somewhere, and so it is. Pacific University continues to thrive on the Tualatin Plains in the heart of Forest Grove and the Willamette Valley of Oregon serving students from around the world.

It's likely that the legislature honored Tabitha, Tabbe, Tabby (as I call her and so she called herself) for her care of children on the Tualatin Plains following the tragedy at the Whitman Mission in the Oregon Territory in 1847. She pushed to establish an orphanage and then to develop a school and university. Tabby tells the story of her later life's work in her long letter known as "The Heroine's Letter," written several years after the crossing to Oregon. I was intrigued not only by her accomplishments but by the woman, the wife and mother and grandmother and the storyteller.

Preliminary research showed that while her oldest son, Orus, and his family and her daughter, Pherne, and her family traveled the Oregon Trail from St. Charles, Missouri, to Oregon, Tabby financed her own wagon she shared with her brother-in-law, eighteen years her senior, and an unnamed driver. Her youngest son, Manthano, did not head west, though it's believed he had originally intended to. Orus Brown did take the Columbia route of the trail while Tabby and the Pringles took the new cutoff. Whether Tabby wanted to go west but was told she couldn't or whether she instigated the family migration is unknown, but given the signs of separation noted above, I chose to make her one who wanted to go but whose family thought that due to her age and disability ought to remain safely in St. Charles. A conversation with a descendant confirmed that view, along with a possible romantic connection with her brother-in-law.

There are many wounded people in this story. Tabby had been lame since childhood, married a pastor in New England, had four children (three survived), and then was widowed at a time when women had few options except the ones we have today: to get clear about what mattered in her life and have the courage to act on that. She kept her family together, taught school, and following a tragedy with her sons' shipping interests, took her family to Missouri. Once her children were grown, she never lived with them while in Missouri nor in Forest Grove nor Salem—until a few months before her death. I thought that was an interesting family dynamic, since so many extended families did share their abodes. Did she prefer that arrangement or was it another pain in her heart? Pherne and Virgil Pringle grieved the loss of a son, Oliver, who died at nine months, and Tabby herself lost a son at the age of six. The Browns and Pringles witnessed tragedy on their journey, were destitute and starving, and were in their mountain crossing the same winter as the Donner Party was caught in the Sierras. Relief parties were more accessible to the Pringle/Brown party, and as news of the other tragedy reached the Applegate followers, there must have been both joy that they had survived and agony of knowing that another choice might have taken them to an even more tragic life-and-death challenge. There are wounds and there is healing. These characters experienced both.

It's a fact that Tabby was well-educated, a voracious reader, and wrote letters that were later published in newspapers back East. Many were preserved and provided a flavor of this woman's personality. As I researched, I found threads of other early Oregonians I'd written about: Eliza Spalding and her family in Forest Grove, the Sager children, even that those taking the Southern Route crossed Soap Creek and thus might have encountered Letitia Carson. Imagine my delight when I discovered that Catherine Sager—also lame—married Clark Brown, Tabby's grandson, and that Eliza Spalding, the mother, taught at the Tualatin Academy. The frontier was a small town in many ways. As a writer, I enjoy the paths that cross the one I'm currently working on.

Who Tabby was before she became an Oregonian intrigued me. What enabled her to continue to shine her light in remarkable ways until the day she died? My speculation about her character is informed by facts, many provided by a descendant, Ella Brown Spooner, in her books, *The Brown Family History: Tracing the Clark Brown Line*; *Clark and Tabitha Brown: The First Part of Their Adventures & Those of Their Three Children in New England, Washington and Maryland*.[2] The latter contained excerpts of Tabby's husband's sermons; a discussion of their congregational problems; the three marriage proposals; as well as the sea exploits of Tabby's brother-in-law and later, her sons; their time as newspaper publishers. The Browns were also friends with Martha Washington, spent time at Mt. Vernon while waiting for the glebe to be ready. How I tried to figure out a way to include that little episode, but alas, I had to leave it out. Mrs. Spooner also noted that Francis Scott Key, author of our national anthem, was a personal friend and responsible for the publication of Pastor Clark Brown's book of sermons that Virgilia, in my story, held as precious.

Virgil Pringle's parents did start the library in St. Charles, Missouri, and began a literary society. Virgil kept one of the most complete diaries of the crossing, especially important since they were of the first party to take the fateful Scott-Applegate Trail. He wrote down more than miles traveled and gave us distinctive images like "romantic sand hills" and "indifferent grass." The originals of his diaries are in the archives of Pacific University in Forest Grove and were reproduced in *Overland in 1846: Diaries and Letters of the California-Oregon Trail*.[3] Pherne Pringle did sketch many landmarks on the Oregon Trail. Her drawings are in the archives at Pacific University as well. Librarian Eva Guggemos graciously met with me on more than one occasion and offered access to the archives related to Tabby and the university. *The Applegate Trail of 1846: A Documentary Guide to the Original Southern Emigrant Route to Oregon* by

William Emerson[4] allowed me to write in the margins and peruse and consider what that fateful crossing required of the human spirit. The book includes excerpts from other diarists who took the cutoff, lists of those providing relief, wagon information, and other details.

Scott-Applegate Trail, 1846–1847: Atlas and Gazetteer by Charles George Davis,[5] a memorial edition celebrating 150 years of the trail, and *Wagons to the Willamette: Captain Levi Scott and the Southern Route to Oregon, 1844–1847* by Levi Scott and James Layton Collins, edited by Brown descendant Stafford Hazelett.[6] This book offered additional details of the politics surrounding the desire to have an alternate route from Oregon to the east that did not require traveling along the Columbia River. (Stafford Hazelett's work also includes some of Pherne's sketches.) Those works also suggest possible explanations for why the trail was not cut out for that first wagon train. My husband and I have driven the Applegate route coming from the east, through the Black Rock Desert, the Umpqua and Calapooia Mountains into the Willamette Valley on a similar route taken by Tabby and her family. Imagining their journey took on new meaning when we had our own flat tire at dusk and were delayed in changing it until after a rattlesnake had chosen to move on from the shade beneath our car.

A contemporary journey on the Oregon Trail gave me Rinker Buck's *The Oregon Trail: A New American Journey*.[7] The book chronicles Mr. Buck and his brother's adventure on a covered wagon pulled by mules from Missouri to Oregon. This history/memoir/travel book was published as I finished the first draft of *This Road We Traveled*. It offered the insight above all that adventurers of all ages and eras must discover for themselves that "no one knows" what lies ahead. One can only do the best one can.

The history of Tualatin Academy and Pacific University and its chartering and funding were all informed by George Williams's shared material and *A Changing Mission: The Story of a Pioneer Church* by Carolyn M. Buan.[8] I'm grateful for her scholarship and willingness to share it.

I can't say enough about The Oregon-California Trails Association (OCTA) and their work to preserve and mark not only what remains of the physical trail but documents related to it. Their bookstore, website, and journals offer rich histories not found anywhere else. The *Overland Journal*, published by OCTA, included an extensive article, "Oxen, Engines of the Overland Emigration," by Dixon Ford and Lee Kreutzer.[9] It arrived in time to perfect my understanding of travel with oxen. It was one of many articles that keep alive the history of a trail that moved hundreds of thousands of immigrants from east to west.

Other historians of great help were George Williams, a descendant of one of the early trustees of both the Tualatin Academy and Pacific University, and his wife, Lavern. He generously shared his six-inch-thick binder of stories, articles, family reminiscences, academy meeting minutes, etc., with me. I asked him what he thought would have happened if the trustees—or anyone—had disagreed with Tabby, and his immediate response was, "Oh, they'd lose." My sentiments exactly. Everything I could read about her suggests she was a stalwart, faithful, active, and determined woman until her death in 1858 at the age of seventy-eight. She is buried in the Pioneer Cemetery in Salem, Oregon.

I also had the privilege of meeting with docent Deni Cadd and other members of Friends of Historic Forest Grove (www.historicforestgrove.org) and received a tour of the fabulous museum housed in Old College Hall, the oldest building of the university having been constructed in 1848 and believed to be the only building in the West in continuous use for education. Tabby's orphanage sat behind this building and is today marked by a stump on the beautiful campus about forty-five minutes west of Portland, Oregon. The docents and the many artifacts (including a violin) presented by descendants through the years and kept by the Historic Friends offer a picture of a remarkable woman who earned her place of honor in Oregon's statehouse and who is worthy of being remembered in the wider history of settlement of the West.

Tabby never wrote a memoir (although Catherine Sager Pringle did—*Across the Plains in 1844*[10]), but Tabby did write numerous letters.[11] I used the device of her working on her memoir to offer insights into those personal discoveries but also as a legacy for her family. Letters written to her by her son Manthano survive. In one he wrote, *"I am sorry to see that you have the same cruel lash for my back that you had while I lived on Sharrette Creek."* He goes on to defend himself against accusations his mother has apparently made about him: *"... shutting my doors against my friends and opening them to those of my wife, but you are badly mistaken for I should be glad if you would throw away your prejudice and make your home with me for life ... I think that I am wrongfully whipped."* Why didn't she stay with him? Was it because he owned slaves? Or were there other reasons? That letter and a few others suggested her strong will, and certainly her willingness to express an opinion could have kept her family at bay. Her claim in her "Heroine's Letter" about her survival with her brother-in-law those three days alone also contained the explanation of how her glove gave up the secret to her financial success, where she lived in Salem, and her description of the pastor's wife she stayed with as *"ignorant and useless as a heathen goddess,"* her journey by boat to the Pacific, deciding to visit Orus and what happened after. No doubt, to disagree with her would be an uphill battle. And yet we learn, too, of her compassion for the orphans from the 1847 wagon trains, the missionary children who also arrived with the disintegration of the Board missionaries following the Whitman tragedy, and her generosity in serving without compensation those early years of the orphanage. From all accounts, she did indeed save her brother-in-law's life.

Fabritus Smith was a real person who came from New York and, according to census information, stayed at the Roberts household in Salem that winter of 1847. Whether that's how he met Virgilia Pringle is unknown, but they did marry and he did become a legislator, and Smith Fruit Farms was still in existence many years after the deaths of Virgilia and Fabritus. We don't know if Virgilia was a poet, but her descendant Ella Brown Spooner was, and her mother was an artist, so I thought perhaps some of that talent might have been handed down through DNA.

The character of Judson Morrow is a fictionalized account, as no name for the ox driver is ever given, though descendants believe that Virgil's nephew, Charles Fullerton, may well have been Tabby's driver. Many young men hired on as drivers as a way to earn their way across the continent to claim that 640 acres of free land.

Nellie Louise Blodgett Morrow is also a fictional character, but she is based on a real contemporary woman whose daughters Claudia Brooks, Ginger Bradbury, and Kristi Morrow donated to the Barlow-Gresham Educational Foundation in return for the privilege of naming a character in one of my books. Nellie Louise was not only the perfect 1840s name, but she represented many on the Oregon Trail who did indeed become disconnected from their families taking a different route while they thought their child was with a relative who had planned to take the same route, but didn't. Some of these families were never reunited, and others might be two years in finding lost kin. I'd already created a personality for Nellie Louise when I asked her daughters for a description and found uncanny connections to the short, dark-haired seamstress who was generous and caring, who loved to read, who looked out for others, including a son with a disability. The lotion mentioned in this book came from the real Nellie Louise, as did her ability to touch her palms to the ground without bending her knees.

A second successful donor, Beth Willis of Gresham Ford, in furthering the work of the

Barlow-Gresham Educational Foundation, gave her character-naming choice to Sue Piazza. Look for Sue's choice in an upcoming novel.

Beatrice's character grew out of my sister-in-law Barb Rutschow's love of chickens and her careful watch of their behavior. Then I discovered that, as a child, Melinda Stanfield, retired physician and Lenten Study partner, had chickens as pets. She dressed them up, trained them, and even got the family dog to carry one on his back. Between the two of these chicken-loving women, Beatrice came alive.

Deep gratitude goes to my support team from Baker/Revell—editors Andrea Doering and Barb Barnes, publicist Karen Steele, marketing director Michele Misiak, and an amazing sales team—and my agent of many years, Joyce Hart of Hartline Literary. Leah Apineru of Impact Author and Carol Tedder kept me from overbooking and also making my presence at events and on social media less painful than if I'd been handling things on my own. Bookstore owners and staff who keep inviting me back for events warm my heart. Thank you. My webmaster, Paul Schumacher, patiently waited for my updates. Several others must be thanked for their continued prayers, confidence, and care: Judy Schumacher, Loris Webb, Judy Card, Susan Parrish, Gabby Spengler, Carol Tedder, Janet Meranda, Marea Stone, Sandy Maynard, Blair

Fredstrom, Kathleen Larsen, and last but never least, my mapmaker and best friend, Jerry.

I hold a special affinity for Tabitha Moffat Brown beginning a grand adventure when she was sixty-six years old. I saw her as in a period of "spent light," as referenced in John Milton's poem "When I Consider How My Light Is Spent." As I enter my seventh decade, answering Tabby's questions about what she was to do with the rest of her "light" cast a reflection of my own journey toward finding meaning. Add to that, while in revision, I fell and broke my foot! For a short time, I was as lame as Tabby.

Friends, family, and faith offer the greatest hope to keep exploring those questions of meaning while facing challenges of life's uncertain journey. It's my hope that Tabitha Moffat Brown offers insight for your journey. My thanks to you, dear readers, for traveling with me.

Warmly,
Jane Kirkpatrick
www.jkbooks.com

Resources

1. "A Brimfield Heroine," *Covered Wagon Women Diaries and Letters from the Western Trail 1840–1849*, ed. and comp. by Kenneth L. Holmes, 2 vols. (Glendale, CA: Arthur C. Clark Co., 1983).

2. Ella B. Spooner, *The Brown Family History: Tracing the Clark Brown Line* (Laurel, MT: The Laurel Outlook, 1929); *Clark and Tabitha Brown: The First Part of Their Adventures and Those of Their Three Children in New England, Washington, and Maryland* (New York: Exposition Press, 1957); and its sequel, *Tabitha Brown's Western Adventures: A Grandmother's Account of Her Trek from Missouri to Oregon (1846–1858)* (New York: Exposition Press, 1958).

3. Virgil Pringle, in *Overland in 1846: Diaries and Letters of the California-Oregon Trail*, vol. 1, ed. Dale Morgan (Lincoln, NE: Bison Books, 1963).

4. William Emerson, *The Applegate Trail of 1846: A Documentary Guide to the Original Southern Emigrant Route to Oregon* (Ashland, OR: Ember Enterprises, 1996).

5. Charles George Davis, *Scott-Applegate Trail, 1846–1847: Atlas and Gazetteer* (New Plains, OR: Soap Creek Enterprises, 1996).

6. Levi Scott and James Layton Collins, *Wagons to the Willamette: Captain Levi Scott and the Southern Route to Oregon, 1844–1847*, ed. Stafford J. Hazelett [descendant of Sarelia Pringle Northrup] (Pullman, WA: Washington State University Press, 2015).

7. Rinker Buck, *The Oregon Trail: A New American Journey* (New York: Simon & Schuster, 2015).

8. Carolyn M. Buan, *A Changing Mission: The Story of a Pioneer Church* (Forest Grove, OR: United Church of Christ [Congregational] of Forest Grove, 1995).

9. Dixon Ford and Lee Kreutzer, "Oxen, Engines of the Overland Emigration," *Overland Journal*, vol. 33, no. 1 (Spring 2015).

10. Catherine Sager Pringle, *Across the Plains in 1844*, published in part in S. A. Clarke, *Pioneer Days of Oregon History*, vol. 2 (Portland, OR: J. K. Gill Co., 1905).

11. To read Tabby's letter known as "A Heroine's Letter" about a portion of her journey through the Umpqua and Calapooia Mountains in 1846, visit the Schlesinger Library online at Radcliff College. What the library has for Tabitha Moffett Brown is both small and entirely available to view online. The digitized collection is available for you to view at this link: http://pds.lib.harvard.edu/pds/view/9748870.

Reader Group

Discussion Questions

1. The author set out to provide evidence for Tabitha Moffat Brown being named the Mother of Oregon, representing the "distinctive pioneer heritage and the charitable and compassionate nature of Oregon's people." Did the author accomplish her goal? Why or why not?

2. Tabby chose to head her memoir entries as either "Feet or Wings" or "Go or Stay." What do these titles have in common, or do they have anything in common?

3. Pherne was attached to her things. Have you ever found yourself uprooted and forced to "downsize" or leave treasures behind? What strategies did you use to manage the challenge? What did Pherne use to endure? What helped turn your hopes to the future instead of the past?

4. Virgilia wears herself out trying to "take care of people." Do you know people who may

well be addicted to rescuing? How did Virgilia discover how to use her gift of compassion and generosity without maiming herself or others?

5. Was it a mistake for Virgil and Tabby's party to take the Applegate cutoff rather than follow Orus down the Columbia? What did they learn about themselves having made that decision? What lessons did they miss?

6. What did Nellie Louise's comment that she was a "forged" orphan mean for her? Does that term have meaning for those of us separated from those we love because of misunderstandings, arguments, anger? Is it possible for the Nellie Louises of the world to be restored to positive life attitudes despite never physically reconciling with their losses? How might that forgiveness happen? How did it occur for Nellie Louise? For Judson? For Pherne?

7. Virgilia's poem "No One Knows" muses about the randomness of life events: accidents, deaths, losses. And she wonders if she'll ever see her gramo again in this life. Does "no one knows" apply to other aspects of the lives of these Oregon Trail emigrants? To our lives? How do you live with the uncertainty and fear that is the everyday?

8. What do you think was Tabby's greatest challenge? Tell a story of a time when you faced a challenge. What helped you endure? What helped Tabby survive?

9. This is a story not only of one woman's resilience in her years of "spent light" but of family relationships. Did the author succeed in filling in the missing answers of why Tabby never lived with her sons or daughter (until a few months before her death)? What does it mean to "not be a burden" in our culture? Does allowing others to help us put us on the same plane instead of above others, as Orus suggested to his mother? Why or why not?

10. It's said that "generosity changes everything." How did generous acts in this story change the lives of these characters and contribute to the settlement of Oregon Territory? How does generosity expand any community? Tell a story of how generosity has affected your life.

About the Author

Jane Kirkpatrick is the *New York Times* and CBA bestselling author of more than twenty-nine books, including *A Sweetness to the Soul*, which won the prestigious Wrangler Award from the Western Heritage Center. Her works have sold over a million copies and have been finalists for the Christy Award, Spur Award, Oregon Book Award, and Reader's Choice awards, and have won the WILLA Literary Award three times and Carol Award for Best Christian Historical Fiction. Many of her titles have been Book of the Month and Literary Guild selections. A mental health professional, Jane worked for seventeen years on the Warm Springs Indian Reservation in Oregon. You can also read her work in more than fifty publications, including *Decision*, *Private Pilot*, and *Daily Guideposts*. Jane speaks around the world on the power of stories in our lives. She lives in Central Oregon with her husband, Jerry, and two dogs. No chickens. Learn more at www.jkbooks.com.

Center Point Large Print
600 Brooks Road / PO Box 1
Thorndike, ME 04986-0001 USA

(207) 568-3717

US & Canada:
1 800 929-9108
www.centerpointlargeprint.com